Blackberry Promises

by

Jan Moran Neil

'Promises and pie crust are made to be broken.'
Jonathan Swift

Produced by: Creative Ink Publishing
Powered by

Blackberry Promises

Produced by: Creative Ink Publishing

Spiderwize
3rd Floor
207 Regent Street
London
W1B 3HH

www.spiderwize.com

ISBN: 978-1-908128-43-0

Dedication

For Muriel, Jimmy and Linda and the cast and crew
of the same name for keeping their promises.

Acknowledgements and Thanks To:

The Chordettes for 'Lollipop' and the Everly Brothers for 'Dream, Dream, Dream,' and 'Til I Kissed You', Bill Haley for 'Rock around the Clock', Buddy Holly for 'Every Day' and 'No True Love Ways', Connie Francis for 'Lipstick on Your Collar', Craig Douglas for 'Teenager in Love'.

Gemma Mount for the cover photo.

P.C. Bunnet 564 - Amersham Police, Jennifer Dannhauser (née Neil) - Criminal Barrister - 5, Paper Buildings, Syd Neil - and Jack Neil who sat at my feet for the duration of writing.

Prologue
The Old Bailey – January 1960
Lily Lee's Story

Footfalls in the corridor; time to tell her story.

"Miss Lee," the usher says, "you're called for witness now."

Lily Lee stares at the usher's polished shoes - *you could see your face in those shoes* - she hears her father saying. She follows the shoes up the short corridor which leads to the number one courtroom. Lily's pony tail, colour of a new thrupenny bit, thrupenny bit, price of a newspaper, swings seriously in time with the beating of her heart. "*He'll swing for this,*" they have said. All that unbuttoned gossip on the main street; pigeons' beaks snapping at crumbs on the pavement. *Snap, snap, snap,* all day long: tittle tattle. And the squawking stillness rises in volume as she approaches the courtroom.

He would swing for it: had it been with a gun, yes. But not with a knife.

"*This isn't going to be a hanging offence,*" that nice solicitor has told her.

Getting closer now. "*Don't you listen to all that tittle tattle,*" her mother has snapped. "*Just you tell the truth the way you saw it, Lily. And if you ask me he deserves no less than he's given. He never was quite the ticket.*" Cecilia's knitting needles has stabbed out the verdict in painful synchronicity. "*He'll serve,*" knit one, "*the rest of his time,*" pearl one, "*inside,*" knit one, "*and it'll,*" pearl one, "*serve him right.*" Knit one, Cecilia. Castle of strength, Cecilia. Moats on all side of her, Cecilia. Powerful Cecilia: lips pulled hard at the edges like an archer's bow, hands stretching wool as tight as her splayed nostrils. Knitting God knows what for God knows whom, but Lily's mother was a busy woman who believed that idle hands did evil work. Cecilia: the Patron Saint of Lily's Virginity. Her mother was medieval.

"Where will the murder ..., I mean where will the defendant be sitting?" she asks the polished shoes when they stop at the courtroom door.

"Straight ahead as you enter - at the far end of the court. He will be facing the judge. He will be sitting in the dock. When you go into the witness box, you will be facing the jury. The defendant will be at the end of the court to your left. He'll be sitting in the dock." For some reason the usher repeats this fact.

She nods and then he adds, "Don't catch his eye."

But she catches the usher's eye. He doesn't know it, but she knows she could go down for 'perverting the course of justice'. If she lost her bottle - *don't lose your bottle, Lily* - how can you lose your bottle? - if she lost it now, she could go down for 'perverting the course of justice'. Where do sixteen year olds go when they are sent down?

Where do defendants go when they get taken down? Down steps. Seen it on the telly. The courtroom door opens. Lily does not expect this. She is strangely expecting a courtroom to be in black and white because she has only seen courtrooms on *Armchair Theatre*. But this courtroom is in colour and she is not sitting in an armchair. She is about to enter a witness box *because I witnessed it – didn't I? Didn't I?*: the gowns and wigs as audience; some willing her to say the right thing, others wanting her to trip up. Then there is the earnest public gallery of neighbourly and newspaper reporter faces above and behind the witness box; her mother's three sisters flown east like birds in distress across the Atlantic: high-heeled and chignoned, a chorus of cashmere moulting mink and BOAC flight bags for this is national news. The vigilant 'twelve good men and true' sit opposite, but there are women sitting there too ... and then him … he would be at the far end. But she could not lock eyes. Not yet. *It's your choice, Lil. It's your choice. Make up your mind. Never could come off the fence. Don't lead me on. I'm not leading you on.* All those chatterbox voices in her head. Little Miss Chatterbox. Lily's Miss Chatterbox is typing out two stories in her head on two different walls in two different back streets and she is not sure which one to tell. How on earth will she not be able to tell the right story?

"*You're the prime witness,*" that nice solicitor has said.

A wigged, gowned and stout man was talking to the judge now. The judge is bony and as old as these walls. And above him, on the wall is the Sword of Justice. Her father Gordon knows all about The Law as he reads the newspapers daily and he says that the courtroom dealing with the most serious crime of the day will carry the Sword of Justice. *This is serious. This is very serious, Lily.* Her father said this last Wednesday August 26th – the date burnt to the front of her fringed forehead - when the black Ford Anglia police car drove away from the pavement; the light from the street lamp making a furnace of the numbers chalked out for hopscotch.

And now they are all sitting beneath the Sword of Justice. Her parents, Gordon and Cecilia are in the public gallery for they have given evidence for the prosecution, whilst Lily is about to give evidence for the defence. The judge's wiry fingers are making slow notes with his left hand as if he is practising his best handwriting. The skin on his hands is translucent. She thinks she can see his bones whilst the barrister speaks in sing song velvet tones, which cracks just now and then, indicating that this has been a long trial. "Ladies and gentlemen of the jury," and Lily looks across to the jury: twelve good men and women true, wearing serious faces and matching suits, "With my Lord's leave I seek to call Miss Lily Lee ..." and Lily watches the defence barrister's red moustache move up and down with these words. This barrister has the velvet voice of God, would look like God if his bits of reddish hair didn't show beneath his white wig. Wig. Le perruque. *Sounds so much better in French, don't you think? Cicatrice. Cicatrice.* French for 'scar'. Scar on my leg. Scar on his face. Oh that deep and rutted scar on his face; it is never going to fade in her head.

This is the Queen's Counsel. Her father has told her that the barristers are QCs and 'take silk'. She thought he said 'take milk'.

The usher places a hand on her shoulder and propels her gently in direction of the witness box. She takes a sharp, nervous intake of air and feels the weight of courtroom eyes rest heavily upon her. *That jury has made up their mind from square one. You can tell by the way they look at him sitting there in the dock.* Her mother has said this looping the wool over the left knitting needle. *Stab, stab.* Where did her mother think square one was? On one of Hudge's Snakes and Ladders' boards?

"Would you take the Bible in your right hand and repeat after me ...?" the usher says. "I promise before almighty God that the evidence which I shall give will be the truth, the whole truth and nothing but the truth," he says, slowly, calmly and with grave resonance.

Help me, almighty God. Don't look ahead. God give me strength, as Aida would say, to do what I need to do. To say what I need to say. "I promise to tell the truth ..." Bibles make her think of Aida and the way Hudge's mother folded and wrapped their words like her pastry: pastry filled with rich dried fruit and thumb prints touching half remembered edges.

She cannot help but look up towards the defendant for the first time. Is he really smiling? Does she keep her promise or does she tell the truth? The whole truth and nothing but …? Lily Lee is suddenly not so sure …

"Can you speak up so that the judge may hear you?" the usher says.

And the bony judge with skin like papier-maché and a robe a much brighter red than the colour of blood, for she has seen the colour of blood, cocks his head to the side. Lily is aware that a woman is typing every uttered courtroom word. Her father has prepared her for this, but all the same the cluck of the typist chatters to the same beat as the words which scatter like bird seed in her head. Pick a grain here, pick a grain there. Nothing but the truth.

"I promise," she says – she has been told to say *I promise* – for she is only sixteen and under age and need not say 'I swear', "to tell the truth, by almighty God, to tell the whole truth and nothing but the truth," she says mixing up all the words. Please help me, God. Lily Lee's heart is swinging, just as it has always done, from the one version of the truth to another altered version.

And the mighty barrister with the red moustache and the red bits sticking out of the side of his perruque leans on his pedestal asks, "Can you give your full name to the court?"

"Lily Lee."

She then hears the barrister telling her to speak 'nice and slowly' and to direct her answers to the jury. He gives a small smile and tells her to watch the judge's pen moving if she thinks she may be speaking too quickly as the judge must take down her words. He continues. "And where do you live, Miss Lee?"

"My parent's grocery shop on the Pennington Road."

"And does the shop back on to the cul-de-sac - Alpha Road?"

Lily's heart is a dull thud on hearing the innocuous names of places she has known all her life become somehow shameful. "Yes, sir," she says.

The barrister's reddish moustache continues to rise and fall with each word spoken. Her father Gordon has talked about these wigs or perruques being barristers, because they go to the bar. Where's the bar? The barrister gives the jury time to consider the map and the scene of the crime whilst Lily considers with a shiver the other tagged exhibits lying cold and impersonal in plastic bags on the table below: that knife, his leather jacket and thank the Lord there was no overall because she has dealt with that … then Lily suddenly sees it ... that camera. But he lost that camera. Why is that camera being used in evidence? *The photos. Oh almighty God, what photos have been taken with that camera?*

For the second time she turns her head slightly towards the dock. She hasn't seen him since the funeral. The camera is a surprise. What is that camera doing there and will this change things? That camera was a silent witness for the camera never lies, does it? But his head is down. She catches only the nape of his neck before she looks back at the red moustache and wig, who is speaking again. "Miss Lee, were you able to gain access to the Oddy's yard by coming the back way through your parents' grocery shop yard and into Alpha Road?"

"Yes, sir." Lily is confused by the presence of the camera. Members of the jury are consulting maps because the fact that Hudge could never cross busy main roads has been so important. Then she looks up to the gallery and she swears that she can see Bessie Fenchurch shaking her peroxided head. What has that woman said?

"And are you or were you a good friend of the defendant?"

God give me strength. She looks to her left. He has lifted his head. And there he is. And she looks into his oh so familiar and beautiful eyes. For a moment, the courtroom disappears and they are alone together as they had been at the funeral. Lily smiles not only with her lips that will tell but with her salty eyes because she wants to give him reassurance that she will keep the promise. But she is not sure that she can. She would like to tell him that she has been able to get rid of the blood stained overall; carefully incarcerated in the Brambles' disused stables. Getting rid of the blood stained overall was very important. It was incriminating evidence, after all. There was so little time to talk at the funeral and it was the only time they let her near him since 'it all happened'.

"Miss Lee, could you answer 'yes' or 'no' to the question? Would you say you are or were good friend of the defendant?"

She replies with a disembodied voice but without hesitation, surprising herself, looking back at the barrister and his very large moustache, "I would consider myself to be a very good friend of the defendant."

"Then Lily, could you give us your version of the events which led up to the stabbing which took place in the Oddy's yard last Wednesday 26th August?"

This is Lily Lee's story: the whole truth.

PART ONE

1

WEDNESDAY 19TH AUGUST, 1959

South of the River Thames on the Victoria Line

Her parents' grocery shop closed on Wednesday afternoons. So well after one o'clock, Lily Lee grabbed the bag of lemon sherbets for Hudge and dashed out through the backyard and garage and into Alpha Road. It was a grey, muggy afternoon and Lily took a deep breath, inhaling the smell of fresh timber. At one time the timber yard's corrugated iron gates had marked the end of her cul-de-sac world. Across the street had been another country. She walked quickly up the narrowing apex of Alpha Road, passing the Oddy's yard and crossed at Carlisle Street, taking steps down to the railway cottages under the bridge. It was the long route to the recreational ground, referred to as 'the rec', but it was a childhood habit to avoid the busy main Pennington Road. And Hudge had never learned to cross main roads *so when they walked with him this was the route they took.* Over the years he had become accustomed to the geography.

The Pennington Road fronted a small parade of shops where Lily lived, above her parents' grocery shop. It was the top stroke of the T-junction. The down stoke was Peterson Road. As a child she believed she had been born in Peterson Road. Babies were born under mulberry bushes in Peterson Road. Her mother said so when she used to teach Lily to read *Janet and John*, on her lap, by the white marble slab of a cheese board with the wire cutter. Janet and John's father had a job. Janet and John's mother didn't. When her babysitter had been sacked, Lily had been sandwiched as a child between her father's early turns on the railways and her mother's shifts in the shop.

Beyond the slab of 'Cheddar of the Day', was Peterson Road, across the main Pennington. Lily had never seen any bushes, or found babies. She had found Des instead, on the other side of the world. Des and his elder brother, Hudge. Des and Lily had long given up sucking lemon sherbets. Hudge still did.

A train rattled past and Lily Lee opened her mouth wide, emitting a scream that she knew would ricochet back at her from stone walls. It was the 'almost' one thirty train which ran intoVictoria, leaving the local station, where her father worked. Lily Lee had no need of watches. She told the time by the passing of trains. *And the trains ran two minutes to every half hour.* She was late for Des. It didn't do to be late for Des.

Des and Hudge were waiting on swings which creaked under their weight - especially Hudge's. Hudge was big both ways and in all ways. Lily opened the side gate into the rec., passing the disused stables where the greengrocer, Brambles, once housed his carthorses and where she and Des hid things. Hudge, eager for the lemon sherbets saw her immediately and waved his arms vigorously, screeching, "Lily. Lily. Have you been to Perrys?"

Lily was breathless from running and nerves. It didn't do to be late for Des. "Sorry I'm late."

Des was looking at his watch and pulling his slightly askew lips tightly together like he did when he was tense. He was wearing that leather jacket which would become such a crucial feature in the trial but for now, something different had happened between the two of them. Des had grown angrier. Like last night.

She spoke to Hudge; Des made her nervous; he enjoyed observing her nerves. Quiet cruelty: everyone in the road always nodded knowingly and said Des Hodge had 'an evil temper'. "My dad took ages to shut up shop this dinnertime and then your mum came in, last minute as usual, wanting half a pound of streaky bacon." She produced the bag of lemon sherbets from behind her back which she had purchased at Perry's Newsagents and Hudge squealed deliriously. Des looked at his watch again.

"Big of you to spare a Wednesday afternoon to see me, Des. Did you speak to Mr Oddy about the job in the caf for Hudge?" Lily took the third swing, to the right of Hudge.

"I spoke to Jean about it." He was pushing his weight back and forward with his winklepickered right foot, speaking down to her stained white plimsolls. "She's going to speak to her dad - tonight," he went on. "Said she'd meet us in the shed at eight and give us his verdict."

"Why her? It's not Jean's caf, it's her dad's." She spoke across Hudge who sat on the middle swing.

"She insisted." Des took a cigarette pack from the upper pocket in his leather jacket: Senior Service with a bearded sailor on the front. "Something I never do." He lit up, throwing the match seriously to the ground.

She knew what he meant. Lily looked at Hudge, who was slumped in the middle swing between them. His features were wide and open, like Aida's - his mother; a baby face stuck on a massive body, in sharp contrast to Des - with his neat dark good looks. Des was a long, moody, razor swift streak whilst Hudge plodded safely and heavily at his heels. Hudge was a Hodge in sight but not by right. Hudge was Des's elder half brother; the surname belonged to Des. Lily would have doubted they were brothers except that they seemed to strangely share the same timbre of voice: like the Everly Brothers.

It was difficult with Hudge around. At times she had silently blamed Hudge for just being there, in between them. She hesitated, and then decided to reply. Hudge wouldn't understand anyway. "You apply pressure," she said, pushing the ground with her foot. The swing began to gather momentum.

"That's exactly what I want to do," Des said looking up and down at Lily, as her swing gained speed. "Who are you keeping yourself for?"

"Keeping? I'm not keeping myself for anybody."

"Lily," Hudge called. "I can beat you." Hudge was attempting to swing as high as Lily. The frame began to shudder.

"What's stopping you then?" Des called at her.

Hudge was laughing wildly.

"Stop it, Hudge," Lily shouted, reaching for the ground and trying to bring her swing to a halt. Hudge's excitement could sometimes be dangerous.

"You never answer the bloody questions, Lily," Des shouted up at her.

"Stop it, Hudge," she screamed at him, "you'll break the chains."

"Cut it, Hudge," Des shouted.

Stillness. Hudge immediately, obediently slowed the swing down and placed his hands in his trouser pockets. "Sorry Des," he said and stuck out his bottom lip and looked down at his tie. Why did Aida always dress Hudge in a tie and sleeveless woollen jumper? It was a proper tie, not the kind of thin ties the Teddy boys or 'Teds' wore with suits: thin ties which the cowboys wore on *Wagon Train.* Hudge looked like an uncle. And he had never been moved from the C stream during his entire school life, despite being held back a school year. It was shocking.

Des threw the cigarette down, stubbing it out with his winklepickered foot and looked back at Lily. "He really needs that job," he said quietly. He rubbed his hands over his face, as if with fatigue. "I'll try to see Jean this afternoon."

"I'll come," she said.

"No." He almost shouted the word. He was looking at his watch again. "I need to go on somewhere."

"Where?"

"See a man about a dog." Des was always seeing men about dogs, but he wasn't smiling.

There's one thing a boy's after. Give him that and he's off. Cecilia regularly stabbed these words out with her knitting needles. *Stab, stab, stab.* It had been simpler when Des murdered all her dolls and insisted she took up conkers. Once he snipped off all the heads of her *Girls Crystal* comic's cut-out dolls. She had so lovingly dressed them in paper outfits and secured them with tabs behind their legs and arms. She didn't speak to him for hours. Being Des's mate had stopped after they discovered 'Postman's Knock'. She thought they could always remain friends, but the first kiss outside the scullery in Peterson Road ended all that. Sometimes they saw Hudge floundering, and it seemed to Lily that their only coming together was when they were preventing him from imminent disaster like his almost stepping in front of forty ton lorries on Pennington or not standing for the anthem at the pictures. "I'm sorry Des. There is something stopping me. I wish I could put that feeling into words, 'the what's stopping me'. But I can't."

"Oh, don't worry about it, Lil. I've got bigger things on my mind just now," he said.

"Oh," she said. "Bigger things?"

He seemed to drag himself up from the darkness where he sometimes lived and said, "Well, I can put 'what's stopping you' into one bloody word," he said, ignoring his 'bigger things'. "Cecilia. Your mother. Fort bloody Knox."

"Six words," she said.

'Practise saying 'no' Lily," Des said, mimicking her mother Cecilia, "and always say 'no' to a boy. That way he will respect you."

When he raised his dark, expressive eyebrows, wagged his nicotine-stained index finger, he *was* her mother. Des Hodge was as shrewd as the flea-bitten cats which shared their concrete territory and Lily loved cunning strays and lame dogs. That was Des and Hudge.

He lit another cigarette and continued. "Your father must have a degree in civil engineering to get through your mother's corsets. She'll have you in cast irons before you're seventeen." His mood was shifting.

Hudge had now collected the word 'corsets'. "Our mum pulls up her dress and takes off her corsets when she's watching telly." Hudge started to laugh. Lily and Des smiled. Aida needed corsets. Des said his mother's first port of call was Perry's sweet shop when his father had run away to sea and joined the French Foreign Legion. This had coincided with the end of sweet rationing and the combination of these two factors had proved fatal for Aida's figure.

Encouraged by their smiles, Hudge carried on. "Then she hides them behind the cushions in the front room when people come to visit or we have a party."

"Hudge," Des warned.

But Hudge carried on laughing. And he kept on laughing, like he did sometimes, so that he couldn't stop, until Lily and Des ceased smiling and Des said, "Cut it, Hudge."

Hudge stopped laughing immediately and stuck out his bottom lip.

Lily sighed. At least Des was here, with her, on a Wednesday afternoon. "You won't be doing any degrees in anything if you don't re-sit your 'A' levels."

"You don't need a degree. You shopkeepers' kids have jobs for life," he came back quickly. It was cutting.

"Jean will work in the caf for life," she said. "I'm going to Teacher Training College."

Hudge looked to Lily on his left.

"We all know your mother says you're going to Teacher Training College and we all know you do exactly as your mother says," Des said.

Hudge looked to Des on his right.

"My mother says you're only re-sitting 'A' levels and going to university to avoid doing National Service," she bit back.

"Yeah, well your mother speaks through her backside."

Hudge had now collected the word 'backside' and was repeating it with obvious enjoyment. Their dialogue had changed little since the days of exchanging conkers.

"Anyway, I'm not stopping in a grocery shop all my life," she said.

"Oh, you and your splendid plans to be great, Miss Lee." There was a trace of a smile on his slightly askew lips.

His desire to be ordinary annoyed her. "There's more to life than baked beans and babies," she said.

Des was now standing above her, next to her swing with that look. "So your mother says. It'll take me a lifetime to get through your cast iron knickers," he muttered, still looking at her, looking at her with those golden flecked eyes which changed colour according to the hue of his mood or tee shirt.

"You do too much smirking, Des." Hudge was wagging his finger at Des as Aida would do and the three of them laughed together. It was just then that Lily experienced an uncomfortable moment. When Des gave her that look it was safe. But she didn't like Hudge staring at her chest. "I sometimes wonder about your brother's inclinations, you know," she said to Des but he was looking at his watch again.

"Inclinations? I'm the leaning bloody tower of Pisa I am," he said.

"You've never been there, Des. You've never been further than cockles and whelks on Margate pier."

He smiled back at her quietly, "And how would you know?"

"Congratulations, Lily. Congratulations, Hudge. Congratulations, my boy. What are you getting me for my birthday, Lil?" Hudge said. "Will Mum bake me a cake?"

"Oh, don't keep on about your birthday and cakes, Hudge. It's only August and you're not twenty two until Christmas."

"We'll buy you a brain, Hudge - how about that?" Des moved behind Hudge's swing and ruffled his hair and they laughed together again. "Or how about some balls from Fenchurch's Exchange & Mart?"

Hudge stopped laughing and said quietly, "I got balls, Des."

Des was starting to move towards the gate. He turned back to his elder brother. "I know you got balls, Hudge. I know." Then he came back and stood in front of Lily's swing, sighing heavily like his mother Aida did and completely changing the subject to whatever happened to be the next thought in his head. He was just like his mother. "It must be me," he said.

Balls on his mind, she knew. "It's not you," she said. All blokes say that. They try and make it personal."

"It is personal. Very personal. It's about as personal as you can get. But don't worry, Lil, just at the moment, you really are not the problem at all."

She was confused. They had been screaming at one another the previous night and now he was saying there was no problem at all. He leant down and was about to kiss her, ah ... that old familiar scent of Des ... and more than a trace of Senior Service nicotine ... when Hudge said, "Very personal, Lily. B.O." Both Des and Lily looked at Hudge who was shaking his head with despair, as Aida did, when the price of black pudding had risen. Hudge was heavily into TV advertisement dialogue and he had collected this from a well known soap product: possibly Palmolive which her dad had put on special offer this week.

They began to laugh softly, but Hudge was looking across the rec. He had seen a figure in the distance jump the fence by Juniper Street and eddy towards the roundabout.

Des was kissing her now and Lily felt ... watched. She was aware of the figure on the roundabout too. Both she and Hudge had been aware. Des had been oblivious to the shadow from the outset.

Then Des placed a finger on the side of her forehead as if to drill a hole. "I love you Lily Lee," he said,"but someday you'll have to make up your mind. Remember this," he said, whispering in her ear so that the words reached the bottom of her spine. "We always pay a price for what we most desire. And don't I know it," he added almost as an afterthought. Then he took off that brown leather jacket and placed it around her shoulders. Des would often leave his belongings with her. He would do this. Leave his belongings with her like he was leaving a part of himself: including Hudge.

Lily's eyes flickered towards a street pigeon which fluttered by - scrawny, bloody and battered and then towards the spinning roundabout. She could now see the figure astride it, just as Hudge could.

Des chose that moment to walk away. Des knew where to leave off. Des knew all the Achilles' heels: every one of them. Hudge followed. Where Des went, he went.

"See you at eight, then. In the shed," she had shouted, as Des looked at his watch and jumped the fence into Juniper Street. He wasn't going to spend that wet Wednesday afternoon with her. Hudge would have followed, two steps behind, up the Pennington Road, towards Peterson where they lived, thinking of the kissing. Hudge was always witness to the kissing,

It was beginning to rain. Lily felt bitter towards Des that soggy Wednesday afternoon. Alone, like the other Wednesday afternoons. This was the first moment she ever saw Geoff Mabs; thick set, tough to see and touch at a glance and in that moment, she made to go. If she had might none of it happened?

But he shouted the words and she was stopped. "Oy, don't."

****

Geoff Mabs drained the beer from the bottle, chucked it aside and leapt down from the roundabout. He jumped the base of the slide and ran to the swings. Even better. In close-up, she had fairy princess blue eyes. Or were they green?

"Don't what?" she said.

"Don't go," he said, placing a hand above him on the swings and towering above her. "I like looking at you."

"Oh yeah?" She blushed. The colour sprang from her throat and oozed up to the eyes. He liked a girl to blush. "Well, I'm going home." She looked up at him. "It's raining." She slipped her arms into the leather jacket.

"Where's home?" Mabs watched the fairy princess eyes inch towards the main road.

"The grocery shop on Pennington Road."

"Lees?" He'd heard his mother speak of them.

She nodded. She looked towards the main road again. A train thundered by.

"That's the 'almost' two o'clock," she said.

She was flinching; he didn't know why she flinched but it was interesting. "You're local then." He couldn't help but add, "Very handy."

She flinched again.

"I'm from the chippie," he said. "Mum's just taken over."

She gave this kind of small smile. A smile with the lips. Nice lips. But not a smile with the eyes. She got up from the swing to go but Mabs placed a hand on her arm. "Let me give you a push on the roundabout."

"Thanks. But I ought to be going."

Geoff Mabs reached for his Ilford Witness camera: a cherished camera. His grandfather had given it to him just before he died and Mabs would never part with it. "Let me take a photo of you then." *Flick, flack,* his grandad would go. "Sit there, son and let me take a photo of you," his grandad would say. *Flick, flack* with its focal plane shutter. Mabs placed his hands on her shoulders, making her sit down again on the swing. Powerful things, cameras. "You look like a fairy princess."

But she frowned.

"Smile."

She didn't.

"Smile," he said. Harshly. *Flick, flack.* "You should always smile for cameras." He remembered his grandfather saying that. Say 'cheese'. Say 'cheese'.

Her blonde pony tail fell down past the bottom of her boyfriend's leather jacket. Droplets of rain had fallen on her sweeping lashes. Those eyes were a very, very deep ocean colour. He was swimming in them.

"Is that your boyfriend?" *Flick, flack.*

"Sort of."

"Only sort of?" *Flick, flack.*

"I ought to go now. My mum ..."

He came round behind the back of the swing and placed his hands firmly on her shoulders. "Looks as though he's buggered off and left you. Who's the fat geezer?"

She pulled a face. "His brother," she said.

He circled her swing and then knelt down in front of her, sizing up the photograph. "You look like my sister." *Flick, flack* . "I saw you shouting at him." *Flick, flack.*

"Can you stop taking these photos?"

It was raining harder.

"Come on. Let me give you that push on the roundabout." He didn't wait for an answer but took her hand and led her, backing his way to the roundabout, keeping his eyes on her. She seemed mesmerised, and, placing her on the roundabout, he looked at her sizing up another picture for the camera. He gently pushed.

"Are you going steady with him? He pushed the roundabout a little harder.

"I ought to go now."

Geoff Mabs pushed even harder. "Where can I meet you tonight?"

"Can you stop? I'm feeling dizzy."

"Where can I meet you tonight?" Mabs was pushing the roundabout with one hand, but with as much power as he could muster. She wouldn't answer. So he spun his circles faster. The girl was spinning, slipping now, thrusting her weight forward to keep her balance. Mabs was exhilarated, could feel his breathing quicken. "Where?"

"The caf," she shouted. "The Oddy's caf. Now let me get off."

Another train screamed across the bridge. "That's the non-stop 'on the quarter'," she screamed at the same volume. What was with her and trains? It was now pouring with rain. But Geoff Mabs was not about to let up. "Meet me there tonight." He was pushing with both hands. She had closed her eyes. Was she beginning to cry? "Don't close your eyes," he shouted. "Don't lose your bottle. Tonight," he repeated. He could feel an attack coming on, his breathing was getting faster. Used to hold his breath as a kid. What a scare that was.

"Yes - now let me get off."

Geoff Mabs slowed the roundabout down. The girl sat in stunned silence for a few moments and then stepped off, trying to regain her balance. She was crying now. He took both of her hands. She was shaking. His breathing had subsided. The train had passed on. He held her. "I'm sorry," he said. "I'm really sorry. I got carried away. I like looking at you." He held her chin in the palm of his hand, knowing he had a way with women. Her skin was ... peachy and felt smooth and cold like ...a pumpkin.

Turn into a pumpkin at midnight, she will. Fairy princess.

The girl drew back and sniffed. "Got to go," she said.

"Oh look," he said. "Your hair's drenched. You're shaking. I'm sorry. Here's my hanky."

"It's not you," she said. "It's Wednesdays."

"Wednesdays?"

"My afternoon off," she said.

"And mine ... fancy a quick ..."

She looked up at him. Very innocent.

"Cup of tea …?" His voice trailed.

"But Des is always doing something on a Wednesday afternoon. I think he's going off me."

That was a good sign. "Maybe he is ... what about coming back ..."

"I'd better go."

He grabbed hold of her hand.

She looked at him quickly as if warning, "Des nearly killed a boy once for having a go at his brother. He might kill you for being with me."

Geoff Mabs laughed. Was she green or what? "Sod that. I'm bigger than him and he's not a Ted. Stay and we can ..."

"He's not been the same since he failed his 'A' levels. He's doing re-sits."

"Thick, is he?"

"No," she said quickly, defiant like. She frowned again. "My mum said he failed his exams on purpose so he could do re-sits and avoid doing National Service."

"You're a fairy princess."

"You're really sweet." She released her hands from his.

He really did have a way with women. "You look like my sister. Where can I meet you tonight?"

She jumped off the roundabout and turned away from him, brushing him in the face with the sweep of her long pony tail. It smelt good. It smelt fragrant. She ran towards the gate. The chippie, now Mabs's chippie, was straight ahead of her on the corner of Juniper Street. "In the Oddy's caf at eight fifteen," she shouted.

He called after her. "My name's Geoff ..."

"Mabs," she shouted back and pointed to the chippie. "I've seen the new sign writing."

She gave one of those little smiles.

"What's your first name?" he shouted. But her backside was off up Pennington. *Flick, flack.*

Geoff Mabs took a cigarette from behind his ear, reached for matches in his suit pocket, lit it, chucked the match over his shoulder and sat on the roundabout. Shark shit. The seat of his trousers was soaked but then he smiled too. Princesses were funny things. They liked being wrinkled now and then.

****

Mrs Brambles, lined with time, having seen a couple of world wars come and go, loading her lettuce, Wednesday night closing (she stayed open all weekday afternoons) looked down the Pennington Road and saw the new chippie boy coming towards her. A camera, too expensive-looking to be owned by the likes of this boy, was slung across his chest like a gun holster. He was thick set with a menacing dance about his eyes. She placed a protective hand on her zipped purse in her overall apron and pulled down the beret on her head.

Flick, flack. "All right, Mother?" he muttered.

"What?" she shouted back, not hearing.

"All right, Mother?" he shouted at her, giving her a grin and walking into the caf next door.

She wasn't his mother. He was like one of her colts with a bit between his lips. Kids.

****

The strange girl in the leather jacket was not in the caf that Wednesday evening. Was it eight o'clock yet? He half hoped but didn't really expect her to keep the date.

The Oddy's caf was not more than twenty feet square, swollen with bodies, like lobsters in a fish tank, thought Mabs, and veiled by cigarette smoke. There was a chipped enamel sink in the far right-hand corner behind the counter, a one-armed bandit and a juke-box which demanded kicking for operation. Just at that moment it was playing that daft tune 'Lollipop' by the Chordettes. Geoff Mabs preferred Presley or black groups like The Platters.

A squat, dark-haired, buxom girl was standing behind the till. She was in earnest conversation with an old man, who frowned as she spoke and fumbled with coffee cups. Two boys were kicking the juke-box whilst others looked on and jeered. People were so ugly in this part of the country, thought Mabs. "Any good lookers here?" he asked a small, swarthy-skinned boy who was chewing gum and looked as though he should still be in junior school.

The kid smiled and displayed fangs for incisors as well as a disgusting ribbon of elasticated gum. Mabs noticed the junior glisten with Brylcream and his eyebrows seemed to have a slimy insect life all of their own. The kid pulled at the collar of his Teddy boy jacket with both hands and spoke to a girl dressed in a yellow and black polka-dotted puffed skirt, "Only me, ain't that right, Teresa baby?"

Teresa gave a high pitched laugh and said, "Sod off, Gary Papanikalou," and she drifted towards the counter. Nice legs. Teresa's 'A' listed feature was obviously her legs because she laughed like an air raid siren.

Papanikalou - that sounded Greek - Papanikalou cleared his throat and said, "Nah. This place is a shit bin. We move on to the Dragon's Head at ten for a pint. You'll get off with a bird there. Come with me and Flick," and he pointed to a big bloke leaning against the juke box, "but don't expect the BBC News out of him - he's spent too long working at the timber yard at the end of Alpha Road to hear what you're talking about, if you know what I mean."

Know what I mean, know what I mean? They all said that in this part of the country. South London dump. Papanikalou's voice twanged with these words.

Mabs looked across to the big bloke who was eyeing him up and down. The big bloke had bad skin: pock-marked, acne-ridden and he was checking him for size. Geoff Mabs knew that he hadn't been born with great height, but he was built solid and he could look after himself. "D'you call him Flick because he flicks a knife?"

Gary Papanikalou looked across to his mate who was flicking a knife, in, out, by the side of his suit pocket. The Greek boy's incisors grinned enthusiastically and then he snorted. "Yeah. He's put that knife to more necks than I've snogged."

Geoff Mabs ignored him and took a seat at a coffee table.

"I work in the timber yard an' all," the Greek boy said sitting beside Geoff. "Where d'you work then?"

"Chippie. Across the road."

"Chippie? On the corner? Next to the rec.?" Papanikalou snorted again. "Mrs Mabs. Phaw," and he waved his hand back and forth as if indicating a strong smell. "Right gypo tart. Just moved in they have. What's your name then?"

He moved his chair in closer to Papanikalou. Almost intimately. "Geoff. Geoff Mabs. Yeah, the chippie's got the rec. on one side and the undertakers on the other." Mabs gave him a warning look, saying that word 'undertakers' with a weight and the Greek kid instantly understood; knew his place.

Teresa, sitting at the counter in her black and yellow polka-dotted puffed out skirt, the one with the high-pitched giggle and legs like an 'A' feature, said, "Your dad gonna let you go to the Dragon's Head on Wednesday night then, Gary Papanikalou? Thought you were only let out on Saturdays."

"Go rattle someone else's cage," the little Greek said, and turned back to Mabs.

Did this boy have a serious case of halitosis.

"Teresa lives in the railway cottages. Her dad works on the Junction. Punches your tickets."

Geoff Mabs then looked across the counter to the dark-haired buxom girl. "Who's that?"

"Tart," Papanikalou said.

The buxom girl approached their table with a notepad and a pen and a smile. She looked just over the age of consent and everything about her was round. Round face, round eyes and a round backside under which there was probably a very round roll on girdle. She was an 'O'. The girl at the rec. was an 'S'.

"Coffee?" she asked. The voice was husky, high-pitched and inviting.

"You work here?" Mabs asked.

"Clever."

That kind of cockiness annoyed Mabs.

"I left school two years ago," she said giving him a small, sly smile, "and we own the caf," she said proudly.

Mabs sighed, looked around the rubbish dump and said, "Nice". She was over the age of consent then. He looked at the girl's legs which were pretty round too, indicated to Papanikalou to shift himself from his seat and patted the chair for her to sit. She sat.

"My name's Geoff ..."

"Mabs," she cut in. I've seen the new sign writing. Milkshake?"

"Coffee. Two sugars," he said, not taking his eyes from hers.

"You get your own sugar," she said, cheeks like suet dumplings, eyes like chocolate eggs. "I'm Jean ..." she said cupping her chin in her hands and leaning towards him.

"Jean what? he asked

"Oddy. Can't you read signs above shop windows?" she said.

He'd made her feel stupid. "I never looked," he said quickly and then turned to look at the caf front door.

"You waiting for someone?" she asked.

"Do you know the girl from the grocer's?"

There was surprise in her wide, dark cocoa chocolate eyes. "Yeah ... I know where she's from ..." she said. "Are you waiting for Lily Lee?"

"Could be," he said. Rule number one: never ask after another woman.

"She's in the back ... in the shed ..." and then she added with relish, "with Des."

Gary Papanikalou leaned forward, and opened his mouth wide, a mouth that was full of gaps where the molars should have been. "Des Hodge nearly killed a boy once." His breath was shocking. The kid was in desperate need of a dentist.

Mabs leaned in closer to Jean. "So ... you've got a shed in the backyard then?"

Jean's eyes were half closed, attempting to look 'Marilyn Monroe' and Papanikalou came between the two of them again and said as if Mabs had not heard him the first time, "I said Des Hodge nearly killed a boy once ... at the rec."

Mabs was becoming irritated with this Greek kid. He moved in closer to Jean. "I'd really like to take your photo sometime."

"Impaled him on the railings," Papanikalou said.

This annoyed Mabs.

Jean leaned back on her chair. "And Hudge of course."

"Hudge?" Mabs asked.

But neither he nor Jean had realised that the caf had gone quiet, the juke box was still playing The Everly Brothers 'Poor Jenny' and their backs were to the counter. They had not seen Des enter through the back scullery door and help himself to a coffee. It was evidence which was brought up later in court.

"Did you have a date with Lily then, Mabs?" Jean said.

"Loosely speaking," he replied.

"There's nothing loose about Lily Lee. She's such a good girl but she's out in the shed with Des and Hudge if you want to go out through the back scullery and into the yard to see her." Jean looked as though she might be stirring shit.

The Greek boy leaned in again, this time he was smiling. "Hudge is Des's brother."

"Oh him," Mabs said. "He's daft."

The juke box stopped playing 'Poor Jenny' mid-tune. Mabs couldn't work out why there was such quiet until a voice from the counter said, "Jean." It was a command.

Jean Oddy looked up behind her and then got up at once. "Jean," the voice said again, "my brother is waiting for his sandwich."

"Sorry, Des."

Geoff Mabs turned round. Des Hodge was standing behind the counter stirring a cup of coffee. Slowly. The two boys made eye contact for the first time. And then Mabs noticed that Des was wearing his brown leather jacket: the one he had seen Des Hodge giving to 'Lily' at the rec. that afternoon. 'Lily' must have seen him since then. Must be in the back, as Jean had said. He watched as Des Hodge whispered something in Jean's ear and she went on tiptoes to whisper something back. Des Hodge looked as though his cage had been rattled badly. The lobsters in the pot were silent. He was new here. He needed to make his mark. *Make your mark, son,* his grandad would always say. *Make your mark.* He felt they were waiting for him to say something. So he did. "Waiting for his sandwich? Your brother can find his mouth then can he?"

He felt the caf breathe. A fat girl with pimples gave a small shriek. It was quiet but from the corner of his eye he could see Papanikalou whispering, "Elephant shit," and Flick half smiling in anticipation. Mabs expected Hodge to come round the counter with fists, but instead his head began to twitch back and forth. The girl with the high-pitched laugh couldn't restrain herself and Des Hodge began to sniff. Sniff, sniff, sniff. He came from behind the counter, slowly. "Jean," he said, seriously. "Jean." Sniff, sniff, sniff. Des Hodge was now no longer looking at Geoff Mabs but seemed to be hunting with his nose. "There's a strange smell ... lard ... chips." The stifled sniggers grew and Des Hodge gave a mock snigger, whilst hitting one of the Teds on his shoulder. Geoff Mabs felt Hodge's nose getting closer. Mabs stood up abruptly. He was ready. Des Hodge and Geoff Mabs were face to face:

leather jacket to Teddy boy suit; the long moody streak to the tough, unshaven squareness of Mabs; the smooth to the rough.

Des Hodge smiled, lips just slightly off balance, Mabs thought.

"I shouldn't think you'd have any problem finding your mouth," Des said.

Papanikalou snorted. The fat girl with pimples shrieked. Teresa in black and yellow polka dot gave out an annoying siren of laughter. Mabs needed to say something. "A little bird told me you're re-sitting all your exams. You daft too?"

"Phaw." Des Hodge backed away and held his nose. His face was contorted with the fake stench he had invented in the air. "You stink of lard."

There was more laughter but before Mabs could respond, Des Hodge had kicked the back of both his knees, forcing him to sit astride his seat. And Mabs didn't like to be forced to do anything. As if finished with his smiling game, Des looked Mabs furiously in the eye, took him by the shirt collar and pulling him towards him in an almost embrace he said, "Re-sit your arse." Then he exited through the back scullery, saying to Jean, "I'll see you later."

Geoff Mabs got that old familiar feeling back again. He knew exactly where it hurt: between his legs. Charlie and his mother Zelda had given him proper training in humiliation: cold nights in a caravan. Old familiar feelings got shoved down into the coal shed: shoved down with a scuttle along with sunless memories.

Teresa looked longingly after the scullery door. "Des Hodge has such tick a tick a good timing," she sighed.

Re-sit your arse. Yes, I'll re-sit it on you, Des Hodge. Des Hodge had just shat on him and Mabs had taken it. In the clench of his jaw a plan formed.

Des Hodge would pay for this. Oh yes, Hodge would pay.

****

"What does 'loosely speaking' mean?" Des was livid, shouting at her in Alpha Road. She had never seen him like this before. He had slammed open the shed door and told her to 'get out', 'go home', 'scuttle'. It wasn't his shed anyway. It was Jean's. Then he had run out after her into the back road, shouting, "I asked you. What does 'loosely speaking' mean?" And he had forgotten to collect Hudge's cheese sandwich.

She had quite forgotten about meeting Geoff Mabs. So she said, "It means a casual arrangement." She had been caught up with the news that Jean had finally nailed the job for Hudge in the caf. But that had only been when Jean had finally accepted the fact that *Des* wasn't going to wash dishes for her. Des wanted the job for *Hudge* and the post was permanent as long as Hudge took his overall home for washing. Des had told her and Hudge without having to wait for Jean to meet them in the shed at eight. Des must have seen Jean this Wednesday, this Wednesday afternoon then.

"Since when have you started having 'casual arrangements'?" he said mimicking her, sticking his nose in the air and raising the pitch of his voice.

"What is this? Am I on trial?" she shouted back. A curtain in the house opposite twitched. They were being watched.

"You never answer my questions. You never answer them," Des said.

How dare he interrogate her when he cleared off every Wednesday afternoon? "I met him this afternoon, when you buggered off and left me again. What do you *do* on Wednesday afternoons?"

"Leave Wednesdays out of this." He kicked a stone into the kerb. Hudge was standing between the two of them, head at a Wimbledon final.

"You see. You never answer *my* questions. I'll ask Hudge," she said.

"You leave Hudge out of this."

"Why?" she found herself saying. "What are you going to do? Beat me up for involving him like you do everybody else?"

"Don't go round telling people I'm re-sitting my exams." He was starting to walk up Alpha Road. He obviously didn't want to walk back through the caf as a short cut.

What had happened in the caf? He stopped still, turned round, walked up to her and held his face very close. Des did this frequently when he wanted to make a point. Aida did it too. Then he said, "Geoff Mabs is welcome to you. He looks like an ape."

"Geoff Mabs looks nothing like an ape."

"I see," he said, lifting a dark eyebrow.

"What have you said to him?" she asked.

"I told him to re-sit his arse." He turned and stormed off up Alpha, his hands stuck in his leather jacket pockets and his head held high. Sometimes he acted like he was eleven again. He never said 'sorry', but he had never been mad about what she was doing elsewhere. Des was quick to play biased referee for his elder brother, but she was out on the playing field on her own. She had never seen him like this before and she suddenly realised that Hudge hadn't moved. He was still standing by the lamp post. "What does he *do* on Wednesday afternoons, Hudge?"

Hudge shook his head. "You never answer the questions, Lily. You never answer the questions."

"Hudge. Des will be waiting for you at the top of Alpha. He knows you can't cross the main road without him."

Hudge looked up Alpha and squinted his eyes in the dying light. Then he thrust his hands into his trousers pockets, stuck his head into the air and strutted off in the same childish way as Des had done. She smiled.

Then she walked back slowly to her own yard and thought about Geoff Mabs and smiled again. She smiled again for a different reason because he had been both wicked and playful at the same time; like his eyes.

Mrs Papanikalou's curtain at 17, Alpha Road was dropped. It was evidence which would later be used in court.

2

FRIDAY 21ST AUGUST, 1959

"It's Friday, six o'clock closing and I can see your boyfriend's mother heading this way up Peterson Road with Bessie Fenchurch." Gordon Lee swiftly turned the grocery shop 'open' sign to 'closed'. "I swear Aida Hodge sets her clock by my closing times. Mrs bloody Omega your boyfriend's mother is. No forward planning that family. She's always the last one of the day and she only ever comes in to buy a loaf of bread or a packet of chipolatas sausages. I think she shops elsewhere and comes to torment me last thing on a Friday." Gordon Lee took his business and his livelihood very seriously but he liked to get bathed on a Friday night and out to greyhound racing at Catford. The Hodges always blighted his betting.

Lily was stacking tins of baked beans. "She does sometimes shop elsewhere, Dad. It's because you sacked her when I was two. And Des is not my boyfriend."

"We employed Aida Hodge as your babysitter, and she used to park your pram outside this shop and stand at this counter with your mother jawing whilst I was paying her wages." Gordon pushed his dark-rimmed spectacles up to the bridge of his nose and resumed his stocktaking which meant counting the number of fruit pies in small cardboard boxes.

The grocery shop bell sounded 'ding dong'. Aida Hodge ignored Gordon Lee's 'closed' signs. "God only tests those he cares about," she was saying to Bessie Fenchurch, "the rest He leaves to the devil."

"To the devil, yes," Bessie said to her stringed shopping bag.

Aida was suddenly mesmerised. At first by Bessie's laquered and peroxided bouffant and then she looked wildly into the air. Lily, Gordon and Bessie looked at her in amazement when she suddenly whipped the stocktaking notebook from Gordon's hand and violently sawed the air before whacking it down on the shop floor. "Wasps," she said. "You want to mind your unwrapped Cheddar, Gordon Lee."

Lily checked that the wasp was deceased. Aida checked Lily. Aida knew how Lily hated wasps.

"Come to tell me how to run my business, Aida?" he replied.

"I'll have a packet of fish fingers," she said.

Gordon went to the frozen food cabinet whilst Aida continued her conversation with Bessie Fenchurch. "And when the Good Lord sets His mind to take me from this earth, I'm passing my organs on to the university ... for research."

Bessie was impressed.

Aida continued. "And if I'd known about the research when my boy Ben was alive, I would have had his organs donated ... but they were very mangled."

Bessie stood beside her in sympathy.

"Did you want these fish fingers, Aida?" Gordon Lee asked.

Aida gave Gordon a brief look of disdain. She had been known to frequently refer to Lily's father as 'that bloody grocer'. Des had said so.

"Yes I do," she said, as though Gordon had just offered her poisoned produce. "I'm not going near that fish and chip shop again. I know they're almost your neighbours, Bessie." The Fenchurches owned the Exchange & Mart three doors up from the chippie on the other side of the main road, "And you won't hear me speak ill of a soul …"

"Ill of a soul … no." Bessie Fenchurch shook her peroxided bouffant and opened her stringed shopping bag to collect the packet of fish fingers Gordon was holding.

"You wouldn't hurt a fly, would you, Aida?" Gordon said.

"But they've been there a week," she said totally ignoring him, "- a week, mark you, and Zelda Mabs smells of whisky and dripping when you meet her on the road."

"On the road …yes." Bessie said.

One of Des's pastimes, as a child, was to go into the Exchange & Mart and ask Bessie if she had 'got any balls'. Des said she didn't have any - neither did Will Fenchurch - who he swore would one day run off with a sailor. They had everything else though. It was a dark little dungeon piled high with frying pans and miscellaneous memorabilia. There had also been rumours around the Teds at the Boys' Games Club that black market could be bought there too. It was a big secret which people told one another one at a time. But the Fenchurches were very cagey about 'black market'and keen to deny it all costs. But the truth was, anything was on offer, at the cheapest of prices, including Bessie's row of sisters, who intermittently opened up shop, had the deliberate hair shades which could only come from a bottle and could shock the knickers off of Lily's mother with the purchase of a tin of pilchards.

"They don't bath," Aida said conspiratorially.

Bessie gasped.

"Gypsies," Aida continued. "And they used to live in a ..." Aida smacked Gordon's stocktaking notebook on Bessie's arm, "caravan."

"And they don't do tick," Bessie said, quickly.

"Where does Aida pick up her unreliable snippets of information?" Gordon mumbled as he spoke down to the baked beans' tins. "And with such speed," he sighed.

Gordon had always said Aida was 'privy to some kind of esoteric circle' (a phrase he had read in one of the 'better' newspapers) which was most likely to do with her being a member of the Prince Philip's Boys Games' Club. Aida Hodge was a short, robust woman who wore woollen coats in the height of summer and never ever wore any stockings at all. She wore corsets though. Hudge made sure everyone knew that.

"So you'd like the fish fingers then Aida?" Gordon Lee retrieved his notebook from her with unmistakeable irritation.

"Well - I'll take two packs if Lily's coming for her tea."

"No. Not tonight, Aida."

A dark pause descended. It was rare that Aida ever stopped talking. This was one of those moments. She frowned at Bessie who frowned back at her. Even Gordon, who had gone to collect another packet of fish fingers from the frozen food cabinet, was surprised.

Lily was still smarting from the 'words' that had taken place between her and Des on the previous Wednesday evening but Aida obviously had other business on her mind. "Well, who's going to see Hudge across the Pennington Road then? He starts his job at the caf tonight – Friday - and I've a shift at the Boys' Games Club. Bingo. Teas."

"Why can't Des?" Lily asked.

"He's got a job. Working nights at the factory. It's just temporary, mind you, Bessie."

"Temporary, yes."

"He's going back to school to do re-sits. I thought he would have told you, Lily. Nights at the Nestles factory. Chocolate. Very sudden."

"He doesn't have to tell me everything, Aida. And besides, I haven't seen him since Wednesday."

Both Aida and Bessie said, "Oh well," and sinking into her double chin, Aida added, "suit yourself, I'll take just the one pack then, seeing as Des said he'd call into the fish shop for his tea."

Gordon placed the packet of fish fingers back in the frozen food cabinet.

"Yes, he's got a job, Lil." Bessie Fenchurch fondled imitation pearls whilst hoisting up a straying bra strap.

"No, I'll come," Lily said.

"That makes a difference does it? Des not being at home?" Aida circled the tiny central display of merchandise with the serious intent of a professional shopper, even though she was wearing her bedroom slippers. She didn't always require answers. In fact, observed Lily, she often clean forgot what she was talking about. Aida embraced the spoken word, for its own sake, her father said, in redundant syllables. In truth, Des not being at home did make a difference to Lily. There was no-one else to see Hudge across the Pennington Road and it was his first night working at the caf, so she would go down to Peterson Road for her tea.

Lily cashed up Bessie's goods and thought about Aida's question. Why did she want to avoid Des? Why could she never even answer her own questions? Most likely, she thought, it had something to do with Geoff Mabs. She hated him for making her feel sick on that roundabout.

She recalled the sensation of having to hold on to the bars with all her force, feeling the weight slip beneath her. She felt as though she were looking in eight different directions at once, but dared not close her eyes. It reminded her of being imprisoned in the spinning rocket at Battersea Fun Fair, when the operators had not fastened the safety belt - but caught it accidentally in the door. She had screamed to explain - but they stood below laughing. Geoff Mabs had not laughed. He had looked.

She had hated him more, for making her cry. Des had never seen her cry. Not even when she had lost at conkers. How could she explain that? Geoff Mabs had unfastened Lily's safety belt and she had come close enough to him to notice he did not smell of dripping. But he smelt of danger ... and she liked it.

But no, Lily had absolutely decided. Her feelings towards Geoff Mabs were totally negative. Yet the recollection of his low, somewhat smudged and insistent voice was gnawing away at that decision. Decisions apart, Geoff Mabs was quietly gnawing away at her.

As an afterthought, but it was quite clearly Aida's reason for shopping, she said to Lily, "And then if you could see him back over the main road at ten, Dolly Chops Daydream - when he knocks off - I'd much appreciate. Jack Oddy's a lovely man - shame about the caf - but he doesn't want to be doing with all that for his employees. Considering his heart ... and all ..."

Bessie Fenchurch examined a jar of Silver Shred marmalade and then looked at Aida with meaning. "Shame about the Oddys, Aida," and Gordon looked up quickly from the Pine Fluid Disinfectant at Aida.

But Aida ignored them both. Lily noticed that her father and Bessie made unusual eye contact. The old people always said, "Shame about the Oddys" and looked at each other in a strange way. It *was* a shame that Jean's mother was dead, this was true. But no-one ever said it about the Hodges. And Ben was dead after all. Lily had seen it happen. From the grocery shop front window when she was eleven. Aida went on and the moment disappeared into the disinfectant. "I've told my Hudge he's a very lucky boy to have a pay packet. I mean, Bessie, when he sat that 11 plus examination, he just kept putting dots where the answers should have been. He didn't answer a single question on the paper and I said Hudge, answer the questions, just answer the questions. Still, he's come ..."

"A long way ..." Lily mimed Aida's words as she stacked the Heinz beans tins.

"... and I just thank the Good Lord He's sent my Hudge a job," Aida said.

"Perhaps you ought to be thanking *Des*, Aida. It wasn't *God* who was originally offered a job in the caf." What Lily was not thanking Des for, was lumbering her with another job: crossing Hudge back and forth the Pennington Road.

"*Saint* Des, now then is it?" Aida said, looking at her quite blankly. And both women combined in a knowing 'ah'. "Of course it was all Des's doings that Hudge has been offered a job but there are better places than the caf to work," Aida pondered.

Bessie agreed, looking knowingly at Aida whilst her hand was making brief contact with the shop door now and then.

"Still - you know what they say about beggars. Not that my boys are," Aida quickly added.

"Oh no," Bessie agreed.

"Buggers more like." Aida let out a resounding raucous laugh - her trademark, which both Lily and Bessie found more amusing than the comment itself. "Give me half a pound of self raising flour, Lily. I'm going blackberry picking on Sunday, Lil, with the Boys' club, so you can come over after Evensong and help bake blackberry and apple pies with me like you do every late summer," she said, catching Gordon's eye as he emerged from the scullery carrying a cardboard box of Bisto gravy powder.

"Okay, Aida," Lily said, placing the flour in Bessie's string bag. The members of the Boys' club would pick blackberries for Aida every summer because she made the best blackberry and apple pies. Piles of them for sale at the cake stall in aid of black children in Africa.

"Look," her father said, "why don't you all go and jaw in the proper place. Go and have a coffee in the caf - the lot of you. And let me run my business."

"Huh," Aida said with a mildish dose of outrage. "I wouldn't be seen dead in the place. Give me two packs of fish fingers, Lily. And charge one up to your father - seeing as I'm giving you your tea." She went to leave the shop and then turned back and said, "On tick," before dropping some coins into the wax child's box which read, "Give to Polio'

"Now remember Lily," Aida said, tying a scarf beneath the wobbling chins, "seven-thirty start for Hudge and ten o'clock finish. Sharp. No lingering at the caf. Hell-hole. Now where's my bag?"

It was later that Friday evening. Hudge was slowly eating his egg and chips at the table in the back room. He pushed back his chair and retrieved a very large handbag from beneath the billowing, checked tablecloth. Lily wondered for a moment if it was true - what her mother had said: that Aida used bed sheets for tablecloths.

"Thank you, Hudge. You're a very lucky boy to get this job, so remember what Des said. Clean those dishes well and don't talk to no-one. I knew Jack Oddy would do me a favour," she said nodding her head and then muttered to herself, "Jack Oddy and me … we …" She quickly changed her tune. Lily noticed that the adults quickly changd tune – usually when they felt they were giving something away. "I'll get away from running the teas at the Boys' Club as soon as I can Lily, so you won't have to wait. Here's the key. Give us a kiss, Hudge."

Aida slammed the front door shut and Lily suspected that Aida running teas would run on and on through this back end of summer and into the autumn. The Boys' Games Clubs had been set up nationally to keep the Teds from standing on street corners but as far as she could see they ended up in Jean Oddy's caf. Aida obviously didn't know that Jean Oddy was doing Des a favour. Jack Oddy didn't do anyone any favours.

She watched Hudge concentrating on a home-made chip he was dipping into a runny fried egg. What was Aida going to do when she went back to school? Even if Des did go back for re-sits in the autumn, Hudge couldn't rely on his brother forever. I mean, as Mum says, where is it all going to end?

"Friday night, Lil. No fish and chips?" Hudge asked her.

"The new people don't do tick, Hudge."

He mouthed an 'oh' and then asked, "Did you get any sweets from Perrys, Lil?"

Lily shook her head.

"Did you forget the fruit gums, Lil?" Hudge let out one of his raucous laughs because he was imitating the Rowntrees' television advertisement.

"You've got to think about your figure. And your teeth. Make sure you brush them now before starting work." Lily had always waited for Hudge to grow up. It was all so much easier when they were younger. When Des was about fourteen, when his father had just run away to sea and 'the French Foreign Legion', Aida would send him up to Perry's for Walnut Whips and Caramel Crunch. Mrs Perry who was about ninety five would reach out for her huge sweet jars: the clatter of Butterscotch Twirls and Liquorice Allsorts hitting the weighing machine was Everly Brothers to the ears. Blackjacks and Fruit Salads for Hudge. Acid Drops for Des, of course. Pineapple Chunks for Lil. Then it was a Friday night feast without the ration books down in Peterson Road with Aida's legs propped up on the mantelpiece and Michael Miles and *Take Your Pick* on the new telly. It had been the happiest of times for the Hodge family, when Reg left. Aida always said, as she bit into her Nut Crunch, that sweet rationing had ended 'in more ways than one', and it had all been easier then.

There would come a time when both she and Des would want, need, to move away. Lily longed for that day. What would become of Hudge then? No thinking ahead - that was the trouble. Her father was right.

Lily gathered up the magazines which lay scattered across the kitchen table. Aida loved to invent impossible holidays. It was one of her favourite pastimes - flicking through the Butlins' advertisements with Pollyanna optimism. Even if she had the money, thought Lily, she'd never get there. She was totally disorganised. Aida covered distances in her head though. Most years Lily went with her parents to a caravan in Bognor Regis, whilst 'Auntie' Rose 'minded' the shop. Auntie Rose was, in fact, Lily's cousin, not much younger than Lily's mother, with honeyed legs and lips and nails which demanded constant attention. On their return from Bognor Regis, her father would always complain that there were very few takings. 'Auntie' Rose hardly ever opened up shop. In fact Gordon had often pleaded with Lily's mother to ask one of her numerous and much older sisters who oozed from every corner if they could mind the shop instead, because he certainly wasn't going to ask Aida. She would filch the profits. But Cecilia's older sisters were always in another country. This year Aunt Iris wasn't taking the flight across the pond from Connecticut and, incidentally, Des had been bloody nasty since Cecilia told him.

As Lily picked up the Butlins' brochures, she realised that Des and Hudge had never been on holiday. She then noticed some forms lying on the orange and green checked tablecloth. They must have been Aida's forms from the university she was always going on about: the ones to do with her organs. But they weren't. They said 'Emigration' on the top. To Australia. Lily's brow furrowed just slightly. Then she didn't give it another thought. Aida travelled miles in her head.

Lily looked fondly at the photo of Ben and Kay on Aida's precious sideboard. Even though her father had sacked Aida when Lily was two there had been no real ill-will. Lily had been one of Ben and Kay's six bridesmaids. Ben and Kay. Kay and Ben. Smiling out in black and white. Six years ago and not long after, smash, crash, mild-mannered Ben had been killed right there in front of their grocery shop, motor bike splayed out towards the haberdashers on the other side. Lily had heard it and ran to the front room window. Cecilia had rushed up the narrow staircase from the shop to pull her away from the front room window. Aida had carried the indelible sadness in her eyes of one who had lost more than letters of the alphabet could ever say. For once Aida had been literally lost for words and Des's father, Reg had left soon after. After the Coronation. When she and Jean went to different schools. *That Reg was a dark horse.* What did dark horses do?

"Can we play snap?" Hudge interrupted her thoughts. His teeth were covered in egg yolk and he was brushing them with a chip.

"No Hudge. You've got work tonight, remember?" She took out her hanky and wiped his teeth clean.

"Yes. I'm very lucky, Lily." He then got up at once to fetch his coat.

Damn, thought Lily. Say anything to him and he thinks it's immediate. Like Christmas. Des and Lily never mentioned Christmas because Hudge would go searching for old socks in June to hang on the mantelpiece. Still ten minutes to go. It took only three minutes to get from the Hodge house in Peterson Road up to Pennington. Never mind.

I'll teach him to cross the road, she thought, as she wiped away the congealed egg from his mouth. *Teach him to cross the road by himself.* That's what I'll do. She would spend her life wishing she hadn't tried.

Lily stood outside the Exchange & Mart, facing the caf and sighed deeply. Pennington was a dangerous through road to the city and the traffic didn't ease up at any time of day. At night, in her attic bedroom which faced Peterson, she fell asleep to the roar of vehicles and the roll of the trains into the nearby station. It would take a miracle for Hudge to get across this moving jungle safely.

"Look right, look left, if the road's clear, then quick march ..." Hudge stepped into the road. "No, Hudge, there's a bloody lorry coming."

"Can we play 'snap' tonight, Lily?"

"Hudge, your mum told you. You're washing dishes in the caf tonight."

"And I'm lucky."

"To get this job, and don't talk to no-one."

"Des said."

"And no handling money," Lily reminded him again.

Hudge nodded. "And bring me overall home for washing."

"And I'll teach you to cross the road, Hudge, if it's the last thing I'll do or I'll be fetching and carrying you until Christmas,"

"What are you getting me for Christmas, Lil?"

"Hudge, look right, look left, is the road clear?"

Hudge nodded and stepped into the road. But Lily placed a hand across his chest and screamed, "It's not clear, Hudge. There's a motor bike."

Hudge sighed very deeply. "You never answer the questions, Lily."

But Lily was concentrating just as deeply on her road. She had seen a quick gap in the traffic. "Now, Hudge, now. Quick march."

Safely into the caf, thought Lily. Goodness gracious, great balls of fire, she sighed as she stepped on to the grocery shop's black and white chequered doorstep and opened the front door.

****

Winnie Brambles, turning the sign to 'closed' on the greengrocery shop door, half past seven, Friday night, stood watching Lily Lee obviously telling Hudge Hodge to 'look right, look left'.

"Aida Hodge would have a blue fit," she said to her huge husband who had just come in through the scullery back door and lived in an old trilby hat.

"I've just checked the coalmen's delivery and they've left the right number of bags this week," he said. "The van's standing upright in Alpha Road and still in one piece. Maybe we should think about building a garage and selling the stables."

Mrs Brambles unzipped the purse in the front of her canvas apron. "As if Aida would ever let that boy attempt to cross this road on his own. After Ben ... and all that business." The Brambles spread plenty of crumbs for the street pigeons but gossip was something they did not share, not even with each other. "Did the coalmen deliver the right number of bags this week?"

"Ah ..." Mr Brambles said, shaking his double chins, "Ben. Poor Aida. She's had a hard time, Aida Hodge, she's suffered in more ways than one." Then he added as he climbed the stairs, "She had King Edwards' on tick tonight, Winnie."

But Winnie Brambles did not hear him. Winnie Brambles, who was to later give crucial evidence suffered herself from poor hearing and was to have a hard time catching what the prosecuting barrister said. But now she was watching that kid with the bit between his teeth taking a photo of Lily and Hudge from behind them, in the doorway of the Exchange & Mart. The chippie boy saw her and placed a forefinger up to her as if giving her a warning. She understood sign language. "Bully boy," she muttered to herself. "You'll come to a bad end."

****

"You're a big bloke, aren't you, Hodge?" Mabs couldn't believe his luck when he walked into the caf that Friday night. He had wondered why Lily Lee was crossing Pennington with Hudge but didn't think the spaz would actually be working here. Mabs watched the daft boy carry two cups of coffee from the counter to his table. Papanikalou and Flick gave a soft snigger as they ate free chips from yesterday's newspaper. Mabs put the beer bottle to his mouth, took a swig and then licked his lips. This could be fun.

"My name's Hudge," the daft boy said quietly.

"I said you're a big boy, aren't you, Hudge Hodge?"

Hudge placed the coffees on the table with shaking hands but he said nothing.

"Can't you answer questions?"

"Des said not to speak to anyone. Just wash dishes, but then Jean asked me to bring your coffees 'cos her dad's upstairs with Angina."

Mabs looked sideways at Papanikalou and Flick. "Who's Angina?"

But Hudge said nothing.

"Are you a big bloke?" Mabs asked.

Hudge began to move back to the counter. Mabs was determined to get a response. "Have you got a girlfriend?"

The spaz began to laugh, was encouraged by the others' laughter. Even the girl who always wore yellow polka dot - was that her only outfit? - laughed too. Hudge laughed some more and more until he seemed unable to stop himself, until it was a crazy hysteria. The youths stopped laughing. Papanikalou's dark eyebrows rose in disbelief. Flick shook his head. Teresa in her yellow polka dot took a sip of milkshake but Mabs had only started. "Come on. Answer the question. Have you got a girlfriend?" he shouted over the daft boy's shrieking and clutching of his stomach.

Hudge cried, "Yes, yes" and stamped his feet with joy. "I got a girlfriend."

"Lucky boy," Mabs said, smiling at the others and downing more beer.

"I am lucky."

"What's her name?"

"No," Hudge's face crumpled. Out went the bottom lip. "Not telling."

"Oh go on, Hudge, tell us her name," Papanikalou said, stretching out his pleading arms. Teresa joined the chorus, "Oh go on, Hudge, tell us your girlfriend's name. Please. Please." It wasn't long before a few of the other Teds were shouting - what's her name, what's her name?

That was enough for now. Steady boy. Mabs lifted his coffee cup and deliberately emptied the contents on the table.

"Look what you've done, Geoffrey Mabs," Flick said, shoving free chips into his mouth. "You are a naughty boy."

"Am, aren't I, Flick? Fetch us a cloth, Hudge."

Hudge moved to the counter to do as he was told when Mabs began to sing, slowly and quietly to the tune of 'Happy Birthday' - Who's your girlfriend, Hudge Hodge? Who's your girlfriend, Hudge Hodge? until the whole caf was singing. Mabs could feel the rate of his breathing increase with the rise in volume of the chanting and something in the simplicity made his mind flicker with recognition. The caf lobsters were shouting it loud now and Mabs suddenly remembered how he had learned to forget. Nasty things got pushed into a convenient dark room.

"Enough, Mabs." Jean had opened the scullery door and she stilettoed her way around the counter to his table. "Or I'll let Des know about this."

Mabs smiled as he watched the short sharp daggers of her high heels clip clop back around the counter.

****

Lily was waiting for the World News to burst into the upstairs front room, before jumping to duty, ten o'clock sharp that Friday night.

On such days of early five o'clock turns at the station, quick shut eye in the afternoons and shifts in the downstairs' shop, Gordon Lee would burst in through the door with a tray full of Horlicks and paste sandwiches. The next morning he would then rise at seven, open up shop and with Cecilia on afternoon shift, he would get to the station for late turn until nine. Even on late turn days, Gordon could return home for the World News and supper. In between all this, Gordon Lee mysteriously sold clocks house to house.

For now, her mother was click, click, clicking knitting needles, immersed in *Wagon Train* - a Western with nice-looking cowboys. Lily was jaded. Now that Des and Hudge both had evening jobs the summer was going to be pretty boring. Pretty boring, she whispered.

"What?" Cecilia Lee quickly glanced at her daughter and then rested her eyes once again upon the television.

"Wagon Train's boring," she said. "I thought I might stay at Aida's tonight - seeing as I've got to take Hudge home." Lily had been contemplating sex. Flirting with the idea more like. Just as Des was flirting with the idea of taking re-sits. Probably nothing would happen with Des and certainly couldn't with Geoff Mabs, could it? But she wanted to have sex before she died.

"Well you can forget that notion as soon as you like." Cecilia Lee click, click, clicked her knitting needles and pulled a strand of wool towards her twin set.

Her mother could read her mind.

"Aida Hodge has only reared boys," she carried on. "God knows what she'd allow you to get up to, given half the chance. She hasn't always worn corsets, that's for sure. And that's that." Cecilia re-adjusted the cushion behind her back, as if to reinforce this statement. She then re-focused on *Wagon Train* and the group of good-looking cowboy pioneers in search of a new life. Her mother identified with this notion on behalf of her sisters. Des said Cecilia did everything 'by proxy' including sex.

"You've always let me stay in Peterson Road every summer before now," Lily said.

"Not this summer. Iris is getting her teeth crowned," her mother said.

"Your elder sister Iris didn't keep her corsets on either, Cis, so don't go throwing bricks at glass houses." Gordon placed a mug of Horlicks on the mantelpiece by Cecilia's chair. The 'almost' ten o'clock city train rumbled by and *Wagon Train's* credits rolled. Gordon was running slightly early.

Cecilia pulled her lips together. "Don't you bring up my eldest sister."

"You brought her up, Mum," Lily said.

"I'll bring your sister up every time you start to talk about other people's morals," Gordon said taking a mouthful of paste sandwich.

"My sister's morals have got nothing to do with me. And she never had a patch on the Oddys," she said waving the sandwich at him across the front room.

"Cis, shush. Jack Oddy's a good man."

She bit into a paste sandwich as if biting back her tongue. As if she knew she shouldn't have said that about the Oddys. There was a local and adult 'shushing' about the Oddys. "Gordon, I think we could run to more than paste at this time of night,"was all her mother said.

"Cis, shush."

These kind of parental repeats frightened Lily. Would she and Des end up jawing like this? Or skirting around subjects like her parents always did when people like Jack Oddy or Aunt Iris were ever mentioned? One of the reasons Lily didn't succumb to a man's charms, as her mother would say was because of Aunt Iris. Aunt Iris had been six years older than Lily's mother and had become pregnant with 'Auntie' Rose at the age of sixteen. This was almost thirty years ago and the effect on the family had been shocking. 'Auntie' Rose had been brought up as Cecilia's sister. The sins ... sin ... of the fathers ..., as Aida would say. Auntie Iris had run off with an American GI, in the same way that Des's father had 'run off' and joined the French Foreign Legion. Lots of running off.

Aunt Iris may have been the family black lamb who was verbally slaughtered periodically for her sin, but almost as regularly, it seemed, she would alight from Cunard liners: a chignoned, high-heeled, transatlantic queen. Latterly, when feathered flight was her preference, she would trail BOAC flight bags, moult mink and nicotine and sit in her youngest sister's kitchen knocking back straight scotch, putting Pennington to rights. Of which she knew absolutely nothing at all but pretended she did. On arrival, Aunt Iris imported all brands of transatlantic baggage and Lily's mother seemed to move to a dark place when her sister arrived. As Fall approached - at Blackberry Picking time, Lily would be packed off to Peterson Road, so that her mother could accommodate her eldest sister's suitcases. It was another of Cecilia's arrangements as the grocery shop had only two bedrooms. So did 47, Peterson Road but no matter.

Aida always moved into Hudge and Des's bedroom and Des had slept on the front room sofa. This left Lily for ten days of every enormous six week summer holiday sleeping in Aida's double bed.

Iris loved Aida. Aida loved Iris's pearl-studded plumage and they would often secretly rendezvous with blackberries and bourbon. Iris would annually stiletto up Peterson and stagger with a swish and a sway of her rounded hips back down to the shop. And secretly Lily loved the feathered-hatted Iris for she knew her aunt was a rare breed. The rest of her mother's sisters were pale but all the same painted shadows of this particular Iris bird and all, with the exception of Cecilia were named after flowers. A bunch of idle cockney sparrows, her father called them, all with the exception of his wife, who although she did love to shop, always opened it up, six days a week.

Lily loved her aunts. Aunts did things without expectation of return payment. Not like Granda Siddy who gave her sixpence and then asked her to pop up to Perrys for a box of baccy. Aunts took you to Trafalgar Square and told you that Admiral Nelson was your great great grandfather. Aunts pressed five dollar notes into your palm and said, "Sssh ..." just as they did when they took you to Verrys on Regent Street for Knickerbocker Glories because they couldn't or wouldn't cook. Aunts bought you *Girls' Crystal* annuals on soggy days and the world was colourless without them. Aunts did all this and all because the ladies loved to be liked.

Gordon Lee said that her mother's sisters flocked together as a pattern in distress and in migration, which gave Lil a feeling of togetherness. All of Cecilia's true three sisters: Iris, Violet and Margaret, called Daisy, had flown west 'after the war', or rather sailed ...

When the Queen Mary or Queen Elizabeth's foghorns heralded sail for Iris at Southampton to New York each September, Lily's mother would sigh and say, "She never had an education. She can't be blamed." Yet it seemed to Lily that Aunt Iris, married, divorced and married again to the same man who dealt in leather hadn't done splendidly badly for herself and all without an examination to her name. Their company – 'Hell for Leather' had made a hell of a lot of money.

This year Iris was not coming. She was getting her teeth crowned.

Lily studied her mother - so upright and proper in her comfortable chair and wondered how her mother had ever been able to have sex. Cecilia loved to sit, and she did it so well. Lily had no brothers or sisters. Cecilia had taken one look at Lily when she was born and told Gordon, so Rose had said, "If you want any more - you can have them yourself."

Her mother only ever liked doing things once, Lily observed. A day trip to Brighton and 'that was that'. Cecilia Lee had no inclination to travel second time around the track and certainly no desire to visit New York which Lily was determined to do. Preferably in Cashmere.

Auntie Rose wanted to go to Connecticut permanently and live with Iris, but Cecilia was having none of it. "I don't like the sound of that arrangement," Cecilia had said to Rose before they went off to the caravan in Bognor Regis and her mother had cried the whole of the week's holiday. Auntie Rose did not go to Connecticut.

"I'm not sure either," she said, pulling another strand of wool up towards her and averting her eyes momentarily from the television, "I like this new arrangement with Hugh." The News had started. Cecilia gave Lily her full attention. Gordon gave The News his. Her mother always referred to Hudge - a childish nickname she and Des had christened him - by his proper name - Hugh. "Aida works most nights at the Boys' club. I mean where is it all going to end?"

"Cis, shush, the News has started."

"I've got that sorted, Mum. I'm teaching Hudge to cross the road by himself."

Cecilia Lee lifted her eyebrows and dropped the corners of her mouth. "You might as well teach him calculus Lily and you know it."

Lily sighed. It was true. Look right. Look left. Hudge didn't know his right from his left.

"But you taught him gin rummy, Cis," Gordon said.

"Gordon, shush."

Laughing voices from the Pennington Road drifted up into the front room.

"Closing time at the caf," Cecilia sighed. "Go through the yard, Lily. If you open up the shop door, they'll be at the till. Besides, your father mortice-locks the door after nine. We'll leave the back door open."

Her father mortice-locked the door after nine; a creature of habit Gordon Lee so there was no way out through the front door unless the keys got stolen of course and Gordon guarded his keys as well as Cecilia guarded her daughter's virginity.

"Oh, Mum," Lily went to protest.

"Do as I say or put an end to the arrangement." Stab, stab with the old needles.

Lily slipped down the narrow staircase, through the darkness of the shop and out by the back scullery door. In the stillness of the summer night the shouting and bitching coming from the main road could be heard distinctly. The noise was a familiar backdrop and was always worse in the summer.

It had been a hot summer - plagued by wasps. Lily told her father she should be paid 'danger money' for working in the shop. The garage was full of debris. You could hide anything in that garage. Lily was certain that the wasps had nested in Cecilia's old coats. She could hear a low hum as she closed the garage door behind her as if they were about to seep out and swarm at any moment. She hated them.

The Lees were one of the few families who owned a garage - a double garage at that - on the road. Many had tried to rent the extra space - but Gordon Lee preferred privacy for his black beetled Ford Anglia, used for trips to the wholesalers, customer deliveries, clock collections and the odd 'Sunday run out'. Cecilia would sometimes say, "Let's go for a drive, Gordon". And that's what they would do. Drive. It was a pastime in itself.

Lily walked up Alpha Road, the all-pervading smell of timber lingering in the warm night air. She passed several yards: Matthews' Glass Engraver's, Perry's Newsagent's, Brambles' Greengrocer's just next to the caf and the Brambles' Ford Poplar van.

Winnie Brambles was as darkly fleshy as her mature purple plums and tended an orchard of fresh fruit and vegetables on the Pennington Road. Lily's father said the Brambles 'descended from a long line of travelling communities'. Percy Brambles regularly brought home stray dogs and men to sup in their tiny kitchen which spilled over with roasted vegetables and dusky grandchildren. He had used his carthorses mostly to transport stock, but he had also collected rag and bone as well as tramps down on their luck. The Brambles' hearts were as huge as autumn pumpkins and as tender as the way Winnie cooked them. They had just begun to adapt reluctantly to the engine, parking it for convenience at their rear entrance in Alpha rather than using their disused stables at the rec. The Brambles missed their carthorses and sighed mightily, wondering at the swift passage of time and where it would all end.

Lily, often called 'Dolly Daydream' by Aida, suddenly realised the Oddy's gate would not be open. *Mr Oddy locked the back door and gate at night,* partly for security reasons but mostly to rid the shed of caf customers who spilled out from the scullery on hot nights. Jean had always allowed Lily and the Hodges access during the day. It had been the childhood clubhouse and a habit. The night time locking would mean walking up to the top of Alpha around Carlisle and into Pennington. And there was always a gang of Teds outside the chippie, opposite the billboards, ready for trouble.

She gave the gate a half-hearted push. Amazingly, it was open. Perhaps if it had remained locked; if there had been no access to the Oddy's yard, perhaps then it might have all been different. The stench from the rotting refuse, on this warm night, made Lily retch slightly. Hudge had obviously been on the look-out for her arrival. Lily could see his huge frame at the window which overlooked the yard. This must be how a mother feels on collecting her child the first day at school. He's probably been standing there, washing dishes, clock-watching and yard-watching. She knew he would be relieved to see her.

The scullery door was open and she winced from the bright neon light, taking two steps up into the cafe. Hudge was drying his hands on a grubby tea-towel, by the chipped enamel sink. Lily detected some sadness in his eyes. "I'm here, Hudge. Had a good time?"

The chins he had inherited from Aida began to shake. He threw his arms about Lily and began to weep softly.

"Oh, Hudge." Lily reached up and stroked his baby-fine hair. "What's the matter? Let's get your overall off." Best to get him home, she thought.

"I got to take it home for washing," he said.

Lily helped him with the buttons, although Hudge could cope quite adequately on his own. She folded it over his arm and taking him by the hand led him to the front door. Jean Oddy and Geoff Mabs were seated in the corner, by the juke-box. What was he doing there?

"What's the matter with Hudge tonight, Jean?"

Jean ran painted fingernails through her dark hair and gave Geoff Mabs one of those looks she often gave Des, tilting her head down and looking up at her eyebrows like Scarlett O'Hara. "Nothing. It's just been a busy night - Friday - hasn't it Hudge?"

Hudge nodded.

"Goodnight then." Lily opened the caf front door and helped Hudge down the step, thinking that Jean fancied the fluorescent socks off of Geoff Mabs. She then heard the door close quickly behind them. Geoff Mabs was standing on the step above them.

"I was wondering," he said in that blurred voice, "fancy coming to the pub tonight, Lily Lee?"

"How do you know my name?"

"Bothered to find out."

Lily looked up at Geoff Mabs. "Thanks. But I've got to see Hudge home tonight." She smiled a little. Lily turned towards the main road, still holding Hudge's hand.

She crossed the road with Hudge, smiled again and wiggled her backside just slightly. Geoff Mabs had very broad shoulders and he definitely liked her.

****

Lily Lee, Geoff Mabs had decided was beautiful. He came to this decision when he traced the knicker line through her denim jeans as she was crossing the Pennington Road earlier that evening. He was now with Jean and generally warm feelings were spare on his pavement. The closest Geoff Mabs came to it, was buying a girl a half of lager.

He had just bought Jean three that Friday night and downed twice as many himself. He was looking across at her as they walked down Pennington. Her ears were pierced with cheap studs which glittered light from an overhead street lamp. In fact Jean Oddy was a bit like those cheap but sparkling decorations his grandfather put on the uprooted tree every Christmas Eve. Geoff looked across from the pub to the church which sang signs.

"The Gates of Heaven are Here," Jean said.

"Eh?"

"On the church signs," she said, indicating the boards up above the Church of the Nazarene.

"If you say so," he said.

On three halves of lager, Jean Oddy was about to give him a piece of his kind of heaven. He was now placing an arm about her shoulder. That made her feel good, he knew; gave her a sense of belonging, ownership even. He hadn't liked to do it in the pub, the Dragon's Head, on the corner of the main road. Papanikalou and Flick might take it the wrong way, either as going soft, or taking the Oddy girl too seriously. Jean wouldn't do that - take things too seriously. He knew her type. Mabs and Jean were one of a kind.

They walked up past the timber yard's warehouse front and Mabs looked up at the grocery shop flat: lights out for the Lees. Where was she then? Did she stay at the daft boy's house? In his brother's bed? He looked down Peterson Road. "That's where the Hodge brothers live, isn't it?"

"Yes and Des Hodge fires up easy, so don't bug him."

That bugged Mabs.

"What's he to you?"

She shrugged and stilettoed on towards her caf, scraping her heels on the paving stones. "Des was very good to me when my mum died."

"I bet he was. Cocky bastard," he went on. "Re-sit my arse. I'd like to give him one of my lessons."

"Oh give over, Mabs. When were you last in a classroom? He only failed his exams to avoid doing National Service. He went to the grammar." Grammar. She said the word in a very important way. Grammar. Her jaw dropped with the word. "Lily and Des went to the grammar." She said it again. "No-one can match Des Hodge."

"I wasn't thinking about giving him an education. I was thinking about showing him the back of my hand ..." Charlie used to say that ...

I'll show you the back of my hand, my boy. "Just for a game, for a laugh," he added.

She ignored his comments. "Why ain't you done National Service then?" The dragging and scraping on the pavement was giving him a headache. She had a big bum too - waddling up Pennington in her puffed and petticoated skirt.

"Asthma," he said.

He hadn't worked out this thing that Lily Lee and Des Hodge had going. Hadn't wanted to probe Jean too deeply on the subject. He wondered then if the Lee girl had said anything about the rec. to her boyfriend. The thought of her sleeping with Des made him take a sharp intake of breath.

"Penny for them?" she said.

Mabs looked down at Jean. "You'd have to pay a lot more than that for my thoughts, girl."

"Don't call me 'girl'." She was sharp and insistent, Jean Oddy. Like a screwdriver.

Mabs realised she had stopped outside the cafe, thrusting her face up to him. Wanting a kiss. Seal the evening with a bit more than a kiss. "I was thinking it would be good to go somewhere a bit ... private."

"We can't go through the caf. Dad will hear us. If we walk up to the top of Pennington and round the back of Alpha, we can get into our yard."

Mabs flinched at the forward planning, but then he too had come prepared hadn't he? Slipped into the lav for a rubber friend, 'because you never know these days'. He put his arm through hers and smiled. He had a winning smile, he knew that. "Your shed?"

She nodded. Yeah, women softened to his smile. Born lucky. The anticipation was sometimes better than the real thing. Sometimes.

They were approaching the billboards on the corner of the main road opposite the fish and chip shop. An almost life-size poster of a Morris Mini-Car stood out against a seedy backdrop. Mabs had stared at it between fry-ups from across the road, during the past week. "Look," he said with passion, squeezing Jean's shoulder tightly. "That car can do over seventy miles an hour because of its low overall weight. It's fast, sleek, and low-down." The way I like my women, thought Mabs.

"Really?" Jean said in a sarcastic kind of way, her round nose seriously facing forward as they were heading for the bridge.

"That's where I'm going to be in ten years," he said, stopping and looking up at the poster.

Jean just laughed. "That's just the stuff that dreams are made of."

"I'm going to make films. I'm going to America. We've got family there. I've got a dark room in our loft where I develop my photos. You can come there sometime. I'm going to have my own photo exhibition some day. Either that or I'll kill myself by the time I'm thirty. I'll cut my throat if I don't make good. I swear I will, Jean."

She took his hand in hers and then she gave a very nasty laugh. "You'll never do that," she said.

Mabs wasn't quite sure whether she meant killing himself or making good. But her comment annoyed him and her laughter shook him up. Anyway, he wasn't going to labour the subject. Didn't want too much chat. Women didn't like you talking about the future - if it didn't include them.

"Come and see where I was ten years ago," she said, and led him around the corner of Carlisle Street.

He quickened his pace and started to drag her into Alpha Road.

"Steady on," she said. She slowed down and withdrew her wrist from his hand. "You were a bit rough on Hudge tonight."

Hudge. Geoff Mabs relished the fear in Hudge's eyes. In the same way as he had done with Lily on the roundabout. "Just a joke - just a game," he said. The way Charlie used to say it.

"This is it," Jean said. "Alpha Road. This is where we grew up."

"A dead end," he said.

"A cul-de-sac," she said.

"Bet you were a beautiful child." He didn't think she was beautiful now.

"Bet you say that to all the girls." She was impressed, he could see.

He moved her at a brisker pace up Alpha Road but as they approached her back gate she gave it a push with her backside and whispered, "I opened the back gate earlier this evening."

Mabs was overwhelmed with Jean’s ‘planning’ and the stench from the rotting refuse which was strewn across the yard. She's done this before, he thought as she opened the shed door. So had he.

He threw his jacket down on the shed floor and placed his camera carefully on an upturned orange box, donated by the Brambles’ greengrocery: the name was stamped on the side. Then he gave Jean's sweaty hand a sharp tug. Down she came. He moved his hand up her short leg and long skirt until he came to her suspender belt. She undid his trousers and he moved aside the crutch of her knickers. She snorted with laughter.

Got her, thought Geoff Mabs. And never had to say I loved her.

3

SATURDAY 22ND AUGUST, 1959

"You've got beautiful eyes," he said, standing opposite the slab of today's Wensleydale in the clear light of a Saturday morning. "Has anyone ever told you that?"

"Consistently," she said, fumbling with the cheese wire cutter and almost slicing her thumb in half.

"What's the colour of mine?" he asked.

"Blue."

She said that too quickly.

"And nice teeth too."

"They're my crowning glory," she said.

"I don't think you're as sure of yourself as you like to make out."

She didn't answer. The colour was again rising to her cheeks. He liked that. Geoff Mabs was very, very sure of himself: with women. Steady with that wire cutter.

"Or else you'd come out with me tomorrow." He had other plans for tonight.

"I help Dad scrap the week's Wavy Line reductions on a Sunday."

"All day?"

"No."

"Right. I'll meet you on the bridge at three,"

"No you won't," she said.

He narrowed his watchful eyes and gave a playful smile as if to say - scared?

"You'll come to my front door," she added.

An old-fashioned girl then, he thought. Or a mother who insists. Okay, charm the mother. "All right, Lily." Then he picked up a copy of her *Woman's Realm* magazine which was lying on the counter and splattered a wasp across the open and closed sign on the glass front door. "Watch you don't get stung now," he said.

As he opened the grocery shop door to leave it sounded - ding ding - and he gave another of those playful smiles and winked - an almost nervous habit - which he knew was charming all the same.

****

Lily fiddled with the wire cheese-cutter as she watched Geoff Mabs cross the Pennington Road, whilst also keeping an eye out for wasps. His hands were thrust into his trouser pockets and he sauntered. And he always carried that camera. He had, what Cecilia would call, bravado. He was *so* attractive when he sauntered. Lily unwrapped a slab of English Cheddar, her favourite, sliced off a sliver of cheese and ate. Once, her mother had scraped a knife on the bottom of the Belfast sink in the back scullery. Lily's nerves had jangled from the centre of her head to just below her sternum. Geoff Mabs made her feel that way.

But he was far from boring. Boredom was a state from which Lily continually tried to escape. It would pop up and wave at her from the Wavy Line reductions in the shop window and say, "Hello, here's Boring. How about some sex?"

The little wax model with the leg brace and polio by the open front door was saying, "I'm bored, Lil. Tell me about sex."

"Divertissements, divertissements," Lily whispered French diversions to the wax model whilst trying to recover from the jangling nerves which Geoff Mabs had just set on edge. He was a 'danger area'. He carried that danger around with him - somewhere between the outer corner of his wide, dancing eyes and the top of his prominent cheekbones. And where there was danger, there was risk.

She had made the decision earlier in the week that her feelings towards Geoff Mabs were ambivalent. But now she wasn't sure, because he was very sexy when he sauntered. She sliced off a larger piece of today's Cheddar, continued eating whilst humming to the tune of 'What's the use of wondering if he's good or if he's bad?', and imagining herself as Julie Jordan in *Carousel.* Anyway, Geoff Mabs hadn't given her much choice regarding this date which actually was ... very attractive. Cecilia said that, 'changing her mind is a woman's prerogative'. Cecilia said that when it suited her.

Agreeing to meet Geoff then, on the Sunday afternoon, came about by the combination of these factors. She stood up in front of the marble cheese board so as to slice off an even larger piece of Cheddar with the wire cutter. The biggest factor was - that it provided a 'divertissement' from labouring painfully over the biggest heartache. Whether or not to make love with Des. And that had become boring - since Lily could not make up her mind when suddenly there he was, heading up Peterson for the shop. "Can I go upstairs and get some dinner, Dad?"

Gordon sighed. "Yes, but not for long, Lily. I pay you two pounds ten shillings a week and it's not to have conversations with boyfriends or eat my profits," he said lifting his head from his newspaper.

"Geoff Mabs is not my boyfriend," she said and then added, "Where's Mum?"

"Where do you think?"

"It's not Wednesday," she said. "It's Saturday."

"How your mother loves to shop," he sighed. "She shops and she sits and she never tires of either. Hurry up with your dinner. I've got some deliveries to make and some clock collections."

Lily opened the door to the stairs when her father saw Des ambling up Peterson Road. He sighed. "Now I'll never get the clock collections done. That family just spend their time wasting mine."

Lily ran two steps at a time up the narrow staircase with the *Woman's Realm* magazine crumpled from wasp swiping. Her mother had left a Shepherd's Pie in the oven on low which she switched up to high. She picked up a packet of custard creams which was on the kitchen table. Then she whipped into the front room and looked out of the window. Des was just crossing Pennington. Come to say sorry. Look disinterested. She lay tummy down on the floor and bit into a custard cream. Flick, flick, flick through *Woman's Realm* ... and by this time ... yes ... there were his heavy footfalls on the staircase.

When he opened the front room door he sniffed. "I'm starving, Lily. What have you got in your oven?"

Lily didn't look up from *Woman's Realm.* "Shepherd's Pie and I thought you weren't talking to me."

He scowled, reached for one of her custard creams, sat astride her waist and spoke to the back of her head. "I never said that."

"If you can wait ten minutes the pie will be ready," she said continuing to pretend to read and feeling his soft breath on the back of her neck.

"Just time for a quick one upstairs in your attic bedroom. That's if we don't trip up on all those principles in this house," he said.

"Your stomach might rumble," she said.

"Your mother might walk in with her principles. Where is Cecilia - oh mighty Fort Knox?"

She thought he sounded hopeful. She couldn't see him. She was still pretending to read the problem page. "Gone shopping."

"That'll make a nice change for her," he said with thick sarcasm. Then he leant over her shoulder so that his face was touching hers. 'Dear Lily, 'can't make up your mind', Lee. In reply to your question should I have sex with Des, consider this ... your shelf life. Yours, Auntie Beryl.' 'It's no good asking a man how he feels, Lily, because more often than not he doesn't know. Men swim with their bellies."

Lily couldn't help but laugh. Des *was* her mother. Lily rolled over and for the first time looked up at him. Des Hodge was as good as milk chocolate.

"She's a saint your mother, ain't she, Lil?" he whispered, tracing her lips with his yellow- hazel eyes.

"The Patron Saint of Virgins," they whispered together.

Then he said softly, "I know I joke about it, Lil. But I do love you."

This was one of the moments Lily would love best about Des: unguarded, open, yellow-hazel eyes looking up from *Woman's Realm* problems. But all she said was, "How's the job?"

He sighed deeply. "Sorry. I forgot virgins is a vulnerable subject."

"You never told me about your job," she said looking up at him.

He took the packet of custard creams from her and ate another one. “I don’t have to tell you everything.” This was pointed. Aida had obviously been reporting home.

“What are you doing at Nestles?”

“Loading chocolate into vans.”

“Sweet.”

A pause hung heavily in the air filled only by the crunch of a custard cream. A stale pause left over from the previous Wednesday ‘loosely speaking’ evening. Lily glanced back at the problem page, he stood up and her thoughts turned to Hudge.

His too. “How was Hudge when you collected him from the caf last night?”

She sat up. “I see. You came here to talk about Hudge.”

“He says you're teaching him to cross the road.” By now he was on to his third custard cream.

“Oh it can't be that, that's upset him,” she said.

“So he was upset when you collected him?”

Lily felt defensive. “I thought he was maybe a bit tired. He kept going on about being a big bloke - bigger than you - bigger than Ben.”

“I'll show him to take the route under the bridge if it's too much bother”

“I never said that and you know he'd get lost - especially last thing at night. I was thinking about asking Jean if she could keep the back gate open permanent so I could wait in the scullery until closing. The caf’s always filled with loud-mouthed Teddy boys. I never mind doing anything for Hudge,” she said still looking up at him and getting a crick neck.

“I know,” he said and held out a hand to her. She took his hand and he pulled her up, close to him. “I know you don’t mind. Promises,” he said softly and kissed her forehead.

“Mix our blood, promises, promises. Always take care of Hudge,” she said.

It was Deslily talk and had its own rhythm. In years to come, she would return to that moment, re-play it, stick it on a groove: Des kissing her forehead and saying that word, “Promises”. The real moment was over.

Then, like Aida, as though it was a fresh thought but was often the whole reason for the dialogue, he said. “I'm working tonight. What about meeting me tomorrow afternoon? Over the rec.”

“I can't.”

“Why?”

“I've got something on.” Lily wondered why she said that. Didn't know why she hadn't said it to Geoff. Didn't know why she hadn't told Des she was scrapping the Wavy Line reductions because of course it would be Sunday tomorrow. That would have done.

“I see,” he said.

“What about meeting me after work tonight?” she said.

“I’ve got something on,” he said.

“What?” And then she quickly added, “And don’t say you’re seeing a man about a dog. Your mother won’t have one.”

He fell serious. “Jean’s been saying she needs to see me about something. I saw her quickly on Wednesday ...”

“On Wednesday?”

“I had to go to Nestles for an interview for the job. I only had time to ask her about the job in the caf for Hudge. She hasn’t said anything to you, has she, Lil?” He looked worried.

“Is that why you were in such a bad mood at the rec?”

He looked taken aback. “Yeah ... yeah. The interview. I was nervous about the interview. Has Jean said anything to you, Lil?”

“Well, you were still nasty later on Wednesday night, when you called Geoff Mabs an ape. And you’d had your chocolate interview by then. “

“I was nervous about the outcome of the Nestles interview too,” he lied quickly. Lily knew when he lied. “Has Jean said why she wants to see me?”

“No. You don’t think it’s about Hudge, do you?”

“No, I don’t,” he said. He seemed absolutely sure about this. “I just thought she might have said something to you. Enjoy your Shepherd’s Pie, Lily,” he said, brandishing a fourth custard cream. “Don't enjoy it too much though,” he said, placing a hand on her hip. “You never know where it might end up.”

He was about to kiss her again, hand on her backside when Gordon opened the front room door. "Lily, I told you about those clock collections." Then her father shut the door behind him.

Des raised his eyebrows and said, "Why is your father always collecting clocks from the council estate?"

But before Lily could say 'higher purchase', Des had gone and he took the custard creams with him.

Lily could suddenly smell burning. She ran into the kitchen. "Oh shit," she whimpered. "The Shepherd's Pie."

Why did he have to see Jean Oddy tonight? And then she sat down on the kitchen chair and cried.

Sod him.

****

"I've got to take Dad's cocoa upstairs, Hudge. Can you take the orders?" Jean said.

"I'm just to wash dishes. Des said."

"Oh Hudge, Dad's upstairs with angina. I can't be everywhere. I won't be long and it's almost closing. They won't want anything. They're off to the pub any minute for a Saturday night booze up. Oy," she shouted across to Mabs. "Get rid of that beer bottle. We've no licence to sell booze and you shouldn't be drinking in here."

Mabs clicked his fingers. Hudge zigzagged towards the table, notepad and pen in hand. The audience settled, and coffee clatter was silenced.

He turned to Papanikalou and whispered, "Look at them. Like gloating lobsters in a fish tank, waiting ..." He very softly began singing to the tune of 'Happy Birthday to You', "What's your girlfriend's first name, what's your girlfriend's first name." All the Teds joined in until the verse built to a crescendo. Flick brandished his knife and carried on a little too long. Mabs silenced him. "So, Hudge. How old are you then?"

"I'm ... I'm twenty-two in Christmas." Hudge wiped the sweat from his smooth upper lip with the sleeve of his white overall.

"Oooh." Mabs's eyes gleamed. "Are you going to have a party?"

"Yes," whispered Hudge, holding the pad and pen redundantly before him and flinching as a stray chip was thrown in his direction.

"A big party, Hudge?" Mabs leaned back in his chair and put his hands behind his head. The ball was rolling.

Flick switched off Buddy Holly's 'Rave On' which was playing on the juke-box - a signal for all, and especially Hudge, that the first round was beginning. Folding his arms, Flick grinned, as if playing the biased referee. The fat girl with shining pimples silenced the crowd. Leather jackets, fluorescent socks, tattoos, grease and nicotine-stained fingers froze.

"A big party? Like your big mum, Hudge?"

Everyone laughed. Everyone knew Aida. Everyone laughed - everyone but Hudge, who went sinking further into his chins and tie.

"Who said Hudge has got a big bum?" Papanikalou hit the table with mock concern.

"Can we come, come, come, then Hudge?" Mabs was encouraged by the little Greek boy's attempt at a double act.

"Please can we come, Hudge ... come ... come ... come," and Papanikalou knelt down before Hudge, spreading his arms out in mock pleading, his black Brylcreamed hair shining like a bug beetle.

Flick bowed his head and tried to stifle his laughter.

"No." Hudge wiped his nose on his overall sleeve.

"Why? Why Hudge? Why can't we come?" Mabs went on.

Papanikalou let out a manufactured groan.

Hudge gulped nervously. "Mum ... Mum wouldn't like you."

"Oooh." The caf made one huge oscillating sound.

Hudge's eyes were pricked with tears.

"Oh dear. Wouldn't like to upset the fat cow from Peterson Road, would we boys?" Mabs passed him a handkerchief. "Dry your tears, son and get us two coffees."

Hudge took the handkerchief and attempted to write down the order.

"Ah, he's crying." Teresa - the girl in yellow polka dot - adopted the same mock parental tone of voice. Others began to chant 'cry baby, cry baby' whilst Teresa began singing - *Cry Baby Bunting, Daddy's gone a hunting, gone to catch a rabbit skin to wrap the Baby Bunting in.*

"Make that four coffees, Mabs," Papanikalou said.

"Four, Hudge." *Flick, flack.* Mabs had taken out his camera whilst Hudge began to cross out the number.

"Salmon paste sandwiches?" Flick threw in, taking the collar of Hudge's white overall.

Flick, flack. Mabs was enjoying this. "Six salmon paste sandwiches, Hudge - and - no, make that seven - and a milkshake."

By now the crowd was in hysterics of laughter. Hudge trembled, seeming as though his legs would give way with the confusion and *flick, flack.* Point, press, re-wind, point, press, re-wind.

"Let's go the whole hog, Hudge and have six bacon and egg sandwiches ..."

"And I'll have a knuckle sandwich," someone else said, until the whole caf seemed to be hanging over Hudge's shoulder and Mabs was very happy. *Flick, flack.* He took a photo of Hudge in tears. Point, press, re-wind.

"It's all right, Hudge." Jean had opened the scullery door and came from behind the counter. "I'll take the order."

Mabs stood up, but couldn't match Hudge's height. "Now, what I want to know, Hudge, is," looking him squarely in the eye, "what's your girlfriend's first name?"

The crowd then began to sing, "Happy Birthday".

"I'm not telling you." Hudge was almost aggressive and his response was met with yet another 'oooh' from the crowd.

"Jean, is it?" Mabs said this as if laying an ace of hearts upon the table. The caf was quiet once again.

"Mabs." Jean's voice had a faint note of warning. She began to pull Hudge away.

"Is Jean your girlfriend?"

"Stop it, Mabs." Jean widened her eyes at him and shook her head.

Mabs looked to the scullery door and placed his beer bottle beneath the table.

"Everything all right?" Jack Oddy was standing behind the counter. "Seems very quiet."

Hudge looked at him, with eyes craving for reprieve.

But Jean said, "Fine. Everything's fine, Dad. Saturday night's a busy night."

Jack Oddy nodded, smiled and retreated back up the staircase.

"Let's play another record," Teresa said.

Jean went to the juke box and pulled the plug.

"That's good for custom. Touchy bitch. Your time of the month, is it?"

"You really are a shit heap, Gary Papanikalou and you stink of Alpha Road timber. Sod off to the pub the lot of you."

To which the Greek boy began dancing and singing to a Charlie Drake number. But Mabs picked him up before he could finish, carrying him out of the caf. This was a laugh. Des Hodge would soon get wind of this. And that was his intention.

****

When Lily came to fetch Hudge, she was relieved to discover that the back gate was open again, but disappointed that Geoff Mabs was not there.

Jean was though. "Come on, Hudge," she said, drumming painted fingernails on the counter. "I want to get to the Dragon's Head before closing."

This was typical of Des. To meet Jean in the Dragon's Head whilst Lily was looking after his brother. Cecilia would never let her go to the Dragon's Head anyway. "I was wondering, Jean," Lily said. "If you could keep the back gate and door open when I come to collect Hudge?"

"So you don't have to come the front way through the caf and meet our unsavoury customers?" she said. "I think that can be arranged. Yes."

Lily wondered why Jean had agreed so readily. She must have her own reasons. Jean never did anything for anyone. Hudge was odd on the way home. He was too quiet; too careful with Lily to cross the road which was quieter at this time of night. When they reached the Hodge doorstep, he turned to her and said, "I don't want to foul things up for Des" and stuck his bottom lip out.

There was actually no need to see him all the way home, but Lily was bored. She thought she might catch Des. She caught Aida.

"Now," Aida said. "Sit yourself down, Lily, and take the weight off your feet with a cup of cocoa. Or perhaps we should have something a little stronger?" She headed for her precious sideboard in the back room. Aida was in one of those moods. Lily loved these moods and Ben always seemed to stare out approvingly from his photo frame as Aida reached into the cupboard for the cooking sherry. "Hudge, if you want to wait up until Des gets in, you can get on with your jigsaw puzzle at the table." She smacked the sherry bottle down on the back table and then took his overall for washing, undid his tie and placed it over the chair. Looking across at Lily, Aida sighed. "I expect you'll want to see Des, Lily. I'm pleased to see you've sorted out your differences. So shall we wait in the front room with a sherry?" Then she looked at the sherry bottle and said, "No, I don't think so. Not tonight."

Lily was disappointed.

Aida went into the scullery and banged some doors, returning with a bottle of gin.

Aida would sit, sometimes with her stockingless feet up against the front room mantelpiece and tell old tales of 'before the war' and 'during the war' and 'after the war'. Sometimes Aida would sit with her legs wide open in the winter, warming them against a coal fire and getting scorch marks on the inside of her thighs. Lily could see right up to Aida's holey knickers. Lily's parents had always talked about 'before the war' and 'during the war' and 'after the war'. Her father would get out the old atlas and show her how Nazi Germany had tried to carve up Poland by their annexe. He showed her the corridor or annexe the Nazis made through Poland. Aida had told her that Mrs Matthews from the Glass Engravers sat up and scoured old newsreels when they came on television; to see if she could see her sister coming out of the camps when they were liberated. But Mrs Matthews had never seen her sister. "As if old newsreels would yield up the truth of the matter," Aida said. The war was a long time ago. Almost fifteen years.

"Now," Aida said, clutching the gin bottle, "you haven't forgotten you're coming to bake blackberry and apple pies with me after Evensong, tomorrow, have you?"

Lily shook her head but she had. It would still give her a couple of hours with Geoff Mabs.

"Where's your Aunt Iris this year?" she asked, already unscrewing the gin bottle top.

"She's not coming. She's having her teeth crowned."

"Now," Aida said. "You can sit there with the digestive biscuits, Hudge until Des gets in and Lily and me will go in the front room for a girls' chat. All right, my darling?"

Hudge nodded down at the jigsaw puzzle of a steam engine. It was the same puzzle he had been doing for years and usually he displayed a sense of achievement when the pieces fitted together. But not tonight. He was used to being left at the back room table when these 'chats' went on. "He wouldn't understand and he might get muddled up," Aida would say. Aida would always tell Lily things she shouldn't really know about people on these 'soirees'. They closed the back room door behind them as the big black woman with the hooped earrings and green turban in the reproduction painting above the mantelpiece smiled down on Hudge.

Lily heard the eleven o'clock city train pass by in the distance as Aida, with sighing relief, pulled up her frock and rolled down her corsets, shoving them behind the cushion on the armchair in the front room. "I didn't always wear corsets," she said and Lily smiled remembering her mother's words. "Oh you can smile, Lily Lee," she said. "Your mother 'd have a pink fit if she could hear some of the things I tell you."

"What's a pink fit?"

"Oh, I don't know." She didn't care. She put the sherry glasses on the front room mantelpiece and poured in the gin.

Lily hoped Aida wasn't going to talk about Ben and Kay's wedding tonight because that was boring. Lily preferred it when Aida told the old tales.

"Doctor Crouch said if I enjoyed a sherry then I should treat myself."

Lily didn't believe her. Aida never went to the doctors. Didn't believe in them.

"Here's my treat," she said, handing the sherry glass to Lily. "Sherry, gin, it's all the same," she said, as she opened the photo album with care. "This is my sister Belle. She doesn't speak to me anymore."

Lily knew. "Why?" Lily felt she was in for a good tale tonight except Aida didn't always answer questions.

There was a long pause whilst Aida turned the tattered pages of the photo album and was transported backward to another time and place where she was young and beautiful. Then she shrugged her shoulders. "Things get broken. Don't let things get broken, Lil. People stop talking and then they get embarrassed."

Lily knew Aida was referring to the row she had been having with Des.

"Forget why they weren't speaking in the first place," she went on. "But by that time, it's broken." Aida swigged her gin down in one go and beckoned for Lily to fill her up. Aida always poured the first glass and liked to be topped up again, and again and again after that. Aida didn't knit like her mother and Aida would say, "Oh, give me another one, Lil." Lily felt she could marry Des on the strength of his mother. Fancy having Zelda as a mother-in-law.

"Broken," Aida said down into the photo album.

"Worked in Petticoat Lane, Belle did, didn't she, Aida?" That was the local East End market for cheap but decent clothes. Lily's mother had told her. Aida had worked there once too.

"She stopped talking to me because I ran away with Des's father. She said I broke my promise. Well, promises get broken. That's all I can say."

Lily held the gin bottle above Aida and her armchair. She looked down at the beautiful re-touched photo of Belle. Belle lived up to her name. And Lily could tell the photo had been re-touched because of the pink in the cheeks on the black and white photo. And the eyelashes looked like the touch of pen had been on them.

"Why? Did she like him?"

"Everyone liked Ben and Hudge's father." Aida answered the questions she either only heard or only wanted to. It infuriated Des. "Teddy Pepper was a mild man."

Lily smiled mildly herself. Hudge's father's name always brought a smile to Lily's lips. She waited for what she knew would follow. "Teddy was a Methodist. Good Living. Not like Reg." Then Aida let out a small shriek. "Reg was never bloody mild. And Reggie could drink for the Empire."

Lily realised this was not the photo album which Aida opened on 'comfort' evenings. "Hard years," Aida was mumbling as she turned the pages. "Hard years all over the world, but especially in the East End. A lot of the people who live around Pennington are from the East End. We wanted to better ourselves." Aida was old, but not as old as Mrs Perry or Mrs Brambles. She must be at least in her forties because she had been born at that odd time in the first decade of the century. "'Flabby, over forty and flatulent,' Dr Crouch calls me," she said, "but bugger me if I know what the last one means," as she looked down on her slim adolescence. Aida hadn't always needed corsets.

"It means to blow off, Aida," Lily said.

They both smiled.

"Well shame on Doctor Crouch, but I don't know where you and Des learnt such big words. I mean you learn French, Lil."

Lily wondered briefly why Aida had been talking to Doctor Crouch except Lily changed tack, for tonight she was on a mission. "Des's father never joined the French Foreign Legion, did he, Aida?

Aida didn't answer this question but said that Des was like his father Reg 'in more ways than one ...' She carried on, draining the gin. "As early as '37, there was a smell of war in the air, changes had started taking place not only at home with The King's Abdication but in Europe."

In the past Lily always tried to look as though she were hearing this all for the first time when Aida repeated herself. But after a while, Des told her not to bother because his mother just enjoyed the act of repetitive jawing.

"Teddy, my first husband was a teetotal," she said offering Lily her glass again.

"No bookies, no playing cards," Lily said.

"Who's telling this story, Lil? When your man either joined up or, when the war started, was enlisted, you didn't have an affair, especially if he was a Methodist."

Lily's gin went down the wrong way but Aida did not notice. Lily was used to the cooking sherry but this was the first time she drank gin.

"I met Reg when he came to fix my bulbs shortly after Ted had sailed for Nairobi in '37. The country needed electricians too and it was on account of Reg being vital to the war effort that he was exempt from being enlisted into the Forces. The electrics at my rented house in Stepney were a disaster and 'being kind' to Reggie meant that Ben and me never needed to see by candlelight."

Cecilia wouldn't call it being 'kind', Lily knew.

"And Reggie was very good with his hands." Aida roared with laughter. "And vital in more ways than one, if you know what I mean, Lil, but I don't expect you do, you're a good girl and you know French." By now half the gin from the bottle had disappeared and Aida's legs were hitched up on the mantelpiece.

Lily was sipping slowly, her eyes not straying from Aida's transported face. "Why did Reg join the French Foreign Legion, Aida?"

"Not only was Reg 'good and quick with his hands' but he kept my feet warm on frosty evenings and knew how to light a fire 'in more ways than one'." Aida let out a peel of laughter here and beckoned once again to the gin bottle. "Oh, yes, the Hodges know how to warm things up," she said, winking at Lily. "I was pregnant with Hudge and I prayed to God that the baby belonged to Ted. It was a very close run thing."

This was something Aida did with passion. She prayed to her God and tasted the guilt 'for straying' but then who could really blame her when Reg was so dapper? And she'd have another gin.

Lily had never before seen Aida so, well, plastered. But by the time that Aida had got just over three quarters of the way down the gin bottle, "Don't worry, Lil, I've another in the cupboard next door," she started to get 'maudlin'. Lily wasn't sure what 'maudlin' meant - when she had asked her father he said it was a college at Oxford University but Lily didn't think that could be right. Aida said that Reg had brought her to live in his house in Peterson Road when she was pregnant with Hudge. "Now that must have been before the war started."

"You said that was in 1937 when you were pregnant with Hudge," Lily said.

"Did I? Oh, get the big Bible down off the shelf."

Lily reached up to the shelf above the television set which Reg had bought for the Coronation and for some reason was called 'the gift of guilt'. Aida had several Bibles, but this one was huge and heavy and was published by the Cambridge University Press. Lily's father had always told her that Cambridge was a million miles away but there was a black and white photo of the Vale of Tears in Jerusalem which Lily had thought must be even further. Aida kept all her Green Shield Stamps in Genesis and all her Littlewood coupons in Leviticus. Her passport - which she had never used - and the boys' passports were kept in Proverbs. Proverbs 17 to be exact because *A friend loveth at all times and a brother is born for adversity.* Addresses went under Amos and so it went on. God had an answer for everything, she said if you cared to look for it, and, "He obviously didn't believe in either Bills or Wills as there are no chapters beginning with those letters. I don't believe in bills or wills either," she always said. "I've only this house to my name and Hudge wouldn't know how to pay the rates. So what's the point in wills?"

Lily and Des had often wondered how Aida ever managed to pay for her bills but then Des said she received money in the post and the envelopes weren't sent from France.

All the facts of her family were scribbled under 'Births and Deaths'. "I know Hudge was born in 1937," Lily said, placing the Testaments on Aida's bulky knees.

"And I got pregnant with Des when the war started."

"Then you went on the buses." Lily looked down under 'Miscellaneous'. "It says here, in your handwriting that Edward Pepper sailed for Egypt in March 1939, Aida."

Aida yawned. The nearly eleven thirty train whipped by. "Well, I could have sworn Ted went to Egypt as soon as he joined up in '37." She wasn't really concerned with detail. "It was a close run thing, I know. And I think Hudge being who he was, was my punishment for running off with Reg. The sin of the father. I know my sister Belle believed that."

"I don't," Lily said, removing the tome from Aida's knees. "And neither do you. You always said that Hudge was a blessing."

"Yes," Aida said, taking another swig of gin, "but we all say things. It wasn't the way Reggie saw Hudge. I do sometimes wonder if Hudge was the reason Reggie ran off."

Hudge had been a difficult baby and toddler and cried and it got on Reggie's nerves. Lily didn't probe but Aida said, "I worry that Des is like his father. He's got an evil temper on him." To which Lily nodded. 'An evil temper' was just another euphemism for 'hitting out' or bruising. Cecilia had told Lily this: that Reg said that Aida bruised very easily.

"Hudge has got Ted written all over him in the same way Des has Reg tattooed on his forehead."

Lily thought of Geoff Mabs and those inky tattoos she had seen on his hairy forearms. "But Reg never really joined the French Foreign Legion, did he, Aida?"

She was totally transported and seeing that the bottle was now empty, she took Lily's glass from her hands and drained her remaining gin.

"Because," Lily says, "Des says that the Foreign Legion is just a euphemism."

"Oh, does he now?" Aida said, poking the sherry glass in Lily's direction. "Well, Des is that bloody clever he failed all his 'A' levels and needs a squib up his backside to get him out of bed in the mornings. And I don't think he should be doing all that smirking and talking gisms to you."

"What happened to Ted?"

"I never saw him after I started working on the buses, when the war started. And Belle never spoke to me after he got killed by a land mine in Nairobi." She shrugged her shoulders. "But what did that have to do with me? She talked to me before he got killed."

Lil was quick with calculations. "You were with Reg for a long time."

"Till the Coronation," Aida said quietly staring aimlessly out of the front room window.

Lily knew that was round about the time Ben was killed. About the time that Reg took off ... and not for the French Foreign Legion. Aida was so plastered Lily felt she could push just a little. Find out why all the adult locals said, 'Shame about the Oddys'. "But he didn't go to France, did he, Aida? Where did he go to?"

Aida suddenly said, "Where's your Aunt Iris? That bird usually flies home at blackberry picking time, doesn't she?"

"She's not coming. She's having her teeth crowned, Aida. I told you."

Aida mouthed 'oh'.

"But Reg didn't …"

Aida sighed. "Reg is not dead, Lil and a good job too as I wouldn't be entitled to any widow's pension like I am with Ted. Though I don't know why everyone else around me dies."

Lily felt a little more than uneasy by Aida's comment.

"I shouldn't say about Reg because I'd have to make you promise to hold your tongue."

"I will, Aida. I can keep a promise," she said.

Aida went to speak when they heard the front gate open, footsteps on the pathway and a key in the front door.

Des was shouting, "Home."

Oh, sod you, Des. I could have at last found out.

Aida leapt up to greet him in the hallway and Lily followed. She observed how the house came alive when Des was at home. How on earth would they do without him, she thought as Hudge looked up at her from his steam engine.

Des flung his leather jacket over the hallway banister and walked into the back room, throwing his keys on the table. "Lily," he smiled. "You waited for me." He was in a good mood.

"I came in for cocoa," she said.

"Oh, I expect you did," he said. "Not get much more from you at bedtime."

Lily widened her eyes at him to indicate his mother.

"Been drinking have you?" Aida said.

Des looked at his mother for the first time since he had come into the house. “Have you been at the cooking sherry again from your precious sideboard?”

Aida half staggered towards the sideboard and picked up Ben’s photo.

“Your mum was just about to tell me where your dad went to.” Lily widened her eyes again at him.

“Lily’s been poking her nose around in my past,” Aida said.

“I never,” she said.

“My mother won’t tell you that,” Des said placing his arms around Aida’s wide girth. “A bottle of cooking sherry won’t be enough to elicit that kind of information from my mother. I’ve tried.”

Aida gave Lily a quick smile and raised her eyebrows. She then watched as Aida stood staring at the photo of Ben with Des’s arms around her and Hudge sitting with his jigsaw puzzle at the table. Des and Aida swayed slightly and his mother said, “You and your big words, Des Hodge. Soliciting. They’ll get you into trouble some day.”

“Don’t wish that on me,” he whispered in his mother’s ear.

It must have been about the only time Lily had seen them touch one another, standing there, swaying to the beat of the back room clock, Des with his arms around her squidgy, corset free waist: touching permitted by the oiling of beer and gin.

He turned to her, as if he sensed her watching. “Would have brought you some chocolate home, Lily, but I know how you like to watch the weight on your backside. So do I.”

Lily raised her eyes to Aida’s dim light bulb above and sighed.

Aida kept staring at the photo of Ben.

Des pulled out a bar of Nestles chocolate from his pocket. “Here, Hudge.”

Hudge smiled slowly and looked back down at his jigsaw puzzle. Des looked at Lily and frowned. Lily shrugged her shoulders back at him.

“How were teas at Bingo tonight, Mum? Saturday is usually the busiest and best, isn’t it?” It was Des’s attempt to change their mood, she could tell.

"An almighty disaster," she said, putting Ben back where he belonged and unscrewing the top of the cooking sherry bottle which had been sitting on the table. "One of the Bingo callers, Roy, you know him, the one who wants to get into Variety, was a Red Coat at Butlins last summer, anyway, he had one too many and got his numbers all mixed up ... two fat ladies became sixty six ... instead of eighty eight and legs eleven was two little ducks." She hiccoughed. "I don't know why twenty two is two little ducks anyway. Why does 'two' make a bloody duck?"

"Watch your language, Mum," Des said, taking a digestive biscuit from the packet on the table. "Why do you think?" he added.

Lily expected Hudge to laugh out loud but he continued with his jigsaw puzzle.

"Then we had no biscuits," she went on not answering him, "so when Mr Snook asked me how the teas had gone, I didn't like to bring them up ..."

Des looked at his digestive biscuit gingerly.

"Because I could see he was on the point of sacking Roy whatsisname ...And I don't suppose Roy would have wept because he says Bingo calling is a day job, which is odd considering he starts on at seven at night. He was a Red Coat at Butlins, you know."

"Tonight wasn't a runaway success then," he said, turning to Hudge.

"I think Roy will be one day. He's got a lovely line of chatter and he does a lovely turn of 'All the Nice Girls love a Sailor'."

"The one who was a Red Coat at Butlins?"

Aida ignored Des and gave the black woman on the wall a gin-sodden glance.

"How were the dishes at the caf tonight, Hudge?" he asked.

"Yes. I won't foul things up for you, Des. Won't get sacked."

"That's right, Hudge," Aida said. "Just you wash those dishes and pick up your pay packet."

"Pay packet," he repeated.

"You get a fair share of mine, don't you, Hudge?" Des said, getting up and taking three beer mugs out of the cupboard and pouring inches of sherry from the bottle into them.

Aida smiled at the sherry, then smiled at Lily and took a mouthful. "You sound more and more like your father, Des."

"Your cross, Mum?"

Aida nodded. "My cross. It was all I could do to get his pay packet from him before he got up to the Dragon."

"Did you go to the Dragon tonight?" Lily asked Des but he just said, "Wherever my father is." Then he ruffled his brother's hair. "And Hudge is my cross."

Aida let out her customary raucous laugh.

"So where is he then, Mum?"

Oh, Timbuckbloodytoo," she said.

Both Des and Lily laughed with Aida but Hudge remained glued to his jigsaw puzzle.

"You're quiet tonight," Des said, as he took her hand on the Peterson Road.

She was feeling guilty about the date she had the following day with Geoff Mabs. She was thinking about saying something. But she said, "So was Hudge."

"It's probably settling into his new job. You know he gets like that sometimes." He put his arm around her shoulder. They walked very slowly.

"Did you see Jean tonight then?"

"No. She was out."

"So you still don't know what she wanted to see you about?"

"No. She was out." He looked suddenly distracted and then as if to quickly change the subject his voice shot upwards in pitch with, "Where's your Aunt Iris? She usually flies home this time of year."

"She's not coming. She's having her teeth crowned. Why do you need to go running round to Jean to see what she wants to see you about?"

"Keeps her happy in a funny kind of way. I like to keep people happy." He stopped at the top of Peterson, just opposite the shop. The main Pennington Road was almost quiet at this time of night. He ran his hand down her long pony tail, looked at her long and hard. "Let's not talk about Jean, Lil. Or Hudge." He took a deep breath and then he kissed her. "I taste sherry," he said. Then he thought for a moment ... and kissed her again. "No, I bloody don't. You've been on the gin."

"Your mother's been on the gin."

"And then she's mixed it with the cooking sherry. She's going to be sore tomorrow. I'm the one who has to pay for these 'soirees' you call them. She gets the same when your Aunt Iris comes up. My mother can't cope with the grain or mixing it with the grape. I thought you knew that, Lil."

"Des. Your mother's old enough to know if she wants to drink gin. I'm not in charge of her." He expected her to be so responsible for his family.

"She'll be murder tomorrow. Just you wait and see." Then he smiled and said, "I don't want us to be the love affair of the century, Lil. I just want to get into your bed before the end of it."

"Oh, Des, why do you keep going on?"

"I want to make you happy."

They would often pull into the haberdasher's for a necking session, but tonight she pushed him away gently. "It's an old chestnut. It's boring."

He backed off from her and started walking backwards up Peterson holding up his hands in defence. "No. For once, I didn't mean that. I meant - I just wanted to sleep in your arms. I think we could be happy. Together. Careful how you cross that road." His voice was becoming distant as he continued to walk backward up Peterson and the last train of the night whistled through. "Look right, look left. Look up, Lily. There's an old dog at your front window. Bon soir."

Lily looked up at the shop and sure enough, there was Cecilia, nosing her way through the curtains. Lily crossed the Pennington Road with a bucket of guilt.

How could she enjoy herself tomorrow with Geoff Mabs when Des had just said that?

Bon soir. Him stepping backward up Peterson Road, tasting of gherkins. The train's siren in her ears. Her mother at the front room window above the shop. Saying he wanted to sleep in her arms and make her happy on Aida's gin soaked evening. If only she had, she would think. Would it have made a difference? Would the timing have been different? Des Hodge had wanted only to lead an ordinary life. Like this.

4

SUNDAY 23RD AUGUST, 1959

"Where are you going?" Cecilia asked Geoff Mabs. They were standing by the savage guillotine of a meat slicer, having scrapped the Wavy Line offers for the past week and posted the new ones in the window.

Cecilia smelling danger, sliced some Sunday tea-time turkey breast and narrowed her eyes at Geoff Mabs.

Strains of 'Some Enchanted Evening' from *South Pacific* drifted down the stairs along with the aroma of roast beef which they ate every Sunday evening after scrapping.

But Mabs, it seemed, had no definite plans for he only shrugged his broad shoulders. "Maybe the park," he said.

"Be back by six." Cecilia arched her back and flared her nostrils. She was on double alert when Geoff Mabs gave an unfortunate wink of the eye.

Cecilia opened the shop door, gave Mabs a small smile and warned, "Lily's going to Teacher Training College when she's finished her 'A' levels next year. To teach French."

"Very nice for her, Mrs Lee," he said. "I'm sure she can teach me a French thing or two."

Cecilia closed her eyes, grimaced and then looked up to the hot heavens.

It was a sticky afternoon. Sun brings freedom but Lily felt pressed and a touch misplaced in her rose print dress. She couldn't stop herself looking at the inked tattoos on his forearms. He had one hand in his trouser pocket, the other splayed across his chest. "Why don't you wear a watch?" she said. She never needed to, she listened to the trains.

"No reason," he said quickly.

"What about Ashfields Park? Couple of miles, isn't it?"

"Yeah - they've got a band there."

"Rock 'n Roll?"

"No," she laughed. "A brass band. In the gazebo."

"A gazebo? That's a deer, isn't it?"

She laughed again. "No, it's a...a..." she waved her hand in the air, setting scavenging pigeons to flight, "a pavilion."

"If you say so. French, is it?" He started walking, one step ahead, at a respectable distance. "Up past the Dragon's Head, isn't it?" Then he pulled his camera out from beneath his suit jacket which was over his arm and was about to take her photo.

"No. Don't do that," she said. "Don't take photos."

"Okay, okay. If you say so."

"Why do you always take photos?"

"My grandad gave me this camera in his will. He used to snap birds." Then he smiled. "I do too." He took the photo all the same.

"I said, stop it," she said mildly. "My dad got a cine camera last year."

Mabs looked interested. "I've heard about how you can make a silent movie of your own and I've looked into the kind of camera needed, the projector and screen. How much did it cost?"

She shrugged her shoulders. "I don't know." Her father always said she never knew how much anything cost. "But we've had a few movie evenings in our front room. Des, Hudge and Aida come up."

He looked away.

She carried on, "We draw the curtains and there we are on this little white screen and when it's finished you get white dots come up. Sometimes we end up on our front room wall. Or sometimes, if the films overlap, Nelson's Column can be running up your backside."

"Uncomfortable," he said without smiling. "I'm going to be a film maker one day," he said.

"Are you?" she replied. "Or a photographer," she said with a sly grin.

He grinned back the same. "You can come and see my dark room sometime. Where I develop." Then he pointed to his camera. "This camera's worth a fortune. I've never told anyone that. If Zelda got wind of it – she'd sell it over my head and buy fur coats. Don't you tell anyone. I guard this with my life. It's an Ilford Witness. Worth a fortune. I'm a rich man, Lil."

Lily's chatterbox mind would drift back like a stuck 45 single to the moment that she had said those words to him. "*Or a photographer ... or a photographer*." And then him saying, *"It's an Ilford Witness. Worth a fortune."* The past gave up clues if we thought long enough. Then he said, "My mother used to be a Tiller girl," he said.

"What? One of those girls who kick up their legs and dance round in circles together on *Sunday Night at the London Palladium*," she said.

"And she says she's Irish extraction," he said.

"Oh, I don't believe that," she said. "She doesn't sound anything like Eamonn Andrews."

He snorted with laughter but kindly and looked at her sideways.

"Oh, you're having me on. She never was a Tiller girl, was she?"

"She needs extracting," he said. He smiled. He bought ice-creams that melted and trickled down to their fingers with the third lick. The band played 'Land of Hope and Glory'. Red uniforms sweltered in the afternoon heat. Buttons and brass drums reflected glaring rays from the sun. The park brimmed with Sunday spare time and roller skates. She wiped the perspiration from her upper lip with the back of her hand as he watched. Then he sat down on the grass, pulled her down abruptly and took his shirt off. He lay back, wearing only his vest, and Lily could see his chest and upper arms were covered in dark blue inked, snaked tattoos. She picked at handfuls of grass and felt more than faintly stirred as well as heavy headed from the previous night's consumption of gin with Aida. She cleared her throat. "How come your parents bought the chippie?"

"My grandad died." He looked towards the gazebo, resting his weight on his elbows. The tone of his voice had changed. It was softer. "The old sod had dough all over the place. Under the sofa...bricks in the wall. He'd never heard of banks...or didn't want to. My old girl went on a treasure hunt. She nearly flipped when she went to light the gas oven.

Thousands of readies. She'd have had a heart attack if that had gone up in smoke." He laughed to himself. "Maybe that's what he intended."

"Was he from around here?"

He laughed again, kind of scornfully, she thought. "Nah. Fenman."

Lily lifted her head inquiringly. He glanced away from the gazebo and said to her, "Flat lands. The Fens. Farmer."

She nodded and let her head drop. "Did you like him?"

'Land of Hope and Glory' was coming to an end.

"I think ..." he said, "he was the only person who has ever loved me."

People applauded.

"He taught me to read," he said.

"How old is your sister?" she asked.

"I never said I had a sister."

"Yes you did. You ..." She felt his hand smooth across her knees and a finger touching her left leg - the soft tender skin.

"Where did you get the scar?"

Lily looked down at her leg as if making a new discovery. The scar had been there for years. "Cicatrice, cicatrice," she said.

"Eh?"

"The French word is so much better, isn't it?"

"If you say so." Mabs shrugged his shoulders and let the corners of his mouth drop.

"A nail went through my leg when I was seven." She waited for him to flinch. People always flinched when she said that. She said it to make an impression, to shock but Geoff Mabs was unshockable.

"I was hiding in an old orange box in Julie's alley-way." He was running his finger up and down the seven-stitched scar. "I wasn't supposed to be there ..." Lily's voice trailed off into the afternoon. "My mother told me to only play in the cul-de-sac, never to stray down the alley-ways." He was still running his forefinger up and down. Up and down the tender skin. It almost itched.

"You don't linger in alley-ways now, do you?"

"No. Jean told my mum. It was the only time I got walloped."

"My old man used to beat me up to pass time. Especially when he'd been down the boozer. In at midnight and wallop, wallop. Time to turn into a pumpkin, boy. Midnight. Back from the boozer and ..." His voice drifted away with some thought he obviously wasn't going to give voice.

"Does he still wallop you?"

Does he still wallop you? The past gave us signs.

"No." He laughed. "I can get Charlie to piss in his own scotch bottle now."

She pulled a face.

"Sorry. It's just that I never played in any back street as a kid. We were always on the move and Charlie and Zelda would leave me ... in the caravan ...during the blackouts and the sirens wailing."

"What did you do?"

"I drew windmills."

"What?"

"I drew windmills ... and pumpkins. Thousands of them. On sugar paper. I still got them. You can come and see them some time." He drew in a little closer. "And my dark room. You can come and see my dark room, where I develop." He raised his eyebrows and gave another small smile.

The band began playing 'All Things Bright and Beautiful'.

Something didn't seem quite right. "How old are you?" she asked him.

"Twenty," came the reply.

"How old were you when you were left on your own and the sirens were wailing then?"

"I dunno. Two?"

"Two? How did you know what windmills were when you were two?"

He smiled - that knowing, charming smile. "I was a bright boy."

"Oh, come off it. How did you know what a windmill was when you were two?"

He was still smiling. "Girls usually go for that line about being left on my own when the sirens were wailing."

"It's 1959, Geoff. Do your sums. You could of been five."

"No-one calls me Geoff. You're different, Lily." Then he kissed her tenderly.

This was a first for Lily. She was sixteen. Des had been the only one who had kissed her before now. But this was somehow different. And as if he could read her mind, he said again, "You're different, Lily"

She smiled and meant it this time.

"I've never seen you smile before. Well, maybe with your lips, but not with your eyes."

There was a silence between them and the band was still playing 'All Things Bright and Beautiful' when he said, "I had a sister."

"You had a sister?"

"She smiled with her lips too."

"What happened to her?"

The band played. He looked into the distance. "You remind me of her. She was like a fairy princess."

Then he kissed her again, long, tender, deep. It made her think of Harvest Festival. His weight comfortable. She enjoyed the weight, the pressure, and opened her eyes slightly, squinting in the sun. "He gave us eyes to see them." Harvest Festival. Red polished apples and dazzling dahlia. She could just make out the outline of his darkish head, the serious darkish lashes touching her face. "And lips that we might tell." His lips were both soft and urgent. She could taste his sweat. He was lapping at her lips, "lips to tell," and now at her neck. It made her feel so...alive...everywhere. It was different. Not think of Des now. This had nothing to do with Des. The hymn made it all so ...innocent. Leaves would soon be falling from the trees ... soon ... soon.

Then she heard herself saying, "Des said you're a gypo." It was about the worst thing you could say to anybody.

He laughed - not scornfully this time. It was soft, she thought, like leaves free-falling in the air. "Des Hodge says I stink of lard. Do I?"

She shook her head and he went to kiss her again. But this time the kiss was harsh and biting. It was a kiss that she was not ready to respond to. His hand went from her hair to her upper thigh and ... The Lord God made them all ... Out of the question with Mabs; possible with Des, not probable, but out of the question with Geoff Mabs.

"No," she said, raising herself to her elbows.

"No. Of course. Not here," he said and sat up.

"We ought to be going."

"What about coming back to my place?"

She stood up. "No."

He got up and took hold of her hand. "*Don't lead me on.*"

She felt stupid. "I'm not. I didn't mean to ... I thought ..."

"You thought what?"

"I don't know ... I'm sorry if I led you on ..."

"Well, you did." And then he picked up his coat, put it on, in the blazing sun and shook his velvet collar saying, "But if you say 'no' then okay."

She looked at the clock on the gazebo. "I didn't realise that was the time. I've got to go."

"Why?" he said, picking up his camera and his shirt.

"I've got business to see to in Peterson Road."

"With Des Hodge?"

"It's Sunday. I promised Aida I'd help her bake blackberry and apple pies tonight."

She ran off leaving him standing but as she turned back and looked she swore she could see him mouthing 'fucking pies'.

****

"Ten to six, and the bells from the Church of the Nazarene are calling in customers," Lily said aloud as she raced back from Ashfields Park. Parishioners, Lily corrected herself, as she looked up at the clock face. She hoped that the quick-striding congregation had not heard. Lily had a reverence for church-goers. She half-expected to see Aida heading towards her. Aida never missed Evensong. Lily was certainly going to miss both the baking of pies and roast beef, but she wanted to see Des.

Her upper back was feeling tight and she wished she had worn a blouse and floppy hat as her mother had advised rather than this low backed rose print dress. It was then that she saw Jean. She was darting across the main road towards the caf, from Peterson: in tears.

Lily turned the corner of Pennington and started to walk briskly up Peterson.

Hudge was sitting on the doorstep. "Don't go in, Lily. They're having bad words."

Lily picked up Hudge's left arm which lay limply in her hands and looked at his watch which he always wore even though he couldn't tell the time. "Nearly six," she muttered. "You should be at Evensong."

"I know." Hudge straightened his striped tie and edged a stone along the ground. He was wearing his 'shiny' shoes. "But Mum went blackberry-picking."

"What's that got to do with anything?" Lily had her hand on the Hodge's front door. "Is Des home?"

"Yes." Hudge pulled a face.

Lily went to open the door.

"Lily?"

She stopped and put a hand on her hip. "What, Hudge?"

"Are you Des's girlfriend?"

"Oh, I don't know, Hudge," she said quickly. Did he have eyes in the back of his head or something? He couldn't have possibly seen her with Geoff Mabs. But there was something strange about his emphasis.

Hudge shook his head and frowned. "But you never answer the questions, Lily."

"Wait there. I'll get your mum."

As soon as Lily opened the front door it was obvious that Aida and Des were having a boxing match. Hudge had been sent, as always, to wait at the gate.

Lily enjoyed these confrontations. They were harmless enough and Des outwitted Aida on most counts. Tonight though, Lily was in a hurry. Cecilia would be climbing the walls with Yorkshire Pudding and Lily wanted to ... she let her hand drop from the kitchen door handle. Something was telling her this was quite different. There was none of the usual banter. She could hear only one voice: Aida's.

"Jigsaw puzzles. Don't you give me any bloody Fan Ann about jigsaw puzzles. He's going to be a lot more interested in your doings than jigsaw puzzles." Slam. It sounded like something metallic being thrown into the kitchen sink. "Blackberry picking. I go bloody blackberry picking. I turn my back for five minutes. Five minutes, mind you and you're up to your shenanikins and on a Sunday of all days."

What was Aida going on about? They had both been blamed in the past for Hudge grazing his knee whilst they had been pre-occupied, but

Hudge looked intact. Was Aida simply hanging over from last night's soak of gin?

"Of course. Never on a Sunday." Des sounded subdued. This was serious.

"You're eighteen. You're almost a man. When you're twenty one you can do as you like on your own premises. But not in my house. And not when you're looking after Hudge. And not on a Sunday."

There was a crash. Lily was not sure if it was Des's fist upon the table or the truth colliding with her brain. Jean. Des and Jean. Jean and Des. Together. Des and Jean.

"What do you want me to do? Move out? Do you? He's twenty one and he's a child. You'd never be able to manage without me. You know it. You'd be stuck. Admit it. All my life it's been 'run Hudge here, take Hudge there, wipe Hudge's nose, wipe Hudge's arse'."

"Don't you get vulgar with me, my boy," she could hear Aida shouting. "Your brother's sitting on the front doorstep and he can hear every word you are saying. And you *promised* me you would look after him."

"I do fucking look after him." Des sounded desperate.

"You can use what language suits you when you're with your brazen little hussy, sitting in your bedroom in her black brassiere as if butter wouldn't melt in her mouth. But when you're in my house you'll wash your bloody mouth out with soap and water, you caustic little bugger."

Then there was this pause. Lily didn't know whether to leave or enter. Des and Jean. Jean and Des together. She then heard Aida say, "There was no love spilled upstairs today was there?"

"What has that," Des shouted, "got to do with love? *You* should know about that."

Suddenly everything went quiet. Lily thought she could hear Aida sobbing. Could hear Aida saying, "God give me strength". And Des saying he was sorry ... she thought. She opened the door, very slightly.

Des was standing with his back to her. Aida was standing by the sink, a colander of blackberries in her hand. Piles of wet blackberries lay plated on the draining-board. And cooking apples. Aida's eyes tracked towards Lily.

Aida put the colander down. “Here,” she said, opening up her hand-knitted cardigan, a gift from Cecilia, and placing her hand upon her heart. “Give this to him, Lily.” She felt him sigh. “Let him wring my heart out and hang it on that clothes horse. 'Cos that's what he's done.” She reached for her woollen coat which was draped over the back room chair. “Now,” she said, dusting off the flour from her Bible which was on the table, “I'm off to church. It would do you good Des, to go and ask for forgiveness for your cardinal sins. Still ... I expect you'll want words with Lily. That's your affair. Now, where's my bag?”

Des reached down under the tablecloth and handed her the bag. Lily couldn’t see his eyes. He still had his back turned to her. But Aida’s eyes were angry with him and she swept up to Lily placing a floured and blackberry-stained hand on her cheek. “You're a good girl, Lily,” she said and as she reached the back door she turned and called, “Oi,” to Des. He half turned towards his mother, not looking at Lily. “I’ll see you later,” she said and closed the door behind her.

Lily would have fled up Peterson Road, but for the fact she was stuck rigid to the linoleum floor.

Des finally spoke. “You *are* a good girl.” The sunlight pierced through the chequered curtains, painting a fine gloss on his dark hair. What a time to find him so attractive, thought Lily, still pasted to her spot.

“How much did you hear?” he asked quietly.

Lily forced an “Everything,” through the lump in her throat. “And I saw Jean. At the top of Peterson.”

He nodded - at the orange and green chequered tablecloth.

At this point Lily might, she just might have been able to give Des the absolution he so obviously required. But he said, “Well - why do you have to be so bloody good?”

“Well,” she said, grasping for any words that might do, “why do you have to be so bloody bad?”

He turned, walked into the scullery and picked at the blackberries which sat on the draining-board. “Well, actually, it wasn't so bloody bad with Jean.”

“Oh well - bloody good for you,” she said taking steps towards the scullery.

He turned round and faced her properly for the first time. "And where have you been? You're sunburnt."

"I've been to the park, actually. I've been to the park with Geoff Mabs."

"He's only been on Pennington for a week. He doesn't know your name is Cast Iron Knickers."

"You bastard," she shrieked.

"Yes, that's exactly what I am." And he turned his back to her and looked out of the scullery window.

She only had his back. So she prodded. "How could you do that? With Hudge downstairs?

"I didn't."

She didn't know what he meant by that and she didn't care. She prodded his back. Harder this time. "Don't you lie to me. It's a lie and we promised."

"We grew up."

"What if he heard something? What if Hudge saw something? He would be so confused. He's confused enough about these feelings without you doing it with Jean Oddy." And prod, prod, prod. She prodded his back yet again, just to get some kind of reaction. "We promised to look after him no matter what and you break promises Des Hodge and you," she shouted, "you are an out and out liar. Just like your father before you." She knew she should not have said that. She knew Aida had said those words in confidence but she said them all the same. "You have an evil temper."

It was then that Des threw the blackberries at her. Not the colander. Just the blackberries. All the blackberries in each of the seven colanders which were on the draining board. They splattered the scullery, the back room and they stained Lily's rose print dress and her blonde pony tail. "Bugger off with your bloody promises," he shouted. And after he had aimed them at her he grabbed handfuls of wet blackberries from the heaps which sat on the draining-board. Then he hurled them at the walls, at the back door and down on to the linoleum floor.

She did bugger off. But not before noticing that Aida had not taken Hudge to Evensong. He was still on the front doorstep clutching his stone. She didn't speak to him though. She cried all the way up Peterson

Road. She heard the front door slam behind her. Des wouldn't come after her. He knew where to leave off. He knew all the Achilles' heels.

She was stained top to toe in blackberries. She wiped a hand across her face to dry the tears. But they kept coming. Des and Jean. Jean and Des. God, she thought, I can't face roast beef and Cecilia like this. My face must be smeared with it. *She saw Gary Papanikalou smoking on the corner, on the haberdasher's porch, his eyebrows knitting together with a question mark.* Think Lily, think. Where can I go? Then she had, what seemed at the time, like a good idea.

****

Zelda's lips were drawn up into a condescending smile at the sight of Lily - blackberry and tear-stained on her doorstep.

"Is Geoff in?" Lily gasped.

"Out. He's out." Zelda looked her down and up. Lily, looking up at Zelda's hard lines felt suddenly very small.

"Oh ..." Lily wondered where exactly her mascara might be. "I'm so sorry to have disturbed you," she said.

The chippie door slammed shut. Lily took a few feeble steps up the Pennington Road and let her back slide down against the Exchange & Mart shop front. She slumped into a heap. How was she ever to face Zelda Mabs across the chippie counter again?

How was she going to face Cecilia? Cecilia would bust a hamstring. The back door would be locked. There would be no chance of cleaning herself up before exposure.

That was the way Lily felt now. Exposed. Like those murderous nightmares of running up the Pennington Road, naked, in full view of the world.

Her skin was smarting from sunburn, her head from the previous night's gin, her scalp was marinated in blackberry juice, and Lily felt a migraine coming on. Two wasps began to hover around her head. She was frightened, embarrassed, humiliated by Des and depressed. Altogether, she was in a very sticky situation.

She looked back into the dark little dungeon of the Exchange & Mart, waving the wasps away. Bessie. Bessie might let her clean up there. She found herself knocking wildly on the front door.

But when Will Fenchurch came squeezing down the tight gap between the ancient stock, keys in his hand, Lily thought she might throw herself there and then, on to the Pennington Road and be done with it.

"Is Bessie in?" she shouted, before he could unlock the door.

"She's gone to see her sister Sylvia. Lily, you look a little ... messy." Will Fenchurch, a small man, was an understatement himself.

"It's Des," she cried. "It's all Des's fault." Lily had absolutely no idea why she was saying this to Will Fenchurch, of all people.

Will said, "Oh dear. Never mind."

Lily tried to pull herself together. The trouble is, she thought, when we try to pull ourselves together - we sometimes get pulled further apart. "I'll go home," she said. "I'll be all right. Don't worry, Will."

It seemed the last thing Will might do. Lily walked back up the Pennington Road, set a pack of pigeons to flight, knocked at the grocery shop door and waited. For Piccadilly Circus.

Lily longed for calomine lotion. Her body was raging with an intense and apoplectic heat.

Cecilia, on seeing her daughter sunburnt, muddied with mascara and blood-stained hit the narrow staircase roof.

"No, no. Not blood, Mum. Blackberries."

"Blackberries? What do you mean, blackberries?" she said with a crazy kind of shriek.

Lily was tempted to say she had gone blackberry picking with Aida. But that was unfair, she knew, to expect Aida to cover for her. 'We must tell the truth at all times.' Cecilia insisted. Rewritten one hundred times in block capitals and pinned to the classroom wall.

"Des threw blackberries at me."

"He threw blackberries at you?" Cecilia said it as if throwing blackberries was the ultimate of all sins. And why do mothers always have to repeat what you say at times like this? Why can't they just read the Sunday Express like Gordon did?

"We had a row."

"That boy has an evil temper, just like his father before him. He used to knock Aida black and blue. It runs in their veins," Cecilia said. "Well, that's that. You're not seeing him anymore and you'll do as I say."

"No, I'm not." Lily overwhelmed by the blackberries and the day, let out a flagon full of tears and rushed up to the attic screaming, "You're right. I agree with you. I'm never going to see him again."

Des and Jean. Jean and Des. Her sunburn hurt. She hurt. She had always considered that the Hodges belonged to her. So that was what Hudge had meant when he said, "Are *you* Des's girlfriend?" Poor Hudge. He was confused. Oh God, what had he seen?

Then Lily drew the attic curtains, lay on her bed looking up at the picture of James Dean she had cut out of a magazine. A wasp was tracing James Dean's nose but she was too tired to care.

She cried throughout the evening, not even coming downstairs for *Sunday Night at the London Palladium* or the plated roast beef dinner on what could only be described as the blackest of Sunday nights.

****

"You must be kidding." Jean's fingers were climbing the right nylon stocking and she stuck her bare foot into the mesh. "I wouldn't do anything like that."

Mabs lay back on the shed floor and zipped up his trousers. It was late. He was tired. After the heat of Ashfields he had dropped into the Dragon for some beers and Des Hodge had humiliated him. Mabs hadn't seen Hodge at first. It was the way that Hodge operated: slinking away in a dark corner and then coming out to cut him at his knees. If it hadn't been for the lump of the barman, Mabs would have slit Hodge's throat there and then. Things were getting serious and he certainly didn't mean with Jean Oddy. No, he needed to step up his game with Des Hodge and make him pay – *make his mark.* He had told Des he would make him pay. Make him pay. And then this thought had just occurred to him. It might well run to a plan. An ace plan. Nothing would get to Hodge more than … his daft brother.

"It's just a joke. Just a game." Just a little joke, just a little game. Charlie had said this, or had it been his grandfather?

"What if Des were ever to hear of it?" She lay back too, on his suit jacket, fastening the suspender clip to her stocking. "If 'it' were ever to happen," she added.

"What would he do?" He stared up at the wooden rafters. Thought about how the bastard Des Hodge had squeezed him beyond words in the Dragon earlier tonight. Cocky bugger. Yes, he wanted to know what Des Hodge would do.

"He'd probably kill you," she said calmly. "And me. It's a stupid idea."

Stupid. Stupid. She chewed the word. Stupid. Des Hodge had made him feel that way earlier in the Dragon. Stupid. He might have hit her then, had she not been so useful to him. "Oh come on, Jean," he said, turning towards her, ruffling her dark hair and planting a smack of a kiss on her cleavage. "The boy needs a bit of love." The boy needs a bit of love.

She sat up on her haunches and folded her arms, scrunching up her unfastened black brassiere and white blouse. "Keep your voice down. Since when have you been bothered about Hudge's needs? I'm surprised nobody's told Des already about how you have treated Hudge in the caf this weekend."

Des, Des. What was the big deal over Des, all of a sudden? "Maybe they have," he said.

"No, Mabs." There was an insistence and surety in the round chocolate brown eyes. Her voice lowered. "If Des knew you were giving Hudge a hard time, he'd be on to you. And you'd be in the General Hospital."

He put his hands to his lips, as if wiping away the trace of a smile. He knew that anyway, when he'd seen Des Hodge earlier in the evening in the Dragon. He'd get back at Hodge where it hurt. "Playing with fire am I?" Playing with fire, playing with fire. He reached for his beer bottle.

She stood up. She adjusted her skirt with the same kind of workwoman like way she folded tea towels. "I've noticed you didn't have a go at Hudge," her voice had a quiet note of triumph, "when Lily collected him."

Mabs wondered if Jean knew about him meeting Lily at Ashfields that afternoon. He looked up at her. She was biting her lip and frowning as she grappled with the hook and eye of her brassiere. Grappling with her piece of power. Her tiny piece of power.

If only Jean would do as she was told. This way was so much better. And more of a gas. It had all started out as a joke with Hudge. But the bloody lobsters were hungry and screaming for more.

He had counted on Hudge not saying anything to Lily. And Jean was right. Mabs did want to keep Lily sweet. This way was so much better. Hudge would be sure not to say anything about this. The daft boy had said nothing to Lily so far. Mabs knew that. Lily would never have let him kiss her like that if she had known about him crowding her precious Hudge.

"Scared are you?" Jean was looking down on him, arms winged like a chicken, still struggling with the back of her brassiere. Cluck, cluck, cluck. "Scared of Des?" Cluck, cluck, cluck.

"Getting me riled up, are you?" he said.

He got to his feet, stood behind her and pulled up the back of her blouse. He fastened the hook and eye. Then he placed a hand on her back and with the other, stretched the elastic strap as far as it would go. Tw...ang.

"Ow." Jean yelped in pain.

"Let's see if I am. Bring Hudge here tomorrow night. That'll rile Des, won't it?"

She turned round. "Give me one good reason, Mabs. Just one good reason why I should."

The smell of her rancid sweat tasted bitter on his tongue. Cocky, jaunty little bitch. He shrugged his shoulders and smiled with his lips. "Me?"

She shook her head. Triumph for Jean. "That's not good enough, Mabs. Out. I've got to lock the back gate. Pick up your dirty beer bottles. You drink too much. And quiet."

At approximately midnight on Sunday 23rd August, after it had taken Geoff nine seconds to leg it up Alpha Road, he was crossing to the chippie at the billboards. Jean Oddy had pressed the anger button and Geoff Mabs would see her pay for telling him to clear out of the shed. Just like he was going to make Des Hodge pay. Make them both pay for humiliating him.

He looked back at the dream machine - that Morris Mini - pasted tauntingly to the billboards. Then he noticed a figure, further down Pennington, at the caf door. The figure turned. It was Des Hodge.

Mabs paused at the chippie door. They were yards from each other. In the shadowy streetlight, they were hyena, stalking the night and waiting for that kill. The street was deserted. Anything could have happened. Anything could have happened on that Sunday night, after the discovery Mabs knew for sure Des Hodge had made in the Dragon's Head earlier. But one was distracted. The caf door opened.

5

MONDAY 24TH AUGUST

He was standing at the grocery shop counter first thing on Monday morning, camera slung across his chest. It was the last time Lily recalled ever seeing that camera on Mabs. After that, it would simply become an exhibit in a courtroom; like she eventually became: an exhibit or a silent witness. Lily winced. "That's a nasty cut. How did you get that?"

He had a raw streak of knotted red running down the left side of his face to his chin.

"Let me tell you later. I need to explain something," he said.

He wasn't his usual self. He looked earnest to see her. Lily had never seen him look earnest before. She also wanted to explain why she had turned up on the chippie doorstep the previous night, in such a state.

"Did Des do that? Last night? Because we went to the park?"

Cecilia, who was pricing up Saxa salt, raised her eyebrows and pursed her lips. It was obvious to both Lily and Cecilia that there was something terribly wrong with him. He was shaking slightly.

"It's nothing," he said.

Cecilia walked towards him and looked closely. "You've had stitches," she said.

"Doctor Crouch," he replied.

"That boy has an evil temper," Cecilia said. "Like his father before him."

"It's nothing. Are you able to come for a walk?"

Lily gave Cecilia a pleading look.

Cecilia sighed deeply. "Lily, you know your father goes to the wholesalers on a Monday."

"Because it's the quiet time. You'll manage, Mum."

Mabs gave Cecilia one of those smiles: the kind of smile where he tilted his head to the side, then he winked nervously and said, "Please, Mrs Lee. I wouldn't ask during shop hours. I mean, I understand, being in trade myself. But I won't keep your daughter long and I'll bring her home safely."

Cecilia seemed lifted by Mabs's polite charm and took pity. "Oh, well. Put like that." She turned to Lily. "But remember your father's back in less than an hour, Lily and he'll need help unloading. And then there's the cold cuts of salami that will need slicing."

"Thanks, Mum."

They walked out on to the Pennington Road. He turned left, walked past the caf and the greengrocers. Lily smiled at Mrs Brambles who was swinging and circling a brown paper bag of carrots in her soiled hands. Mabs couldn't smile. Lily thought the stitches must be hurting him. It was a savage, deep slash. How could Des do that? It was drizzling. "Lord help my mother and her nails if she ever had to help Dad unload the wholesaler's order," Lily said, for want of something to say, because her mother had no care for nails. It was 'Aunt' Rose, like the rest of her 'sisters' who manicured. Mabs looked as though he was carrying a load himself.

But he tightened up. "Mothers," he said. "What about the rec.?"

She was about to mention that she had seen his mother the previous evening but he caught her looking down towards Peterson.

"Okay," she said.

They walked in silence. He grasped her hand, tightly as they crossed over towards the 'Exchange and Mart', as if he had some special license to do so. As they passed the undertaker's and then the chippie, she said, "Not on a shift today?" She could see Zelda parcelling fish into yesterday's newspapers for a customer. She thought he might say something about why she had called the evening before.

"Later," he said.

"Des found out I'd been to the park with you yesterday afternoon. He went mad and threw blackberries at me." That was a good way of finding out if Zelda had said anything but he seemed pre-occupied. "Des Hodge needs a head examination," was all he said.

"He's never fought over me before. For Hudge. But not me." For a moment, she was distracted herself. Des must care then? She was faintly flattered but then again, when she looked at Geoff's wound, she wasn't.

As Mabs opened the rec. gate, it started to rain: hard. He kept hold of her hand and led her towards the disused stables. She was surprised Mabs knew about this place. Lily always felt it had been her and Des's private place where they hid stuff as kids. Mabs tugged at the brass handle on the graffitied wooden stable door.

"I'm not sure I should ..."

"Look. I don't want anything from you. I need to tell you something. I need to explain ... about me. So you understand."

He looked almost desperate.

She watched as he turned the brass handle to the right and push the stable door open. She turned to go, she shouldn't be here, when he said quickly, "It's about my sister ..."

She turned back.

He swung the stable door open. There was a musty, disused smell in the air. The Brambles must have used these stables for storage. There was an old cart and a disengaged wheel. "He's not long got rid of the horses," she said.

"Who?"

"Mr Brambles. Used to do greengrocery deliveries on the horse and cart up until last year. Now the old man's got a gammy leg and they've sold the horses off and bought a van. I can even remember the horses watering from the troughs on the main street."

"My grandad had horses."

"Did you live on his farm?"

"Kind of."

They sat down on stinking straw. On the damp. In the dark. She was aware of his breathing. It was shallow. His chest wheezed slightly. He was still shaking.

"You seem in a bad way," she said.

He snorted. "You could say that." He looked around the dank stable. "This reminds me of sitting in the caravan with my sister."

"Oh, not that caravan again."

"Just listen, will you?"

It was that harsh kind of command she'd heard on the roundabout the previous Wednesday. She wondered if anyone had ever listened to him. "Go on then."

He went to his suit pocket and brought out a packet of Woodbines.

"You can't smoke in here. The straw. Fire," she said.

"Playing with fire, am I? If you say so, then." He put the packet of cigarettes back in his pocket, but lit up all the same, blowing the match out and putting it in his suit pocket.

It did occur to Lily that with a cigarette in his hand, he couldn't really be a threat and certainly he didn't seem to have 'that' on his mind.

"I don't mean in the caravan with the sirens wailing and all that. This was after the war. When I was about ... I must have been about ten. My sister was a few years younger than me. Charlie and Zelda kept us in the caravan, wherever we went. The school board man was always on our tail."

"Did you really get visited by the school board man?" Lily gasped. "I've never met anyone who's been visited by The School Board Man before. Aida always threatened us with The School Board Man if we said we didn't want to go to school. But we never saw The School Board Man. He's been as elusive and scary as The Bogey Man."

He just looked at her and said, "Right." He took a drag on his cigarette. "Charlie and Zelda would bugger off sometimes for days. We had the dog, and a lot of the time we had just the tap and the dog's meat."

"Oh, Geoff. Don't make up stories." His wheezing was increasing. "You don't need to make up stories to just impress me. I like you already."

"But I'm trying to tell you something."

"Well, why now?"

"Because suddenly this has become important to me." The wheezing in his chest was now beginning to take hold: the cigarette precariously hovering above the damp straw.

"Watch that cigarette now," she said.

"She was such a beautiful little girl, Lily."

His breaths became short and sharp and he was going red in the face.

"Can I do anything?" she said.

He waved his hand, stubbed out the cigarette and shook his head. "Need inhaler," he gasped.

She got up to go. "I can go over to the chippie and ask."

He reached up for her hand and pulled her down to the ground. He shook his head again. "Be ... all right soon."

She sat next to him and rubbed his back. It was firm, strong and she felt his back shudder with the erratic breathing. A few minutes passed and the short raspy breaths began to subside. Slowly. His breathing became more even.

"You don't need to talk," she said.

"It's okay. I think talking about her brings it on."

"What is it?"

"Asthma. I've had it since I was a kid. Damp bloody caravans."

"You shouldn't smoke."

"I shouldn't do a lot of things." Then he took her face in his hands and began to kiss, small kisses all around her mouth, her chin, the sides of her face. She felt the thick, unpleasant weave of his stitches on her own cheek. "You'll always be my friend, won't you, Lil?"

You'll always be my friend, won't you, Lil? Then he kissed her on the lips just as she was going to say, 'yes' but instead of asking what he had to tell her, instead she said, "Have you been drinking?" Moments get lost in the cart wheels. If she had asked him there and then what he wanted to tell her, could she have stopped it all happening?

He carried on kissing her. "It's the stink of our front room on my clothes. Charlie drowned in Glenfiddich last night."

She could have said, "What do you mean?" and he might have then told her the dreadful things that had happened the night before. Instead she said, "I shouldn't be here."

"Shouldn't," he kissed her neck, "shouldn't," kissed down to her breasts, "shouldn't," and further.

"No, I shouldn't," she said, enjoying herself. "I'm thinking about my dad's delivery."

"Well, don't." He smiled. Kissed her on the lips. Pulled at the zip on her denim jeans.

"No," she said.

He sighed. Pulled out the packet of cigarettes from his suit pocket, placed another cigarette in his mouth and lit it with a match. He blew the match out and said, "You're safe with me. Okay?"

"Okay," she said.

Then he said. "I want you to be my girl."

"I can't do that."

"Because of Des Hodge?"

"I've known him all my life like a brother."

"That doesn't sound like the best basis for sex," he said, taking a deep drag on his cigarette and seeming fully recovered from his attack.

"Who's talking about sex?"

"Who wants to *talk* about sex?"

"Is that important to you?" she asked.

He laughed. "Strangely so. Yes."

"What's so important about it?"

"When you hold back, I want it."

"I always feel you're so nice and tender - and then, then you get ... rough. It scares me," she said.

"If I didn't get rough, would you do it?" He leant across and kissed her gently on the lips. "You see, Lily, it could be really right with you. It could be perfect."

In the darkness of the stable, she was almost tempted but then Des intruded. After all, a friend loveth at all times. "Geoff. Des is my friend. I ... I know him. And I'm not going to be disloyal." But then she started to change her mind when he surprised her because he stood up abruptly and said, "Okay, okay. Some day maybe then?"

It surprised her, especially as he was bearing the scar which Des had inflicted. She knew what he was saying though. "Maybe," she said.

"And you'll always be my friend?"

Lily thought that was a stiff request. After all, as sexy as Geoff Mabs was, she had only known him a few days. But often people did not require answers to their questions because he raised his eyebrows and said, "'Cos I can do with all the friends I can get." He opened the stable door wide open.

She leaned back against the wall and raised her voice as he turned, "What was your sister's name?"

"Oh, that was just a game, just a laugh - to get you up to the stables." He smiled.

"I don't believe you," she said.

As he walked away, she saw him pick up a stone and throw it, hard into the distance. His shoulders were angry, his back was broad.

****

Jean winced. "That's a nasty cut."

"It needed stitches." Zelda Mabs emptied a tray full of chipped potatoes into the fat fryer. "Gherkins?" she asked a thick-set, dour-looking man who was dropping and counting coins into the palm of his hand.

The chips instantly hissed and Zelda gave them an aggressive poke with a fish slice.

"Where did you get it?" Jean picked up a jar of pickled onions, seemingly examining their contents.

"I walked into my old man," he said, not bothering to lower his voice.

Zelda slammed the till shut. "He was in a fight with Des Hodge last night and we had to call out the doctor for stitches."

"Doctor Crouch?" Jean asked sidling to the corner of the Formica-topped counter. She put the pickled onions back on the counter. She looked as though she was about to say something else, she looked confused. Did she know what had really happened? How he had really got his face slashed? After all, Mabs had seen Des Hodge on the caf doorstep at midnight last night but she quickly said, "I need to talk to you, Mabs" in a hushed tone. Mabs had heard this phrase many times on *Armchair Theatre* nights. BBC plays were full of 'I need to talk to yous'.

"Talk here," Mabs said. The cut was stinging. It was one of the last things he felt like doing.

"Not here."

Mabs had come to realise that Jean Oddy could not be easily manipulated. She did things on her own terms - for herself. In a secret kind of a way, he admired that. Even if he didn't admire *her*.

"We're going upstairs," he said.

Jean smiled. Zelda's mouth was set in chip fat. Mabs looked back as they disappeared up the steps, watching her watching them from the corner of her eye, as she one - folded - two - the chips - three - automatically - four, into a neat package for her sullen customer.

Mabs opened the front room door and Jean placed her hands on her hips, observing the freshly-stained carpet. "Had a party or a booze up in here last night?"

He didn't reply. There were things he might have told Lily Lee about last night, if he could have brought himself to do so, but not Jean Oddy.

"Where did you get that cut?" she asked again.

"I told you. I walked into my father." She'd only broadcast the full story all over the caf.

"Your mum said Des Hodge did it."

He removed a Sunday paper from the sofa and threw it to the floor. Yesterday's photos had been stashed away in his bedroom. That's where they would stay. He couldn't believe that he had almost told Lily Lee. Information was power. When she'd said she was loyal to Des Hodge, he couldn't chance it. He'd keep the photos in a dark room.

A faint gluey sheen of sweat covered Jean's skin. For once, she was stripped of make-up, her eyes red and puffy. "You look tired," he said. And like a stranger, he thought. He was used to a painted Jean, in the caf, in the pub, in the shed ... Monday morning and out of place, he was not sure how to react towards her. Or what she wanted. Jean always wanted something. "What do you want? Not pregnant are you?"

Jean paused at long and hard and seemed to enjoy this moment but then she said, "Oh, give over, Mabs. God - it stinks in here." A stale stench of alcohol dominated the room - like flats above public houses. The smell of alcohol had over-ridden the seeping fat and even Mabs noticed it. She pulled up the sash window, perched her bottom on the sill and folded her arms. "I've come to tell you, you can have what you want," she said.

It was Monday morning. He had pain like acid at his mouth, and that's not what he wanted.

Jean's eyes ran to the dark blotches which stained the faded candy-striped paper on the wall opposite. “This business with Hudge.” She stared back at the scar on his chin.

Mabs took a step towards her. He was interested. “Yeah?”

“Well,” she said. “It might be fun.”

There was a pause, whilst the two ‘lovers’ weighed up each other's motives. Then Jean's eyes narrowed. “You're a sex maniac, Mabs, aren't you?”

“Yeah,” he grinned. “Why have you changed your mind?” He hadn't the faintest idea.

“Let's say,” she yawned - as if to emphasise this was no big deal, “I have my reasons.” He’d heard this phrase bandied about on BBC plays quite a bit, as well. “Well,” she added. “Someone’s given me a good enough reason.”

Mabs was not about to labour the point by asking questions. She had changed her mind. But he did say, “I am a good enough reason then?”

“What do you want me to do?” she said quickly looking out on to the Pennington Road.

Caught, thought Mabs. Ace - I've got her. “Take him to the pub. Then maybe to the shed...”

“And the rest.” She laughed nervously. Then her tone changed abruptly. “Lily won't like it.”

“Who cares?” He was quick to reply.

“Doing her out of a job.”

“She's got enough on.” Mabs wished he hadn't said that. He moved towards her, placing his arms about her waist, side-tracking away from the remark. The cut itched like crazy.

She looked up at him with narrowed eyes again. “And Des won't like it.”

They were quick to clock each other's reactions - looking for the dead give away.

“That’s what it’s all about, isn’t it, Mabs? You want to get back at him for showing you up in the caf, don’t you?”

"If you say so." The caf, yes, but the Dragon's Head pub, last night. He would never, could never ever let Hodge get away with that, for making him squirm, even if it had been private. "And you? Why are you going ahead with this?"

"I've told you. I've got my reasons. Don't get boring."

Seal the deal, thought Geoff, and he bent down to kiss her lips.

"Don't give me that on a Monday morning, Mabs." She pulled away and walked across to the sitting-room door. "And that cut must sting like hell." She leaned against the open door and gave a spiteful grin. "You want to be careful. The caf might think Des did it."

That was the last thing he needed. Geoff Mabs knew all about people and their power and right now Jean Oddy was holding it in her dirty bitten fingernails. Then, once again, he remembered Des Hodge on her caf doorstep the night before. "How do you know," he said, "that he didn't?"

Jean's face twisted. "Let's start with Hudge, tonight," she said, and closed the door behind her.

Mabs fell into the settee. How unlike a fairy princess Jean Oddy was.

Papanikalou put a shilling in the juke box and Bill Haley's 'Rock around the Clock' began to roll. Teresa clicked her fingers in time with the music and Papanikalou took her hand. They swayed to the beat and he swirled the black and yellow polka-dotted dress as the rest of the Teds began clapping and stamping their feet. If there was something the Greek boy could do, it was rocking and rolling. Down to the floor the couple went, turning on to their stomachs, walking the floor with their hands and Teresa wickedly smiled as she threw the diminutive Greek beneath her legs. Mabs was mesmerised by Teresa's legs as they scissored across the tiny caf floor.

Hudge also looked mesmerised. He began to clap too, spotless in his white overall and taking a break from sweeping the caf floor. He seemed more relaxed tonight for so far, Hudge had been in remission. Until Geoff Mabs gave the signal to Flick. Flick moved to Hudge and took his broom, throwing it over the counter. Then he swirled him. Papanikalou stopped dancing and pushed Hudge around in a circle.

Hudge began laughing uncontrollably and the youths in the caf joined him. Bill Haley stopped singing.

"That's enough, Flick. You're going too far," Teresa said.

But they continued to swirl Hudge into circles until he was dizzy, losing balance. Jean Oddy sat on Mabs's lap.

"Take a seat, Hudge."

"I got work to do," he said, trying to stand upright and grasping for a table to steady his moving feet.

"That's all right, Hudge," Jean said standing up. "Take a rest."

Hudge did as he was told.

"Do you think your girlfriend would mind if Jean sat on your knee, Hudge?" Mabs turned a chair about and sat astride it, leaning forward towards him. "There doesn't seem to be a spare seat for her."

There were plenty of spare seats. Late-night stragglers leaving the caf in semi-congo style, were singing to the beat of 'Rock around the Clock'. Papanikalou, out of breath, from his performance, said, "Who gave you that cut?"

"My old man," Mabs replied. "But you should see the state of him."

"Nah. Bet that'd be Des Hodge done that. For sniffing round his girl."

Jean pulled a face at Mabs, put her hand on her hip and cocked her head. Mabs shrugged his shoulders and said to the Greek, "Oh, go and piss yourself, Papanikalou."

"Well, I saw the state of Lily Lee running up Peterson last night. Covered in blood. So if he duffed her up, Jesus knows what he was going to do to you. Des Hodge nearly killed a boy once."

"Oh, yeah," Mabs said. "What for?"

"For having a go at him," and he pointed to Hudge who was silently seated and listening, "if you know what I mean ..."

"Look," Mabs said to Papanikalou, "I'm pissing in my pants." Then remembering what the plan was supposed to be he said," Jean, wouldn't you like to sit on Hudge's knee?"

"Sod off," she said,

She was obviously smarting from Papaniklalou's remark: that he had been sniffing around Lily Lee. Mabs was worried that she would go back on the deal. He got up and whispered in her ear. “Do this, Jean and I promise you I’ll do anything for you.”

“And I said ‘sod off’,” she said.

“You know,” Flick leaned across the table pointing a place mat at Hudge, “Jean's very fond of you. Know what I mean, Hudge?”

“My mum says Jean’s a brazen little hussy.”

Everyone laughed loudly and Jean placed her hands on her hips, angrily. “Would you hold my hand?” she said.

Hudge shook his head.

“But I got you a job, Hudge. Remember?”

“Pay packet,” Hudge said. “I’m a very lucky boy.”

Jean placed a hand on his head and began to caress his hair.

“About to get luckier,” Mabs said, still sitting astride his chair.

Jean circled Hudge’s chair and then came and knelt at his feet. “Why don’t you come to the pub with us tonight?” The tone of her voice had changed. It was low and inviting.

Hudge looked up at her. “Lily doesn’t go.”

“Lily’s not invited,” she said, pushing his legs apart.

Teresa knelt down beside his chair. “Kiss him, Jean. Go on. Kiss him.”

Some of the other youths started to say quietly, “Kiss him. Kiss him.” Papanikalou chewed his gum. Flick folded his arms and grinned. Mabs watched. And waited.

“Doesn’t Lily boss you a bit?” She placed a finger on his ear lobe.

“No,” Hudge said. “I got to go home. Wash my overall.” He went to get up. Mabs placed a hand on Hudge’s chest to restrain him. “We’d really like you to come to the pub, wouldn’t we, Jean?” he said.

“Kiss him, Jean. Kiss him. Wouldn’t you like Jean to kiss you, Hudge?” the fat girl with pimples said.

“Des says you’re a tart,” Hudge said.

Jean’s jaw was tight. Then she stretched up to Hudge and took his face in her hands and kissed him long and hard. The caf was silent. Flick’s jaw dropped. Teresa, kneeling by Hudge’s chair looked amazed. Mabs cocked an eyebrow.

It was Papanikalou who spoke first. “Des ‘ll kill you, Jean. He’ll kill you.”

Jean turned to him and said, "Then Des Hodge will swing for it. Come on, Hudge, help me shift some cokes from the cellar before closing." And she took him firmly by the hand, around the counter and through the scullery.

"We're gonna have some fun tonight," Flick said.

"I'm having nothing to do with this," Papanikalou said. "Des'll cut you up again, Mabs. Again."

"You can tell him, Papanikalou. But not yet. Let Hudge have his fun first," Mabs said.

"Yeah," the Greek boy said, as if to convince himself, "she'll only be playing Monopoly in the cellar with him. He wouldn't know a bosom if it bumped him slowly in the eye," Papanikalou said giggling stupidly.

It was at that point that Lily appeared at the scullery door. She looked around the caf and then at Mabs. "Mabs. Where's Hudge?"

"Shifting cokes from the cellar."

"You were covered in blood last night," Papanikalou said.

"Blackberry juice," she said, coming around the counter and walking across to Mabs.

Papanikalou looked confused. "Look what Des gave Mabs," Papanikalou said quickly.

"I know," she said.

"Well," Mabs said. "It's nothing."

"I told him yesterday that Geoff and I had spent the afternoon together and he went crazy last night... so I finished with him."

Papanikalou and Flick exchanged a look of realisation. Papanikalou mouthed the word, "Geoff," and placed his hand on his cheek in a girly kind of way. Mabs had not expected Lily to say this. He was tempted to ask her to the pub, but there was more fun to be had with Hudge and Jean and besides, princesses fared better when they were made to wait.

She waited. He clocked the disappointment in her eyes. Then Papanikalou said, "Des nearly killed a boy once for having a go at his brother."

"Oh, we only put that about to give Des clout. That boy fell on the railings at the rec. He's still alive," Lily said, looking about the caf.

Mabs let out a roar of laughter and Papanikalou's dark eyebrows collided in confusion.

"Where's Hudge?" Lily said.

Hudge's overall was thrown across the counter. "He's here." It was Jean. "Perhaps you can give this to Aida for washing. Hudge is coming to the pub with us."

Lily said his name with disbelief, but Hudge smiled broadly with only a whisper of guilt in his face.

"Well," Lily said, "I'll come too."

"Give Hudge a break, Lily. What are you? His keeper?" Jean said.

Lily waited. As if for reinforcements. But they did not come. Jean continued the attack. "Me and Mabs will see Hudge home."

"I promise I'll see him home safe," Mabs said

"That's if you can trust anyone else to do the job," Jean said to Lily.

Lily snatched up the overall. "I'll see you tomorrow night, Hudge."

She went to the front door, making brief but bitter eye contact with Jean and then decided to add, "And don't drink any alcohol, Hudge. Remember, your tummy." To which everyone burst out laughing and repeated in a girly whine, "Your tummy".

"There you are, Hudge," Jean said, taking firm hold of his hand. "Easy isn't it? You're free now."

Geoff Mabs looked up at her. Jean Oddy was bathed in a powerful halo of neon light. Halos slip, he thought. Become nooses.

One day she might strangle herself. Or he might do it for her.

It was easy too, to spike Hudge's pineapple juices with double measures of vodka. In a smoky corner of the Dragon's Head, Hudge was getting high on vodka. He snorted loudly and cracked stupid jokes to which his equally 'unsavoury companions' - this is the way Jean had described them - would match in laughter. Hudge now had friends and was having the time of his short life.

Jean, Mabs thought, had pressed all the right buttons. But Jean would not go through with it. He was certain. Why should she? Even when she slipped off to the lav, "for a Rubber Johnny," and returned, gulping down her remaining lager - she had knocked back more than her share tonight - her knees dropping in a jig with the music, saying "To the shed ..." he was certain she would not go through with it.

Out into the humid night air with Jean was hanging on to Hudge's arm, giggling and heading up the Pennington Road, Mabs felt sure they would stop at the top of Peterson.

"No wonder Hodge cut your face open." Flick had spoken for once.

"Sniffing around his girl," Papanikalou said.

Mabs took hold of the Greek's jacket. Gary Papanikalou always went too far. "Keep your mouth shut about that. You let on to Jean about me seeing the Lee girl and I'll cut you open. 'Know what I mean?'" And he threw him backward.

Papanikalou put his hands up in defence. "We won't breathe a word. Didn't know she was that important."

Mabs wasn't sure if Gary meant Jean or Lily. He looked ahead. Jean was pulling Hudge up past the T-junction. Why was she doing this then?

"It's just," Flick said, "I'm surprised Hodge got the better of you."

"He nearly killed a boy …"

Geoff Mabs seethed with anger. He looked at Papanikalou. "Shut it."

Jean and Hudge were gathering speed towards the billboards. He needed that public fight with Hodge. Hodge didn't seem bothered about him going with Lily, never even mentioned that in the Dragon last night. Well, this would get him going.

"Jean's really going to go through with it," Papanikalou whistled quietly. "She's really going to go through with it."

Flick stopped at the top of at the billboards. "I'm going home," he said, and he walked off up Carlisle Street.

"And you can bugger off too," Mabs said to Gary.

"Yeah," he replied, backing up towards the bridge. "I'll leave you to pimp."

Mabs ran round into Alpha. There she was. At the back gate. Pushing with her backside.

"Sh ...ush Hudge," she was saying. "Keep your voice down."

Papanikalou was right. She was going to go through with it. She was actually going to go through with it. Why? He was running up towards the back gate. They were into the yard now. She must be doing it for me. She must have fallen for me. He looked up: a full moon. He could take photos without a flash bulb and set the camera to a 'B' setting. He was up to the shed door. He put his hand to the door when it was wrenched open from the inside.

"Oh no, Mabs." Jean pushed at his chest. "Not you and your sidekicks. Get scarce. This is my business."

****

"Blackberry and apple pie, Lily?" Aida's round face collapsed gaunt and tired.

Lily refrained. She was not quite sure where the blackberries had been.

A late-night city train shrieked across the Pennington bridge. Lily found it a reassuring sound. That rattling and shrieking had been a part of her waking and even sleeping consciousness but now it just signalled that time was moving on and still Hudge had not returned from the pub. Aida looked at the clock.

"There was nothing I could do, Aida. Hudge insisted. So did Jean."

"She's a brazen little hussy."

"Geoff Mabs promised me he'd see Hudge home."

"His eyes are set too close together.

"I think he's nice ..."

Aida gave Lily an old-fashioned look.

"Anyway it's early yet," Lily said.

"Des'd be up the pub like a shot, but he's not back from the factory for another hour," and then Aida quickly added, "and I'm not letting you go. You should never have lied to me about what Jean Oddy's been up to with my boys."

"I never lied," Lily said. "I didn't know. And Hudge has only gone to the pub with Jean."

"That's true. You don't lie. You're a good girl," and then as an afterthought. "But ignorance is no excuse."

There was no beating Aida. She got up to wash some dishes. "Aida?" Lily was speaking to Aida's bulbous back. It was easier that way. So many intimate questions are asked of backs. "Aida, what is it with Hudge?" Lily had not liked to use the word 'wrong'.

Aida's back did not speak. Lily listened to the heavy tick of the kitchen clock. The dip, dip, dip of dishes into water. She could almost hear soap suds sliding from the plates. It was a rare Aida silence.

Lily had really wanted to ask Aida what Hudge had seen the afternoon before. Des and Jean. Jean and Des. But she felt that would be going too far - even for backs.

"There you are, Lily." And for the want of something to say it seemed, Aida said, "Put plenty of sugar on. The blackberries weren't quite ripe enough for an August picking," because Lily knew the blackberries were ripe: they had saturated her head the night before. Aida sat down at the kitchen table with the two basins. They picked up spoons that she had stuck into the ample slices of blackberry and apple pie. Aida took a mouthful, moving it around her mouth, as if sampling vintage wine and stared into space studiously. "Every child, Lily, has a guardian angel, who looks into the face of God."

Lily thought nothing of this. Aida plucked biblical references out of the midnight air. And Lily knew that this was some kind of delayed response to her question about Hudge.

"It's just," Aida went on, trowelling the blackberries with her spoon, "that Hudge's angel loved him too much to let go."

Lily did not know what to say. Her spoon was poised in the air. "I'm teaching Hudge to cross the road."

"I know," Aida cut in quickly and shook her head. "That's the difference with Hudge. He'll never be able to cross the road."

"He will."

"He won't," Aida said. "He can't grow up." She sighed and then thought she heard a sound at the kitchen door. Both she and Lily looked hopefully. Nothing. They sighed together.

It was true. He was not progressing with the kerbside drill. Even tonight - on the way to the caf - look right, look left, and there he was - stepping in front of a motorbike. He would have come to grief, had she not been there.

"Every bone in my body is bruised." Aida got up and moved to the back room door.

Cecilia said that Aida bruising easily was a lot of Fanny Ann.

Aida sighed again. "God give me strength. I think I need a dose of liver salts." She disappeared into the hallway.

Hudge had not grown out of his skin. He would always be six. Lily had hoped he would progress. In the past, that it was not possible for him to progress, was almost impossible to think. Not only for him, but selfishly Lily was thinking about herself. The sooner he learnt to cross the road by himself, the better. For everyone. But sooner or later, Lily was realising, she needed to accept that he would not progress at anything at all.

As Aida returned into the room carrying the huge Cambridge University Press Family Bible, Lily was thinking how Aida's skin had expanded over the years with all of Mrs Perry's sweets. It was as though Aida had given up on her body and carried the weight of generations on her bulging back in the same way that Bunyan's Christians carried bundles on the back of theirs. Lily had seen illustrations in Des's copy of *The Pilgrim's Progress*, presented to him on his confirmation and scrawled over by Hudge. Just as Hudge had scribbled over Des's complete works of D.H. Lawrence who had once taught at the secondary modern school years and years ago, before the war. Hudge needed carefully drawn boundaries and he needed also, to be shown how to colour within the lines. Hudge. The clock ticked.

"Here they are." Aida dropped the weight of the Bible on the kitchen table and sat down. She began turning the pages of the Bible. "Now," she said. "O."

"Oh?" Lily said looking at her with a question mark.

"Yes. O for Organs. My papers. In Obadiah."

Aida found the book of Obadiah and there sure enough, was an envelope. She took some papers from the envelope and smoothed them out with the palm of her hand. "I need my glasses. Now - where's my bag?"

Lily felt underneath the billowing checked tablecloth with her foot and drew up Aida's trunk of a handbag.

Aida rummaged. She put on her glasses. "This is my copy - see?" She perused the papers and smacked the palm of her hand on the kitchen table. "There you are, Lily."

Lily was not sure where she was. At Obadiah, maybe. She looked with furrowed eyebrows at Aida.

"My papers," she said. "My papers from the university."

"University?"

"Now that's where my organs are going should anything happen to me. To the university." She looked pleased with herself. "So if Des doesn't get there at least someone in this family will. Lazy bugger, failing all his 'A' levels. He needs a dose of liver salts."

'If anything happened' to Aida, - that was another one of Aida's euphemisms – I mean things happened to people all the time but when Aida said, 'if anything happens' it meant 'Death' - 'if anything did happen' to Aida, what would become of Hudge? Lily did not ask Aida this question. She knew her answer. Des would look after him. It went without saying.

"I know what you're thinking, Lily."

Lily was suddenly disturbed.

"Girls pair up from kindergarten. Boys are all over the place."

At times, it was difficult for Lily to tack down Aida's thread of thinking, but she guessed she was referring to Des and Jean.

"I would have loved a girl, Lily. Lots of mothers with boys feel like that. Especially three. All those shirts to iron, Lily. And no frilly knickers in the drawer."

Lily instantly understood why Aida had appointed herself as her babysitter. A door had opened on Aida. But, as always, Aida's butterfly mind fluttered sideways.

"'Course your mother …" Aida stopped herself.

"What was that, Aida?"

"I'm not sure any of my boys have grown up," she said. Lily thought she may be confusing her tenses. Ben.

Aida's elbows were on the table. She rested her chins in her hands - a sign that she was deep in thought. Aida carried that indelible sadness in her eyes which bereaved parents do. Lily did not like to speak of Ben. "You don't think Des has grown up?" Lily sometimes thought that Des had grown up before his time: that he carried about with him the luggage of premature responsibility. Des was waiting for the right skin to creep up.

"My gift. Des is my gift. He'll always be your friend. A friend loveth at all times and a brother is born for adversity. Proverbs 17, 17. Des knows that. I've taught him that, Lil. If he's learnt nothing else my boy knows that." And then suddenly Aida looked straight at her. "You'll have to go to him, Lily." There was something different about her face which was right up close to Lily's now. Lily couldn't work out what the difference was. "I know he's done you wrong. He knows it. That's the thing about Des," she said, pointing a finger at Lily. "When he's had time to think, he comes round. He rushes in where seraphims fear to bloody place their big toes. Acts first," she said, hitting the kitchen table with the palm of her hand, "and thinks last." She shook her head. "But he won't admit it and he won't come to you."

His mother knew Des better than she did.

"Well - you're here, aren't you?" Aida said. "Where is he? It's almost midnight." She got up and began to stack the dishes. Her squab, stocking-free legs displayed fine blue lines.

Lily observed their pattern. "And me?" she said. "Have I lost my guardian angel?"

"Your mother always dressed you in blue, didn't she?"

Lily sighed deeply and looked up at the clock. She should be going. Cecilia would be waiting.

But Aida was up and fetching her photograph album. "There we are," she said. "Six bridesmaids in colours of the rainbow and your mother insisted on blue for you. Your mother wore a red hat to Ben's wedding. Funny choice."

"And you said to my mum 'red hat, no drawers'."

"She didn't think it was funny," Aida said.

Lily looked at Aida sideways from the photograph album, she could see Aida's lips twitching, wanting to relax into laughter. But somehow, not tonight. "She's had a hard life, your mother. You give your mother the benefit."

"Why do you say that?" Lily asked. "And what were you going to say earlier bout Mum?"

"Where's Iris this late summer?"

"She's not coming, Aida. She's having her teeth crowned."

"You said." Aida kept looking at the 'comfort' wedding photo album. "How old were you at Ben's wedding?" Aida said instead.

"Ten."

"And Mrs Brambles supplied the tea roses."

Their sweet scent seemed to linger for weeks afterward, Lily recalled. "And Jean wore lime green and hated the dress."

Aida's lips turned downward, her chin dimpling with disdain.

"Why have you never liked Jean, Aida?"

"Because she's a brazen little hussy."

"No, I don't mean just Sunday night." She caught Aida's eye as she looked up from the photograph album. "I overheard you shouting at Des, Aida. I heard it all."

Aida ignored her and carried on looking at Ben's wedding photos.

"You haven't liked her much since she was eleven."

"Jean Oddy," she whispered. "Sin of the father."

"What?" Lily said. Aida really wasn't making sense tonight. What did Aida mean by 'the sin of the father'? What had Jack Oddy done? As far as Lily could see Jack Oddy did as little as possible and everyone on the road always said, "Shame about the Oddys".

"I've never seen six bridesmaids look so lovely," was all Aida said.

Six of them, in colours of the rainbow. Ramni from new Indian restaurant, gleaming darkly in a shade of amethyst. Arranged marriage for Ramni. So much simpler for Ramni. Aida, wearing stockings, looking dapper with a feather in her hat. Des and Hudge, smiles fixed, a moment caught up in time, signed, sealed and packaged forever.

"Oh, look at Des." Aida laughed. "He'd just passed his 11 plus."

And Ben. Of course Ben. Looking faintly, thought Lily, like Des does now. Ben and Kay. Kay and Ben.

"So few of Hudge," Aida said.

"He's always hated his photo being taken," Lily said. "Kay looked lovely," she said, losing count of how many times this same conversation had taken place. Kay, with her big Adam's apple.

"She's a nice girl, Kay," Aida said. "She's a bit daft, but she's a nice girl. A good daughter-in-law. She's never re-married in six years. Married to that Pekinese dog more like. What she called it?"

"Nanky-Poo."

Aida raised her eyes to the unshaded light bulb overhead and cupped her double chins in her hands.

"Des named it for Kay. He told her it was the name of a character in a Gilbert and Sullivan musical," Lily said.

"And she believed him, I suppose. He's full of wind that boy."

"There is a musical, Aida."

"Oh, I don't doubt it, but I wouldn't put it past Des to have Kay on the end of a piece of string. He could never have married Kay."

"And Ben?" Lily said, clearing an imagined rasp in her throat. There was a long pause whilst the kitchen clock ticked heavily and Aida stared up at Ben's photo on the precious sideboard. "Where was his guardian angel?"

Aida let out gulps of laughter which galloped around the kitchen. "Oh Lily. There's not much a guardian angel can do when you're racing down the motorway on a motor bike at seventy miles an hour. I'm off to bed. I'll lie awake upstairs until Hudge comes in and you can wait here for Des. Night, night, my darling. Put that album in my precious sideboard, now."

Aida had motorways on the brain seeing as one was being built this very year. 'Devils' roads', she called them. But of course Ben was killed right outside their grocery shop. There were no photos of Des's father, Reg. Spikey man, Reg Hodge. They had been removed. It took Des and Lily years to realise that the French Foreign Legion was a euphemism for clearing off. She closed the photograph album, remembering how Des had always wondered, dressed in his boys' scout uniform, standing at the corner of Peterson Road, looking at Ben stretched out across Pennington, why his parents had been on different sides of the road. Silly thought. And then she fell asleep, head on the family Bible, at the kitchen table.

****

"Did you enjoy that, Hudge?" There was laughter from inside the shed.

"You were bloody good, Jean."

Mabs could hear Jean giggling. He took the cigarette from behind his ear, lit up and leant against the shed wall. He had taken some nice shots through the shed window.

"Des said you weren't so bloody bad."

"Did he?" Jean sounded pleased.

"Yes, he said you were a tart."

Then was then a long silence and a scratching around, probably getting her knickers on, Mabs thought.

"Stop that, Hudge. Stop staring at me like that."

"I'm smirking."

"Well, don't," she said.

"You don't wear corsets."

"No. Why? Does Lily?"

"Des says she does."

Jean laughed. She was drunk and then Hudge joined in, shouting, "My mum hides her corsets under the cushions."

Jean was obviously getting annoyed because Hudge just kept laughing and she said, "Quiet, Hudge. You'll wake Dad."

Then after a short silence he could hear Jean asking Hudge if he fancied Lily and him saying, "No, because she's Des's girlfriend." But then Hudge seemed confused and was talking about 'bad words' and Des throwing blackberries at Lily. Then Jean asked, "Do you fancy me?"

"Have you been keeping yourself for me, Jean?"

"No," came the reply.

"Did you make your mind up about me?"

"What do you mean by that?"

"To do what we did."

She was now sounding desperate. "Don't tell anyone, Hudge. It'll be our little secret and I won't do it with you ever again if you tell."

Hudge was promising that he would keep the secret. "I promise, Jean. I promise. But does that mean I can touch your bosoms again?"

Mabs could hear Jean getting up, moving around. She must have put the high heels back on, because they were clunking and scraping the floor. Hudge was asking if she was his girlfriend and then he added, "now that Des says he wouldn't touch you with a pole."

"It's time I got you home."

Mabs moved to the yard gate. Hudge was saying he was lucky now he had a girlfriend and Jean was saying she would open up the caf and let him cross the Pennington Road on his own, "because I'm not going to baby you like Lily Lee does."

That was good. Mabs would have had to leg it up Alpha or hide down one of the alley ways if they'd come through the back He was about to scram when he heard Hudge Hodge say, "I love you, Jean Oddy."

"You dare mention my name again to anyone." She was bloody annoyed.

"But I love you Jean Oddy, because I made up my mind."

"If you mention what's happened to anyone, I'll say this never happened and I'm not your girlfriend. You never tell anyone I'm your girlfriend. Do you understand?" There was a pause. Then in another angry, strangulated whisper, she said, "Answer me. Do ... you ... understand."

"I do. I promise I won't tell, Jean," came the reply. "It's our secret."

And mine, thought Geoff Mabs, as he caressed his camera: gift like a Trojan horse this camera, he thought. His bloody grandfather had told him the story of the Trojan horse: a gift to enslave a nation.

As he headed up Alpha, smell of timber in the air, he thought about what he had just seen in Jean Oddy's shed. They had a word for it, he knew. Watching. Watching two other people. Mabs had set up this 'love match'. But quite strangely, that is what it had almost turned out to be. For Hudge Hodge, this was his first time. For Jean Oddy, it wasn't. She had taken the lead, shown him what to do. And there had been a tenderness in the act. An act which Geoff had watched with intense curiosity. Geoff Mabs's act with Jean - or anyone else for that matter - was always quick, urgent, as if they might want to run away, as if he were anxious that the feeling of high might run away if he didn't hurry up. It had always been over too soon: diving into the fleshy softness and then ... nothing. But for Jean and the spaz, there had been what they call ... intimacy. Jean had kissed the boy as if she wanted the love. And kissed him afterwards. Slowly. Geoff Mabs had not expected this.

Their intimacy was also a private act. Geoff knew that. And he felt sick at the thought of himself - and his past.

****

Lily woke at Aida's back room table to the sound of Hudge singing, "Until I kissed ya," - an Everly Brothers' number. He's been drinking, she thought.

She opened the back room door. Hudge smiled stupidly at her and then the smile slipped. "Oh no," she said, as he rushed to the kitchen sink in the scullery. He was painfully sick. "I'll murder Jean Oddy for doing this," she said as she cleared his vomit from the Belfast sink and gave him a tea towel. Just at that moment, the front door slammed closed and she could hear Des shouting through to the scullery, "Hudge. Hudge. Get me my bottle opener will you from my tool box, will you?"

Des had been drinking too. She could tell. "I'm going home, Hudge," she whispered and went through to the scullery.

Hudge left her in the scullery and went through to the back room. There was a heavy rummaging through the tool box until Hudge had obviously found the bottle opener. She didn't want to see Des now. Not when he had been drinking. And not when Hudge had been drinking. Des would hold her responsible. She stood behind the scullery door, deciding that she would go the back way out and through the Hodge's side gate when she heard Hudge say, "Des, are you Lily's girlfriend?"

"I dunno. I dunno, Hudge." Des's voice sounded tired and a little defeated.

"I don't think she loves you." Hudge had obviously clean forgotten she was in the scullery. How much had he been drinking?

"Why?" Des said.

"Because she can't make up her mind."

Des was laughing softly now and she could hear bottle tops being removed. "You eavesdrop too much for your own good." For a moment Lily thought he had seen her but then he said, "Lily has big problems with the word 'yes'. She can't make up her mind about anything. She never comes off the fence."

Bloody cheek. There was a long pause. Lily now did not know what to do. She felt a cough coming on. How would she explain this? And she would be heard leaving by this kitchen door if she went now. The pause went on. What was happening? Then Hudge said, "Mrs Slattery's fence?"

"You always pay a price for what you most desire."

"For black pudding?"

"For freedom, for truth, for ..."

"Mum says she has to pay Mr Lee too high a price for black pudding."

"For Lily Lee."

Lily was infuriated, outraged.

Hudge snorted. "Lily's not a black pudding. Black pudding's slimy and fat."

There was another pause whilst Lily looked across to the scullery draining board where blackberry and apple pies sat in neat sugared rows, the plated edges pressed with Aida's thumbprints; the excess pastry having been shaved off with her sharp knife.

"How's the job going?" Des was asking.

"I've got lots of friends."

"Have you?" Des sounded surprised.

"Yeah ... Mr Oddy doesn't spend any time in the caf 'cos he's upstairs with Angina. But I've never met her. Jean takes them cocoa."

"Has Jean been good to you?"

She wanted to burst through and give the pair of them some home truths but Hudge was asking Des if Jean was his girlfriend.

"No," Des said.

"I got a girlfriend."

"Who?"

"Not telling," Hudge said.

"Lily?"

Why on earth had Des asked Hudge that question?

"No." Hudge sounded indignant. "She can't love you. She can't love me."

Lily suddenly felt black. She loved them both. She was standing feet away and she wanted to tell them both how much she loved them, albeit in different ways. Why did Hudge just say that? Then he said, "She wears corsets."

There was a sound of gulping and some laughter. "Hudge," Des was saying. "I swear I never know what's going on in your head, but sometimes you speak a lot of truth."

Lily wished she had never heard this conversation.

"You must always keep a promise," Hudge said.

Lily could barely hear Des's voice. "Yes, you must," he was saying. "Promises unlike pie crust are not meant to be broken."

Lily thought how original Des was in his thinking, but years later she would fall across a quotation of Jonathan Swift's. *Promises like pie crust are made to be broken.* If only she had known then, at that moment by the scullery door, the truth of those words. Des, it's harder to keep a promise than we thought …

Then she heard Aida. Aida must have been so relieved. "My boys," Aida was saying. Oh God, what if she came into the scullery? The scullery door opened and Aida was in her dressing gown. Lily put her fingers to her lips and shook her head. Aida frowned. Then she opened the scullery back door and said, "Off to bed, boys. I'm just putting the cat out."

"Okay, Mum," Hudge called.

There was a soft silence before Lily heard Des's voice. "What cat?"

Lily closed the scullery door, leaving the sweet scent of cooked pastry behind her. The weight and varied textures of those cooking fragrances would float on into the future, touching the half remembered thumb edges of the past. It was the last time she ever heard their words or saw their faces together as a family. Grief searches these moments out, discovers them and dwells.

****

"Slipped my mind last night ..." Tight-lipped and 'all angles' Zelda Mabs attacked the cauliflower with a kitchen knife the same way as she did life.

Mabs stood still, at the kitchen door. What was she going to say now? What more could she say now after last night?

"Another one of your tarts called last night," she said.

"What tart?" Mabs kicked at some Cash and Carry cardboard boxes which littered the floor and threw his front door key down on the table. It was midnight. What was the woman doing slicing cauliflower?

A smell of fat seeped up from through the ceiling, despite kitchen cooking. Zelda took a swipe at a bluebottle with a tea-towel, which was hovering above a greasy joint of yesterday's roast beef. "Where the bloody hell have you been? I had a rush on tonight. Go down and switch those fat fryers off."

"Where's Charlie?"

"Where do you think? Flat on his back cradling Johnny Walker."

Mabs strongly suspected his mother had been at a bottle of her own Johnny Walker's; it was the way she talked through half closed eyes and the stench on her breath that gave it away. "What did Jean want?" His suit jacket was slung over his shoulder.

"Christ knows what any girl'd want from you but it slipped my mind last night. Remember last night? I said, do you remember last night?"

"Yeah, I remember last night."

"When you got in a muddle over your night off and sodded off with that tart - Jean - from the caf? Found an alley way with her, did you? Real alley-cat she is."

"What slipped your mind?"

"The grocery girl."

So ... Lily had come looking for him later last night. She never mentioned it in the stables earlier.

"What a state she was in. Covered in God knows what. Red wine probably. Drunk as a bloody lord with all the airs and graces of a bloody lady. And on a Sunday." Her thin white elbow jogged up and down in staccato bursts with each quick carrot slice. "Is Geoff in?" Zelda drawled in a breathless husky whisper.

Mabs watched the hard lips attacking the words that Zelda seemed almost to spit out. "My God, they're only shop people."

Lily's lips were soft and moist.

"Think they're a cut above, they do."

Cut, cut, cut at the carrots. Lily caressed words. He would like to stuff Hodge full of his anger. He would like to stuff the cauliflower into

Zelda's mouth and watch her squirm. Lily's mouth had been warm ... yielding.

"Cecilia Lee walks around as though she's a broom stuck up her backside. And the way her daughter prances about swinging that pony tail, she thinks she's Doris bloody Day. I ask you."

The hairs on the back of Mabs's neck stood upright, the same as they had done when Des Hodge had come within inches of him. His mother wished she was Ava Gardner. Had a subscription for *Eve's Film Review*.

"Snobs." Zelda wiped the back of the knife on her skirt and pointed it at Mabs. "And no tarts in your room."

"She's no tart."

"That's the one you've been taking photos of, isn't it? I've watched you from this window. Watched you in the rec. taking photos of the Lee girl. Not getting enough of it, are we? Despite all the talk. Runs in the bloody Mabs's family."

"Don't you start again."

Actually, he was getting enough, but from the wrong direction. Zelda took a swipe at the bluebottle and then a swig of her Johnny Walker. She pointed the peeling knife at him once again and said, "And stop giving those Teds from the caf free bloody chips," and then sashayed to the kitchen window, singing *It's so damned hot, It's so damned hot.* "I should 'ave been a film star, me. Legs like a Tiller, I had. *It's so damned hot, It's so damned hot.*" Here she went again. God, this woman was an embarrassment.

Her real name wasn't really Zelda. It was Margaret. Margaret Mara. Mabs had seen it on her passport. In the week before they had moved to the chippie, his mother had slung every which bit of paper or ornament or frying pan or tobacco tin in cardboard boxes. She had unashamedly stripped his grandfather's house of every nail and light bulb it possessed. His grandfather had only been gone weeks when they were on the move once again. But this time it was to their own property. Bought 'with the proceeds of your father's house, Charlie'. 'Zelda' wasn't going to fritter the inheritance away. But the chippie upstairs flat was like a London bombsite which Mabs had never seen during the war. Littered with unpacked boxes of goods: just in case she had missed something of any worth, which was a laugh, him sitting with his Ilford Witness. His grandfather must have thought a lot of him to leave this treasure to him. But maybe Zelda had been searching for something else. What he found last night. The flat was splitting at the sides with rubbish, like Aida Hodge. Like his head.

"Can you see that rubbish down there? I'll have to call the dustmen. I think every blessed soul in Juniper Street leaves their rubbish up my back alley."

"Yeah, you're stuffed full of rubbish, you are," he said.

Zelda turned on him and pointed her knife. "Remember last night, sonny Jim? I can give you a few more home truths if you want, you little bastard. Now get downstairs and switch those fat fryers off unless you want your right cheek sliced open as well."

Mabs moved quickly.

6

TUESDAY 25TH AUGUST, 1959

"Had a good time with lover boy last night?" Mabs whispered to Jean and Papanikalou immediately moved up to the juke box by the counter and slipped on Presley's 'Don't be Cruel'.

Jean leant across the counter. *Flick, flack.* He had to take a photo of her face. It was priceless. Hudge was slowly buttering bread. "Nothing happened," she spat back at Mabs. "I took him home after the pub and put that bloody camera out of sight, Mabs or I'll have you put out on to Pennington. You're crazy."

"Yeah, well, I followed you both down Alpha Road right into your unopened back gate last night."

"And I said nothing happened. We played 'I Spy'."

Mabs thought this was really funny. "And I've got some lovely snaps in this camera to prove it. Funny way to play 'I Spy'."

Jean looked quickly at Hudge, his buttering knife hovering above the uncut bread.

"Quiet, Mabs. Don't let this get out. You got me drunk last night. If Des finds out you're finished. Now give me that bloody roll of film in your camera." She reached across to take the camera but Mabs only grinned and patted it.

"Give it to me," she said.

"I'll give something better later," he said.

She scowled back at him. "If Des finds out ..."

This was Papanikalou's cue, "Jean's right. You wanna be careful. Des Hodge might do you over again. This time, not because of his girl but because of his daft brother. You know he nearly killed a boy once."

If Mabs heard this Greek say that once again, he would take him apart organ by organ, he swore. "You know, Papanikalou," he said turning to him by the juke box, Presley still belting out 'Don't be Cruel', "the way you chew gum, the way you do anything is disgusting. And I told you, Des Hodge didn't give me this cut."

"Well, why did you let the grocery girl think you did?"

"Well, you know," he said, pulling at the collar of his velvet lapels, "birds like to feel sympathetic, don't they?" he said elbowing the kid. "Eh?"

Papanikalou at first looked confused and then grinned, showing those incisors. "Yeah," he laughed. "Oh, yeah, yeah, I get it."

Mabs grinned.

"Why did Jean go with Hudge then?"

"For the love of Mabs," Mabs said.

"For the love of Des Hodge more like," Papanikalou said.

Now Mabs was confused. "What do you mean?"

"Des is ... was ... I dunno ... doing it with Jean. He comes out the back way, into Alpha. Timber yard's closing time when me and Flick are clocking off. Maybe he's dumped her. Maybe that's why Jean's gone with Hudge. You only got to put two and two together, haven't you?"

"And you're able to do that are you?" came the answer. But Mabs was stunned.

"Nah, Jean 'd never go for you," Papanikalou said.

"She's mad about me." And with that Mabs looked across the counter but Jean simply pulled a face.

Papanikalou laughed. "She's gotta funny way of showing it."

Mabs was irritated. He looked again at Jean who was now smiling at a paying customer. He would wipe the smile from those painted lips. Reduce her tiny piece of power and have her hanging in shreds. "I can get off with her any time I like," he said. "Watch me." And he placed his camera on the counter.

Papanikalou spat his chewing gum on to the floor and Mabs whistled. "Hudge. Here Hudge. Come here, Hudge."

Hudge tightened and Jean moved round the counter to Mabs's table. "What do you want?" she said but Mabs quickly grasped her arm, pulling her on to his knee. "Let me go," she shouted at him.

"Hudge," he shouted across the counter. Tonight he meant business. "Hudge, let me introduce you to my girlfriend."

Slowly, Hudge laid down his buttering knife and came round to the table. Mabs went on. "This is my girlfriend - Jean. Jean, this is Hudge. Say 'hello' to Hudge, Jean."

"Mabs, don't," she said, sitting still on Mabs's knee.

"No, Jean," Mabs said. "I won't say that you are anybody else's girlfriend because you are my girlfriend, aren't you, Jean?" Mabs said the words as if underlining them, his eyes fixed on Hudge, his grip firmly fixed on Jean.

"Yes I am, okay, I am your girlfriend. All right," she said, looking at Hudge who stood before them. "Now, just let me go, Mabs. Let me go."

Mabs released his grip but not before he pulled Jean's head towards his and gave her a hard and penetrating kiss. She liked it. He could tell. He looked up and saw the backward boy studying them. Then he realised it was almost closing. "That'll do for starters," he said, placing a coin in the juke box slot. And then suddenly he could feel another asthma attack coming on. It was smoky in here. He needed to get out quickly. His breath was short. He couldn't be seen to be having an attack in here. Not in front of all this crowd. He would never live it down. And he was needing air. He managed to squeeze out the words. "Tomorrow night we're really going to have fun. I'm going out into the yard for some fresh air," he said to Papanikalou and Flick, whilst the one-armed bandit pulsated and spewed out coins with a continuous clatter. He made a quick exit. He couldn't have an attack in front of the crowd.

Mabs tugged at the back gate and took a seat on the pavement, leaning back on the caf wall. He searched his pockets for his inhaler. Shit. He'd left it at home. The Everly Brothers' 'Dream, Dream, Dream' wafted out into the sultry night. Voices on the Pennington Road were getting louder. It was almost ten. He had to catch his breath. He looked up towards the timber yard, then back at the graffiti-ridden wall. He picked up a nearby stone, feeling a need to make his mark and rid his head of words that had been running around on a railway track for days and was about to chuck it away in frustration when a garage door slammed. There were footfalls on the pavement. In the clear light of a full moon he could see Lily stooping down to stroke a cat.

"Hello old cat," she said. "Where have you been?" The cat rubbed its body against her leg and then circled her. She lost her balance, and then, as if feeling eyes touching her, she looked up Alpha Road. "Oh. Hello. You startled me."

The cat sprang across the road and disappeared down an alley way by the timber yard. She walked towards Mabs. "I haven't seen that cat in ages, but it's been around as long as I can remember."

He stared at her, like a dog maintaining eye contact when guarding his territory. He said nothing.

"It's a nervous cat." A tiny gulp of laughter emitted from her throat. She looked behind her, as if indicating the cat, not wishing to maintain eye contact.

He took out a packet of cigarettes and lit up, a stupid thing to do, he knew when he had just had an attack. The stone was still in his hand. Then he offered the cigarette to her. She accepted, took a small puff and coughed. He smiled knowingly. She passed the cigarette back. "Cloudless sky," he said, pointing up.

"Sorry?"

"Stars are there and no longer there. By the time the light reaches us, they could be dead," he said.

"Who could be dead?"

"The stars," he said. "Dream, dream, dream ..." The Everly Brothers' velvet tones drifted into Alpha Road. "It's amazing. That light can take all that time to get here - millions of years. Light years they call it. Miles are measured by the number of years it takes light to reach me and you. And by the time it does, the stars are gone. Exploded. Nothing. It doesn't seem possible. You're seeing it now but it's gone already."

Lily felt like Julie Jordan on the 'Carousel' again. It was romantic. Des never talked like this. "Like cine films?" she said.

"Or photos," he said. "Or dreams …"

She sat down beside him and he offered her the cigarette again but this time she declined.

"My grandad said that explosion was the price stars paid for shining. When I was twelve, it was hard to understand that things could be there and yet not there. Like dreams, he said. They're there but they're not. Sometimes dreams are remembered ages after they take place, but it doesn't make them any less real. I believed everything the old man said. 'Make your mark, son.' My grandfather called me that. He called me 'son'. Except I wasn't ... wasn't anything to him."

"But you told me he loved you," Lily said.

Mabs shook his head. The Everly Brothers' ballad was coming to an end. "I wasn't his. Had nothing to do with him. Charlie told me on Sunday night. Zelda had cheated on Charlie. The woman's an absolute bitch." Coming from a long line of Irish navvies, he thought. He felt Lily take hold of his left hand which still held the stone. Warm, comforting. He said quietly, "You're my strange girl in the leather jacket. Dream on." She looked up at him. Beautiful eyes.

She smiled and looked back at him. He was smiling too. He kissed her very softly, her body seemed to fold into his.

"Be my girl," he said. After all, she'd finished with Des. He needed to make a move quickly before she changed her mind. Then she did something strange. She looked down at their hands, opened his palm and took the stone. "Look. Let's write it on the caf wall. Me and you. For everyone to see." She was scratching out on the wall. Any moment now she would pass him back the stone. What was he going to do with the stone? Her back was to him when she said, "It was Des's leather jacket, but that's all over now. Let everyone know that it's me and you together. We can make our mark." And there she was stretching out the fucking stone. He couldn't think about what she was doing for the both of them. All he could think about was – what was he going to do with the stone. "There we are. Look what I've written about us."

"What has Des told you?" He was accusing. He meant to be.

"Told me what?"

"About me."

"Nothing. Let's forget him. Let's make our mark." She was holding the stone out towards him. He took it quickly and turning, seeing the cat, he aimed and hit. The cat screeched in pain. Mabs jumped up. "The shed door is open," he said quickly, abruptly. He took her hand, tugged, but she shook her head. A train screeched across the bridge. "Oh come on," he said. "Don't lead me on again."

She put her hands on his chest and pushed him away, brushing the hair away from her face, but Mabs pulled her into him and went to kiss her again.

"No," she shouted. "Stop it."

It occurred to Mabs for the first time that she had never done it before. That would be even better. Tender, like Hudge's first time with Jean. He grabbed her hand. She gave a quick, sharp intake of breath as if to scream and he placed his hand across her mouth.

Another train screamed across the bridge and as he opened the back gate of the caf he heard a voice shouting, "Lily, Lily, where are you?"

"I'm here, Hudge," she said. He heard her sigh with relief. "I've come to fetch you."

Mabs walked off up Alpha Road. Those Hodges stopped him having what he wanted. Then he stopped; realised he was at a loss. Something was missing. His camera. The roll of film, a whole week's work but that meant nothing now: his Ilford Witness. How could he leave it alone? He'd had the asthma attack and then Lily came but how could he forget it? He ran back to the caf yard and kicked open the gate. No, he hadn't had his camera when he left the caf and met Lily. It must be inside. Lights out. Lily must have already collected Hudge and be walking up Peterson by now. Jean must have gone up to bed. He went to the scullery door and hammered hard. No, the Oddys would never open up after closing. It would have to wait until tomorrow. He turned round and started walking up Alpha.

As he turned the corner of Alpha Road he saw a figure, the 'A feature' legs he recognised, on Carlisle Street, just by the railway cottages: Teresa 'legs' Dossing. Maybe she knew who would have picked up his camera.

****

"Would you let me touch your bosoms?"

Lily kept walking. The chances were, if you ignored Hudge's odd questions long enough, he forgot they were asked in the first place.

She tried to stay calm. Calm. Lily Lee did not feel calm. This was the last question in the world she wished to be asked - considering the brief interlude which had taken place with Geoff Mabs in Alpha Road.

Why did she feel this way? Frightened ... but excited. Lily Lee was excited by Geoff Mabs. By his dark, symmetric, foreign terrain. It was marred with whirlpools and every time Lily dipped a big toe in, to test out the water, it enticed her in further, not despite of, but because of its very danger.

Des was the stuff that marriages were made of, but Des wasn't feeling that way now. Geoff Mabs was ... but there was something else ...

"Would you let me touch your bosoms, Lily?"

Hudge's question was not going to go away. What had he seen that Sunday night with Des and Jean? He had obviously opened the door on them. This was all Des's fault.

"You never answer the questions, Lily."

Lily stopped and looked up at Hudge. "Hudge. I can't even answer my own questions." She was angry. She had enough problems of her own, without Hudge continually adding to them. "Besides. That's not a very nice question."

Hudge's lower lip protuded and he looked down at the pavement. I've upset him again, thought Lily. He was standing clutching his white overall, his chins quivering. Lily knew this signalled oncoming tears. In order to prevent them, and for the want of something to say, she said, "Do you want me to carry your overall?"

"No." He took a step back.

"Why?"

He only shook his head.

"Have you been into Perry's to buy more sweets?" she said. "It's okay. I won't take them away from you. You don't need to hide them from me."

"Geoff Mabs is a bad boy, Lily. A bad, bad boy." He was standing hunched up, holding his overall close to him.

Lily failed to see any connection. She was surprised. She laughed and put her arm around him. "Have you been reading inside my head?"

The back gate had been closed when Geoff kissed her this evening. Hudge couldn't possibly have seen anything.

But that wasn't the only thing on her mind. She had realised tonight that Geoff Mabs probably couldn't read anything at all. Hudge could at least read and write some, but Geoff Mabs threw the stone at the cat because he couldn't write - and probably couldn't read sign writing. It was why he never wore a watch. It seemed to Lily that Geoff Mabs could be as handicapped as Hudge - but maybe in a different way. Had his fight with Des on Sunday night been something to do with Geoff not being able to read? "Why is Geoff Mabs bad, Hudge?"

"He ..." Hudge looked from the ground and up towards the caf. "He ..." Hudge then attacked the word 'kissed' with a stutter, "Jean."

Oh well, thought Lily. That answers my question. Geoff Mabs was a two-timer.

She shrugged her shoulders. "It is," she was picking her words carefully, "all right to kiss, you know, Hudge."

He shook his head. "But she didn't like it, Lily. She didn't like it."

"Oh well then," Lily said, thinking how unusual it was for Jean to be loyal to Des. "Then it is wrong."

"Yes. It is wrong, isn't it, Lily?" He held the white overall to him closer, like a child with a new puppy. "And I am lucky, aren't I, Lily?"

"Yes, Hudge." She ushered him to the front door.

"To have a friend like Jean?"

"Very lucky, Hudge. Goodnight."

Lily stood for a few moments on the Hodge doorstep, just in case someone came to the closed front door. Then she walked up Peterson Road very slowly, just in case she bumped into somebody. The curtain in the flat above the grocery shop was drawn back. There was the old dog at the window again. Above this was her attic bedroom window. How she wished Des could sleep in her arms tonight. She was to spend her life wishing he had.

7

WEDNESDAY 26TH AUGUST, 1959

When Jean turned up on the shop's black and white chequered doorstep the next day, with a surreptitious, 'I need to talk to you', Lily wondered if she was pregnant. Jean possessed a keen sense of drama. When Jean's mother had died she had rather enjoyed the drama of it all.

It was Wednesday morning and Lily had spent a good half hour swatting wasps in the shop. There had to be a nest in the garage. "Can I take Jean upstairs, Dad?"

Gordon Lee was stacking cardboard hamburgers in the frozen food cabinet. "Of course, Lily," he said. "Don't let the shop interfere with your social life."

Lily mounted the steps to the kitchen. "So ..." Lily said angrily, as she turned and folded her arms to face Jean, her back to the kitchen sink, "what did you want to talk about?"

Jean took off her leather jacket and placed it over the kitchen chair. How on earth could she wear such an item in this hot weather? But then Jean did everything for effect. Jean sat down, crouched her head over her knees and ran unfortunately varnished nails through her dark, curly hair. She looked around. "Don't suppose I can have a cigarette in here?"

"No." She waited for Jean to speak.

Jean rubbed her forefinger on the kitchen table. "Has Hudge said anything to you? She swallowed hard and looked up at Lily, blinking in the bright sunlight.

Lily shrugged her shoulders. "About what?"

Jean continued to look down at the kitchen table and bit her lip. "About the caf."

Lily went on. "He didn't like Geoff Mabs kissing you."

Jean put her head back and looked up at the ceiling.

"Hudge seems to think you're his friend." Lily then tutted.

Jean suddenly seemed to relax, fell back into the chair with ease. "Yes," she said. "Yes I am."

Jean never ever had any problems with saying the word 'yes'. Lily went on. "Hudge also said that Mabs had been calling you names, but how dare you take him to the pub like you did on Monday and top up his pineapple juices with vodka. He was as sick as a hamster, but I don't suppose friends like you clear up sick, do you, Jean Oddy?" Lily was cross.

"Actually," she said. "It was Mabs I wanted to speak to you about. Are you still going with him?"

"Well, I am surprised with this line of conversation, Jean but how did you know?"

"I saw you on Pennington with him - on Sunday. You looked very much together." The grin returned to Jean's dimpled face. "And he did slip out to see you last night, in the yard, didn't he? I mean, he said he'd gone for fresh air. But fresh air is dangerous for his lungs."

"What's the point of all this, Jean?" Lily was not prepared to give Jean any more information.

"I don't want you to be upset, Lily, if you and Mabs are going out. But the point is..." She tightened again.

So, thought Lily, she's come to tell me she's going out with Geoff Mabs too. Well, Hudge had already told Lily this.

But to Lily was astonished when she said, "The point is ...that Geoff Mabs has been bullying Hudge." Jean looked up at Lily. "At the caf."

Lily didn't believe her. Why had Hudge said nothing? There was this awkward pause. So that was why he had made a friend of Jean. She had been protecting him. Jean had taken over Lily's role of Supreme Protector. Lily hated her.

Of course, Hudge would want to have kept his job. What had he said? 'Not want to foul it up for Des.' And the pay packets. The pay packets were so important to him. Hudge would have known she would have told Des. Des. Jean must have told Des ...the cut on Geoff's face. It must have been what Jean had wanted to see Des about all week.

But then Jean said, "I think you ought to tell Des."

Lily bit back at once. "Why don't you?"

"Me?" she shouted. "Me - tell Des? You've spent your life putting walls between me and Des. When my mother died," Jean never referred to her mother as 'mum', "when my mother died," Jean repeated, because her eyes were welling up with tears, "Des tried to get friends with me and you never let him."

"That's not true, Jean. When your mother died it was Aida who stopped you seeing Des. It was round about the time you failed your eleven plus and went to Peterson Road Secondary Modern."

"Oh, yes, the eleven plus, Lily. How could I forget? Anyway, you go parading up Pennington with Geoff Mabs and then run down to Des and tell him to stay away from me."

"That's not true either," Lily said.

"You sent Des round on Sunday night to finish with me and I really wanted to hurt him…"

Lily looked to the kitchen floor and thought that Des must have resolved to chuck Jean on the Sunday night and then went looking for a fight with Mabs, all for the love of Lily Lee. It was odd. Something wasn't sitting right.

"I know you all call me a tart and an exhibition." Jean started to choke, in an effort to keep back the tears, and then seemed to give way to them, willingly. "Whilst all the time you keep your sacred clean little place with Des. And Hudge. You've never let me be friends with them. You took everything on offer from me and threw it back in my face like everyone else. You've always been there, Lily. Taking the biggest slice of the cake."

That was true though. After Jean's mum had died, her father gave her Knickerbocker Glories to feed the whole street and a shed. Knickerbocker Glories which cost two and sixpence. Knickerbocker Glories which Jean adorned with cream like she was a sculptress. "You've never let me be your friend and you never let me make any." Jean was suddenly eleven again, gauche and unguarded and crying over the death of her rabbit. Or was it the hamster? She had not tried to keep

Des away from Jean on this instance. He must have come to that decision himself. But it was true. She had never returned Jean's friendship. She was frightened of what she might lose in the exchange and she had tried to keep Des and Hudge apart from Jean in the past.

"Well, you've always got a lot on offer, Jean. Like your Knickerbocker Glories."

"You're a prig, Lily Lee."

Lily thought. She was about to confess that well, yes, she was and she was about to move forward, to touch her, to say 'sorry' when the kitchen door opened. It was Cecilia.

"Lily, I'm going to ..." Cecilia, armed with empty shopping bags, peered around the door at Jean and then gave Lily a questioning look. "Jean, why on earth are you crying?"

"Oh, Des came round to me a couple of nights ago and I told him I was seeing someone else. He got mad and had a fight with them."

Des had got mad, for once because of her, not Hudge, not Jean.

"*He got into a fight because you were seeing someone else?* He fights the world, that boy. Lily, I'm going to catch the shops before they shut. Then I'm off to see Auntie Rose. So I'll be back about nine. Don't forget to lock the front door tonight and be a good girl. No smoking in here now." And she diplomatically closed the door behind her.

Jean wiped her eyes and took out a packet of cigarettes from her jacket pocket. "You are always so good," she said.

Lily fetched a saucer for the ash, gave a small smile and a small cough. Then she sat down next to Jean. "Why do you tell lies like that to my mother? You've just told me Des came round to finish with you on Sunday night."

"Because it makes me feel better. It's what I want it to be. I'd love the world to think he loved me. I'd love to think that myself and sometimes I pretend. I love Des, Lily." And she wiped her nose on her wrist. She looked at Lily with wide, round chocolate eyes. "You love him too, don't you?"

"I do ... yes, I do. I suppose I do. But I never told him to stop seeing you. He must have made his own mind up about that."

Jean lit up a cigarette and looked at Lily hard. "What's your kind of love, Lily?"

Lily thought for a moment. This was the first time she and Jean had ever talked this way. And looking at Jean now, swollen-eyed with her recent confession, Lily felt that she deserved some kind of reply. So she said, "I don't know, really. *Woman's Own* can't provide an answer. Well, not the kind of answer I'm searching for. Aida loves Des and Hudge. And they love one another in a kind of a way. I mean Des would die for Hudge, wouldn't he?"

Jean blew a smoke ring in the air and flicked some ash away from her trousers.

She waited for Jean to at least smile, but she didn't. "You said so much of what you had was 'on offer'. Why Jean?"

Jean didn't answer but took a puff on her cigarette.

Lily went on, "Dad says when goods are selling at too low a price then people don't give them much value."

Lily really wished she hadn't said that. Jean gave her a sideways look and then she sounded urgent. "You've got to tell Des to collect Hudge tonight. I heard Mabs talking to the timber yard boys this lunchtime. He came into the caf this morning on the war path. He can't find his camera and he thinks Des has nicked it."

"His camera? When could Des have nicked his camera?"

"They're going to have a go, tonight. Lily, you must believe me. Mabs is a danger area. You must tell Des. I know for sure that Des doesn't know what's been happening. You've got to tell him."

Lily thought for a moment. "How can you be so sure?"

"Just am," Jean replied stubbing out the cigarette on the saucer with finality.

Des would get very cross indeed at Jean for not telling him sooner. If Des had got into a fight with Mabs over me, she thought, what would he do to him if he knew about the trouble with Hudge? Geoff Mabs would end up in Emergency Ward 10.

"But Des will kill them. I can't."

"Lily - just for once - forget about your high ideals and get involved. For Hudge's sake."

For Hudge's sake. Lily looked at the kitchen clock. Five to one. If she was going to catch Des she should leave now, or he would be having his afternoon kip before his night shift at Nestles.

She cleared the cigarette butt end from the saucer and opened the sash window. The kitchen was thick with heat and smoke. If she told Des what had been happening at the caf he was sure to get into a fight on Hudge's behalf. Jean was right. Des didn't know about Mabs ribbing Hudge because any problems with Hudge and Des was there.

Oh why couldn't Jean tell him? She must have some reason for keeping quiet. Jean kept her own secrets.

And if I do tell Des, she thought, the responsibility of his actions will be on my shoulders. She would have to make up her mind fast.

What was she to do?

She didn't have to make up her mind. Because at that precise moment her father opened the kitchen door and said, “It's one o'clock closing and Mrs Omega is down in the shop. She wants to speak to you.”

Lily got up to go when he said, “She sounds upset, Lil. Turn the ‘closed’ sign.” Customers were only allowed upstairs by prior invitation.

The almost one o'clock train was coming into the station.

“Hudge came in last night ... so...” Aida shook her head, “so...” she had difficulty in forming the word, “upset.”

“Did Hudge say why he was upset?”

“Oh...” Aida's 'oh's' could go on forever. “Beyond me,” she sighed. “Des has chucked in his job at Nestles. He's says he's sick of the sight of chocolate and he's going back to school to do re-sits. That gives you a break tonight, Lil. I've told him to fetch and carry Hudge to the caf tonight and to come round and patch up the differences with you.”

“Is he going to?” Lily asked.

“He said after he's called into the chippie for cod and chips. You know what he's like.”

“I know.”

“I've been in to see Mr Oddy and given him two nights' notice on Hudge’s behalf. Finish up Friday. And give me two dozen chipolata sausages, will you, Lily?”

“Isn't that a bit drastic, Aida?”

“A dozen will do then.” She pulled out a large crumpled handkerchief from her woollen coat and blew her nose formidably. “Oh Lily,” she said, wiping a tear from each eye. “Hudge was so upset.”

****

Wednesday, no half day closing for Winnie Brambles and it’s thirty five minutes past six. Mrs Brambles, swinging a brown paper bag between thick fingers, watched her customer's pug-nosed child spit cherry stones on to the pavement. Spanish oranges had sold well today. Clean out, sweep down and feet up by seven thirty. Reconcile Wednesday's takings. Peaceful night in front of Hughie Green’s *Double your Money*.

She zipped across the purse in her canvas apron, adjusted her beret and proceeded to load parsnips into lightweight wooden crates.

“Need any help with those crates, Mrs Brambles?”

Mrs Brambles looked up and saw Des Hodge, not knowing where he had come from.

“*What did you say*?”

“The crates,” he said, pointing to the two on her shop doorstep and raising his voice. “Want anything shifting?”

“No. They’re lightweight, Des.”

She saw him look at his watch, look towards the Lee’s grocery shop, hesitate and then run across the Pennington Road. Good-looking boy, Des Hodge, she thought, as she watched him slide down Peterson Road.

Next door, Hudge Hodge was coming out of the caf, a spotless white overall held over his arm. Two brothers couldn’t be more different. What was he doing there so early? Caf didn’t open until seven thirty.

He walked slowly to the kerb. Look right, look left - the road wasn't clear. Mrs Brambles was ready to shout. A lorry came thundering down the road. A motor bike turned left out of Peterson. Look right again, and Hudge Hodge marched briskly across Pennington.

Mrs Brambles narrowed her eyes and watched Hudge Hodge plod up towards Juniper Street.

Presumably, she was thinking with parsnips in her hand, for the chippie.

****

Mabs had spent that Wednesday lunch hour in the Dragon's Head pub. In fact he started drinking beer early that day and he had already been in the caf in the morning demanding his camera back.

As soon as Mabs entered the caf on that Wednesday evening he caught Jean's arm and pulled her on to his knee again. Tonight he was mad. "Jean. Give me my bloody camera back."

"I told you this morning. I haven't got your camera. Now let me go," she said struggling to pull herself away.

"You've nicked my camera because of those photos I took of you and Hudge." He spat the whisper into her ear.

"I never touched your camera."

"Hudge, Hudge." Mabs whistled.

Hudge continued to dry dishes, his huge back at the chipped enamel sink; staring out ahead of him into the yard.

"Hudge. Come here."

Hudge came forward to the counter.

"Where's my camera, Hudge?"

Hudge simply shook his head, his face was drawn, his lips pulled tightly together.

"You didn't meet my girlfriend last night," Mabs said.

Jean was trying to wrench herself free. "Let me go, Mabs. I've got work to do."

"Hudge. Come here and say 'hello' to Jean."

Hudge dried his hands and walked around the counter. "I know Jean."

"You know Jean, do you?" He released his hold on her wrists and ran a hand up her chubby leg. Hudge watched the hand. "Yes, I do believe you do. You do *know* one another, don't you?"

Jean whispered. "Just say 'hello' to me, Hudge. Just say 'hello'."

Hudge said quietly, "Hello".

Mabs put a squeeze on to her wrist. "Louder, Hudge."

"Hello," Hudge said.

Mabs squeezed harder on the chubby wrist and said to Hudge. "Say 'hello, Jean'."

"Hello, Jean."

"Now, Jean," Mabs said. "Say 'hello' to Hudge."

"Hello, Hudge."

****

"Hello, Des."

"Hello, Lily." Des was at last on her black and white chequered doorstep, his hand outstretched holding a red and gold wrapped bar of Nestles chocolate. The slightly askew mouth broke into a lop-sided smile. Lily knew then, that nothing had happened. He had not seen Mabs at the chippie. She would need to tell him.

"Mum said you wanted to see me," he said.

"*She* wanted you to see me," Lily said indignantly.

"Ask me in then."

Lily closed the door behind them and fiddled with the lock. Her fingers, like her heart, were knotted and Des put his hands over hers and turned the key. As he did so, she closed her eyes. She had missed his touch. He had not touched her in four whole days.

She had been caught up in his touch. No, she could never really remember if he had actually *turned* the lock. It had been important evidence but she could only tell the truth.

He quickly retrieved the bunch of keys and stood jangling them, looking at her inquiringly.

"Did you have cod and chips for your dinner?"

"Lil," he sighed. "I had sausages. Is this important to you?"

"We had better go upstairs," she said to the frozen food cabinet.

So many miles to cover, thought Lily, as she climbed the narrow staircase. The business with Jean. The business with Hudge. The city train rumbled by. Two minutes to nine. She gave the kitchen a cursory glance. Cecilia would be back from Auntie Rose's soon and bound to be on patrol. Lily opened the front room door. "Dad - is it okay if Des comes up to the attic?"

Gordon Lee lowered the Daily Express and lifted his eyebrows. "Where's the keys?"

"There you are, Mr Lee." Des came into the room and handed Gordon the keys. "Bachelor Boy. Kempton Park. Three o'clock tomorrow."

"Why, thank you Des." Gordon Lee went in search of a Biro and Lily and Des crept up the second flight of stairs to the attic bedroom.

****

"Hudge says his brother is collecting him tonight." Jean whispered into Mabs's ear, her lips held tight in a single blood-red streak across her face. "So watch it."

He was looking forward to it. Des Hodge most likely was behind the theft of his camera. He had seen Des Hodge eyeing his camera in the Dragon's Head on the previous Sunday night. Mabs was riled. And he was going to place Hudge right down amongst the pit-bull terriers to coincide with his brother's arrival.

First, he had to whip the dogs into a frenzy.

"Good. Now we all know one another. Now, Hudge. What's your girlfriend's name?" Mabs was running his hand up and down Jean's thigh.

Hudge held his head low, but watched.

"I said what's your girlfriend's name?" Mabs shouted. "Answer the question."

But Hudge stood and watched.

"I said answer the fucking question you fucking dummy."

****

"So..." Des said, as he threw his leather jacket on to her children's wooden armchair and flopped on to Lily's bed. "*This* is the bedroom."

He had seen the room before of course. When they were younger. Cecilia had later drawn the boundary.

Lily opened the window which faced Peterson Road. The attic was thick with dusty heat. She stacked some Buddy Holly 45s on the record player. She looked down at Des. He had put his hands behind his head, crossed his legs at the ankles and stared at her bookcase. She was faintly embarrassed by her *Girls' Crystal* annuals and *Anne of Green Gables* hardback. Despite this, he looked at her seriously. She wondered if he thought he had been brought to the bedroom for other reasons.

"Did you see Jean?" she asked. The oppressive heat was thawing Lily's anger towards Des. And she was finding him very, very, desirable lying on her bed.

Des lifted his head with his hands. "That's over, Lily. I went round to see her on Sunday after our row."

"I know."

"You *know?*"

"But have you seen Jean this *evening*?" she said, thinking Jean may have already broken the news.

"You *knew?* Then why didn't you come round and see me?"

Lily bunched her hair up at the back of her neck, feeling the sweat at the nape and picked up her brush from the dressing table. "Have you seen Jean this evening?" She said the words slowly, as if speaking to a small child. She watched him in the mirror, brushed her hair and then picked up her Yardley Pink Magic lipstick.

"I didn't go to the caf to see her tonight. I went to take Hudge." He stared up at the James Dean picture above him.

"I know. But did you see her?" She turned, asking the question again, as she swivelled the base of the lipstick.

"No. Happy now?"

"I'm not happy, no. Did you see Geoff Mabs?" She looked at her lips in the mirror and applied the Pink Magic.

"No." He buried his head in the pillow in mock sorrow. "I haven't seen Jean Oddy or Geoff Mabs. I haven't come here to talk about them." He looked up at her. "I thought you wanted to talk about ... other things."

His voice off shot into a high-pitched note on the 'other things'. She took a deep breath. She would have to tell him about the 'other things'. But not the 'other things' that Des, so obviously, had on his mind.

She was about to do just that, when Des spoke first. "Jean told you then?"

So ... she had told him. Lily nodded and with Pink Magic lips picked up her brush again.

"Trust Jean," he said. "She can never keep her mouth shut."

"About what?" Lily frowned.

There was a long pause whilst Des was stared at the poster, still stretched out on the bed. Finally he said, "About me doing it with her."

"But I know that."

A pause lingered in the dusty heat of the attic. Lily looked away from Des to the bedroom door. She was trying to work out what Des had just implied.

Then he said slowly and very quietly, "So you did."

Well, there were an awful lot of things that she did not know. She stared down at the brush and said, "You'd done it with her *before* that Sunday, hadn't you?" Then somehow the brush leapt out of her hand and was heading directly at him. "*Hadn't* you?"

He put his arms over his face in defence. "Well ..." he said, speaking into the pillow, "not much." He said this as though the infrequency was some kind of excuse.

"What has Hudge seen? Last night he kept asking me if he could touch my bosoms and he was hiding something under his overall, I know. He's confused. He's not himself. What has he seen?" she said.

"Nothing." He sat up on the bed. "Nothing. Mum keeps on about this. Just because Hudge keeps talking about bosoms. But you know how he gets hung up on words, Lily. I mean I'd like to get hung up on the real thing, but I swear, it's all been out of Hudge's way. Except for last Sunday night with Jean. He was doing the jigsaw puzzle. He never came up. Honest."

Lily did not see why she should believe him. Both he and Jean had lied to her. Lied. Or said nothing. It was the same thing. Silence is a sin. But she did believe him. She believed him because sometimes truth rings out from the corners of old friends' mouths, as it did now, with Des.

"Where did you do it with her then?"

He picked at some hair in the teeth of the brush. "In the shed. Afternoons."

"When I was working at the shop?" Truth hurts.

"Five thirty. Just before the caf opened, if you'd like the exact time. But never on a Sunday - because the back gate was locked."

"Wednesdays?"

"Sorry?"

"Wednesdays, Des. Did you do it with her on Wednesdays?"

Des didn't know what to do with the hair he had gathered from the brush. So he let it drop to the ground.

"You bugger. So when I met Geoff Mabs at the rec. - you were doing it with Jean Oddy."

"Met him at the rec., did you?" He was laughing now.

Geoff Mabs. What was the time? She had been side-tracked. She should tell Des about Geoff Mabs. What was happening to Hudge now? She felt an itch of neglect.

"Des," she said softly.

He was again staring up at the slanting roof, at James Dean, unaware, Lily knew, of what was about to come.

"There's something I should tell you about Geoff Mabs."

****

"That's better," Mabs said. "Now. Tell us your girlfriend's name."

Flick pushed Hudge on to all fours so that he was kneeling before Mabs and Jean.

"I promised not to tell. Got to keep a promise," he said.

"Well, Hudge. This is my girlfriend." And he went to kiss Jean but she pulled away, so he threw her aside. Then he got up and took a step towards Hudge. Flick placed his knife at Hudge's throat but Papanikalou shook his head at him in fear.

****

"Whatever's happened between you and Mabs," Des said, still staring up at James Dean. "It's not important. He swung his legs round and sat on the side of the bed. "It doesn't matter, Lily." He looked up at her. "I would forgive you anything. You must know that."

Lily thought that under these circumstances it should not be important. That's if 'it' had ever happened. Which it hadn't. There was nothing to forgive. She was about to sit down beside him and explain. When there was a creaking on the second flight of stairs to the attic. The door opened abruptly. Her plaid dressing gown went swinging to the ground. Cecilia stood sentry. "Lily. It's well past nine."

"We're coming downstairs in a bit, Mum. We've got to collect Hudge."

Cecilia's eyes narrowed and settled upon Des. He looked up, attempting to smile.

There they were. Soldiers. Soldiers having a private war of their own making. There her mother was, standing in her bedroom just before the nine thirty train had been due at the station. *Her mother was there, standing talking to Des.*

"I'm going back for re-sits next week, Mrs Lee."

"How very sensible, Des." Her nostrils twitched. Her permed curls twinked. "No hanky-panky and downstairs by ten."

Lily waited until she could hear the front room door close. Then she closed the bedroom door which Cecilia had left wide open.

"Hanky panky." He sighed deeply and shook his head. "Hanky panky. That's what I'm up against."

Lily sat down on the bed beside him. Somehow Cecilia's invasion had melted her anger. "Why did you fight with Geoff Mabs?" She had almost forgotten about that.

"Fight Mabs? Why should I?" He took hold of her hand. It was the first time he had really touched her for centuries. They both sat on the side of the bed, confused.

Lily shook her head slowly. "Didn't you give him the cut on his chin?"

"Why should I do that?"

Lily was a trifle incensed. After all, he had thought Mabs was doing it with her. "That's true. You'd never fight over me, would you?" she said quietly. "You'd fight for Hudge, though, wouldn't you?"

"That's different," he said, stroking the palm of her hand. "Hudge can't defend himself. You can."

Then why, she thought, did Geoff Mabs let her assume? Then again he had never said that Des had hit him. Mabs had lied too then, by avoiding the truth. Yes - avoiding the truth was the same as a lie.

Des placed an arm about her waist and pulled her back onto the bed. "Just lie here beside me," he said. "In my arms."

And there they both lay, looking up at James Dean's eyes on the slanting ceiling, with Buddy Holly's 'No True Love Ways' dropping down with a click and filling the semi darkness of the attic. Lily felt secure. She felt at peace. She felt his fingertips drum softly on her waist. Her longing for him was an ache and almost a pain. She heard the drone of the television below. Her stomach rumbled. Then the rattle and the siren of the city train shot across the bridge. The almost nine-thirty train. What was happening to Hudge?

****

Let's see him squirm, thought Mabs. Let's see him beg. Des Hodge would soon be here. Mabs would get his camera back. He rested his eyes upon his victim. Mabs waited. The caf waited. It had been quite some while since they had been treated to a performance. And this was the first time he had included Jean Oddy. Humiliate her too.

"Mabs," Jean said quickly and quietly, running her painted fingernails over the reddened wrists. "Let's go into the yard."

"Flick, what's the time?" he said.

Flick looked at his watch. "Nearly quarter to ten."

Lily's collection time was just after ten o'clock. He had time. "Okay," he said, giving Flick and Papanikalou a knowing smile.

Nine forty-five and Geoff Mabs followed Jean Oddy out to the back through the scullery as the fast city train screamed in the distance. And Hudge took up his post of washing dishes at the enamel sink.

****

The city train had screamed and then rumbled on. It was getting darker. She could barely see James Dean above her. What was happening to Hudge?

"What are you thinking?" he said.

"Hudge," she whispered. Lily was torn between what might be happening to him and feeling responsible for Des's actions.

"What about Hudge?" he said.

Lily bit her fingernail. Hudge was in the caf. What was Geoff Mabs doing to Hudge? It was so peaceful here. She was reluctant to let go of that peace. She had never ever felt so close to Des. Lying there in the darkness, feeling his arms about her. Nothing else seemed to matter.

"Des, what's going to become of him? Where is it all going to end? I mean I'd like to think he has a guardian angel but I can't be sure."

"Guardian angel?" he said and smiled sadly. "My mum's been talking. Don't let Hudge come between us. He's not here."

For once, she thought - although neither of them would ever say it. "I mean, if you're going to do re-sits, then university, then maybe National Service."

He pulled his weight up on to his arm, and then rested his head on his hand, looking down at her. "Lil. Mum's not well."

"What do you mean 'not well'?"

"When she came back from Evensong last Sunday ... you know ... after the blackberries ... she told me. It's why she's organised her organs ..."

Lily didn't know what to say. Aida. Not well. He lay his head back on the pillow. They both stared up at the ceiling. At James Dean. The almost ten o'clock train rumbled by. Then he said very quietly, "I read somewhere that death is the price we pay for sex." She had never heard him so serious before. Then he added. "The way things are going ... if I die too soon I wouldn't have had much value for money."

She turned to him, kissed the side of his long tapering neck and prayed Cecilia wouldn't walk in. "No, Des," she said. "Death is the price we pay for life."

He sighed. She sighed. James Dean remained as always.

Lily sensed black shadows in her stomach. And what was Hudge going to do 'if anything happened to Aida', she suddenly thought. "Hudge will always need caring for, won't he? Always."

"We can't do that, Lil."

Lily was surprised by his sudden agreement.

He turned in to her, propping his head up with his hand. He was talking seriously. "I couldn't ask you to do that for the rest of our lives. I've thought about it. Mum's leaving the house to me. Hudge can have it. We'll get someone to look after him ... when it comes to that." He took a strand of her blonde hair between his fingers.

Her father could be wrong: at least one of the Hodge family was capable of forward planning. A very gentle summer breeze fluttered the magazine pages lying on the dressing table. "You've never asked too much of life, have you?" she said.

He shook his head, let go of her strand of hair and looked upward to James Dean. "No. You've always had splendid plans, Lil. I don't want to be a hero. I've just wanted to get by. To live quietly." Then he laughed softly, kindly. "Baked beans and babies will do me."

"I love you," she said.

"I love you too."

James Dean looked down at both of them.

"Does that mean ... it's all right?" he asked.

Des kissed her. Lily's scruples were dissolving rapidly - right down the river - soft peaceful kiss that it was. She would have liked to have wallowed in that kiss forever. Keep the spell going. Lily felt a surge inside. Then the surge inside became one of guilt. Oh no, thought Lily, the kiss becoming more intense, it's hardly worth even telling him now. Push down those scruples. But up they came. She could see Hudge waiting, watching for their arrival at the enamel sink. His last night. It was gone ten.

"Des," she said, breaking off from the kiss. "About Mabs."

****

"What's it all about, Mabs?" Jean smoothed down her hair behind her ear with nails that were bitten and torn at the cuticles. She folded her arms. The stench of the rotting refuse mingled with the odour of her cheap perfume was sickening. Geoff Mabs could hear voices on the Pennington Road getting louder. People were beginning to leave the caf. The show was over. He didn't have much time.

"What was it like doing it with Hudge, Jean?" His breathing was becoming a erratic. He needed to get this over before he had an attack. "Remember - I watched."

"You're shit on my shoe."

He was going to enjoy watching her dangle. Play with the strings. He'd make them do what he wanted them to do. "Why did you did you do it with Hudge, Jean?" His breathing was getting faster.

She leaned back on the shed wall and looked down at the yard's crazy paving, pushing an empty cigarette packet up and down with her foot. He could see the scowl on her face from the fluorescent light in the caf.

"To get back at Des?" he said.

"You tell Des and I swear I'll kill you, Mabs." Her face looked up at him, bitter and twisted - just like Zelda's.

"Changed your mind, have you? Gone too far? I wouldn't have thought 'going too far' had any meaning for a tart like you," he shouted it at her.

Jean Oddy's left hand came up delivering a scalding slap to the left side of his face, stinging his cut.

He was close enough to her to see the thick, caked layer of fake sun tan cream - her lashes clogged with mascara - her face ugly with hate. She was a mess. He shrugged his shoulders and placed his hand above her, threateningly, on the side of the shed. Jean Oddy had used Hudge to get back at Des Hodge and now she was regretting it. He would make her pay. Pay for cheating him. For using him as a pawn. Jean Oddy was cornered. Defeated. "What was it like doing it with Des Hodge, Jean?"

"Better than you." Her face was thrust up towards him as she said, "You fuck like a little boy."

Boy ... Geoff Mabs felt like killing her ... killing her ... boy ... his hand went to the back of her neck ... the other round her waist ... strangle her ... boy ... I'll strangle the bitch ... fuck like a ... pull her down ... force her down ...little boy ... she's choking ... she was trying to get her breath .. he was trying to get his own ...

****

Des was kissing her neck. Lily caught her breath.

Buddy Holly was singing about it just being the two of them …

"It doesn't matter," he was saying softly. "Whatever's happened between you and Mabs ...it doesn't matter. What's important is us now."

And if she had carried on with what was important to them both then maybe, it might have all been so different. Except she knew, he would never have forgiven her. So she said ... "But it does matter. It does matter, Des," she said sitting up and breaking the spell altogether. "It's not about me and Mabs." Lily looked down on Des's confusion. "It's about Hudge and Mabs."

He sat up slowly. "What do you mean?"

Now. It was now. "Jean told me he's been teasing ... bullying Hudge."

Des looked away towards the dressing table.

"In the caf," she went on. "That tonight Mabs and the timber yard boys were planning something ..." But Lily was unable to finish her sentence.

"Lily," he shouted as he jumped to his feet and looked at his watch. "Why didn't you tell me before?" He swung the bedroom door open and the urgency of the World News came pounding up towards the attic.

She grabbed his arm. "I didn't tell you, because I don't want you involved."

"Lily," he said angrily, holding both arms tightly, "sometimes you have to get involved."

He picked up his leather jacket fom the chair and threw it at her. "The keys, Lily." He was shouting at her. "Get the keys from your dad."

"We've got to go the back way. He won't open the front door at this time of night."

They started down the stairs.

"I love you, Des. Please be ..."

But Des was rushing down the narrow staircase and she was following, poking her hands through the armholes in his leather jacket he had thrown at her: through the shop and yard, heading out into Alpha Road.

****

There was a crash as the caf scullery door flew open. Mabs released his hold on Jean. A figure came rushing towards them in the darkness of the yard. Jean screamed and leapt away. She flung the back gate wide open and ran out into Alpha Road.

Mabs turned to call her name but he had no air to speak. Her footsteps echoed. But the figure was on his back. Pushing him. Shoving him. Pushing him towards the open back gate. He dug his elbows back into soft flesh. The figure grunted and swung him round. Geoff Mabs looked into the face. "You..."

But he was unable to finish the sentence. The face was shouting at him. The hands were tearing at him. Out into Alpha Road.

Geoff Mabs felt a grinding thrust. The knife. Get hold of the knife. Get it. Get hold of the knife.

The thrust came again and again. On each thrust came the word 'girlfriend'. "She's my girlfriend. She's *my* girlfriend. She's *my* girlfriend."

****

Des had his hand over Lily's mouth. "Sh... don't call his name," he whispered.

Lily froze. Her eyes were wide with terror. They were fixed to the centre of the street. A body lay stretched out like a fresh scar.

Then her eyes creased with the pain. She wanted to bite into Des's hand. She wanted to say, 'Mop it up. Mop it up.'

Des took a few steps forward. Then he was down on his knees. Lily flinched. She watched as Des placed the side of his head on the body's chest. Des looked up at her, rivulets of blood trickling down towards his plimsolls. "Is he dead? Is he dead, Lily? Is he dead?"

She hesitated. And then slowly she moved forward and reluctantly crouched down beside the body. There were a few fitful breaths and then one which rattled throughout, bringing the body to stillness. The head turned to them. The eyes did not close, but looked sideways towards Des. This time Lily's hand went to her mouth. She groaned. For now, in the clear moonlight, she could see who it was. The smell of blood. Such a smell of blood.

"Is he dead, Lily? Is he dead?"

Was he dead? Lily remembered bringing a dying cat into the front room. Spreading it out by the coal fire. Witnessing the cat's fitful breathing, just as she had done now. And that rattle before rest. Something then, inside of her had said that this was going to be all right. Until with split-second timing she realised that this stillness was to do with death.

So much blood. She was steeped in blood. She looked at Des and nodded. "We're covered in blood, Des." Almost black blood. 'Mop it up,' she wanted to say. 'Mop it up.'

It was only then that Des looked up at Hudge. His white overall splattered with the blood. His right arm held limply by his side, holding the knife between his thumb and forefinger, looking hang-dog, like a child who had just spilt ink on a new carpet.

"Where did you get the knife, Hudge?" Des said quietly.

"She was *my* girlfriend, Des." Hudge looked to the ground and shook his head.

"Where did you get the knife?"

"Geoff Mabs was a bad boy."

"Where did you get the knife?" Des's voice was insistent.

"It's *your* knife, Des." Hudge's chins crumpled and he began to cry where he stood. "I got it from your tool box. You won't tell will you Des? You won't tell?"

Lily looked at Des. For some reason she could not go to Hudge. Could not even look at him. But Des was staring up at him.

"Promise you won't tell." Hudge was still crying. "I give it you back."

"I promise," Des whispered. Then he looked quickly up and down the road. "Did anyone see you?"

Hudge sniffed, held his shoulders taut and shook his head. "Jean run off."

Des scrambled to his feet with purpose. "Give me the knife."

"Des. You can't touch it. We should just phone the police," she said.

"Lily. Let me do this my way. Give me the knife, Hudge."

Hudge obeyed. Des was hurriedly unbuttoning Hudge's white overall.

"What the hell are you doing, Des?" she said.

He then wiped the blade and handle of the knife on the overall. "Now wipe your face and hands on the overall." Des was looking furtively up and down the road.

"Don't want to, Des."

"Wipe them or I'll tell." Des was shouting now.

Des was wiping his brother's face, his hands, his hair. Hudge was crying, "Please don't tell, Des. Please don't tell."

"Des. What are you doing?" Lily watched incredulously as he wiped Hudge's shoes with the overall.

He was now kneeling at Hudge's feet. He looked up at her. "Go and tell your dad to phone an ambulance and the police."

"Not the police, Des. Not the police," Hudge cried.

Des stood up and held Hudge's arms firmly. "It's going to be all right, Hudge. It's going to be all right. Quiet." He turned to Lily. "Hurry Lily. It's important you tell them."

"Okay," she said faintly.

"Tell them we saw Hudge and Mabs fighting."

She nodded.

"And tell them you've just seen me stab Geoff Mabs."

"No."

Des leapt towards her with the overall, putting his hand on her mouth. It wouldn't have mattered if she had screamed the word. It would have been lost in the chaos of shouting and whistling that drifted across from the Pennington Road. She wrenched his hand away. "You're mad," she said, still holding his hand. "I won't do that.

"Please, Lily, please." Des was now holding her hand tightly. "Look at him."

Hudge was now sitting on the kerbside, rocking back and forth to give himself comfort, repeating the words, "Please don't tell, Des. Please don't tell."

"They'll hang you, Des."

"With a gun, yes. But not with a knife. Hudge will never get out, Lily." He pulled her into him and whispered into her ear, "They'll lock him up forever."

She said nothing. She looked down at the stained overall which dangled at her side. Then across at the body. Then to Hudge, still weeping on the kerbside.

"Please don't tell, Des," he said.

"No. I promise." Des was still holding her close as he said this.

And finally she nodded, so that his face could feel her agreement. A decision which was going to change the course of their lives.

He pulled away from her and gave her the overall. "Get rid of this," he said quickly. "I've got to stay here and give Hudge the right words to say. Hurry, Lily."

She stood rigid, looking at him. Then he shouted, "Hurry."

Lily turned, took a few steps forward and then for some reason looked back. As she did so, she saw Hudge still sitting on the kerb, hunched up over his knees sobbing. Des was standing above him saying, "It's all right, Hudge. I won't tell. I promise. It's going to be all right."

The greengrocer's curtain twitched above them. And Geoff Mabs's body lay stretched out between them, under a starlit sky, completing the triangle.

It was going to be all right. It was going to be all right, thought Lily, as she raced towards the double garage.

It was not going to be all right. There was no way they could protect Hudge from all this. Des was expecting her to lie. For Hudge's sake. The overall. What was she going to do with the overall?

From the tiny window in the double garage she could see the glimmer of a light in the shop. What had happened? What could possibly have happened? Her father never switched the light on until she rang at the front door on her return.

She looked down at the overall. Geoff Mabs's blood. Geoff Mabs's blood smothered the overall. Geoff Mabs's blood was on her shoes, on her denim trousers, on Des's leather jacket.. Geoff Mabs's blood was everywhere. And so was the smell ... Lily retched. Her heart beat fast. Think fast. Act fast.

And all Lily Lee could think was that Cecilia would go crazy. Crazy at the sight of the overall in her hands.

So she wiped the front of Des's leather jacket with the overall as she heard the low buzz of the wasps' nest. Then she stuffed the overall behind her mother's coats amongst the pile of debris in the double garage along with wasps and the decision she was unable to make.

Jean was there. With Gordon and Cecilia. Crying. She had to get away from Geoff Mabs. He was trying to ... rape her, she said. *Someone* had charged out of the back door. She ran off up Alpha - round into Pennington - past the crowd at the chippie. The caf lights were still on - she didn't want to go in in case Geoff Mabs was still there.

Lily heard it all. From the scullery. Jean was sitting on the chair beside the meat-slicing machine, behind the counter, inhaling deep, noisy breaths. Gordon and Cecilia were facing her, with their backs to the scullery, telling her to calm down, catch her breath, but she was wildly out of breath.

It was Jean who saw her first when she stepped up into the shop. "Lily," she heard Jean saying, "is Hudge all right?"

All right? Hudge. Was Hudge all right? Lily's eyes glazed over. The shop's fluorescent lighting strip cast shadows about the room. The shadows were moving, dancing. Round and round, in a kaleidoscope of colours. Was Hudge all right? Mop it up. Lily Lee began to shake uncontrollably.

"Lily, are you all right?" the shadows said.

"Where's Hudge?"

Hudge? All right?

Shadows had footsteps. Arms around her. "Are you all right?"

"Mum." It's all she could say.

"Lily. Your feet. Your trousers. Lily - what on earth has happened? What has happened? What on earth are you doing wearing Des's leather jacket?"

"Phone an ambulance - the police." That's what he had said wasn't it?

"Lily, are you all right? What has happened?"

"What should we say? What has happened?"
What had happened?
"Say..." she said. "Say that I've just seen..."
"Lily, what have you seen?"
What had she seen?
Eyes that see. Lips that tell.
"Seen ...Geoff Mabs stabbed."

People came crawling and running from the woodwork. Cecilia insisted that the girls went upstairs for a cup of Horlicks. Lily would have none of it. Desert Des and Hudge at this time? For Horlicks? What if Des had changed his mind? Perhaps she could persuade him to do so?

Gordon Lee left immediately by the back door after telephoning for aid and instructing Cecilia to contact Zelda and Charlie.

Jean had slumped dramatically across the frozen food cabinet crying, "It's my fault. It's my fault." And Cecilia, with her finger poised on the scullery telephone was saying, "Is he dead? Who stabbed him? Lily, what has happened?"

Lily was not about to answer Cecilia's questions and Cecilia, who tried to block the back door with a besom, and managed to do so for a good few minutes, finally found herself powerless to restrain a daughter who would go.

Jean knows nothing. Jean knows nothing. Lily ran to the beat of the words. As Lily ran into Alpha Road, a police siren heralded Lily's increasing isolation. Lights were being switched on in the terraced houses. Curtains were being drawn back. The world had come to view.

The police car's headlights lit up the area and Lily saw Gordon speaking to Des and Hudge, who were both now seated on the kerbside. As she approached them, Gordon was shaking his head, saying, "Des, this is serious. Very serious."

Des looked quickly at her as two uniformed patrolling constables jumped from the car. The caf back gate was swung wide. Geoff Mabs's once beautiful eyes were still open. Lily closed hers tightly.

If only ... thought Lily, if only they had stayed in the attic bedroom. She could hear the scratching of a walkie-talkie above Hudge's gentle sobs. "F.M.E. called for," the voice was saying. "Life suspected extinct. Cordoning off area."

More lights dotted the terraced houses. Doors were being opened. Lily kept her eyes firmly shut.

"Are there any other victims?" she heard another voice say.

Lily felt like crying. But the tears would not come.

"Constable," she could hear her father saying, "this boy says he stabbed ... but it's not possible."

"All right, sir. Let's take it a step at a time. Can we all move further up the road?"

"I did it." It was Des's voice.

Lily opened her eyes. So much light. And Des was still holding the Swiss army knife. Standing there in his black tee shirt and denims. Holding the knife.

Gordon had his arm around her, with the other he was steering Hudge to the top of Alpha Road, where more police cars drew up. Des was moved away. The constable was speaking to him. If only... Someone was taking him, moving him towards a police vehicle.

It was an almost robotic statement uttered by the police constable. "Did anyone see what happened?"

"Yes," Gordon Lee said. "My daughter. My daughter saw what happened."

Sliding into September

August slipped unnoticeably into September. September. Name tags and new pencil cases. Polished shoes - shoes you can see your face in - and the true beginning of the year: the cleanest of clean sheets of paper.

September. Lily had to close the attic windows. For insects crawled in from the woodwork. Wasps get angry in September. Daddy Longlegs filled the tiny attic and were smashed across James Dean's eyes. Gordon Lee announced that there was a wasps' nest in the double garage and something had to be done.

Something had to be done. It was on such a September night that Lily Lee also slipped unnoticeably down to the double garage, removed the bloodied overall, walked up Alpha, across Carlisle, down the railway steps and deposited it in Mr Brambles' disused stables.

Had it not been for fear of starting a fire, she might have taken a match to the overall and reduced the damned thing to ashes.

8

DECEMBER 1959

Lily counted thirteen at the funeral when there should have been only eleven.

But Des was flanked by two prison officers. The handcuffs, invisible to no-one at all were being partially hidden by a raincoat.

"Now unto him that is able to keep you from falling, and to present you faultless before..."

Weren't there supposed to be tears at a funeral? Lily looked across the gaping divide at Des. He was hunched up and weighted down with unseen responsibilities. Then she looked at Hudge. His hands were clasped respectfully in front of him, like the other men.

"...dominion and power, both now and forever. Amen."

"Amen. Amen. Amen."

"Mrs Omega," she heard her father whisper. "The last plot in the cemetery." Without seeing, she could feel him shake his head. "No forward planning."

She did see his hand slip into Cecilia's, so that together they formed one white and multi-knuckled fist.

The prison officer unlocked the handcuff. Des stooped, and picking up a handful of earth, he scattered it on his mother's casket. And Hudge did as Des did.

"So ..." Cecilia sighed heavily, searching the ground to place her stilettoed foot, "that's that."

Kay, who had cups of tea on the brain, invited the prison officers into the tiny terraced house. But they refrained.

"I didn't know whether to cater for the policeman," she said to Lily, as she poured from the brown china tea-pot in the kitchen. "It's very nice of them to allow Des in, isn't it?" she said, poking her nose through the chequered curtain. "Even though one of them is guarding the back door."

Lily's foot brushed against the billowing orange and green checked tablecloth. Aida's handbag was still beneath the back room table.

"Tragic, isn't it, Lily?"

Lily didn't know which one of the four Hodges Kay was referring to, so she simply nodded her head and arranged the sandwiches into a pattern on the plate.

"It's very nice of you to help, Lily. Considering ..." Kay's frothy voice trailed away. "Well ...considering it all ..." her sentence went on aimlessly. A little nervous squeal emitted from Kay's Adam's apple. Kay's Adam's apple was the first thing Lily had ever noticed about her: that and this little nervous high-pitched squeal. Lily had observed that Kay's Adam's apple was extraordinarily large and seemed to pulsate with nerves, the very first time Ben had brought her home for tea.

Kay began to pour cheap sherry into glasses. "I hope everyone likes sherry. I asked the manager of the Boys' Club to say a few kind words," she said confidentially. "But he was a bit busy with the Bingo rota so I asked your dad. I know in all honesty it should be Des. But under the circumstances..."

Lily began to pile the sandwiches erratically. Kay was the kind of person who could only respond to her own blunders with yet another. "I thought the service went very well," Kay went on.

Lily nodded and gave one of her small smiles.

"Yes," Kay said and smiled too, gratefully. "Very nice. I'll send Des through. I expect you'll want a word." She went to the back room door and looked up at the stain on the wall. She seemed disturbed. "What's that, Lil?"

Lily looked up at the floral wallpaper. "Blackberry juice."

"Oh." Kay was confused.

Lily bent down underneath the table and retrieved Aida's handbag. She hadn't been allowed to speak to Des before now. By his own admission of 'guilt', combined with Lily's statement, bail had been refused before the case came to trial. Gordon had explained that self defence was a complete defence and that he should be set free. Cecilia had been less optimistic. "You could be done for perverting the course of justice if you haven't told the truth. You have told the whole truth, haven't you, Lily?"

As Des stood in the kitchen doorway, Lily remembered that the last time they met here, Des had thrown blackberries at her. Only now their positions were reversed. But the space between them gaped as wide ... if not wider. Lily stood with her back to the scullery. "I'm sorry," she said.

"Sorry?"

"I mean about your mum."

"Yeah ..." They asked me which name should go on the headstone. You know..." he said awkwardly, "my mum moved in here when Ben and Hudge were kids. Mum and Dad never married. I said leave it as Hodge." He nodded as if to agree with himself. "Mum left the house to me - but it's here for Hudge." He looked up from the linoleum floor with a kind of desperation. "You will look after him, won't you, Lil?"

She placed Aida's handbag on the table. "The welfare officer was round yesterday."

"Mum doesn't ... didn't want any of that."

"I know, Des. But we've got to be practical. He can't stay at the shop forever. We had to contact them."

Des stared seriously at the tablecloth, as if the answer lay somewhere between the folds of the orange and green squares. He looked defeated and he looked now like his mother had at the very end when Des was charged with murder. Aida, who had always fought so furiously, for and with her sons, had been suddenly silenced. Lily had been unwilling to see the new Aida of the past few months.

"I was wondering ..." he said. He stopped. And Lily was wondering how much more Des could ask of her. "I was wondering ..." he seemed to be fighting back the tears, "if I could kiss you."

She moved towards him, pulling him round so his back was to the big black woman with the green turban and she held him and filled him with a kiss of 'if onlys'. The last time he had kissed her had been minutes before it all happened. Lily shuddered within, and as if sensing this, he broke away and said, "I've been thinking about the blackberries." He looked down at her. "I've been trying to remember her face when she saw them all over this room. It was funny at the time, but ..." His voice started to quiver and Lily held him close to her. "But I can't remember, Lily. I keep trying but I can't remember her face."

Lily stroked his hair as he cried softly into hers. The heavy hand of the clock ticked away those remaining minutes. When Des kissed her again, she opened her eyes and, looking through the chequered curtains she saw the policeman gazing at them from the yard. All those wasted years stretching out ahead. It wasn't fair and she was going to tell him so.

She looked up at him. "I've been thinking about the promises..."

He frowned, just slightly.

"I won't let them lock you up. Des, it's not fair. I can tell them. Hudge did it. I..."

His eyes tracked towards the back room door.

"Lily. Where's Jean?" Hudge had been there long enough to witness the kissing.

Des loosened his hold of her, folded his arms, standing with the big black woman looking down on him.

It was Lily who spoke to Hudge. "They've moved, Hudge. To a council estate. Remember?"

"The welfare officer says I can come back here to live. I'm very lucky 'cos I'm twenty-two."

"I know, Hudge."

"Will Chrissie come here to live, Lily?"

"No. She's the welfare officer, Hudge. She's got her own house. Like you now. But someone will be here for you," she said.

"You?"

"No, not me. But someone."

"You, Des?"

"No." Des took out a pack of cigarettes from his suit pocket. "It was my knife that killed Geoff Mabs, wasn't it, Hudge? Remember?" he whispered. He looked across at Lily and then back to Hudge. "He had a fight with you because you found him being nasty to Jean. And then I came along ..."

"With your knife," Hudge went on as if memorising lines, "and stuck it in." Hudge shook his head and looked down at his shiny shoes. "I didn't tell Chrissie I took it Des. I won't tell no-one."

Des lit his cigarette, put his forefinger to his lips and shook his head. "Sssh ..."

She suddenly understood love so well. It was to do with protection. And Lily would have thrown her arms about Des and told him so, had Hudge not done it first.

"I won't let them take you away, Des." Hudge was crying on to his brother's shoulder. "I took the knife, but they took you. I don't want to stay in this house without you."

Kay put her head around the door. "Ah ... finished your tea? I think Mr Lee is ready now," she said, swallowing so hard that the Adam's apple jumped and squealed, "to say a few words."

"Right," Des said, and stubbing his cigarette out in the ash-tray he shook his head at Lily.

It was no good. He would never forgive her if she told the truth.

"You look very smart today, Des," Kay said. "Yes ... very nice. In we come then."

Lily followed the others through to the front room where everyone was gathered, holding sherry glasses like props in a play. Cecilia wore a serious expression and a black tailor-made suit. On seeing Lily enter the room with Des, she quickly took her daughter by the hand and sat her next to Bessie Fenchurch. Bessie was sitting at Gordon's side, on the three-seated sofa. Will Fenchurch receded into the background and Gordon Lee looked at his watch. The shop was closed until his return.

Mr and Mrs Brambles, big people, and smelling of raw vegetables, took up quite a bit of space. They were telling Des who stood next to them, that that 'needed to get away as soon as possible'. Autumn had been very busy, trade had been brisk and winter was a good time to take stock: clearing out the stables to make way for the new van. Des with Hudge, was bunched up by the mantelpiece and not making eye contact with Mr Brambles. Lily could feel Des watching her as she studied the Axminster at her feet.

Mr Brambles turned his attention to Gordon and was asking him if he still was dealing in clocks but Gordon was reaching into his jacket pocket for his speech which was written on the back of the bookie's betting form. He stood up, stroked the stem of his sherry glass, loosened his tie, put his hand in his trouser pocket and rocked back and forth in his squeaky shoes. Lily listened to his feet speak.

"Kay has asked me to say a few words on behalf of the Hodge family." There was a pause whilst the shoes spoke in the silence of the dusty room. Bessie Fenchurch reached for her handkerchief and blew her nose. Kay's Adam's apple squeaked again.

"As you all know, Aida Hodge was a lovely lady ..."

"Lovely lady," Bessie Fenchurch said, tucking her handkerchief into her polka-dotted sleeve. Cecilia nodded and took a sip of her sherry.

"A chip off the old block, I might go as far to say. Her passing ..." he loosened his tie once again, "is a sadness to us all."

Cecilia sounded in agreement.

"Sadness." Bessie Fenchurch retrieved her handkerchief and Gordon looked down at her with a small frown.

"She was a good worker at the Boys' Games Club ... and um ..."

Bessie Fenchurch was teetering on the brink, about to repeat his words, when he came thrashing in with an "And," and he reached into his trouser pocket to jangle his car keys, "she was a very good mother ..."

Lily looked up with a trace of a smile at Des. He had a hand over his mouth, disguising the laughter, but then he looked at her, puzzled.

"And she brought up two sons," he went on, whilst Kay lifted her eyebrows and looked out of the front window. "Yes, two good sons ..."

People looked down at their sherry glasses for fear of catching anyone's eye. Bessie Fenchurch was unable to restrain a cough. Gordon Lee was nodding at his sherry glass.

"Who will sorely miss her. So let us raise our sherry glasses in remembrance of Aida."

"Aida," said all and sipped at the dreadful sherry.

When Bessie Fenchurch spoke to Lily in a subdued voice, she barely heard her. Gordon was saying to Cecilia that they needed to go back and open the shop as he was on late turn at the station and anyways, the prison officer would be wanting the two of them to leave as soon as possible, them being witnesses for the prosecution. Kay was thanking Gordon, saying she had to get back to the dog too.

"Come on, Kay," Cecilia said, as if relieved that 'that was that'. "I'll collect these sherry glasses and wash them up in the kitchen and you collect the side plates in here and bring them through."

"Sorry, Bessie. Troubling you, did you say?" Lily said.

"Troubling me, yes. Yes, let's just go through to the back room. Quieter there."

She followed Bessie and her husband Will through to the back room with the picture of the big black lady with the turban. She gave Des a quick smile.

Lily followed Bessie through to the back room, a weight in her heart.

"Troubling me, yes," Bessie said. "I think I ought to go to the police, but Will's not so sure."

"Police?" Lily said as she watched people filing into the hallway. Will Fenchurch closed the back room door with meaning, crossed and closed the door to the kitchen and then crossed back to the back room door like they had decided to do this. Will then stood sentry with his hands behind him, shaking his head ruefully.

"About Hudge, you see," Bessie said.

"Hudge?"

"Hudge. Yes. He came into the Exchange & Mart, the night before...before...you know...it all happened."

Lily said nothing but looked at her.

"With the chippie boy ... and so on. Yes."

"Came into you?"

"Came into me. Yes. About six o'clock. On his own."

Lily laughed. "Well, that's not possible, Bessie. He doesn't go anywhere on his own. He can't cross roads."

"Cross roads? Oh yes. He can. Mrs Brambles seen him. Cross roads. All on his own."

Lily looked into Bessie's face – a game of noughts and crosses - and wondered what she was going on about.

She did go on. "It's not that, Lily. No. It's that he asked to buy a gun."

"A gun?"

"A gun. Well, we don't sell guns. Wouldn't have sold him one if I did. I mean we don't have a license to sell guns." She looked quickly at Will who shook his head again and took a couple of paces into the room, towards the fireplace and the picture of the black woman with the green turban.

Bessie was whispering now: a hoarse frightened whisper. "You can get into all sorts of trouble for selling guns without a license in this day and age." Her voice was now a low murmur. "My sister was in the shop. She said then, 'Why should he want to buy a gun? And he shouldn't be going round telling people you sell guns, Bessie.' Why should Hudge want to buy a gun, Lily? I mean Des did it, didn't he? Everyone says so. Des had given the chippie boy the cut on the face, earlier, hadn't he? Everyone knows they were at odds. Over you ...or something. I don't know. The chippie boy was waiting for Des to come in that night and was raring for a fight. Everyone says so.

"I mean I know Hudge got involved. He had bruises on his chest from the fight. Aida worried about that. But I never mentioned the gun to Aida. She was so poorly at the end. She was such a God-fearing woman. When the police came to search the house for that camera she just sat and read her Family Bible, Lil. Never moved from the Word of God. Maybe Hudge was more involved than they think. I mean they did bully him at the caf, didn't they? But thank God the pair of them didn't have a gun. That's a hanging offence, isn't it? What do you think, Lily? Lily?"

Bessie's voice was like machine-gun fire. Hudge. Crossing roads? Buying guns? There were things that Lily did not know about Hudge. Having Des's knife was like pick-pocketing. For no real end. But guns. It all seemed so calculated. Pre-meditated - wasn't that the word?

"What do you think I should do, Lily?"

"Keep schtum," Will whispered from the fireplace.

The back room door creaked open. Lily looked up. What she saw was not the young boy she had always known, but a man who had finally caught up with the skin that had been waiting for him all the time. Des looked at her, uncertain. But how long he had been standing behind the door and just exactly what he had heard, she did not know.

"Lily?" Bessie Fenchurch said with her back to the door, and Will gave a small cough indicating Des's presence.

Bessie Fenchurch looked behind her and up at Des, frightened. "Oh ..."

But Des turned and walked back into the hallway as Cecilia opened the scullery door. "Right, any more sherry glasses?" Her mother gave Bessie Fenchurch a tight, sideways glance and Lily thought she should change the subject quickly. "Are Aida's organs going to the university, Bessie?"

"The university? No." She shook her head forlornly. "They wouldn't take her. She was riddled with cancer, Lily. The body has to be in near perfect condition for all that."

"Lily. It's time for Des to go now."

Lily looked up at her mother, her skull feeling as though it might crack open. She had been lost in thought on the three-seated sofa in the front room. Fresh evidence, she had said to herself. What else didn't she know about Hudge? He had planned it all. He couldn't buy a gun, so he stole Des's Swiss Army knife. He must have known exactly what he was doing. Why had Hudge done it? Had she been that naive to believe that he was protecting Jean? That he acted on impulse? That he just happened to be carrying a knife, like a Biro pen. Could Hudge possibly have had the ability to think through something like this? To cross roads? To ask for guns? The only Hodge capable of forward planning?

"I promise. I promise, Des. Mix our blood. To look after Hudge. Always. Mix up our blood and mop it up." Bonding in backyards. Commitments to the past.

Damn the Hodges. Where was Hudge's guardian angel now? He was flapping his wings and hanging on to Lily Lee's back. She looked down at her feet. And there were those damned promises, small and big, crowding round and lining up to face the truth.

"We must tell the truth at all times."

Even if it meant now telling the truth, saying what *really* happened would perjure herself and Des? Perverting the course of justice. We were out of the playground now and into hard schools of detention. Was she prepared to carry the weight of Des's sentence over the years? Tell the truth for the love of Des or lie for the love of Des and the sake of tiny promises? Would he, could he, ever forgive her for not keeping the promise? Would she ever be able to forgive them for Geoff Mabs?

She could explain away the incident of the gun. In a fit of temper Des said he could kill Geoff Mabs. Hudge took things literally. Talk of Christmas and socks get hung by the fireplace. Lily Lee was the only witness. The only one. Hudge's public innocence or guilt lay in the palm of her sweaty hand. And she hated it. Hated it.

Seal the eyes and lips?

But Lily Lee had seen what really happened. Some people go through life never seeing anyone die. She had seen Hudge covered in Geoff Mabs's blood.. She had heard Hudge shout, "She's my girlfriend. She's my girlfriend." For Jean. Why? What was Jean to Hudge that he could cold-bloodedly plan Geoff Mabs's murder?

And what of Geoff Mabs? 'Eyes to see with ... his eyes had been bright had been beautiful ... And lips that we might tell ...' and laughter like free-floating leaves. Geoff Mabs had been alive ... with whatever faults he might have had ... and deserved still to be so. Didn't he deserve a fair trial? Geoff Mabs was at her right shoulder, and would remain there, never to leave her.

Geoff Mabs's blood. The stench of it and the overall. Still in the disused stables. She could maybe get the overall back. Come clean. Clean. If that was ever possible. Cecilia ... what would Cecilia say?

"I thought you might like to say goodbye." Cecilia was looking down at her with a sympathetic smile.

Lily looked up again at her mother. Spatter patterns. Spatter patterns had not been consistent. It was just her evidence. Lily's evidence. Would Hudge ever be able to remember what he was told? He didn't know his right from his left, let alone right from wrong. And Des could be wrong. How did Des know what would happen to Hudge? Hudge might get the kind of care he needed.

"Lily. I think you're only half awake. Are you coming to say goodbye?"

"Yes," she said. "I should say goodbye." She got up from the three-seated sofa with unsteady feet and spatter patterns on her mind. And hadn't Des played 'Happy Families' long enough? How long could Des go on living Hudge's life for him? "Oh Lily. There's not much an angel can do when you're racing down the motorway at seventy miles an hour."

Would Des ever forgive her? "*That's the thing about Des. When he's had time to think he comes round in the end. But he won't admit it and he won't come to you.*" They had been Aida's words. She walked towards the door, the tiny promises scrambling at her feet.

Rules were rules. Mop it up. Mop it up.

What was she to do?

Lily entered the crowded hallway. Luckily Mr and Mrs Brambles had already left. They had needed to get on and take stock. Des dutifully shook hands with everyone, although Bessie Fenchurch winced as she retrieved her right hand from his.

Then he turned and looked at Lily as a voice from behind said, "Chrissie asked me if I had any friends."

It was Hudge's voice, but she continued to look at Des.

"I said Jean was my girlfriend and Chrissie asked if she ever gave me my tea or took me to work. I said you did that, Lily. I said you did everything. And Chrissie said I was very lucky and she'd speak to you about still helping me."

Des closed his eyes and sighed.

"Well," Cecilia said, standing in the kitchen doorway, "it's not going to be as easy as all that, Hugh. Things aren't the way they were, I'm afraid. People grow up. And that's that."

Hudge stuck out his bottom lip and Gordon frowned at Cecilia who whispered to her husband, "And I hope he's not going to ask her to wait, because that won't last long."

Des put his arms around his brother.. "Okay?" he whispered. Just as he was about to draw away, Lily saw him give Hudge an extra squeeze.

Then he put his arms about Lily and hugged her so that she could hear her bones speak. "The promise ...," he said quietly as if to say more but it was at that moment that the policeman opened the front door.

Gordon Lee had to hold Hudge back when the prison officer locked the handcuff in Des's at the open doorway. As the nameless uniform led him down the front path, Lily's heart went bouncing along with them.

Cecilia, Gordon and the others dispersed into the front room to watch the departure from there. Only Hudge remained on the doorstep behind her. She watched Des get into the waiting car. It started up and reversed.

"Lily," she heard Hudge say. "Do you think I'm lucky?"

It was an awkward three-point turn and narrowly missed a tree. Another city train thundered across the bridge. She continued looking at the car. Des was seated in the back between the two policeman. "Yes, Hudge," she said, her eyes still fixed on Des. "I do think you are lucky. I think you're very lucky to have a brother like Des." The car drove off up Peterson towards Pennington. He didn't look back.

"And people don't always keep their promises do they?"

She turned and looked up at Hudge. He was frowning down on her. He really wants my answer, she thought. He really wants to know what I think. She faltered for a moment, smiled and then said, "No."

"I told Geoff Mabs that Jean was my girlfriend and she made me promise to keep our secret. I broke the promise." This came out in the usual Hudge gabble.

"Sometimes it's not possible to keep a promise. Sometimes you realise you made a mistake," she said.

He looked at her. "I ask questions inside my head and no-one answers. That's why I've made up my own mind."

"To do what?" she asked.

"To ask you to break your promise to Des and tell the policeman I took the knife. Tell Des. Tell Des. He listens when you kiss him. It was my mistake."

Lily looked up at him, his shoulders hunched, his bottom lip trembling. A final door had opened on Hudge. He loved his brother as much as she did. "But do you understand what will happen if I do break my promise?"

"You won't have to wait," he said.

This was so important. Important that he knew what he was saying and doing. "Do you understand what will happen to you?"

Very quietly he said to her, "Des and me will swap. Lucky Des."

"Yes ... you or Des." A gust of December wind slammed the front door shut.

"Answer the question, Lil," he said as Cecilia poked her head into the hallway. "You choose."

She let the tears come. Sod the conkers. "Happy Birthday, Hudge," she said.

Hudge gave a small smile, shook his head and said, "No cake this year."

She never really got to speak to Des after the funeral. Cecilia stood on permanent guard. It wasn't until after the trial she realised he had stood the other side of the slim door and listened.

PART TWO

9

The Old Bailey
JANUARY 1960
Witnesses for the Prosecution

Des's Hodge's Story

Des Hodge, the defendant, has been sitting in his funeral suit, his only suit, now his courtroom suit, whilst mostly looking down at shoes you could see your face in. *You can see your face in those shoes*, Gordon Lee always used to say when they were kids, polishing with a bit of spit and plenty of elbow grease. *Here, Des lad, I'll give you a thrupenny bit if you can shine my shoes the way I can. Shine them up like Lil's hair.* It was the way Des learnt to polish his shoes. Up in the flat above the shop, looking on to the down stroke of Peterson Road. Gordon has been more of a father to him than his own father has ever been. Where was his own father when his mother died? But Gordon standing for the prosecution, Christ's sake, was a Judas betrayal.

Sometimes the defendant catches the eye of a visitor in the public gallery. Sometimes he holds their gaze, knowing they are trying to make their own judgement: tiny decisions about the defendant's guilt or innocence. They make judgments based on looks. Keep those shoes shined; half the battle is looking like a man who wouldn't murder. Des Hodge is being tried for murder. People in the public gallery come and go whilst members of the jury have been here for weeks. Cecilia's flamboyant sisters sashay and squeak in stilettos as the public gallery door is held open and closed. Des has been here since the beginning of

1960. Des has been remanded at Her Majesty's Pleasure since August 26th 1959.

There is one person in the public gallery who has not come and gone, but been here since the case began: a middle-aged man, swarthy-skinned, permanent five o'clock shadow. He has asked to see his son but Des won't see him. Des looks up at him frequently but won't send him a visitor's order. Des can look up and eyeball him. Des used to think his father was God. But the judge and jury are a combined God now.

His father loved notoriety.

Sometimes, Des the defendant gets scared. When he listens to the testimonies and knows they are false. *Neither shalt thou bear false witness against thy neighbour.* His mother was very keen edged about the commandments. All ten of them.

Sometimes Des's thoughts are scattered. His thoughts scramble from one memory to another, scarper round and then he begins to wonder why juror number seven: the pretty dark member of the jury with the big mole on her face is frowning. This scattering of concentration scares him because he is supposed to be listening to all the evidence so that he can 'build a defence case'; report back to his barrister: Mr Williams: Mr *Boyo* Williams with his tufts of red hair matching his tufts of red moustache and nicotine-stained lips.

At other times Des's thoughts are centred and he takes notes. He does this sometimes to impress the jury. He knows that Mabs was stabbed in the back and that the prosecution barrister, Mr Stevens-Sinclair QC, would like to prove that Des entered from the caf scullery *with the intent to kill or cause grievous bodily harm.* Either would do for murder. Mr Stevens-Sinclair QC would like to disprove self defence as self defence would bring about 'a complete acquittal'. Des has learnt all these phrases since he spent time 'inside' and with Mr *Boyo* Williams. Mr Stevens-Sinclair QC needs to prove that Des left by the shop front door, or earlier enough to go up the back of Alpha, on to Pennington and through the caf front door. But despite false witnesses, and Lily will not be one of those, Des is not about to lose his bottle.

All Lily had to do was to keep her promise; the prime defence witness who will say he acted in self defence.

And here is Gary Papanikalou, teeth like broken knuckle dusters ...

Gary Papanikalou's Story

"My Lord," Stevens-Sinclair says, "I would like to call my first witness, Gary Papanikalou."

A slight figure, dark brows permanently raised as if in small surprise, Gary Papanikalou wouldn't have known if he was kicking off for the defence or the prosecution. He clears his throat and swears to tell the truth, the whole truth and nothing but the truth. The little Greek has a first class Language degree in swearing.

"Could you give the court your full name?"

"Gary Papanikalou, my Lord." The little Greek clears his throat and seems mesmerised by Stevens-Sinclair's nose. Draw a cartoon of Stevens-Sinclair and you'd have a pair of nostrils. What a conker, Honker Conker, Des can hear Papanikalou thinking.

"Can you give the court your full address to the court?"

"Indeed I can, my Lord. 'Tis 17, Alpha Road, my Lord," Gary says, speaking to The Nose.

"And can you give the court your place of work?"

"Yes, my Lordship," Papanikalou says speaking to Stevens-Sinclair, the barrister, which makes Des smile with his slightly askew lips. "Indeed I can, your Lordship," the boy goes on. 'Tis Lewis's timberyard at the bottom of Alpha, my Lordship."

"Yes, Mr Papanikalou. The judge is 'My Lord'," Stevens-Sinclair says with a touch of irritation and indicating the old man on a high chair.

The old man, older than the Perrys or the Brambles, peers over his glasses and raises his lips like he's got painful constipation. *He needs a dose of liver salts,* Des can hear his mother saying. His mother would spoon out Syrup of Figs as punishment, whenever, she said, any of her three sons gave *her* 'the unmentionables'. Des has them now and has had them for some months. He tries to concentrate. The Huge Honker Conker talks again and Des watches the little Greek stare at The Nose. "It's perfectly acceptable to just answer my questions and direct your answers to the jury. May I remind you, Mr Papanikalou, I am a barrister and my name is Mr Stevens-Sinclair QC? The judge is 'Your Lordship'."

"I'm sorry, your Lordship," Gary says to the old man on the high chair who carries on writing with his left hand whilst a the stenographer taps away at something which looks like a typewriter when Gary or anyone ever speaks. Tap, tap, tap. Tap bloody tap.

"Protection is something important in the area you live and work, is it not?" Mr Stevens Honker Conker Sinclair asks, but doesn't seem to really ask, seems to know the answers before he asks. Mr Stevens-Sinclair is a tall, reedy man and those nostrils are so large they seem to be doing all the talking. You can see right up these nostrils. Every now and then Mr Stevens-Sinclair strokes his big nose and then pulls his heavy black gown up by the lapels. He takes time to think.

"It was not, yes, Mister."

"Let us return to your first meeting with Geoffrey Mabs. How did Geoffrey Mabs strike you?"

"He never striked me."

"I'm sorry, Mr Papanikalou. I do apologise. Forgive my obtuse question. I'll re-phrase." Mr Stevens-Sinclair smiles quietly down at his notes, or rather his huge nostrils spread and Gary notices the bunch of people opposite doing the same. This wasn't a laughing matter, was it? you can hear Papanikalou thinking by the raising of those slimy black eyebrows.

"What did you think of Geoffrey Mabs when you first met him?" Honker Conker asks.

"Well, he was a Ted for a start. And he never seemed to be wrinkled, like, by Des Hodge."

"Why do you say that?"

"Well, that Wednesday night Des Hodge comes into the caf and starts saying Mabs stinks of lard."

"That's Wednesday 19th August: the Wednesday preceding the night in question?" the barrister says.

"Yeah – when Des Hodge hit Mabs."

"Des Hodge hit Geoffrey Mabs?" Now Stevens-Sinclair seems surprised by this. Gary seems surprised that Stevens-Sinclair is surprised. Gary's probably told the police enough times. Signed a sworn statement.

"Yes." Gary is again pleased to be saying this word.

"Where?"

"Back of the legs. Like this." Gary Papanikalou indicates this by dropping his knees and dropping his mouth open. Then he raises those dark eyebrows at the jury opposite, especially at the pretty dark haired girl: juror number seven. "To break his legs like. Des Hodge was always saying he was going to break people's legs."

Des Hodge has never said this in his life.

"Can you say why this contratemps between Des Hodge and Geoff Mabs took place?"

Gary's inky brows meet in confusion. "Contrawhat?"

Mr Stevens-Sinclair's nostrils spread with his lips and he smiles down at his big books again. The judge on high does not smile. His skin is set like cement. His face looks bored to hell.

"Let me re-phrase that question, Mr Papanikalou. Why do you think Des Hodge and Geoff Mabs were 'at odds' with one another at their very first meeting?"

'At odds'. Funny little phrases they use these barristers.

Gary Papanikalou hesitates. He does not want to look up to the dock. "Been sniffing round his girl." Gary nods a lot here.

"Who was Des Hodge's girl?"

He looks unsure. "Lily Lee, the grocer's girl."

"I see."

"And after Hodge hit Mabs he says, 'Re-sit your arse." Gary chuckles to himself and then chuckles at the jury opposite. The fat man runs his hand over his head and yawns.

"Hodge said, 'Re-sit your arse'?" the barrister with eyes like bird beads says to Gary Papanikalou.

"Yeah," the little Greek says, "then he went out into Alpha with his girl and his brother and then he went mad."

The barrister cuts in quickly. "Yes, but that is by the by, Mr Papanikalou as you weren't in Alpha Road that Wednesday night, the 19th August, the Wednesday preceding the night in question, when Des Hodge 'went mad' with his girl. So if we may move on ..."

"No," Gary says. "But my mum was."

The barrister takes a very deep breath and then, "Well, she will give evidence in due course. How did things proceed between Geoff Mabs and Des Hodge later in the week?"

"On the Monday. Mabs had the cut on the Monday and got it on the Sunday."

Stevens-Sinclair looks down at his notes; pulls the lapels of his heavy black gown forward. "That's Sunday 23rd August – the Sunday the deceased received the cut to his face but you saw him on the Monday 24th August – the Monday preceding the night in question?"

"Tis so."

"Do you know how he came to have that cut on his cheek, Mr Papanikalou?"

"Des Hodge give it to him."

Des shakes his head in disbelief. He knows he is not supposed to react. 'It doesn't help," his re-haired Welsh barrister has said, 'if you start reacting to witnesses' evidence. The jury will be watching you much of the time and it doesn't help'.

"You know that?"

"Yes."

"How do you know that?

"Geoff Mabs told me. Des Hodge gave Geoff Mabs a good hiding on that Sunday night."

Mr SS QC as Des refers to the prosecuting barrister in his head takes a sip of water. Des looks across to his defence barrister who is searching his papers. Williams should be on his feet objecting, surely. This is hearsay evidence. Stevens-Sinclair goes on. "How do you know that? How do you know that Des Hodge gave Geoff Mabs a good hiding?" Stevens-Sinclair's 'good hiding' vowels are clearly cut. Received Pronunciation, they call it. Gordon told him.

"Geoff Mabs told me."

Des Hodge shakes his head again. Whenever would Geoff Mabs have said he had been given 'a good hiding' by anyone?

"And where were you on the Sunday before the stabbing, Mr Papanikalou?"

"At the top of Peterson." The little Greek nods his head with a smirk.

Des didn't know this. It is at this point that the jury is provided with maps; maps of Des's home ground. They peruse the maps, are shown the road where he lives, by Stevens-Sinclair saying it was adjacent to this and … what was Papanikalou doing at the top of Peterson but the boy goes on. "Yes, round about seven before the churchie folk tip out of the Nazarene."

"And what did you see, Mr Papanikalou, when the churchgoers were coming out of their Sunday evening service?"

"I sees Lily Lee running up Peterson coming from the Hodges house."

"Yes."

"I sees her covered in blood."

Mr Stevens-Sinclair, or Mr SS QC as Des has begun to think of him, leaves off here with one of those pauses where you can hear the court breathe and seats creak; says, "Mr Papanikalou, I have no further questions for you at this time but if you could just remain where you are, my learned friend may have some questions to ask you." Very good place to leave off, Mr SS QC. Des wishes that Stevens-Sinclair was representing him because now Williams, his defence barrister is standing up and Williams must be about as much as the state can afford.

"Mr Papanikalou," Williams says, "I do have some further questions for you. I am Mr Williams QC and I represent Mr Hodge." He clears his throat. "You say you saw Lily Lee running up Peterson Road covered in blood," Williams says.

"Yes."

"Did you see Lily Lee the next evening - on the Monday - when she usually collected Hudge Hodge from the caf after work?"

"Yeah. I was in the caf on the Monday night when she came to collect Hudge."

"When you saw her on the Monday evening, did she have any wounds?"

Gary pauses to consider, as if he has never thought about his before, and he probably hasn't. "No, sir."

"You said she was covered in blood on the Sunday evening when you saw her running up Peterson Road?"

"Yes."

"Would you not expect her then to suffer some wound, say some scar, albeit temporary, after such a supposed assault?"

Gary shrugs his shoulders.

"Is that a 'yes' or a 'no', Mr Papanikalou? For the record the witness has shrugged his shoulders."

Stevens-Sinclair is on his feet – no wonder they talk about barrister 'being on their feet' – they're up and down like Jack-in-the-Box – objecting – saying this is 'expert' evidence and the question should be withdrawn but Boney Judge allows Williams to continue with his line of questioning.

Gary swallows hard, you can see his Adam's apple bulge.

"Let me repeat the question - would you not expect her then to suffer some wound or scar after a supposed assault? You said she was 'covered in blood'.

"I dunno. You're mixing me up."

"Mr Papanikalou, how far were you from Miss Lee when you saw her running up he road supposedly 'covered in blood'?"

The boy shakes his head, looks swamped in that suit, shrugs his shoulders. "I dunno."

"Well I put it to you that you were a considerable distance away Mr Papanikalou and that you can't be sure at all that she was covered in blood. Can you?"

The boy looks at Williams in earnest. "Looked like blood."

"But it is possible, it is possible, is it not that what you in fact saw Miss Lee covered in, was not blood but another substance?

Papanikalou's eyes widen in confusion. "Another substance?

"Could she have been covered in say ... blackberry juice?"

Des listens to the court laugh, watches the fat man on the jury fold his arms and throw his head back and grin, sees Gary's humiliation and remembers the night of the blackberries.

Everything in his life changed that night, everything which had once been solid got broken. It wasn't even the night of the stabbing which was marked with a cross or a red letter for Des. It always remained that bloody, black Sunday.

When he had thrown the blackberries at Lily, he had been angry. Angry at her for saying he was like his father and angry at her for saying he couldn't keep promises. He had been so angry he had left Hudge on the porch, gone to the Dragon's Head, knowing that his mother would be back from Evensong for Hudge within minutes. He hadn't wanted to carry Hudge that night. He wanted to just have a few beers in the corner of the pub. And the Dragon was always quiet on a Sunday. Mabs was standing at the juke box, didn'tee him when he walked in. Lily going out with Geoff Mabs had no significance for Des. Des had forgotten about it. What had remained in his mind was this.

The barman threw a coin at Mabs and said, "Put on Craig Douglas's 'Teenager in Love'. I like it." Des watched Mabs flip the names of the discs. Mabs seemed to be having trouble. The barman got irritated. "It's number ten," the barman called. "Number ten."

Mabs finally banged the side of the juke box and threw the coin back across the counter at him, saying, "I don't like that track."

"Hey," the barman shouted back, twenty stone and big as a side of beef, pointing a stubby forefinger in Mabs's direction. "Watch your behaviour, boy or I'll have you barred."

Mabs took a swig from his beer bottle and shouted, "Don't call me 'boy'." It was then that Mabs saw Des at the door.

He realised why Geoff Mabs had not put the coin in the singing machine for the barman. Des was still smarting from the blackberries and the prodding of three women's forefingers at his shoulder blades. He walked up to Geoff Mabs and whispered, "You can't read, can you?"

Mabs's look confirmed it. Mabs might have killed him there and then if the twenty stone barman had not been present. Des could see it in Mabs's eyes.

Des nodded at him. "Even my daft brother can do that. But you be a good boy and your secret is safe with me."

It was unforgivable. Des realises this in the months and weeks to come. He learns a lot about a victim he has scarcely said more than a couple of dozen words to, but who would change his life to the extraordinary. Our lives changed by those we crash into, he thinks. As Des sits and listens in number one courtroom, minutes turning into hours and tea breaks, weeks turning into adjournments and extra evidence, he listens to Geoff Mabs's story. And as the tale of Mabs's unfortunate life begins to unfold, Des realises that he has been guilty of vandalising the little self esteem Geoff Mabs must have possessed. How he wishes he could steal those words back.

Mabs took hold of Des's jacket collar and the barman shouted, "I'll have the pair of you out of here, so cut your gas."

All Mabs said was, "I'll pay you back some day."

And right now Des was drawing the devil's dividends.

Mabs hit the bar with his fist and left. But there was worse to come.

"Des Hodge nearly killed a boy once for calling his brother names," Gary says. He hadn't liked the courtroom laughing at blackberry juice.

"It would be safe to say, wouldn't you agree Mr Papanikalou that Des Hodge was merely protecting his vulnerable brother during this first meeting between himself and Geoff Mabs?" the defence barrister says in his sing song voice.

Des wonders why the Greek had been able to make a statement like that in court. Des has never nearly killed a boy once for calling Hudge names: it was just something he and Lil had put around to stop Hudge being ribbed. Why has his barrister let that comment of Papanikalou's go?

"Yeah, that's safe, but that's because Des Hodge was always protecting his brother from being crowded."

"What do you mean 'crowding'?"

The court sees the little Greek mouth boy something with his lips. Des sees the little Greek boy mouth the words, 'elephant shit' because Des has seen him mouth off in the caf before. Gary looks sideways, his eyes dusting defensively over the dock. Gary doesn't know what to say. So dumpy Williams with his sing song voice and red tache repeats the question. "Mr Papanikalou, you said, 'crowded'. How and where was Hudge Hodge 'crowded'?"

"Des Hodge nearly killed a boy once for crowding his brother so no-one was likely to do that, were they?"

Williams lets Papanikalou's statement go again and says only, "What, not even Geoff Mabs?"

"Not even Geoff Mabs."

"So, Mr Papanikalou," Des's barrister says, "on the night of the stabbing, Wednesday 26th August 1959, when did you last see Geoffrey Mabs?"

"In the caf. Then he left."

Williams the asks the jury to look at their bundles, directing them to more photos of the caf. "Which way did Geoffrey Mabs exit?"

"Behind the counter, through the scullery."

"Why?"

Gary shrugs his shoulders again. "He followed Jean out to her shed."

"Did Geoffrey Mabs seem angry to you?"

"Yeah, he was riled all right. Someone had nicked his camera."

"The camera was important to him?"

Gary laughs. "Yeah. He said his grandfather had given him the camera just before he died. He'd have killed anyone who dared touch that camera. He was always taking photos. Of anyone, anything. His camera was always slung across his chest on a strap. It was like his camera was, well, was like ...I dunno." Gary's words fall out fast.

It is at this point that Des's barrister asks for the jury bundle at tab F and the Ilford Witness camera is held up to the jury. "The Ilford Witness," Williams explains, "could be purchased for £122 six years ago."

Gary's mouth fell open. Des gave an audible sigh. The camera had been found under his bed. Why had Hudge stolen it from Geoff Mabs and why the hell was Williams using it as part of the defence case? How was Mabs able to own something as expensive as that?

"Mr Papanikalou, considering the value of this camera, in your opinion, do you think Geoffrey Mabs was capable of rape that night ? Or more ... murder even?"

Mr SS QC is up on his feet. "My Lord, the witness is not in a position to to know what Mr Mabs was thinking or was capable of on that or any other night."

Boney Judge then gives the defence barrister a warning and tell him to move on with his questioning.

They object so much, Des thinks it might lead to a punch up. This is nothing on the caf. His defence barrister is saying he as 'no further questions', the judge is asking Stevens-Sinclair if there is any re-examination from him and then looks at his watch and at the members of the jury. Gary Papanikalou sneaks a glance at the defendant. Des places his head between his knees, something the other inmates have told him to do when he needs to think, needs out of the court. His upper lip perspires. But these are early days and I'm already serving time and the little Greek is probably thinking, it's four o'clock, Friday and time for a pint. Oh for a pint. Des's dad has been upstairs in the audience. "Mr Papanikalou," and the judge looks down at Gary over his spectacles, "I hope you understand that you must not speak to anyone about the evidence you have given in court today."

"Why's that?" Gary asks.

"Because that's the rule, Mr Papanikalou and you will remember the warnings I gave you at the outset of the trial and for those reasons, members of the jury, I must ask you to do the same. We shall re-convene at ten o'clock on Monday morning."

Des is staring now at his polished shoes and wishing that he could return to just before ten o'clock on that Blackberry Sunday evening. Let's say two minutes to ten, as the outward bound city train was making its way into Pennington.

Des spent a few hours on that Sunday evening sipping beer slowly in the corner of the Dragon's Head, thinking about calling in on Lily, except he was in no mood for Cecilia. So he returned home about ten. Des sits in the dock and wishes he could place his key in the lock of his house, number forty seven as the city train rumbles into the station and change it all; except it had been waiting to happen all along. All he could have changed was how he had reacted.

He found his mother not home. Hudge had gone up to bed. Des checked on him. Hudge was fast asleep and Des sat in the back room, thought about clearing up the seven colanders of discarded blackberries he had thrown at the walls earlier that evening, and worried for the first time in his short life about his mother. It was almost eleven o'clock. There was no Bingo on Sundays. Finally the key was placed in the lock and the front door slammed shut. His mother walked into the back room and raised her eyebrows to the stained wallpaper. "What the bloody hell has been going on here?"

"Had a row with Lil."

"I can see." She put her handbag under the back room table, placed her Bible purposefully by Des's elbow.

"Where have you been?" he asked.

She shook her head. "Walking. I just took off after church. I listened to the minister speak and I needed to get things straight." Aida sat down in her unbuttoned overcoat amongst the chaos of the blackberries at the kitchen table. Her body shook heavily with a sigh. "Ohhhh." Her 'ohs' could go on forever.

"I'll get cleaned up, Mum," he said. "I'm sorry." He wasn't just apologising for the mess, he was saying 'sorry' for swearing at her, for calling her a tart, for calling himself a bastard. He just didn't have the words to say it.

"Oh, I'll bake the pies tomorrow," she said. "The Games Club's cake stall is not until the end of the week. I'm just not in the mood tonight. But I'll bake blackberry pies tomorrow. They'll be ready for you after your shift tomorrow. You like your pies, don't you, Des?"

He said, "That was a long walk. Why did you go walking? You've been gone hours."

"I'll tell you this, Des," she said, wagging the famous forefinger, "the sin of the fathers weighs down to the third or fourth generation. No escaping."

"What do you mean, the sin of the father?"

"Breaking commandments. And it wasn't just your bloody father who's done that except the good Lord knows he must have broken every single one of them bar murder."

"Oh, Mum. I'm sorry about what I said earlier this evening." He was about to tell her that she had been a good mother, but the words got caught in his throat. *You've been a good mother*. He spent the rest of his life wishing he had taken that moment to say those words. But the moment floated and was gone. He might have said it, had she not come in with, "I've sinned, Des."

The clock ticked heavily.

"Haven't we all?" he said. He was thinking about the words with which he had dishonoured his mother earlier that evening, thinking of his stolen hours with Jean in the shed and the cherries stolen from Mrs Brambles' stall, the way he swore and took the Lord's name in vain, not only on a Sunday. Oh, Des Hodge had been brought up on a shaky Moses' tablet of stone.

"Yes, well some more than others," she said. "You take care you don't turn into your father."

And Des tried to work out the sin of the father. How Hudge would hide under the bed when his father returned from the Dragon's Head whilst Des was trying to protect his mother's head. Parents passed on not only a legacy for the future but the legacy of the past. He had continued to protect his elder half brother.

As if she could read his mind his mother said, "I'm sorry if you've had to be responsible for Hudge."

He looked across the table at her. "He's my brother," he said.

Aida nodded her head and smiled, "And you're my gift, Des, so be a good boy." Then she said, "I did go walking, but I also went to see Jack Oddy."

"Jack Oddy?"

Jack Oddy's Story

Monday morning, 1960 and Jack Oddy takes the Bible in his unsteady right hand, swears to tell the truth, takes a handkerchief to his brow and removes his spectacles to wipe them clean. Jack Oddy glances not up towards the defendant but to the public gallery where a man leans forward. The clerk of the court frowns upward. Des knows who the man is.

"Were you aware that Hudge Hodge was being bullied in your cafe?

Jack Oddy swallows hard, looks up for the first time towards the dock. "No," he says. "No, I never saw any evidence of that at all."

Des shakes his head again in disbelief.

"But if there had been any ribbing, any teasing, any bullying so to speak, you would have been aware?" Stevens-Sinclair says turning over a page, looking up towards Jack Oddy.

"Yes - yes, of course. And my Jean would have told me."

"Jean is your daughter?"

"Yes."

"Mr Oddy, how much time during the last summer, did you come down to work in your cafe?"

"My health has never been good since my wife departed and I think a lot fell on my daughter." He glances up again towards the public gallery just as the clerk of the court is shaking her head in that direction, warning the member of the public probably to stop leaning forward. "But I was always there, always keeping a check on things, so to speak. I know we lived in an unstable area. I would never have left young people to manage a business on their own. She always was such a good girl and I just can't understand what has happened. I can't understand how this came to happen in our yard ... I feel so guilty about her ..."

"Mr Oddy, on the night in question, did you see or hear anything?"

Des places his palms together tightly as if in quasi prayer.

"There was always noise. Noise during the evening from opening hour until we closed at ten o'clock." His voice is cracking slightly. "I did hear something a little later ..."

He pauses. Des tightens.

"My girl screaming, I ..."

Was that all you heard, Mr Oddy?

At this point, Jack Oddy becomes breathless and he grips the rails of the witness box and begins to weep gently. "I never knew that she was involved with this boy Mabs. If I had known I would have put a stop to it ... I ... The way things turned out for my girl, I blame myself. I was selling up, you know. I had the papers signed, but the buyers have pulled out. Jean didn't want me to sell. If only I had done it earlier."

The judge looks dispassionate. The prosecutor now leans on to his pedestal and softens the tone of his voice. "Mr Oddy, I understand that the memory of this may be difficult for you but on the night in question but it is important that your evidence is heard. On the night in question, did you hear anything else apart from your daughter screaming?"

"No," Jack Oddy says.

Des is relieved. Jack Oddy heard nothing, did not hear Hudge screaming.

"I'm so sorry for what has happened to the Hodge family ..." Once again Jack looks upward but the members of the public are seated back on their benches, "my daughter thought the world of Des Hodge ... they were so close ... giving Hudge a job, it was my way of helping ... I ...I thought I was helping Aida ... oh my God, poor Aida. I ..." Jack Oddy just cries. Someone in the gallery is about to get up but refrains.

Poor Aida. Des looks up towards his father in the public gallery. *The sin of the father.*

The judge looks over his spectacles. "I think this may be a good time to adjourn for lunch. And if you have any questions, perhaps Mr Oddy will be more able to continue after the break?"

"No questions, my Lord," Mr *Boyo* Williams says.

No questions for Jack Oddy? No questions for Jack Oddy

Jean Oddy's Story

Des does not understand why Jean is being called for the prosecution. Why is Stevens-Sinclair calling Jean Oddy? She saw nothing, she heard nothing. How could so many people who knew him prosecute him?

Jean Oddy swears to tell the truth, the whole truth and nothing but the truth. She confirms her name, past and present address. Jean looks up the courtroom and her eyes sweep over Des.

"Miss Oddy, how long have you known Des Hodge and his brother, Hudge?" Stevens-Sinclair says.

"Since we were ... " she clears her throat. She is dressed in an understated deep blue with a brooch on the lapel. Since when has Jean Oddy worn a brooch? "Since as far back as I can remember."

"And how did Hudge Hodge come to work at the caf?"

"I persuaded my dad. Hudge Hodge got the job because of me."

That was what Jean thought. But she was wrong. Des knows more than the witness. He looks up at his father but his father is watching

Jean Oddy, or what he can just about see of her as he leans forward in the gallery. Of course. His father would be interested to see how Jean Oddy turned out. But who is the woman seated beside his father?

The people he has known all his life do not look at him. On the shed floor during those knickerless and bottom filled Wednesday afternoons. And now you won't look at me.

"Why did you do that? Why did you ask your father to employ Hudge Hodge?"

"To please Des Hodge."

His father is not looking at him now. Neither is the woman seated beside him. They are focused on the witness.

"Did you like to please Des Hodge?"

"Yes."

"And were you intimate with him, Miss Oddy?"

"Yes."

Des cannot remember what intimacy is. Don't lose your bottle, Lil. Stick to our story. I'll get off on self defence. His father whispers to the woman seated next to him.

"When were you intimate with Des Hodge?" asks Mr SS QC.

"In our shed, in our yard, on Wednesday afternoons. My afternoon off. We open up for breakfast, then at lunchtimes till about three and then in the evenings. But Wednesday afternoons is off."

Des lifts his head. Stevens-Sinclair is a very clever man. Whenever Des has felt that the line of questioning was redundant, Sinclair-Stevens has mostly proved it to be relevant. Des wishes that Stevens-Sinclair was representing him and not acting for the Crown, but Mr SS QC is out for blood all the same. How like Cecilia Lee, Stevens-Sinclair is.

"And was Hudge Hodge ever bullied in the caf, ribbed, teased, that kind of thing?"

"Yes, on the night of the stabbing, but mostly before that I didn't really know that much, because I was upstairs with Dad and his angina or in the scullery."

Des waits for his defence to rise and object. Jack Oddy has said there was no bullying of Hudge in the caf because he was downstairs in the caf most hours. Jean is now saying her father was mostly upstairs.

Why doesn't his lawyer rise? Des is trying to plead self defence. Prove that Mabs was a dangerous case, for God's sake, will you?

"You went to tell Lily Lee earlier on that Wednesday night in question that Hudge was being ... teased?"

This was a leading question by the prosecution. Why wasn't his lawyer on his feet?

"Yes."

"So why didn't you tell his brother Des?"

"Well, Des had an evil temper, everyone knew that."

Des sees the jury member with the permed grey hair and who looks like a headmistress sigh a little. He swears he sees her sigh a little. Williams has told him that defending too many 'bad character' statements can look as though there is something to hide but Des can't help feeling he is being bad-mouthed during this trial.

She skirts the dock, skims the jury opposite. "I told Lily that Wednesday lunchtime, before the killing that night. That was about the first free minute I'd had because I work all lunchtimes but Wednesday. On Wednesdays we shut up shop and I told Lily and she would have told Des everything...."

Stevens-Sinclair folds his arms, breathes in through those big nostrils and nods with meaningful emphasis. "She told Des everything," he repeats. Slowly. And takes a sip of water.

The grey-haired woman arches her pencilled eyebrows in two upturned 'u's. Good motives for the defendant to kill: ribbing and sexual jealousy. "And were you intimate with Geoff Mabs?"

Des looks up towards the witness box. "Yes," there comes the answer. He looks down at his funeral shoes. Where? In the shed. When? The week before he was stabbed. After closing.

"And did Des Hodge know that you were intimate with Geoff Mabs?"

"Yes, he did."

Des looks up at her quickly. He's been told by his barrister not to react to witnesses' evidence, it doesn't help, he's been told. But why is she saying this?

"Did Des Hodge at any time express any jealousy about your liason with Geoff Mabs?"

As if Jean would have a 'liason' with anyone. She didn't know the meaning of the word, couldn't spell it. He checks his arrogance again but he could have laughed at the idea that he might be jealous of her 'liason' with Geoff Mabs. This will be all too difficult for his father, Des knows.

"Well, on the Sunday before the Wednesday when this all took place, I went down to see Des Hodge in Peterson Road."

"What happened?"

Jean stops and starts and stumbles and looks up towards the dock before saying, "We had a fight because I said that Lily had been leading Hudge on, getting him to like her in that way, but Des never thought that was possible."

"That what was possible?"

"That Hudge could you know ... like a girl ... in that way."

"Sexually, you mean?"

"Yes." Jean reddened up.

"And then what happened?"

"I smacked him across the face and then his mum came in and told me to go home."

His mum came in and told her to go home. Des looks up at his father. The story was familiar.

"Why did you smack Des Hodge across the face?"

There is a pause. Jean seems uncomfortable but all the same, as Jean does, she enjoys her dramatic moments. "He was really angry when I said that I had been with Geoff Mabs."

Des wants to jump up and say, "That's a lie' as he has seen on *Armchair Theatre* but he doesn't.

"When you say 'been with' you mean having had sexual intercourse?"

There is a pause whilst Jean thinks. "Well, sort of."

"Intimate relations, shall we say?"

"Yes, I don't have it away."

Des raises his eyes to the ceiling, folds his arms and sighs and realises that at least one of the jury must be watching him. He feels heads turning his way. What had they been doing in the shed then? Or maybe it was just one more thing that Geoff Mabs was unable to do. He doesn't care. He remembers Jean Oddy in his bedroom the Sunday night of the blackberries. In her black brassiere, as his mother would say.

He had taken Jean up to his bedroom on that Sunday, it was true. He had been trying to see her all week. He had phoned her from a local telephone box on the previous Tuesday like he always did, to arrange their Wednesday afternoon off.

"Jean," he said, from the telephone box outside the station, "I can't stop tomorrow. I've got an interview for a job at the factory. Did you speak to your dad about the job for Hudge?"

She had started crying down the phone. This immediately worried him and worried him further when she said, "Oh, Des. Something dreadful's happened ..."

She wouldn't tell him over the phone. He had an interview the next day and might start work after that. It took until the Friday night in the caf, the Friday night of Hudge's cheese roll and 're-sitting arses' when she had whispered in his ear and riled him. "I'll speak to you tomorrow night,"she had said. It had been in front of the whole caf and then he had forgotten the cheese roll for Hudge and gone ape at Lily in Alpha Road. Then Jean had been busy on the Saturday night. He had been in a bad mood all week and now on this Sunday he needed to know.

Jean had immediately taken off her top, saying, "Your kitchen's filled with bloody blackberries." It was Blackberry Baking Sunday.

"Oh, no, Jean, I didn't ask you here for that," he had said. She was disappointed. Saw the look on her face. She could be such a responsibility. He had, of course, taken her upstairs, left Hudge down in the scullery to do his steam engine jigsaw puzzle, taken her upstairs to tell her they were finished, well as long as she wasn't pregnant. But he was never able to get that far. Jean had said, "Well, this is your bedroom. What are you going to do, ask me to marry you then?"

"Oh, get serious, Jean," he said.

"Thought we were serious," she said. "Thought I was your girlfriend."

This worried him. The Saturday night before, when he had pulled Lily into the haberdasher's porch, he felt he could make her happy. That was when he decided there and then to let Jean go. Jean needed too much. Lily never did. He'd wait for Lil. But then it all went wrong.

"What did you want to see me about?" he said. "You told me last Tuesday you wanted to speak to me about something. Now's your chance."

Jean said Hudge had taken a bit of stick. "But then we all have to take a bit of stick now and then, don't we?"

Des was slightly relieved that she hadn't said she was pregnant. "What do you mean? Stick?"

"Oh, I'm sorry," Jean said, standing there in the middle of his bedroom in her black brassiere, "Your name is Des Hodge. You don't take 'stick' do you?"

He had kept on. What did she mean 'stick'?

"Everyone knows Lily delivers and collects him and is teaching him the Kerb Drill – how to cross the stupid main road. She might as well be teaching him calculus."

Jean must have heard that one from Cecilia Lee. "Oh, Jean, you don't even know the meaning of the word," he said. "You failed all your 'O' levels."

"You and Lily think you're so clever, don't you? Swanning around in the A stream whilst I was stuck in with the simple Cs." This seemed important to her. "Well, you were so clever, you failed all your 'A' levels."

"I had Hudge to look after."

"Oh, that's always your excuse. Lily babies your brother and it doesn't help with the boys from the timber yard."

Des kept asking her, had they given Hudge stick. He realised later that maybe Jean had tried to tell him there and then. Maybe he could have stopped it before it got to all this. Maybe he would have taken the next day, the Monday, off work and gone into the caf and sorted it, if he'd stopped and listened or asked the right questions. Instead this is what happened.

"No," Jean said. "I wouldn't let anyone give Hudge stick. But Lily doesn't help."

"Lily knows what she is doing with Hudge."

"She kisses Hudge."

"Oh, give over, Jean."

"She's not the angel you think she is."

"Jean, you wouldn't know the difference between a peck on the cheek and having your tongue down someone's throat."

"She encourages Hudge."

"Of course she encourages him."

"He fancies her."

"Oh, give over. He thinks a fuck's a game of soldiers."

"He fancies me."

Hudge fancying Jean. It was laughable. He had seen Hudge looking at Lil's chest now and then, but he would never have known what to do. "Oh, do me a favour, Jean. I can understand him having feelings for Lily. But you? That'll be the day."

Then she slapped him. Then she apologised. "Sorry." The apology slipped out on the tail of the slap.

He had been tempted to slap her back, except he remembered the way his father had lashed out at his mother. He said, "Put your top back on, Jean."

"Yes," his mother had said, coming into Des's bedroom, "put your top back on, Jean Oddy and get out of my house. You really are an exhibition."

Instead of leaving immediately, Jean then said something strange. "Why have you always said I'm an exhibition when I wanted to be just friends with Des?" Jean stood there glaring defiant, the plain dark chocolate eyes widening at his mother.

"Well, you look as though you're 'just friends' now, don't you?" His mother had stood looking face to face with Jean. His mother had hatred in her eyes for her. He had never seen that before, never seen hatred in his mother's eyes before.

No. Stop. This was what was strange. Even more strange than the hatred in his mother's eyes. He is remembering now. Jean then said, "Des only wanted to be my friend when my mother died. You called me an exhibition then. Why did you do that, Mrs Hodge? I was only eleven."

His mother had said nothing.

"When I was eleven I started Peterson Road Secondary Modern where Hudge was and I asked you if I could take him to school. You made Des and Lily do that when they were at the grammar." Jean repeated, "Why did you do that, Mrs Hodge?"

"And on the Sunday night, did Des Hodge turn up on your doorstep?"

Stevens-Sinclair's voice brings his thoughts back to focus. Sunday night, cut on Mabs's face.

"Yes, he rang the caf bell."

"What time was this?"

"About midnight."

"Was that the night that Geoff Mabs received his cut to his face?"

There we are.

"Yes."

"What did Des Hodge want?"

Jean's throat emits a tiny cry. The members of the jury frown again in sympathy. Des knows Jean will not tell the truth. Oh, far too painful, Jean. He looks up again at his father. Only now is his father omniscient. Bloody absent in the past. His father still refuses to look at the dock, but the woman seated beside him looks his way for the first time and he now knows who she is. Can see the resemblance.

On that Blackberry Sunday the Hodges had visited the Oddys. His mother had been to see Jean's father after Evensong. Des remembers asking her that question around midnight on Blackberry Sunday.

"So why did you go and see Jack Oddy, Mum? Was it about Hudge's job?"

His mother gave a nervous laugh. "I had to sort out the sin of the father."

"What do you mean?"

"I knew tonight that Jean's father had come clean with her. I knew when she stood face to face with me in your bedroom in her black brassiere that Jack had chosen his time to tell her now. Jean Oddy stared me out. But at least she had the goodness, Des, to not say it in front of you." Aida got up and opened the sideboard cupboard. She took out the sherry bottle, but it was empty.

"Tell her what? Tell Jean what, Mum?"

"Son, Jean's mother never died ..." She leaned back against the sideboard, her right hand holding the empty sherry bottle.

"So, what has that to do with us?"

"She's in Hartlepool."

"Shit football team."

"Don't joke, Des. Your father's living there too."

He looked down at Hudge's jigsaw puzzle and the pieces fitted together. "Well, I worked out that he'd never joined the bloody French Foreign Legion."

"I chose to tell you kids that he'd run away to France. It was only a little fib and by the time you grew to know it wasn't true, you didn't care. It was a little fib so that Hudge could chew on it." She plonked the empty sherry bottle on top of the steam engine, sat down and rubbed her face with her still powdery white hands. Des remembered her hands being still floury white from earlier in the day.

"Well, it would have been something to know he was in Hartlepool."

"Well, little fibs grow into big lies, that's true. It was different for Jack with a girl ..."

And as they sat in the naked light of that unshaded light bulb, Des listened to his mother's story of how Gwen Oddy and his father Reg had conducted an affair from round about the time Ben and Kay had got married.

Oh, she expected Des would live out his days to be the same as his father. Dallying here, dallying there, God help Lily. To be honest, she had done the same thing. Left Ben and Hudge's father when he was serving his country. "Teddy Pepper was a good Methodist. But somehow, Des, I can't see life like Cecilia Lee."

Des shook his head with misunderstanding.

Aida went on to explain. "With all her principles."

"They don't pay rent, you know."

"You've told that joke too often. No. I never saw adultery as the biggest of sins. Cecilia may do. God may do, but I don't agree with Him. Oh, I could have taken Gwen Oddy keeping my man warm at night. I knew when Ben and Kay were getting married that your father wasn't interested in bridesmaids' dresses but he always turned up to the fittings, Des."

She paused here. He wished there had been some sherry to punctuate the pauses but they had knocked it back with Lily the night before. He couldn't get worked up about this affair of his father's with Jean's mother. So what if his father went to bridesmaids' fittings?

"And that's 'cos Gwen was there with Jean. I wouldn't have been that bothered about your father bringing her here to this house."

And so his mother wasn't that bothered either. "What you mean in your bed, Mum?"

"No. You see, he didn't do that. He took her into your room and Hudge's."

"And ... so what?"

"I don't know why Ben rolled up that night on his motor scooter."

It was a bike. A big bike. But she always called it a scooter. Ah ... so that was what she was leading up to.

"I'll never know why he called round. Kay could never say why. But it was Ben who found your father and Gwen in your bedroom. You and Hudge were out bobbing and jobbing. Then I come up the stairs and see the pair of them standing there in your bedroom like you and Jean were tonight and Ben at the door. Course, Ben gave your father a mouthful and in returns your father told Ben what he thought of his father Ted. Your father had a dreadful tongue on him and I knew he didn't always mean what he said. But he had a shocking temper on him in drink. He told Ben that Hudge had been a handicap and he'd only stayed with me because of you. You being his and a Hodge. Your father told Ben that Kay was simple."

Des tried to hide his smile.

Aida playfully pushed the side of his head with her hand. "Oh, I know what you think of Kay, but let's face it my love, Ben, God rest his soul was short of a shilling too. Not like you, except you're a lazy bloody bugger who needs a squib up his arse." It was an interesting image. She went on. "It was all to cover his embarrassment of standing there with Gwen Oddy in nothing but your bed sheets."

"Did Ben storm out?"

His mother looked at him slowly, with a strange, sad smile on her face. She shook her head. "No. If only he had done. Your father sat down at this back table with Ben and Gwen and the three of them got drunk. I know your father would say the most dreadful things and then regret it. All he could do was say, 'Let's have a drink and forget all about it'. Your father was a charmer and Ben was like his father. Ben was a Pepper. Such a meek boy. Daft, you see. Easily led. Ben and Hudge like their father."

"What did you do when they sat down and got drunk?"

"I went and told Jack Oddy. If I'd stayed in the house then maybe I could have stopped Ben getting on his bike that night. He turned out of Peterson. I was in the caf. I turned round. I heard the screech, I saw him stretched out in front of the Lees. I didn't think at first it was Ben ...Seeing you and Jean in the same room brought that all back to me. It's maybe why I slapped you. I was slapping your father really." She cupped her chins in her hands.

"It was why you and Jack were on one side of the road and Dad and Mrs Oddy were on the other."

"The pair of them left. They'd got him drunk. They pissed off to Hartlepool. Forgive my language, Des but you use worse and you shouldn't. Jack said never to come back again, if she wanted her share of the caf. Don't darken my doorstep, Gwen Oddy. Jack told Jean her mother was dead and I said your father joined the French Foreign Legion which was easier. I agreed to say I'd been to the hospital. Seen Gwen dead. I wanted her dead, believe you me. She'd got my boy drunk and he was in the mortuary. But I lied. I lied for Jack. That's why he gave Hudge the job in the caf."

Des almost smiled again to himself. Jean thought she had used her influence with her father. Jean had never had any influence. "Poor Jean," he said.

"I know. I feel that was my biggest sin. To lie to the girl. I've felt guilty about that, but I've also felt guilty because I could never forgive her mother. Not that her mother pissed off to Hartlepool, forgive my language once again, with your father, but that they got Ben drunk. I could never forgive Gwen Oddy for spending those last sweet hours and minutes with my eldest. Whilst I was spilling it out to her husband. I hated her for that. Not that she's spending a lifetime with your father. He never was my husband. He's her husband. But that she might even have been the last person to speak to my son."

So ... his father was married to Jean's mother.

"Sounds messy, Mum. When did Jack tell Jean the truth about her mother?"

"Last Tuesday."

Des sighed with relief. Was this what Jean had wanted to tell him then? Oh, thank you kind, kind God.

"He's exchanged contracts on the caf and Gwen will get her share. I don't think he was going to keep it from her forever. I feel awful about the lie I have told that girl. How can she ever forgive me?"

He had been terrified that Jean was pregnant. But this was obviously something she had wanted to share with him. He had been in a dreadful mood the whole week. Jean said she 'needed the right moment' to tell him. He had been foul to Lily that Tuesday night, quarrelled with her, worried on the Wednesday when he met her at the rec. Jean had wanted to see him 'for the usual' in the shed that afternoon but he'd had to go to Nestles for his interview. Then he had been relieved this evening when she had only talked about Hudge 'getting stick'.

His mother was reaching down into her bag for a hanky and it was after this that the tablets of stone got shattered. After she said again about the baking of pies. After she said once again like a mantra, "You like your pies, don't you, Des?" it all changed.

As Des stares down at the polished shoes you can see your face in, he wishes he could return to that unknowing moment before it all changed. After that feeling of huge relief, that maybe, just maybe, Jean Oddy wasn't pregnant, came something much worse. That's what happens in life. When you think something is bad and it turns out okay, what you weren't seeing pops up like the rusty, coiled spring of Jack in his rancid box. He almost wishes he did not ask the next question. But he did.

"Are you all right, Mum?"

"I'm not well."

His mother didn't say this when she had a cold. It was a euphemism which was applied to anyone who was 'very sick indeed' as Doctor Crouch used to say. Not that his mother had ever visited doctors. She had only ever believed in calling the doctor out for sons with high temperatures. Personally, she saw no need. Whenever anyone died and he asked, "What of?" his mother would say, "He wasn't well." And Des would say, "Well, we knew he wasn't well. He wasn't bloody well, he's dead." Des knew too well that the three words were a euphemism but all the same, he said, "What do you mean, you're 'not well'?"

"I've been to see Doctor Crouch."

This was serious.

She went on, "It's why I've organised my organs for the university, Des. I'm not well."

He sat there in the bright light of the unshaded light bulb and looked into his mother's crumpled face. She was years younger than Mrs Brambles but tonight she looked like the air had been sucked dry out of her. From that moment, things changed. Life in the light of the unshaded light bulb became suddenly red raw and uncertain. Fragile.

"What shall I do?" he said simply.

"About Lily?" she asked.

"About Hudge."

Des wasn't expecting any practical advice from his mother. He knew her better than that. Filling in the form to the university about her organs had been a major mission Des had thought his mother was only filling in forms to make a strong statement about his inability to get to university himself.

Instead of practical advice, she placed a hand on her Bible at his side. "The minister said today, 'A friend loveth at all times and a brother is born for adversity'. Proverbs 17. I asked him to read it."

"What does it mean?"

"I never really knew why my sister stopped speaking to me. It happens in life."

Des knew that his mother never answered questions directly. She had always insisted that Hudge answered questions, but she answered them in her own fashion, in her own time and for her own reasons.

"You've said something, you've done something and things get broken. Don't let them get broken." She said this as she stared at one of the dishes he had smashed earlier. "The longer the silence goes on, the harder it is to mend. People get embarrassed."

They sat, unashamedly, in a different kind of silence of their own, amongst the chaos of their lives: the smashed plates, the smear of blackberry juice, the unwashed cups, the empty colanders and Hudge's steam engine silently steamrollering through.

"It'll be fine with Lil. Lil'll be fine."

"Too late for me and my sister Belle. She's gone now and you boys are the only ones in the world I have left," she sighed. "You boys must look after one another. The house is yours, Des." Then she looked up across the table at him. "Children are a blessing, Des however they come. But take care. Women like the Oddys can get you pregnant. They lie with you and lie to you."

The last train on the quarter before midnight sped by. He reached for his leather jacket.

"Where are you going?" she asked.

"I need to see a man about a dog."

"But it's almost midnight."

He went to see Jean.

"What did Des Hodge want?" Stevens-Sinclair says.

Jean Oddy shrugs her shoulders, touches her diamante brooch and gives a small smile. "Me."

When he left his mother just before midnight on the Blackberry Sunday, with the intention of telling Jean what he hadn't been able to tell her earlier in evening in his bedroom, because Jean had side tracked him, talking of Lily 'encouraging' Hudge - he saw Geoff Mabs across the street, on the doorstep of the caf.

But then Jean had answered the door and Des had much bigger business on his mind. It was just that seeing Geoff Mabs across the street later turned out to be rancid Jack-In-The-Box. The court kept bringing it up. The fact that Des had left the house at midnight on that Sunday night. If he maybe hadn't been to see the man about the dog ...

Jean wanted to take him into the back scullery. Through to the shed. "No. Not that, Jean."

He stood and looked at the juke box, thought about how one operated in life if you couldn't read a title of a track, turned his back to the juke box and looked Jean Oddy straight into her desperate brown eyes.

"Mum's told me everything," he said.

"Did she tell you about the baby?"

"The baby?" Des's back froze against the juke box. He knew his true nature only too well. He would have to support any child of his. It's just the way he was. Would probably have given himself a life sentence with Jean. But then she said something which gave him a second chance.

"He couldn't have been in a fight with Geoff Mabs," she said earnestly, standing in the witness box. The brooch was a butterfly. "He was with me. He hadn't been in a fight. I could have told that, if he'd been in a fight. And he stayed with me a long time." She even looked up towards him as if to say, I'm fighting for you, Des.

"Yes," the judge leans forward, beneath his Sword of Justice and says, "If you could confine yourself to just answering the questions, Miss Oddy."

"But I needed to tell you this." Jean Oddy says.

"But you must abide by the rules because that is all we have," the judge says, picking up his pen and writing very important words to indicate that his dialogue with the witness has finished.

Mr Stevens-Sinclair places his hands in his dark pockets and says, "Just a few more questions, Miss Oddy."

"What baby?" Des asked again, his back to the juke box.

"We've both got a little brother," she said.

Relief came quickly, right down the back of his spine, up against the top twenty as he leaned on the juke box.

"Joseph Hodge. 'S'nice name, isn't it? Does that stop us getting married?"

"It was wrong of your dad and my mum to lie about your mother."

"We're moving."

Things were getting better. "I could come and see you," he said.

"We're going to Dad's family in Plymouth."

Better still. "Well, that's not a million miles away."

"What about us getting married? I could come and live in Peterson Road."

The idea was absurd. Des needed to think quickly. "Where would Hudge sleep?"

"Hudge, Hudge, Hudge," she said quietly.

Des didn't know what to say, so he turned his back on her, pulled out a coin from his leather jacket and hit number four on the disc listings. It had been a long day. It was gone midnight. His mother 'wasn't well'. His father was living in Hartlepool with Jean Oddy's mother. He had a half brother who had nothing to do with Hudge or Ben but a half brother in the way they were half brothers. He didn't need any more half brothers. But Jean wasn't pregnant. As Connie Francis's Lipstick on your Collar ... 'told a tale on you' filled the tiny caf, he felt Jean's arms around his waist, her head upon his back.

"How did you feel when your dad told you she was alive?" He said the words softly but to the juke box. Lazarus from the dead, he thought. It was the way he was feeling now, in more ways than one.

"When my mother died ... when they *said* my mother died ..." he could feel her lips move on his back - he would have lipstick marks on the back of his leather jacket, "you were so tender with me." He turned round and looked down on her. She looked up and said, "There was no-one else for me and I was eleven. I loved you then, Des Hodge and I love you now." Her eyes filled with tears but he couldn't help thinking that Jean enjoyed her dramas. And he couldn't help thinking about Lily either.

"Jean, we can't get married if our parents are married. It makes us step-related," he said suddenly. He wasn't sure if this was true but he thought it was worth a shot.

"I'll live with you, Des. It's what your mum did with your dad."

"But what about Hudge? You don't like him."

"I do like Hudge. I've been looking after him since he's worked here."

"He doesn't like you."

"He does."

"We'd have Hudge with us for the rest of our lives."

"Your mum can have him."

"He's my responsibility."

"He's your mother's responsibility."

"She won't always be there," he shouted. He felt trapped by the juke box and Connie Francis at his back, Jean's hands on his arms. He felt trapped by his mother 'not being well' and he felt trapped by Hudge.

"Put him in a home where he belongs," she shouted back.

Des went to hit her. Stopped himself. Needed to cool down. Jean fell on her knees and put her arms around his denimed legs. She was sobbing now. "Let's go into the shed, Des, please. Let me come and live with you in your house. Please let me come and live with you, Des. I don't want to go and live in Plymouth. I want to live in your house, Des. Come into the shed, Des, come into the shed." She reached up for his hand and was pulling him towards the counter.

He pushed her away as gently as he could.

"And on the night in question, on the Wednesday, tell us in your own words, what happened."

Des had a nasty feeling that this was coming round to the prosecution's real point.

"Well, Mabs was getting nasty with Hudge. I thought it best to take Mabs out into the yard for some fresh air, so he could cool down a bit." At times, Jean's focus flitted from Stevens-Sinclair to jury to judge to her fingernails. She was beginning to look more confident, at ease with her role, for the first time in her life playing to her mother in the public gallery. And her father. For there they were, in the front row of the public gallery: Jack Oddy, Gwen Hodge and his father. This was Jean Oddy's moment.

"Why did Geoff Mabs need to cool down?"

"He'd lost his camera. He was angry. I thought he might do Hudge some harm, so I took him out of the back of the scullery and into the yard."

"What happened when you went in to the yard?"

"Mabs got really nasty. He wanted to try it on with me but I wasn't having any of it. I said, 'Go away. You're being very childish." Jean looks almost demure in that understated deep blue and sparkling brooch. She'd probably said 'Fuck off, you prick."

"And then?"

"Then the next thing I heard was someone shouting and Mabs let go of me and I just rushed out of my yard and into Alpha Road."

"Someone was coming from where?"

What was Jean likely to say?

"From the caf back door."

"Do you know who this was?"

Jean shakes her head. "No. I couldn't see anything."

Relief came again like a slow shower.

"Male or female?"

"A male voice."

"Shouting what?"

Des fixes upon Jean. If she did hear Hudge, this could change everything. He has counted on her not hearing anything. How could she have heard nothing?

Jean stops still. She places a hand upon the sparkling brooch on her lapel. She shakes her head again. "I don't know."

She is a witness for the prosecution. Of course she heard and saw nothing. Des thinks he is relieved, but he is not absolutely sure.

"And where did you go when you rushed out into Alpha Road?"

"I rushed up to Carlisle Street and into Pennington. I didn't want to go back into the caf the front way, I was too afraid."

"Where did you go?"

"I went down Pennington and into Peterson Road ... to get Des."

She went to my house?

"And was he at his house?"

"No. His mother said he had gone to fetch Hudge from the caf. She said he had packed in his job at the chocolate factory. Then I went to the Lees' grocery shop - to see if Lily was there."

He saw his mother only once after the stabbing. She came to see him in prison the following week. Wednesday afternoon. She had to wait until Gordon could bring her in his black Ford Anglia which he only ever really used for trips to the wholesalers, those strange clock money collections and the odd trip to Brighton on a Sunday. His mother's next trip was in the ambulance on Doctor Crouch's insistence. She hated hospitals.

But she hated prisons more. She seemed sapped of energy: a lifeless plant, yellowed and curled at the edges. He looked into her eyes and saw something he had seen years before. When Ben had been killed. That indelible sadness as Lil always said. Sadness and defeat. They looked at one another.

"What were you doing?" she had simply said.

"Looking after Hudge."

"And what will happen to him if you spend years inside?"

"I'm not going to go down. It was self defence. I promise you, Mum, I won't go down."

"What were you doing? They're trying you for murder, son. Which commandment is that?"

Number six. The devil's number.

"It's the sixth commandment," she went on. "It's the worst sin of the bloody lot."

It was noisy. Inmates were talking loudly. Des wanted to return to his back room in Peterson Road, to talk to her in the stillness of their home. It would never happen again. He knew there would never be a quiet time with his mother again and he felt angry in the noise.

She asked if he had been angry with Geoff Mabs because he was 'doing things' with Jean in the shed. Des was surprised. "I don't care about that. He was crowding Hudge. I was protecting Hudge." He knew this wasn't the truth, but what could he say?

"But Jean's telling everyone that she was your girlfriend. And that's not true, is it, son?"

"When I left you that Sunday night ..."

She looked at him, not understanding.

"The night of the blackberries," he went on.

She nodded.

"I went to finish with her properly. I went to the caf. She told me Dad and her mum had a little boy."

She nodded again and said, "That's not important now, son. Jean came round the night this all happened. She was looking for you. I asked for her forgiveness for the truth I kept back about her mother all those years. I said I was sorry. I feel sorry that I wanted the woman dead, in truth. I'm not sure Jean Oddy took it in at all. Her mind was obviously elsewhere. That I can work out now. But I asked her all the same. She rushed back off Peterson and then they said you'd gone in the police wagon. But son, how are you ever going to forgive yourself for taking that boy's life?" She looked into his eyes. "What happened, son? You couldn't have done it."

How could he tell her the truth? He had to protect his brother. "It was self defence. Lily will tell them." It was all he could say. It was all he could hang on to. "You don't go down for self defence. It's a complete defence." He had heard his solicitor say this or Gordon had said it but he had also heard his solicitor say that stabbing an unarmed victim thirteen times didn't look like altogether reasonable self defence.

"They're saying you could get a life sentence."

"You mean Cecilia bloody Lee is saying it."

"Watch your language."

He dropped his head. As if language mattered now. They didn't speak for moments. Visiting time was coming to an end.

"Oh, Des. Thank God they did away with hanging two years ago." Then just as she was getting up to go, she hesitated and then whispered, "I can't conspire, Des, but always remember, the Bible will reveal all. The Alpha and the Omega."

That was the last thing she ever said to him. It was pathetic, he knew. It was truly pathetic and all he could do was to watch her across the visitors' table. How could he burden her with the truth? Sometimes it's kinder not to. When she left, she never said anything about looking after Hudge, she just stretched out her hand across the table and pulled his head towards her. She had kissed his forehead, got up, turned away and didn't look back.

Then it was the hospital. She would have preferred Des to fetch her a drop of water and see angels at the foot of the bed in her own home.

But he hadn't been there for her; had been denied bail. People wouldn't let them be at home.

"And was Lily Lee at home, Miss Oddy? When you saw Mrs Hodge and rushed off back up Peterson to the Lee's grocery shop, was Lily Lee at home?"

Des is brought back to the moment.

"No. She came in a few minutes after that. That's when she said Geoff Mabs had been stabbed."

"Did she say anything about a fight between Geoff Mabs and Des Hodge?"

"No."

"Did she say anything about Des Hodge needing to defend himself?"

"No."

Mr Stevens-Sinclair folds his arms and strokes his nose and once again the court goes very quiet. Lily Lee has said nothing about Des needing to defend himself immediately after the murder ... with his own knife. Des feels the present and for the first time, the future, slipping away from him.

"And who would you consider to be Des Hodge's girlfriend, Miss Oddy? You or Miss Lee?"

Des knows this is a very important question. Des has watched Mr SS QCfor the past few weeks of this long trial. And it is a trial; arduous. Des remembers back to the night of Wednesday 26th August when their lives changed. When he saw Hudge shouting, "She's my girlfriend, she's my girlfriend." What is Mr Poker Player Eyes up to? Would Jean tell the truth or would she say what she wants to be the truth?

But Jean looks straight up to the defendant dock and for the first time in this trial, someone looks him straight in the eye and Jean says clearly in one line, "Lily Lee was Des Hodge's girlfriend." And then she added, "I wasn't anybody's girlfriend, even if they thought I was."

"Thank you, Miss Oddy, I have no further questions."

As Mr Williams rises, Des thinks what an odd statement of Jean's this is. He thinks about Hudge's cries, *"She's my girlfriend, she's my girlfriend*'.

"You didn't think it was Des Hodge who ran out of the caf door to intervene between you and Geoff Mabs then?" Williams asks.

Who was Hudge's girlfriend?

"I didn't know who it was. I was in shock."

Why has Des always presumed that Hudge had meant Lily? Des thinks back to the talk he has had with Hudge the previous summer: the Monday night when Des asked Hudge to get him his bottle opener from his tool box. Which was on his Swiss Army knife. Des had asked Hudge if Lily was his girlfriend. "No," Hudge had said vehemently. Who then? Hudge wouldn't say. Des had forgotten it. But Jean had been in the yard with Geoff Mabs.

"Yes, but running out of your yard and up Alpha Road, through Carlisle Street and then down Pennington and to the Hodges' house in Peterson Road must have taken what - four minutes, at least."

If Jean had known it was Hudge who had entered from the scullery into the yard, why was she protecting him? It wasn't making sense.

"I don't know. I've never timed it."

"Didn't you think during all these minutes you were rushing down to Peterson Road that if Des Hodge had been rushing through the caf door that this might have literally been a pointless exercise?"

Oh, that was a good point, Mr Williams.

Stevens-Sinclair is on his feet. "My Lord. The witness has already said that she didn't know who the intruder was."

"Move on, Mr Williams," Boney Judge says.

"You didn't hear what the words were which were being shouted from the - let us call him - for convenience' sake - the intruder?"

"No, I was in shock."

Des has a strong sense that Jean had heard but does not know why she doesn't say. Des knows the timbre of his voice is similar to Hudge's, but Jean would have known the difference by the tone of their voices.

"Do you consider Des Hodge capable of murder for the love of you?"

But before Mr SS QC can get to his feet to object, she looks at the court and jury and then to the judge. "No. No, I don't."

"I have no further questions, my Lord."

When he told her it was over, she cried like he'd never seen a woman cry before. He'd never seen Lily cry and never expected to see hard-nutted Jean break down in this humiliating way. She told him then that she loved him, went down on her knees and asked him to stay with her.

"But I never was in love with you."

"You were mine. My boyfriend."

"I never pretended to be your boyfriend."

"I am your girlfriend." This seemed very important to Jean and Des realised there and then that these tears really had nothing to do with him. It came from a grasping insecurity, a grasping need to just be loved and sitting in the dock now, he wished he had showed more compassion and less arrogance.

Because then he said with Jean on her knees at his feet, "Lily's my girlfriend."

And Jean said, rising, "I'll get you for this, Des Hodge. I'll get you where it really hurts."

It was the last time he saw her, until now. For the life of him, he couldn't think what she could do or take away from him that would really hurt.

"If you got into a fight with the deceased on the Sunday, boyo, get straight with me now." Williams has removed his hairpiece, but his baldness is no surprise. They have met several times before the case came to court when Williams was wigless. They are down in the cellar at the Old Bailey and Des is noticing moisture on his barrister's red and bristled moustache. His barrister is trying to get Des serious, to get him to understand the seriousness of this situation but Des concentrates on the perspiration above the upper lip.

"I'm telling you the truth. I was with Jean just before midnight on the Sunday. She testified to that."

"And before that?"

"I was with my mother."

"And she's dead."

Des wishes his mother back for more than one reason of loving her. "And Jean Oddy wasn't my girlfriend. I went round to finish with her."

"The Sunday's not looking good for you, boy. The grocer's girl running wild around the neighbourhood after seeing you. The court may have thought the little Greek boy a fool but the jury may have believed him."

Des watches the red moustache rise and fall in synchronicity with the rise and fall of Williams' Welsh accent. Des can't always concentrate on the words in hand because there are so many words. Words get thrown at his head like it was an empty tin drum, or like rain on the corrugated shed roof. There are so many different versions of the truth and try as he may, his mind needs to switch off and examine the glistening drops of residue on his barrister's tache. He is trying to work out who exactly Hudge meant when he cried *She's my girlfriend* when Williams says, "And the police have interviewed the barman at the pub."

"What are you talking about?"

"The barman. The barman who saw you take Geoff Mabs by the collar earlier on that evening. You didn't tell me about that." Williams throws some papers on to the desk and takes out a pack of cigarettes from his drawer. He lights up, breathes in the nicotine deeply. The room is windowless. Des notices the lack of sunlight during these dark days and weeks. Sunless. He longs for the sun. Even the watery sun on grey rec. days. Or he longs for the urgent rain on a shed roof spelling out that all is well. He longs for a cigarette.

Williams notes this and offers him the pack of cigarettes. Des takes one, lights up, sighs and thinks 'barman'. He hadn't thought it was that important. In truth, he had felt ashamed about his behaviour in the pub that night. "Mabs took *me* by the collar because I worked out he couldn't read."

"Well, barmen have short memories." Williams smoothed a hand over his shiny scalp: a scalp you can see your face in. "And he's testifying for the prosecution this afternoon. Along with the local doctor."

"Doctor Crouch?"

"He did a house call on the Sunday night to sew up Mabs's left cheek." The barrister stares down at his papers on the desk, hand on hip, takes another draw on his cigarette.

"No-one can prove I got into a fight on that Sunday night with Geoff Mabs," Des says. "Jean says I was with her and I was."

"You're not telling me everything, are you boyo?"

They stand across the desk from each other: Williams's eyes bulging, his face puffed and his breath raspy. He is not a happy man. Des longs, in this second, for Stevens-Sinclair's calm demeanour. He has to keep his secret.

"You were told from the beginning by your solicitor to come clean with me. There's nothing I can do for you if you don't come clean. And there's something mucky about your story"

Des goes on the attack. "Why didn't you challenge Jean Oddy when she said her dad was upstairs? Jack Oddy was lying when he said Hudge wasn't being crowded by Mabs."

"I can't go in too heavy about the ribbing. It gives you too much of a motive. Why did Mabs fight with you before you stabbed him? Was it over a girl?"

"I've told my solicitor. He was jealous of my relationship with Lily Lee."

"Or did you steal that Ilford Witness?"

"No."

"The camera was found in your house." Williams sighs.

Des shook his head. "I don't know why Hudge took it. He doesn't like having his photo taken."

"The camera was an expensive piece of equipment."

"Hudge doesn't understand about money. Doesn't handle money."

"You've got to tell me everything. Don't send me into court blind. The plea you make is your choice but you have to tell me everything if I'm to get you the best sentence I can."

"I've told you time and time again, I was carrying my Swiss army knife to fix Lily's record player. I went up to her room and fixed her record player and we left together just before ten. Lily saw everything."

Williams looks him straight in the eye. "I'm worried that you're relying too much on this girl's testimony. Witnesses can be unreliable once they are on the stand."

Des stares up at the ceiling. He takes a nervous drag on the last of his cigarette. Why did these rooms have no windows? How much has he asked of Lil?

"Well, the Lee couple are testifying for the prosecution tomorrow," Williams says with an air of finality about their interview. "Let's hope they don't blow your story, Boyo."

Gordon Oddy's Story

Gordon Lee takes the stand, holds the Bible in his right hand and swears to tell the truth, the whole truth and nothing but the truth.

Gordon pushes his spectacles up to the bridge of his nose.

"Was the Hodge family, in your opinion, reliable?"

Gordon thinks for a moment and speaks formally as if he was addressing the Queen but he knows that he is addressing Mr Stevens-Sinclair. Gordon has most likely read about Mr Stevens-Sinclair in the newspapers. Mr Stevens-Sinclair is a barrister with a reputation. 'Either prosecuting or defending those who were 'disputed to have attacked the jugular vein', Mr Stevens-Sinclair has brandished as many metaphoric knives and sliced as many metaphoric veins'. Like Des, Gordon would have read this in the newspapers. Gordon would have ordered a selection of newspapers from Perry's newsagents so that he can be well-informed about this trial. He knows that Mr Stevens-Sinclair read Law at Trinity College, Cambridge after the war, and before 'coming to the Bar'. Cambridge, Gordon Lee also knows, is a million miles from the Pennington Road.

"No. Alas, no." Gordon needs no time to think. "You could never rely on the Hodges. Reliable, no." He shakes his head. "Aida, Hudge, no. And Lily always seemed to spend a good time waiting for Des to turn up last summer. Especially on Wednesdays - her afternoon off. The father, Reg, well, he had an evil temper..." Gordon feels he is rambling. Stevens-Sinclair seems to let him talk. Barristers do this. Let you just drift on until you say something you never wanted to say. Gordon looks as though he wishes he hadn't mentioned Reg. Gordon's eyes sweep up to the public gallery. Gordon knows Reg Hodge is 'in' then. That's what the inmates say when friends or relatives turn up in the public gallery. They are 'in'.

"Everyone locally has been very patient, very understanding. Ben was killed on his motor bike quite soon after he was married. Once he told me he loved to feel the wind in his ears. He loved speeding. Well, God bless his soul, he paid the price. He paid the highest price. We all pay a price for what we most desire."

This was one of Gordon's pet phrases. *We all pay a price for what we most desire.* Des has always told Lily that he considered her mother was too high a price for her father. But Des remembers having said this to Lil at the rec. *Before it all happened.* He remembers saying this when he wanted her to make up her mind about lovemaking. Lil had big problems making up her mind. Des is wondering if Lil has made up her mind about which story she will tell. Lil changes her mind. Des, for the first time is also trying to work out now if his brother's innocence is worth the price he, the defendant must pay.

"I felt after Ben's death that a lot came to rest on young Des and consequently on our Lily."

Des bites his lip, hard. Mr Stevens-Sinclair does a lot of humming in agreement, and then whips swiftly onward. "Yes, so we can safely establish that in your opinion, you did not find the Hodge family reliable," Mr Stevens-Sinclair says, stroking his long nose and then folding his arms. "And what was the relationship between the two brothers? In your opinion."

"In my opinion, "Gordon says truthfully, "They thought the world of each other and Hudge would have done anything his brother Des told him."

Stevens-Sinclair strokes the long nose, raises his eyebrows, purses his lips, looks down at all those papers on the bench before him and pauses for a long, long time before he repeats Gordon's words, "Hudge would have done anything his brother told him."

"Yes."

The stenographer continues to tap and record the dialogue between the two of them.

"Indeed. It is not in dispute that your daughter was teaching Hugh ... my Lord," Stevens-Sinclair suddenly places his hands upon the bench in front of him and looks up towards the judge, "it's probably clearer to use the boy's nickname to avoid confusion?"

Gordon looks to the skeletal judge who nods back at Stevens-Sinclair.

"Mr Lee, did your daughter succeed in teaching Hudge Hodge to cross the road?" the beady-eyed barrister says.

"Is this really relevant?" asks the judge.

"If I could just be permitted some flexibility with my line of questioning, my Lord, I intend to show how Hudge Hodge's ability or inability to cross the road is hightly relevant," the prosecution states.

Gordon Lee goes on. "Ah, no. You could never teach Hudge to cross the road. But our Lily has always believed in miracles. She wanted to go to Teacher Training College." Gordon Lee pauses and looks up towards the Sword of Justice.

Wanted to go? Had Lil changed her mind about her future then?

Stevens-Sinclair looks disinterested. The judge opens his eyes wide as if trying to keep awake but Des sees Gordon looking suddenly visibly disturbed at the mention of Hudge crossing the road. Had Gordon overheard something at the funeral?

The prosecution continues. "During the week leading up to the stabbing, was your daughter also responsible for collecting Hudge Hodge after he had finished his hours working at the caf?"

"Yes. My wife never liked our Lily having to enter the caf when the Teddy boys were emptying out, but Lily insisted."

"What time would this be?"

Des realises now perhaps where Stevens-Sinclair was leading Gordon. Stevens-Sinclair was a clever man. "About ten. When I am on early turn at the station, I always make the supper and watch the News on the television at that time and Lily, who always sets her time by the city trains would leave when the two minutes to ten shot through." Gordon looks quickly at the jury. The fat man yawns. Gordon then says, "You can hear the trains go by from our flat. The local station's not far away and the trains run through at the top of Carlisle."

"And what route did your daughter take to get to the caf?" Stevens-Sinclair's dark beady, bird-like eyes are now becoming more serious.

"If you like we can say my wife and me came to a compromise. Cecilia, my wife, she insisted that Lily go through our scullery and yard and into Alpha. This meant she could collect Hudge by the back, by the scullery from the caf and not have to pass the Teds through the caf's main door when they were leaving. My girl's a pretty poppet, if you understand my meaning, sir." Gordon looks briefly again towards the jury. The pretty dark girl with the unfortunate mole on her cheek coughs. Gordon looks back again at Stevens-Sinclair, carefully and at all times, avoiding the eyes of the defendant.

"And why did you allow your daughter to collect Hudge Hodge at this time of night?" Stevens-Sinclair's tiny black eyes narrow until they almost seem to disappear.

Gordon looks blank. Off balance. "Well, why not? Aida would never have allowed Hudge, to cross that road at night. Ben, her eldest lay stretched out at the top of Peterson. Six, no seven years ago now. Crash helmet and all. Stretched out like a scar he was. No. Aida would never allowed Hudge, as I say, to cross the road on his own."

"Slow down, please. Slow down," the judge says.

Mr SS QC asks Gordon to watch Boney Judge's pen as he is writing so that he does not speak too quickly and Gordon apologises and repeats very slowly indeed, "Aida would never have allowed Hudge to cross the road on his own. Especially at night. We didn't have the heart to tell Lily that Aida would never have allowed it even if she had succeeded. But Aida hated that road. Called it the devil's horseback. And she never allowed Des to have a motor bike. Devil's horses she called them."

"Thank you, Mr Lee," Steven-Sinclair says. "And on the night in question, did your daughter indeed go to collect Hudge Hodge at this time, at ten o'clock?" The barrister's dark eyebrows arch, his eyes now widen and penetrate. The defendant closes his.

Gordon becomes uneasy. We're off balance again. "I can't be sure."

"Why? Was she not with you when she left to collect Hudge Hodge?"

"No, she was upstairs in her bedroom."

"On her own?"

"No, she was with Des Hodge."

"And did she leave at ten o'clock with Des Hodge?"

"I ... I ... I can't be sure ..."

"Why can't you be sure, Mr Lee?"

"Because there was a set of footsteps on the stairs from the attic a little earlier …"

The defendant tightens.

Cecilia Lee's Story

When Cecilia Lee swears to tell the whole truth and nothing but the truth she looks straight up towards the defendant and even catches his eye. This was no longer a private war but a very public one.

"What did you think of Geoffrey Mabs, Mrs Lee? Did you like him?" Stevens-Sinclair asks.

"I only spoke to him on one occasion. He was polite enough."

"What did you think of Des Hodge?"

"Well, I always called him trouble on legs. And the trouble with young people is that they think they will always be young."

The defendant looks up from the floor and Cecilia cannot help but look in his direction. She then looks up to the public gallery. There is movement but this is probably her sister, Iris. Cecilia speaks, "They don't look ahead or think beyond their noses. It all goes too quickly and now this. Lord knows where it will all end."

Des listens to her words. Fort Knox. The Patron Saint of Virgins.

"I'm not sure I would ever have trusted Derek Hodge. But if you're asking me about Derek Hodge and Geoffrey Mabs, I'd say they were two sides of one bad penny. The rough and the smooth. Geoffrey Mabs was definitely from rough stock and I'm sorry that our daughter ever had anything to do with the pair of them. I think it's a tragedy what has happened and they are to blame. The pair of them in equal measure."

"Let us now think back to the lunchtime of Wednesday 26th August. Did you go out?"

"Yes, on Wednesdays I always left before lunchtime closing to catch the city train, to do some weekly shopping in town. Then I would come back to Pennington and visit my sister Rose."

Cecilia looks up to the public gallery, as if she can smell the scent and distress of her four sisters.

"Yes, on that Wednesday lunchtime, Mrs Lee, did you speak to your daughter before you left the grocery shop to go shopping?"

"Yes."

And was she with anyone?"

"Yes, she was with Jean Oddy."

"And what kind of emotional state was Jean Oddy, in. In your opinion, Mrs Lee?"

Cecilia looks up to the judge and gives a small smile. "Well, in my opinion," she says, pausing effectively here, "I would say Jean Oddy was very upset indeed. She'd been crying."

"Did she say why she had been crying?"

"Yes. She said she had told Des Hodge that she had been seeing someone else and that he was going to sort this other chap out."

"Why should Des Hodge feel that way?"

"Well, presumably because Jean Oddy was his girlfriend. Des Hodge had been cheating on our Lily and our Lily thought she was his girlfriend. Now you tell me," she says.

"Well, let's put it this way, Mrs Lee. Could *you* tell *me* and tell the court, Mrs Lee who, in your opinion, was Des Hodge's girlfriend?" Stevens-Sinclair says.

"Does it really matter?" Cecilia says.

The judge peers down over his spectacles and over the big book in front of him. "Mrs Lee, when the barrister asks you a question you can take it that your valued judgement matters quite a bit indeed."

"I think he played one off against the other, like young boys do."

"And on the Sunday before the stabbing took place, with whom did your daughter spend the day?"

"She spent it with Geoff Mabs but then she went to help Aida Hodge bake blackberry and apple pies. She does this every year. That was the arrangement as far as I know and my daughter would never tell a lie."

"And what time did your daughter return home on the Sunday evening?" the barrister asks Cecilia Lee.

"I'd say it was about eight o'clock because it was well before *Sunday Night at the London Palladium*."

"And who did she say she had just been with?"

"With Des Hodge at their home in Peterson Road."

"And how did she seem?"

"Well, she was very upset. Very upset indeed. And in a dreadful mess."

"And on the night in question, on Wednesday 26th August, Mrs Lee, when your daughter was going ostensibly to collect Hudge Hodge from the cafe after work, at what time did she leave the flat above your shop?" Stevens-Sinclair was speaking still.

"Sensibly just after ten. The News had already started. We were in our front room."

"And was she with you?"

"No. She was in her bedroom."

"And when she left, was she on her own?"

Cecilia stops. Cecilia places her head on one side. Des realises that the witnesses for the prosecution have become more serious as the trial has progressed: a joker, an old man with a heart condition, a tart with a heart for the defendant, Gordon and now this ... He knows it's the 'batting order'. Place your most powerful witnesses at the end of the line.

"Well, of course. She left from her bedroom."

"Was she with anybody?"

"Look. I know my husband says she was with Des Hodge but my husband is mistaken. I always check my daughter's bedroom as I had done that evening and she was alone."

The courtroom leans back. The courtroom mutters.

"She had no one in her bedroom?"

"No, she did not."

"You are quite certain there was no-one in her room."

"Quite certain."

"So that means Des Hodge must have left your flat before you checked the room. At what time did you check your daughter's room?"

"I checked about nine thirty."

"So that means that Des Hodge could have left by the front door of your shop if it had not been locked?"

"Well, I suppose so, yes. Our daughter wasn't going to entertain him for any amount of time knowing what had happened between them, now would she? And certainly not in her bedroom."

Stevens-Sinclair goes to sit down when he says, as if he has just recalled, "Just one more question, Mrs Lee. Did you hear the records being played from the attic?"

"Yes. All the time my daughter was in her room." Then she raises her eyebrows to the courtroom roof. "Buddy Holly's 'No True Love Ways'".

That at least was the truth and Des feels the prosecuting barrister smiles. "Thank you, no further questions."

It's going to be your word, Lil, against your mother's.

Mr Williams stands. "And you wouldn't have liked to have seen a boy in your daughter's bedroom, would you, Mrs Lee?"

"No, I would not. We have principles in our house."

A crowded house living with all those principles. *You've told that joke once too often.* Des has always felt that Cecilia's principles were losing him his life but never so seriously as at this moment.

"And your daughter knows that?"

"Yes, she does."

"Is there space in her L shaped attic bedroom to hide someone?"

"Well, there is space but ..."

"And did you tread quietly on the stairwell, as you went up to the attic, Mrs Lee? I mean, just in case someone heard you and tried to dupe you and hide before you entered the room?"

"Well, we need to be on the lookout."

"Quite. But on the way down, your footfalls might have been heavier?"

"Possibly."

"And you went into the front room immediately."

"Oh really, I really can't remember. I may have gone into the kitchen for some cheese on toast."

"So when your husband says he heard someone coming down the stairs from the attic bedroom earlier in the evening, this could have been, in fact, you?"

"Well, yes I think it certainly was me. I don't believe Des Hodge was ever *in* my daughter's bedroom." Cecilia, placing an emphasis quite emphatically on the word 'in'.

"But your daughter wouldn't have taken a boy to her attic bedroom with the intention of having sexual intercourse?" the barrister asks.

Cecilia Lee flinches at the phrase. "You must be joking." She gives a nervous laugh. "My daughter Lily wouldn't do anything like that."

****

"But you *saw* Des in Lily's bedroom on the night of the stabbing, Cecilia. How could you stand in the witness box and tell a lie?" Gordon whispers and stirs his tea in the coffee bar across from the law courts.

"Oh, Gordon, it was a small lie to protect our daughter," she whispers back for even wife and husband should not be discussing court dialogue. "Poached eggs for us both and toast," she says out loud to the approaching waitress, who turns sullenly on her heel, and then in sote voce again, "and I will protect her reputation. She's our daughter. Imagine what people would say if it got out that he had been in her bedroom."

"What does that really matter?" Gordon asks her placing his head to one side.

"Exactly," Cecilia says, stirring her tea and taking a sip. "What does a small harmless fib really matter?"

"No," Gordon says. "I mean what does it really matter whether Des Hodge was in her bedroom or not."

"It doesn't matter," she whispers back.

"It matters indeed that we tell the truth."

"How on earth can you say that? How on earth can you make a statement like that? We must tell the truth. We must tell the truth. Why? Why?" Cecilia is finding it hard to whisper. "How can you say it doesn't matter that the country, the whole country knows that our daughter had a boy in her bedroom? We will be an embarrassment before the nation. At least my sister Iris's affair, or whatever you want to call it, was a private one. But this? What ever happened to truth according to us? To protect us? Good Lord, it's as though all that has returned to haunt me."

They both lean back from the table as poached eggs land in front of them. Cecilia slices the poached egg with her knife and the yolk spills out on to the white dinner plate. Her right knife hand is shaking. So is her voice. “Where’s the toast?”

“I did hear a set of footsteps coming down the attic stairs,” Gordon whispers on, “and I’ve told the court that. But that was you, Cecilia, wasn’t it? You went up quietly so Des and Lily wouldn’t hear you and you came down normally. Good God, Cecilia we could hear the pair of them having one of their arguments upstairs. Des never left that bedroom without Lily. They were there together until after ten o’clock on that Wednesday night. I feel dreadful.”

“Ah, the toast is coming.” She glances above Gordon’s head. But the plates are for another customer.

“And how can you expect Lily to say he left earlier when he didn’t?”

“Lily will say as she is told.” She cuts again into the poached egg, her right hand slips and the yolk goes shooting across the cafe table. Her lips tremble. She stares down at the mess of egg.

Gordon reaches out across the table, takes her ringed left hand in his, moves her wedding rings around her finger. “What is this all about, Cis?” he says softly.

“Oh, Gordon.” Cecilia is crumpled, can no longer sustain her whisper. “There’s something not quite right about all this and I’m frightened. I feel she’s holding something back and ...”

“Well, if she’s doing that she could have a criminal record for perverting the course of justice. For telling lies,” he says.

“Thank you, Gordon,” she says, releasing her shaking hand from his and reaching into her Mackintosh pocket. “That’s going to really help me when I go in the witness box again this afternoon.”

Gordon looks about the cafe to see if anyone is listening. They have been told not to discuss the case in public, but everyone used this café just around the corner from the courts. Certainly he and Cecilia as witnesses should not be discussing the evidence but who could stop them?

“What would our little fib matter in the bigger picture?” she says. “No-one will find out and I’m so worried for her.” She wipes her wet cheeks but the tears keep coming. Gordon keeps looking around the cafe, sees the waitress leaning on the till watching them. He fixes eye contact with her and she looks away.

"I'm so worried for her. For our baby." Her words were indistinct now. "I mean what about French and Teacher Training College? Gordon, there's more to life than baked beans and babies." She shakes her head at the egg mess, "Oh, please don't go back on the stand and say anything different. I'm trying to protect her, Gordon. I've spent my life trying to protect her. She's so precious."

"I know, I know," he says, taking her now hankeyed hand.

"What would that second baby have become, Gordon?"

"Cis, shush."

"Where would she be? She would be fifteen now."

"Cis, shush."

"I should never have listened to Iris," Cecilia said. "I know she meant it for our best but I've always blamed myself. We could have managed, Gordon. I know it was the war and we were hardly surviving but ... every time that baby's anniversary comes round and then to have all this happen at the same time of year ..."

"Now, now, Cis, leave it alone. Shush." By now the poached eggs had been neglected.

"You've never told Lily about how we ... how we ... what we did ... how she might have had a sister if we hadn't... have you, Gordon? You've not told her?"

Gordon shakes his head.

"And you promise you never will?" she says.

This time Gordon nods his head but changes the subject. "What about this fresh evidence you're thinking of giving?" Gordon whispers again. "I mean overhearing Bessie Fenchurch's idle tittle tattle is hardly cause to go rushing to the police." He is pleased to be changing the subject. "It's 'hearsay' and that won't be accepted as evidence in court."

"Whether I saw Des Hodge in Lily's bedroom, it doesn't matter, Gordon, but I did hear what Bessie Fenchurch said to Lily at the funeral and Lily is prepared to inform the police. It will help her."

"Lily won't inform the police of hearsay, Cecilia." He uses her full name. He is obviously cross. "Good Lord, Bessie Fenchurch is a seasoned gossip. Everyone knows that."

"Oh, Gordon give me strength for my cross examination this afternoon. Des Hodge is part of the past, dead and buried and Lily has to face that fact. And if he isn't already finished now, he will be by the time I let Stevens-Sinclair know just what I heard Bessie Fenchurch tell Lily."

****

"Buddy Holly was playing perfectly well according to the Lee couple." But Williams looked calmer all the same. They were back to the windowless room.

"No True Love Ways."

"What?"

"I'd fixed it immediately. I left the attic with Lily just after ten."

"Well, at least the grocer seems to agree with you." Williams sighs. "But that bloody grocer's wife ..."

"I saw Mabs fighting Hudge in the Oddy's yard because he was bullying him so it's important to cross examine the witnesses for the prosecution about the ribbing in the caf ..." Des says.

"Don't tell me how to do my job. They all deny any ribbing of your brother. Even the boy with the flick knife. What was your brother doing in the yard?" Williams is getting angry now, bulging eyes stare back at him.

"Putting out rubbish at the end of the night when he disturbed Mabs annoying Jean. Then when I arrived Mabs attacked me, shouting 'She's my girlfriend, she's my girlfriend,' meaning Lily. In the struggle, my knife fell out of my leather jacket and Mabs picked it up. I got it off of him and my only defence was to stab him." Des has written this, said this so many times, he knows the speech by heart, almost believes now for it to be true. He pulls deeply on the cigarette. Enjoy this cigarette, he thinks, it's currency.

Williams takes a deep breath and then looks Des straight in the eye. "I don't want to go too hard in on Mabs bullying your brother. It gives you far too strong a motive for murder. Sinclair-Stevens is trying to prove it is a motive to kill whilst referring to a bit of harmless fun or teasing. He's a clever man."

God, his barrister can't even get his learned and very clever colleague's name right. How did he expect to retain all these details?

"Hudge was bullied and I didn't know about it until Lily told me that night. I went to protect my brother in adversity, that's all."

"Big words. Truth doesn't matter. It's what gets inferred, suggested. I'm going to bring in some character witnesses: the Fenchurches, the Brambles woman, then the Lee girl but lastly your brother. They are the prime witnesses for self defence. But first I've got to prove Mabs had it in for you. That he was psychologically unbalanced. That's what our first few witnesses will testify. Right now we have the last of the witnesses for the prosecution. And they will be our biggest chance of proving the victim was psychologically unbalanced."

"Mabs's parents?"

"It's going to be a miracle if I get you off on self defence and unlike your grocery girl, I don't believe in them. Mabs had no weapon. So far, no real motive to attack you – apart from the theft of his camera which you deny - and thirteen stab wounds don't look like reasonable defence to me."

"How can you prove he was unbalanced?"

"The photos."

Zelda Mabs's Story

Zelda Mabs, 'the most pitied woman in England' takes the witness stand for the prosecution and looks up, as if directed, towards the defendant with brimming accusation. She is, at first, unable to hold the Bible. The judge speaks in low, sympathetic tones, "This may be difficult, Mrs Mabs. And the court understands and feels for your plight. But if you could just repeat after the usher ..." Boney Judge's voice trails off as the stenographer – Des has learnt what this woman is called - taps every uttered syllable.

Zelda Mabs swears to tell the truth with strange sounding syllables, like Des has heard when Cecilia speaks on the telephone. "I, Margaret Mara," and Des is surprised at the name, has she not married Charlie? "swear by almighty God," she says and blows her sharp nose clear of mucus. She has bought a dead fox probably especially for this occasion.

It is wrapped around her neck, the little snout visible at her throat, the little paws poised upon her left shoulder. Zelda arrives in the witness box looking as though she might be taking part in the TV show *Double your Money* with Hughie Green. Here is fame, if not infamy, and she looks as though she is secretly rather enjoying it and that this is some compensation for losing a son.

"Of course," Zelda tells the judge and jury, the barristers, the court of, "the excitement our small family of three felt when we moved to the Pennington Road, with Mr Mabs's inheritance." At last a house, after the arduous journey of living in a home on wheels. Has Zelda looked up the word 'hard' in an old dictionary in the Exchange & Mart' and got 'arduous'? Everything about her seems hard and as acidic as the gherkins she sold him once before it all happened.

No, the name 'Hodge' had never been mentioned. Yes, she knew the trades' people, the Lees at the grocers, the Oddys at the caf. Thought Geoff was making friends ... wished now, looking back on it all, she was still living in her caravan. "After all," she continues with her spotlighted tale, "it took weeks to get him back next door to the undertakers with all the forensics over like lice. And police all over the house like bluebottles round the backyard dustbin. His suit has never been returned, you know." Was she looking for financial compensation? But Zelda is now looking towards the front bench of 'exhibits' whilst a red rattle rash appears at her neck and the dead fox's snout. And she's terrified.

The prosecution sits.

The defence rises. "Mrs Mabs, you refer to your 'small family of three'. Do you, or have you ever had, any other children?"

"No." Zelda squints her eyes at the barrister and then looks back at the table of exhibits with concern.

"But your son, on a number of occasions, is recorded to have referred to a younger sister."

Zelda sighs impatiently. "Oh, that was one of Geoff's little ways."

"Little ways?"

"I knew he gave a girl a line. That was an old line about having a little sister he adored and how they all looked like his little sister."

"He made up the line?"

"Well, you know kids. Especially boys."

"Please go on."

She sighs impatiently again. "Well, boys only ever have one thing on their mind. Geoff wasn't past telling a story to pull at the heart strings." She touches the deceased fox's little black snout at her neck.

"He told lies?"

"Fibs, I suppose."

"Fibs?"

She reaches for her hanky and blows her nose. Does she have a cold? "Well, all that story about being locked up as a kid in a caravan and fed dog meat. We had a dog and he idolised the dog in the same way as he idolised his grandfather, but he never had to eat dog meat. That was just a line for the girls. Geoff actually killed the dog." 'All angles' Zelda Mabs looks as though she's dropped something she shouldn't. "Or was it Charlie who killed the mongrel with his poaching gun?" she quickly adds. "I can hardly remember and does it really matter now?"

"So, we could say, he wasn't averse to telling the odd fib to get his way?"

"Well, he was a boy."

"Thank you. To your knowledge, did your son ever bully the elder Hudge Hodge?"

"I told you. I never heard the name 'Hodge' before this all happened. Geoff wouldn't have hurt anyone, but he didn't like dogs in general."

"On the night in question, how did your son feel about the loss of his camera?"

Zelda and her fox fur bristled. "Well, he was f …" She stopped herself. "He'd been jumpy all day about having the camera nicked." She says this aggressively, suggesting that the camera is a cause for concern. "Weren't we all when we realised how much that camera could have fetched?"

"When, to your knowledge did he lose the camera?"

"The Hodges stole it the night before."

"On the Tuesday night?"

"Well, he asked me if I'd seen it on the Wednesday morning. You know, the morning of the night he was … murdered." She took a small gulp of air. "I said I hadn't."

"And why did you think that the Hodge boys had stolen it?"

"Because he said later that day that he had seen Des Hodge with it."

"But you said that you had never heard the name 'Hodge' before your son was stabbed?"

Zelda cocks an eyebrow; touches the little snout again. "Oh, that must have slipped my mind."

"So did he say where he saw Des Hodge with the camera?"

Zelda shrugs her shoulders.

"And he told fibs?"

"Well, why was his camera found under Des Hodge's bed, then?' she says.

The judge makes her say 'yes' or 'no' to the question and so she says, 'Yes, he told fibs'.

"And your son liked taking photos?"

"Yes."

"Of girls?"

"Yes."

"And he quickly set up a dark room in your attic and developed photos?"

Zelda looks confused. "What the bloody hell are you going on about? Geoff had a dark room? A dark room? He probably had a dark room in his head, but not in my attic. How could Geoff have set up a dark room in the attic inside of a week of us moving to the chip shop?" she says.

"No," Williams said, "but that is what he told people."

At this point Williams asks an assistant to pass some photos to Zelda Mabs. The dead fox looks as though it feels hot around her collar.

"Have you seen these photos before, Mrs Mabs?"

Zelda Mabs holds the photos with red varnished nails and her hands look like the pointy paws and claws of the animal which dangle from her shoulder. In fact she and the dead fox look as though they are doing a double act. She looks down at the photos in disgust. "These photos have nothing to do with me," she says and this time she touches the paws on her left shoulder, crossing her body, as if in protection with her right arm and hand.

"If the jury could take a look at these photos ... There are blood stains across the photos but they are photos taken of a small child."

Members of the jury do not linger over the photos: they pass them on quickly. The pretty dark girl with the mole on her cheek looks down at her feet. The grey-haired woman who looks like a Scripture teacher actually places a hand to her mouth.

"A small child ... in distress," Williams goes on quietly to match the mood of the court. "Mrs Mabs, are these photos of your son?"

"Where did you get those photos?" she says.

"Did you know about them?"

"I found them in the old man's stuff when he died. I meant to destroy them."

"Did you know your son had found them?"

"He found them on the Sunday night. I told him a few home truths about Mr Mabs. Geoff would never face up to the fact that his grandfather ... Geoff idolised his grandad, but that idol wasn't true, your Lord above," she says looking up to the judge. "Old man Mabs was a snivveling, nasty piece of work," she says to him, "and he took those photos. You should burn those photos."

"My Lord, I fail to see where this line of questioning is leading." Stevens-Sinclair has risen to his feet gingerly, placing his words carefully before the judge.

"My Lord, I am trying to establish the true nature of the deceased's character and background." Williams is nonchalant, matter-of-fact.

"I'll allow you some leeway for the moment Mr Williams," Boney Judge says, "but please come to the point quickly."

"Well I don't think he should have leeway," Zelda says. "My son's been ruthlessly murdered and you don't think his nature is true?"

"Mrs Mabs," the judge says, "we are trying to discover in this court of law if your son was murdered or not. Now, the rule is that my learned colleagues ask the questions and you answer them to the best of your ability. Do you understand?"

"Yes."

"Did you or your husband take the photos?" Williams says.

"I don't know how you can ask me that question."

"It is his job, Mrs Mabs," the judge says. "You must answer it. Did you or your husband take these compromising photos of your son?"

"No. That was his grandfather." Zelda loosens the snout so that it drops down to her pimple of a bosom. "And if you ask me, leaving that fancy camera in his will to my son was some kind of joke on the old man's part."

"How do you know his grandfather took the photos?"

"Because I found them in the old man's belongings after he died."

"Your son's grandfather's belongings?"

"I've already said that."

"It is important to establish that fact. And when did your son find these photographs?" Williams says.

"On the Sunday night. When he came home."

"And did you tell him some home truths about his grandfather that night?"

"Yes, I certainly did tell him some home truths, all right."

"I am sure you did. How did he react?"

"Well, Geoff made things up. He thought his grandfather loved him and well, I suppose he did in a kind of a way. In the same way that he loved my son's father. You ask Charlie." Des notices that the strange syllables have now flattened out and Zelda sounds like she did in the chippie when she sold him the gherkins.

"Did you know your son's grandfather had taken these photos?"

"No. Never. Not until I found them in his belongings. After he died." Zelda looks frightened now. She seems to be trying to cover her tracks. "I just told him Charlie wasn't his father."

"And where was Charlie at this point?"

"In the front room with me."

"And by this time, did your son already have the cut on his face?"

"Yes."

"And was his face bleeding?"

"Yes."

"And had you, at this point, yet attended his bleeding face?"

Zelda was becoming confused. "Yes, I had but it needed stitches."

"And about what time did your son come home with his face cut, on that Sunday night, Mrs Mabs?"

"I don't know."

"Well, think back, was it late evening"

"Yes."

"Eight, nine, ten, eleven o'clock?"

"I can't remember."

"Well, try to remember, Mrs Mabs. This is very important. What time do you usually close your fish and chip shop on a Sunday evening?"

"Ten."

"And did your son come home after closing?"

"I don't know. He came in the back way."

"And where were you when your son arrived home?"

"In bed. My husband called me to come down."

Through all this interrogation, Zelda embraces the dead animal and Des knows that she is lying, because he was able to see Geoff Mabs clearly in the light of the street lamp on that Sunday night and he will tell the court when he gives evidence, but who will believe him?

"Mrs Mabs, I suggest to you that your son was not in a fight with Des Hodge on that Sunday night. That he had not got into a fight over Des Hodge's girl. I suggest to you that your son, had, as it is reported he said, walked into his old man - Charlie Mabs. I suggest that your son was subjected to violence from both you and Charlie Mabs in his short life and that in fact it was Charlie who inflicted this wound upon him on the Sunday evening."

"Well you can make all the suggestions you like," Zelda says, "and I've been made plenty in my time, but it doesn't mean anything will come of them. My son said Des Hodge gave him the cut on the cheek and stole his camera."

"And your son told fibs as you yourself have said. But these photographs, no matter who took them, indicate that your son was a disturbed young man, who had, by some hand, unknown, been abused, humiliated and violated."

Zelda pulls her lips together tightly and narrows her eyes at Williams. Des is barely listening to him. His eyes see a sharp woman as flat as a fish slice but his mind sees the soft, dimpled curves of his mother. How lucky he and Hudge had been.

"I suggest again, Mrs Mabs, that your son mercilessly bullied Hudge Hodge and that the defendant was, in fact, acting out of self defence when they fought together on the night of Wednesday 26th August. I have no further questions, my Lord."

Zelda looks fried alive and as though she might spit chip fat. She looks sweaty under her fox fur collar. Her mood quickly reverts to smugness when Mr SS QC re-examines her saying that he is relieved that Mr Williams has no further questions as he suggested more than requested and she is able to bring a tear to her eye. She wipes her nose several more times and tells Mr Stevens-Sinclair that when she said 'home truths' she was just trying to help her son through the misery of finding these awful photos. She asks the court to burn them and she bursts into tears. Then, wiping her tears away with the fox fur, she looks up to the barrister and says, "When all this is said and done, will the Ilford Witness be returned to us?"

Des Hodge hopes the photos along with the Ilford Witness will be burnt in hell alongside her and the dead fox.

****

The Chippie – SUNDAY 23RD AUGUST 1959

Charlie was stretched out on his back, the Sunday paper in one hand and a bottle of Johnny Walker whisky in the other. Straight from the bottle, thought Geoff Mabs. Great lump of Chivers' jelly. He went to go when he noticed some photos lying on the front room floor. Either Charlie or Zelda had been half unpacking a removal crate.

"Hey," Charlie called. "Was your shift downstairs tonight."

"I did two hours last night."

Mabs picked up the photos. He sifted through them. His memory was hazy. He felt the nausea rise in his throat with a growing memory.

"Sundays. Sundays is," Charlie pointed his finger, "your night." He swigged at the scotch, half closed eyes leering up towards Mabs.

"What's these?" he said.

"Sunday's your night, boy."

Boy. Boy. Boy. 'Boy', was like red flags to bulls for Geoff. Boy. 'Boy' was knocking broomsticks on ceilings for Mabs. Boy. 'Boy' was knocking so hard that plaster cracked, ceilings fell in, the world was crashing around him. Ready for a fight was Mabs. 'Boy' was taking the lid off pressure cookers and in went Mabs, screaming and pulling Charlie to his feet by his vest and trouser braces.

"I can buy you and sell you, boy," Charlie said to Mabs, not for the first time in his life.

"No," Mabs shouted into Charlie's face and throwing him against the candy striped wallpaper. "No, you can't. You see, you little bully, when did you become a dwarf?" he said towering above Charlie. "And don't call me 'boy'. 'Boy', you bastard."

"No, no, no." Charlie laughed, swaying sideways and full of Johnny Walker. "See boy, *you're* the bastard."

There was something different about the way Charlie said it. It was the glint in Charlie's eye; as though, this time, this time, Charlie really meant it. And he went on. "You and your sacred bloody grandfather. I could tell you a thing or two about your bloody grandfather. He's no more your bloody grandfather than Noddy is, boy. He wasn't saintly, he wasn't your grandfather, 'cos I'm not your fucking father. So how could he be your grandfather? Eh? Eh? Your mother a bicycle? She could freewheel her way through capital cities let alone the village."

"Where did you get these photos? Did you take these photos? You answer me or I'll slam your head so hard against this wall, you'll never taste a drop of Walker again, do you hear me, you snivelling runt?"

"I never took those photos. Your so called grandfather did, boy. That's why he gave you the sodden camera, boy."

Zelda was standing witness at the front room door: lips pulled into a line, curlers taut against her head, winged spectacles like daggers. "What the fuck is all this about?"

Mabs picked up the photos and held them up to her like a deck of cards. "Who's this? Who's this then?"

Zelda took a quick glance. "Where were you tonight? You had a shift downstairs. I'm not making a living for three, you stupid pair of bastards."

"I told him he had a shift tonight." Charlie said pointing a shaking index finger at Mabs.

"I'm not taking this chippie on to slave for the pair of you. You can just clear out, the pair of you," Zelda said, hitting each of them on the shoulder.

"It's my father's money's paid for it. I'm not clearing out of my home. This is my home," Charlie said, raising his voice and jabbing his forefinger on Zelda's right shoulder blade. "D'you hear me?" he shouted hitting her left ear. "My home."

"Yeah - I can hear you," she screamed back at him, swiping him across the head, "and we've got mortgage to pay and I'm the one bloody well paying it."

Mabs held the photos up to his mother. "For one last time, who the fuck is this?" he yelled at her.

She smacked Geoff across the face. "You shouldn't go snooping around in other people's business. You weren't meant to see those photos. They were in your grandfather's stuff," she said.

"What?" Mabs stood staring at her.

"My grandad wouldn't have taken photos of kids like these."

"It's you, boy, it's you," Charlie said, laughing and displaying those huge discoloured teeth as he sat himself down on the sofa. "That's what your beloved grandfather got up to when he was babysitting you, boy. I know all about it, boy, don't I?"

It was then that Mabs picked Charlie up from the sofa and threw him against the wall with candy-striped paper. Charlie clutched his bottle of Johnny Walker. Down came the bottle of Johnny Walker, smash on the candy-striped wallpaper and up went Charlie's hand in defence, holding its remains.

Mabs backed off - his mouth dripping with blood, feeling quickly to see if his tongue was still in place. As he did so, the offensive photos in his right hand went to the protection of his bloody, left cheek. Charlie looked ahead, cringing small with terror.

But Zelda looked down and cried, "Oh my God," There were stains beneath them. Johnny Walker stains. "Look what you pair of bastards have done to my carpet."

****

Charlie Mabs's Story

Charlie Mabs takes the witness stand: eyes like light bulbs, big teeth discoloured from nicotine and his nasty nectar. He says he is going to tell the truth. Charlie shakes his head, strokes his chin, takes a deep breath in, as if to deliver some massive quote to an unsuspecting customer when he says that Geoff had come in about midnight and found the photos. Charlie then called his mother who was in bed. She saw to the cut on his face, they called the doctor and Zelda told her son that Charlie was not his father.

"And did a fight ensue?"

"A fight in Alpha Road, yes, with Des Hodge."

"Yes, that is what is reported your son said happened."

Charlie does not get side tracked and when Mr Stevens-Sinclair asks him, "Mr Mabs, did you at any time strike your son?" he answers, "No. I didn't." This is the truth, the absolute truth, he says.

"And did you take these photos of your son?"

"No. I didn't. We found them in my father's personal fects."

"Thank you. No more questions, my Lord."

When Charlie leaves the witness box, having never admitted during Williams' cross examination of any fight between himself and his son, he shakes his head and muttering, "Poor Geoff," Des thinks he really means it. It's what Des is thinking anyway.

"But what difference does this make to me?" Des asks Williams. Nothing was happening.

"It's what gets passed from generation to generation."

His barrister was a philosopher and a slate miner's son from Snowdownia. "So what?" Des says.

"I'm trying to prove that Geoff Mabs was sexually abused from childhood, by his grandfather or father. It's my case theory; I'm laying the groundwork for my closing speech. But I'm blocked, boy. I can't keep going in on the ragging of your brother. It gives you too much of a motive to kill. Your brother would have got off with a more lenient sentence in the light of this evidence. I wish I had been representing him. I could have shown that Stevens-Sinclair a thing or two." There is a twist of bitterness as he reaches for the pack of cigarettes.

Des goes to speak and stops himself. It is always best to stick to the story, he thinks.

"The prosecution are determined to allude to the fact that you gave Mabs that cut on the Sunday night. There's no proof. It's all allusion. I don't see that anyone will know the truth of what happened that night. But I'd lay odds it was one of those two Mabses that gave him the cut."

Des stands a few feet from his defence, smelling the stench of nicotine and he tries to remember the sweet scent of Lil, but all he seems to recall is the smell of Geoff Mabs's beery and bloody dead body.

10

Witnesses for the Defence

Teresa Dossing's Story

After Des gives his 'sticking to his story' evidence comes Teresa Dossing: little Teresa Dossing with her nice legs, now stripped of her yellow polka dotted puffed out skirt and dressed in a neat white blouse and straight black skirt. She takes the Bible in her right hand and swears to tell the truth, the whole truth and nothing but the truth.

The judge places a hand to his left ear.

"Speak up, please," Williams says.

"I live at 132, Carlisle Street, just at the top of Alpha Road in the railway cottages just off the Pennington Road," Teresa Dossing says, doing as she is told and speaking up.

"Yes, I do. My dad's a railway clerk."

"Did you frequent the Oddy's caf?"

"Sorry?"

"Did you meet friends in the Oddy's caf on the Pennington Road?"

"Yes."

"When did you first meet Geoffrey Mabs?"

"On the Wednesday before the stabbing."

"What was your first impression of him?"

Teresa screws up her face. "An odd ball." This is the first time she looks at the members of the jury. The pretty dark girl with the mole on her face watches Teresa intently, but the lean young man with the dark rimmed glasses yawns and is concerned with something foreign at the end of his nose. This has been a long trial and he is being kept from leading his normal life outside the courtroom. He'll probably return his verdict quickly.

"Can you explain in our language what 'odd ball' means?"

Teresa looks down and up at Williams. "It means strange."

"Why's that?"

"Well, first of all, no one ever wrinkles Des Hodge and Mabs did that the first night he met him."

His father is watching him now. No-one wrinkled Reg Hodge. Gwen Oddy, or rather Gwen Hodge has left the public gallery. She has obviously just made an appearance for her daughter's sake and presumably Reg must feel he has to be present whilst his son is. He wonders if Gwen Oddy, he means, Gwen Hodge, bruises easily too.

"Anything else?"

"When Jean kissed Hudge Hodge, Mabs seemed to enjoy it. I think he was an odd ball."

Williams stops. Is surprised. Takes another of his deep breaths. Des takes one too. *When Jean kissed Hudge.* But Williams skims over this. Moves on. And it's unlikely of course that Mr SS QC will pick up on it although Des sees the momentary lift of the barrister's eyebrow. *When Jean kissed Hudge.*

"Was there anything else which made you feel Geoffrey Mabs was 'an odd ball' or strange?"

Teresa looks sheepish. "Well, yeah."

"What were you doing the night of Tuesday 25th August of last year, the night before the murder?"

"I visited Geoffrey Mabs's room above the fish and chip shop. To see some of his drawings"

There was an audible snort from the gallery. Teresa glances quickly up towards the dock.

"What were the drawings of, Miss Dossing?"

"Pumpkins."

"I'm sorry, could you speak up, so that I may hear you?" The judge is speaking and frowning and putting his left hand up to his ear again.

"Pumpkins ...," she calls up towards the judge, "and windmills."

The judge is writing all this down with his left hand.

"Pumpkins and windmills," Williams repeats and Des is not sure if his barrister really knows where this is leading. "How many?"

Teresa looks up towards the court. "All over. His walls were covered all over with them. It was strange."

"Did you find anything else strange about Geoff Mabs, Miss Dossing?"

"Photos."

"Photos?"

"Yeah, he told me he developed photos in his dark room. In the attic. He was always taking photos."

"Were you at ease in Geoffrey Mabs's bedroom?"

Teresa does the same hunch of the shoulders and lift of the lips. Well, would *you* be, she seems to indicate as she says, "No."

"Why was that?"

"He was really ape about losing his camera. He said he had important photos on that film that he wanted to develop. He said Des Hodge must have nicked it. I liked Des Hodge."

Des never knew. But he wishes his defence lawyer would state again that he was doing a shift at the chocolate factory that night and couldn't have nicked the camera. Des had mentioned this when he gave evidence but would the jury remember?

"And the following night, on the night of the murder, when was the last time you saw Geoff Mabs?"

"I left early."

"Miss Dossing, did you feel that Geoff Mabs was capable of rape?"

Boney Judge is saying this is conjecture and Teresa need not answer the question.

"But I do think he was capable of rape," she goes on. "He had a screw loose. Hudge Hodge probably had one loose too, but Geoff Mabs's head was very strange."

"Miss Dossing," the judge placed his pen slowly on his paper, "you were not required to answer that question."

Teresa hunches her shoulders again.

"Mr Williams you may continue, but no more questions of conjecture please," the judge insists.

But Williams had already got what he wanted. "No more questions, my Lord."

Up Stevens-Sinclair gets, annoyed at his learned friend's underhand tactics.

"Miss Dossing. Why did you go to Geoffrey Mabs's bedroom?"

"To see his drawings he told me about."

"Did you find Geoff Mabs attractive?"

She gives a surprised, embarrassed smile. "Sort of."

"Did you fancy him?"

She frowns.

"Did you fancy him?" Stevens-Sinclair repeats.

"Is this relevant?" Williams ask.

"My Lord, if I can just be permitted this line of questioning for a moment longer?"

"I will allow you some leeway, Counsel, but get to the point quickly, Mr Stevens-Sinclair. Please answer the question, Miss Dossing."

And she answers the learned gentleman with, "Sort of."

"Well, if you go to a boy's bedroom, one might assume then that you did fancy the boy?"

"Well, he was nice looking."

"And did Geoff Mabs have intercourse with you?"

"No." Teresa looks taken aback.

"Did he try?"

"No."

"Why was that?"

"He said he was tired. He was worried about his camera. He just kept asking me who took it and I didn't know."

"And did he at any time, to your knowledge 'rib' Hudge Hodge?"

Teresa's chin shakes slightly. Her eyes do not meet the barrister's eyes. She looks away and then says, "No."

"No more questions, my Lord."

The court sits back; papers are turned; someone leaves the public gallery.

"This seems like a good place to adjourn for the weekend." The judge obviously had Friday night plans. "We will re-convene at ten o'clock on Monday morning," the judge says.

"I didn't know your brother had anything to do romantically with Jean Oddy?" Williams says when he sees Des in the cells.

"Neither did I," Des says.

11

The Old Bailey

The Fenchurches' Story

"Mr Fenchurch, are you aware that Hudge Hodge, at any time, came into your shop and asked for a gun?" Mr SS QC's question came as a bolt from the grey horizon.

Oh, God. Oh, God, no. How did the prosecution come to know this? What had he heard Bessie Fenchurch tell Lily? Had Lil revealed this in her statement? Was it true what his defence had said? "Witnesses can be unreliable when giving evidence on the stand." Lily was his only hope but how did the prosecution know this?

"No, we don't sell guns. Wouldn't have sold him one if we did. But we don't. We have no guns." Will Fenchurch has no balls.

"On the Sunday preceding the stabbing, did you encounter Lily Lee?"

"Yes, she knocked on our shop door. It must have been just gone seven o'clock in the evening. The church bells from the Nazarene had just gone off."

"How did you find Lily Lee?" Stevens-Sinclair asks.

"She was in a terrible way."

"How do you mean?"

"She looked very messy and she was very upset indeed."

"Did she say anything?"

"Yes, she said, 'It's all Des's fault.'"

"Thank you, my Lord," Stevens-Sinclair says. "No further questions."

Thank you, Will, Des thinks and wonders why Stevens-Sinclair has not pursued the line of the gun with Will.

Bessie Fenchurch has no problem repeating her oath. She tells the whole truth as she sees it. She tells Williams how Mrs Brambles has seen Hudge cross the road - on his own. About him coming into the Exchange & Mart on the Wednesday: about him asking for dirty magazines.

Des relaxes.

Stevens-Sinclair stands to cross examine. He pulls at the lapels on his gown. He pauses. Des doesn't like it when Mr SS QC pauses. Every time Mr SS QC has pauses before starts, something wicked follows. "Dirty magazines, Mrs Fenchurch? Dirty magazines? Really? Think again."

And Des looks down at his polished shoes. Oh God, no.

"Are you absolutely sure that Hudge Hodge came into your shop and asked for dirty magazines?"

"Dirty magazines, yes."

"Pornographic magazines?" Stevens-Sinclair strokes his nose and folds his arms.

"Well, you can call them whatever you want, but I told him, 'I don't sell mucky magazines. Wouldn't sell them to you if I did'."

"And what did Hudge say?"

"He told my sister they were for his brother Des."

Des sighs. What does Mr SS QC know?

"Oh, really? Well, I put to you Mrs Fenchurch that Hudge Hodge came into you to buy a gun. Is that not so?"

Oh ... shit no.

"Buy a gun? How did you know that?"

"Well, that's our job, Mrs Fenchurch. To seek out the truth. And remember you are on oath. So let's begin again, shall we? Hudge Hodge came into you to ask for what?"

Bessie twitches. Pauses. The fat juror folds his arms: the young, bored juror with the horn-rimmed glasses moves back in his seat: the girl with the mole squints seriously. "A gun," Bessie says.

Shit.

"And did Hudge Hodge say what he wanted the gun for?"

"No, I told him we don't sell guns and left him in the shop with my sister."

"Mrs Fenchurch, why would Hudge Hodge think to come to you and ask for a gun?

"To us ... for a gun? I've no idea, sir, no idea at all."

"Could it be that you and your husband did at one time, sell guns?"

Bessie twitches again. The colour of her pearls matches her bleached hair. "Well, once or twice, yes." She is almost inaudible.

"Please repeat that," the judge says leaning forward as Bessie jumps slightly and for the first time ever has a problem with the repetition. "Once or twice, yes."

"And you have a license to sell guns?" Mr SS QC asks.

"Well ..." There is a catch in Bessie's throat. Des thinks she may burst into tears at any moment. He thinks he may do.

"Did you have a license to sell guns, Mrs Fenchurch?"

"No."

"No." Stevens-Sinclair, who probably tossed a coin when choosing careers between Law and The Stage pauses once again, just here. A point has most definitely been scored. "So it could have been that Hudge Hodge had heard talk that the Exchange & Mart was the place to buy guns on the hush hush, so to speak?"

"Hush hush?" Bessie asks. "Hush hush?"

Will Fenchurch has told his wife to 'hush hush', not wanted his wife to give evidence about guns. Des has overheard this, standing outside the back room door in the cold funereal hallway.

And Des is dismayed that his defence has no further questions, has been taken by surprise. No re-examination? How did the prosecution know about Hudge asking for the gun? Bessie has not revealed this. Has Lily mentioned this in her statement? Oh, for a half hour with you, Lil. Mr SS is out to prove that Des had asked his brother to get him a gun; pre-meditated murder. How much worse can this get?

Then Bessie Fenchurch's sister, Sylvia Backman, Sylvia with the beetroot hair and matching pencilled eyebrows, takes the stand and swears to tell the truth, the whole truth and nothing but the truth. And upon his cross-examination, Stevens-Sinclair robustly puts to her that Hudge Hodge had come into buy a gun and that this is the truth, isn't it?

Sylvia with the beetroot hair says, "My sister said she didn't have any guns, don't sell guns. Then my sister went into the back to make a cup of tea and I asked the simple boy what he wanted a gun for."

"And what did he say?"

"He said he wanted one to give to his brother."

As the prosecuting barrister is thanking Sylvia Backman, Des places his head in his hands. Done for. He doesn't even hear Williams re-examination asking if Hudge had actually said his brother had told him to run the errand.

"Believing that his elder brother was incapable of crossing the road on his own, and we have heard witnesses say this over and over again, would he have asked his elder brother to cross the road and run this errand?"

"I don't know."

And Mr Williams sits down. But Des is thinking Sylvia Backman knew that her brother-in-law didn't have a licence to sell guns. Sylvia Backman probably got cross with Hudge, probably upset him to the point that he would have said, 'Des told me to get a gun'.

Tell them I did it, tell them I did it. The seeds which Des had planted with his elder and less able brother all those years ago were now growing amok. It had been easier for Des to defend himself against his father.

Sylvia Backman had probably thought that Hudge Hodge was a loose cannon when it came to the subject of guns. Sylvia Backman would have been right.

Mrs Brambles' Story

When Mrs Brambles is called to the witness stand, Des sits back in his seat and relaxes for a short while. At last, a defence witness who would really defend him. She gives the defence a good character reference. Des is even surprised when Stevens-Sinclair bothers to stand and cross-examine the greengrocer's wife.

"Mrs Brambles, your greengrocery is next to the caf and opposite the Exchange & Mart on the Pennington Road?"

"Yes."

"And on the night of the stabbing, did you see anything 'out of place' shall we say?"

"Well, I saw Hudge Hodge crossing the road on his own. I'd seen Lily trying to teach him, but as clear as I can see you now, I watched him cross the Pennington Road." Mrs Brambles wears the same flower-patterned frock and red felt hat that she did at his mother's funeral. *Red hat, no drawers* his mother used to say.

"Did you see anyone else?"

"Yes. Des Hodge. He asked me if I needed any help with the parsnip crates."

"What did Des Hodge do?"

"He looked at his watch and then ran across the Pennington Road and down Peterson. This was before I saw his brother Hudge cross the road on his own."

"And what time was this?"

"Half past six. Closing up time."

"And what time does the caf open?"

"Half past seven."

"Did you think it odd that Hudge Hodge had been dropped off at the caf before it opened?"

"Yes, yes I did."

The courtroom speaks its own quiet language with the shifting of backsides, the shuffle of papers, the habitual stroking of the prosecuting barrister's nose and hitching of his gown.

Des recalled that Wednesday evening. He had not wanted to bump into Jean, after the episode with her on the Sunday night. True, he hadn't checked to see if the caf was open. Foolish, foolish. But after his mother had gone out to the Boys' Club to do teas, Hudge had been eating his sausages.

"What time do you have to be at work, Hudge?"

"Now."

"But it's six o'clock. What time does the caf open?"

"Now," Hudge said, clutching his white overall to him tight.

So Des wolfed down his chipolata sausages, got Hudge safely across Pennington and thought about calling into to see Lily. But Mrs

Brambles had distracted him and he thought he would go later, about eight and then collect Hudge after.

If only, if only, if only, Des thinks, he had called into Lily earlier, this all wouldn't have happened after the caf closing. Maybe he would have asked Lil if she wanted to go out for a drink. Maybe they would have walked on further than The Dragon's Head, gone to The Cherry Tree on a summer's evening, sat outside with a couple of bats flying around and the evening breeze warm in their words. They might have then been together when they walked into the caf to fetch Hudge - there wouldn't have been all this talk of which ways to enter the scene of the crime.

But what had Hudge been doing during all that hour before the caf opened?

Stevens-Sinclair seemed to answer Des's question, "Time for Hudge to do his brother a favour, no doubt, time to buy a gun and then return home to Peterson Road."

"Well, I wouldn't know about all that."

Dear Mrs Brambles. Down to earth Mrs Brambles. But Mr SS wasn't speaking to his witness, he was speaking to the court. "And you are able to see from your back bedroom window into the caf yard and Alpha Road below?"

"I beg your pardon?"

He repeats the question.

"Yes," she says.

"On the night of the stabbing, did you come to your back bedroom window?"

"Yes," she says.

"What made you come to the window?"

"There was shouting," she says.

"At what time?"

"Just after ten," she says.

"And what was the shouting?"

"I heard someone shouting, 'She's my girlfriend, she's my girlfriend'."

Oh ... no.

"What did you see when you looked out of the window?"

"I saw both of the Hodge brothers," she says.

"Did you see anyone else?"

"No, just the two brothers," she says.

"And whose voice did you hear shouting 'She's my girlfriend?"

"Well, that was Des Hodge's voice."

The defendant closes his eyes. His tunnel has become a vortex.

The silence is broken in the court and Mrs Brambles says, "But that doesn't mean that Des did the killing, or that it wasn't self defence, does it?"

And Mrs Brambles leaves the stand, never hearing Hudge Hodge give evidence: a woman in need of a hearing aid who had spoken to Des's elder brother on only a small handful of occasions.

Mr Williams looks a little more than uneasy. For the defendant, dependence upon his prime witness's testimony was growing.

"This is not looking good. Not good at all. Why didn't you tell me about your brother going to buy a gun?" Williams asks him.

Des says nothing. Someone has said it was snowing outside: a cold February. Someone has said that the Queen has given birth to a second son.

"That's pre-meditated murder. You could have been hanged for this a couple of years ago."

"I didn't do it."

Williams looks at him across the table. Williams says nothing. Des glances at him briefly before saying, "I mean I never planned to do it. I got into a fight with ..."

"Will your brother tell the truth?"

"My brother will say what I have told him to say," Des says slowly and quietly.

"He may indict you by saying that you told him to get the gun."

"He only said that because Bessie's sister got angry with him. If he thinks he's in the wrong, he'll say 'Des said'. Or he'll say *Des did it.* It's what he learnt to do as a kid, because ...' Des hesitates, "it's what I used to tell him to tell our Dad, if he did something wrong."

"It's not helpful."

"No. Hudge isn't always helpful. He has his own language, his own way of interpreting the world and it's those around him, closest to him, who understands that world." Des is hearing the words he is speaking, not realising he has always known this about Hudge. "That's why you've got to ask him why he said, 'Des said'. You've got to show that Bessie's sister got cross with him. Backed him into a corner. When he gets backed into a corner, he'll say 'Des did it'. Hudge understands about keeping promises but he's ..." Des was about to say that at this point that Hudge probably wasn't aware of what might be a truth, what was a lie or that he was confused by loyalties. But he didn't say any more.

Williams shakes his head, takes his forefinger and thumb and rubs his eyes. "It's not looking good. The Brambles' woman hearing you shouting, the Lees saying you could have left earlier and by their front door, the cut on Mabs's cheek earlier in the week, Geoff Mabs's camera, found under your bed without a film. Why did your brother steal that camera?"

Des doesn't know but only Hudge could have put it there. Stolen it, in the same way that he had taken Des's Swiss Army knife. But Des doesn't say.

"They say the camera never lies," Williams says. "Well, if only that camera could speak. Why was Mabs's film removed?"

Hudge obviously didn't like the photos Mabs had taken. But Des doesn't say.

"The prosecution is making a case that your brother does what you tell him. It's looking like collaboration. He could be charged as an accessory, if the prosecution think they can prove you both came out of the caf scullery together. Of course he would have to be tried …"

"What the fuck are you saying?"

"I'm saying, Des," Williams has hardly ever said his name before and Des has been used to being referred to as 'Hodge' in recent months, "I'm saying it's not looking good. You've pleaded self defence, but it's not looking good. Geoff Mabs was unarmed. It was your knife. It's looking like murder."

First degree, the Americans would say. Not the kind of degree his mother had hoped for.

"And Hudge?"

Williams shakes his head. "You say his father is dead?"

Des nodded.

"He has no guardian but you."

"No guardian but me, no."

"Life in care at best. You're going down for a number of years if we don't get self defence through. Who will look after him?"

At best. A life in care. Des could hear Lily's words *What's going to become of Hudge? I mean I'd like to think he has a guardian angel, but I'm not sure.*

"And if Hudge had been provoked by being ribbed?"

"That might have been a different matter." Williams' voice is low, subdued. "Geoff Mabs had probably been abused by some family member. He was unstable. If your brother had been provoked to killing then ..." He looked up quickly from the desk at Des, "but I'm not representing your brother. I can't go in too hard on Geoff Mabs's treatment of your brother. I'm trying to get you off on self defence."

Des flickers for one moment with the idea of changing his sentence: but apart from Hudge there was Lily and 'a perversion of the course of justice' to consider. No. He couldn't involve Lily in all of that. No. He couldn't go back on his promise to Hudge. And anyway, Des has given his evidence. Stuck to his story.

"Hypothetically, speaking," Williams says, now watching Des, "hypothetically speaking, if some evidence could have been raised to show that your brother had been provoked," Williams continues, taking a cigarette from his pack on the desk and poking the end on his papers, "then the burden would lie on prosecution to prove to the jury, beyond reasonable doubt, that there was no such provocation. Provocation would reduce any charge of murder to voluntary manslaughter; this changes a mandatory life sentence into a complete discretion on sentencing at the hands of the judge. At the very most he'd do a few years with good behaviour. The chances are he could have walked free."

There is a pause. 'Could have walked free'. 'Could have'. Des smells the cloud of nicotine which wafts across the desk. "I didn't know any of that." If only Des knew all this before he gave his evidence.

"No. But that's why I'm doing what I'm doing and you're …" his voice trails in a nicotine haze.

"But he didn't do it. He didn't do it."

"No. As you say." Another nicotine silence.

Des reaches across the table and helps himself to his barrister's cigarettes. Thus, they have become accustomed to one another.

Williams sits down. "But the fact is he's going to get your sentence time in an asylum. There's no-one there for him."

No, their mother had died since.

Then Des asks the question that he has so far avoided. It is something he hasn't wanted to consider before now. "How many years would I go down for - at the worst?"

Williams shakes his head slightly, purses his lips as if to hazard a guess. "With these aggravating circumstances?" There was a painful pause, which Des felt in his bowels. "Fifteen years."

Just of late, Des Hodge's bowel movements have been erratic. He has thought his mother's favourite punishment of a dose of Syrup of Figs, by comparison would be mild. He thinks about what Williams has just said. Fifteen times three hundred and sixty five of slopping out for all the years ahead of him minus maybe the few months he has already served. Serving. Serving time. Deserving time. Serving and no sex. Fifteen years of no privacy and no Lily. No kids and no home. No true love ways. No ... no ...

A friend loveth at all times and a brother is born for adversity. His mother had said that. Hudge had been born in adversity. Des didn't really want to be born *for* it. He suddenly doesn't want to be noble. Des suddenly, oh so very suddenly, just wants to live and make love and make bonfires and work till Friday in a factory and sleep in Lily's arms.

Perhaps she will change her mind, break her promise and tell the truth … After all, how did the prosecution know about Hudge asking for a gun? The Fenchurches – not on their life - would have have disclosed that information. Not on their life … his life … "Fifteen years?" Des says looking at Williams.

Williams stubs out his cigarette. "Fifteen years," he sighs. "Maybe more."

****

Lily Lee's Story

The defendant listens to her giving the evidence the way she has seen the whole story.

He listens to Lily saying that she left her bedroom with him just after ten o'clock on Wednesday 26th August 1959, even though she hesitates nervously, looks up motherways to the public gallery, when Williams asks her this question. So … Lily did not always do as her mother said. He listens to her say that she heard Jean Oddy run off Alpha Road, that they entered the yard, saw Geoff Mabs fighting with Hudge. Listens to her say ...

"that Des took over."

"Took over?" Mr Williams says.

Des places his head in his hands, his heart thumps.

But she hesitates. "Des's knife fell from his pocket."

"From which pocket?" Mr Williams asks.

"His denim trouser pocket."

Des begins to sweat. His denim trouser pocket?

Lily corrects herself. "No, I mean his leather jacket pocket, where he keeps his Senior Service cigarettes."

"And what happened then?"

There is a pause. Who of the three would she say picked up the knife?

"Geoff Mabs picked it up."

"Picked up the Army knife?"

"Des and Geoff struggled."

"And then?"

"Miss Lee, keep your eyes on Mr Williams who is asking you the question," the judge says, seeing her look up towards the dock.

Williams repeats his question clearly in sing song rhythm. "When Geoff Mabs picked up the knife, what happened next?"

"Hudge ..."

Des cannot prevent himself looking up towards her. She is going to tell the truth. Oh, God, Lily *tell the truth, tell the truth ...forget the promise ...*

"Miss Lee," the judge says, "keep your eyes on Mr Williams who is asking you the question."

"I mean ... Des fought, must have tried to get the knife from Mabs ... accidentally must have ... or tried to protect himself ... stabbed ..."

She keeps her promise to him. He lets out a small groan. His head is into his hands and lap as Mr Williams sits and the prosecution rises. "Now," Stevens-Sinclair says, "would you say that the Hodge brothers were close?"

"Yes."

"Would do anything for each other."

"Yes."

"And Hudge would do anything his brother told him?"

He looks up. She looks confused. He wishes he could tell her what all the previous witnesses have said. How they have told the truth according to themselves. She is mouthing the word 'yes' and being asked to speak up so that the court may hear her. Yes, Hudge would have done anything his brother told him.

"Did Bessie Fenchurch tell you that Hudge Hodge had come into her shop and asked to buy a gun?"

She hesitates and then, "Yes. Bessie told me at the funeral."

Lily must have said something in her statement. He couldn't remember. Surely this indicated that she was having second thoughts – dare he think it – changing her mind – about indicting Hudge?

"Did Des Hodge ever talk to you about getting hold of a gun?"

"No."

"But you taught his brother Hudge to cross the road?"

"Yes, but I didn't think he could."

"And you've said he would do anything for his brother." Stevens-Sinclair is getting viciously faster. "Were you Des Hodge's girlfriend, Miss Lee?"

"Yes."

"And was the defendant cross with you on Wednesday 19th August when he fought with you in Alpha Road, we have witnesses to that effect, because you had arranged a date with Geoff Mabs?"

"He was cross. But it wasn't usually over me."

"Why was the defendant's leather jacket found in your possession after the stabbing, Miss Lee?" Stevens-Sinclair is balanced now, a careful pace and rhythm to his speech.

She falters. "He gave it to me ... after the struggle."

"The defendant stabbed the victim in the chest thirteen times in self defence and then gave you his leather jacket?"

There is a heavy pause in the courtroom. Des remembers that leather jacket slung round Lily's shoulders. His first thought in the bedroom had been to get to the caf. He had thrown his leather jacket at her. Of course he had no knife in either his jacket or trouser pocket.

"We have established ... you say that you left the attic of your shop at just after ten on the evening of the stabbing."

"Yes."

"Where were you going?"

"I was going to collect Hudge from work with Des."

"You say Des Hodge was with you?"

"Yes, he had spent all evening with me. From about eight o'clock."

Stevens-Sinclair scratches his nose, folds his arms, looks directly at the witness and hitches his gown. "What time did Des Hodge arrive at your shop on Wednesday 26th August?"

"Just after eight o'clock."

"Did you lock the front door after he arrived?"

"I tried to lock, but the key was stiff. Des helped me lock the door."

"You saw him lock the door."

"I *felt* him lock the front door."

"What do you mean - you felt him lock the front door?"

"I closed my eyes. I don't know why I closed my eyes but I did. I didn't *see* him lock the front door, I *felt* him turn the key."

Des closes his eyes and sighs. Lily has not listened to this evidence, all this evidence, which has been tap, tap, tapped on to a typewriter all these weeks. Lily is just telling the truth.

"And which way does the key turn to lock?"

"I ... I can't be sure ... to the right I think."

"And then who had the keys?"

"Des. He returned them to my dad when we went upstairs."

"I see. Well, I suggest to you, Miss Lee that Des Hodge did not lock the front door. I suggest that he spent some time with you in your bedroom, but left down your stairs before your mother came up just before ten pm because you told him you had met Geoff Mabs in the Brambles stables on the previous day. Is that not so?

"No. My mother doesn't like me having boys in my bedroom ..."

"Precisely. And according to your sworn statement, you met Geoff Mabs alone in the Brambles' stable on the Monday prior to the stabbing, didn't you?"

Lily murmurs 'yes'. Des keeps his head down. He is surprised but not jealous. No sex would have happened and at this point, Des would not have cared anyway.

"Were you aware that the defendant was carrying a knife when he was in your bedroom?"

Lily's brow creased. "No," she said.

Des watches Williams's shoulders heave. Oh, they have been so foolish.

"I suggest that in a fury Des Hodge left his leather jacket with you on this hot August evening and returned home for his knife. He did not bring his knife into your bedroom to fix, as he said, your record player, did he, Miss Lee?"

"Oh, that ... I forgot."

"You forgot?" Stevens-Sinclair says. "I put it to you, Miss Lee that the defendant left by the front door of your parents' grocery shop which he did not lock. He then returned up Peterson Road for his knife and entered the caf by the front door. I suggest that he saw Jean Oddy with Geoff Mabs through the scullery window and then rushed out shouting, "She's my girlfriend', which Mrs Brambles heard from her upper window, meaning you, Miss Lee. I suggest that you left later by your back way and entered Alpha Road as Geoff Mabs was being stabbed by Des Hodge in pre-meditated murder."

"Not pre-meditated ... no ... self defence."

As Lily Lee is guided down the steps, Des watches the last scrap of her pony tail and young person disappear. Des knows that Cecilia who he can almost hear sigh with relief, will never let him see her again, whatever the outcome, let alone sleep in her arms.

Hudge Hodge's Story

Before Hudge is called to the witness box, Des rapidly looks up to the public gallery. Would Lily be there, now that she has given evidence? But there are no Lees. There is his father, the Brambles, the Fenchurches and the Mabses, but Des fears that the Lees are no longer interested in this story now that their roles are over.

Hudge Hodge knows his name, he knows where he used to live. He understands what has happened - what is happening. He says he understands what is happening. Hudge looks out at the wave of people, as if trying to find his brother. Des tries to catch his eye but Williams speaks. Des hears his barrister asking Hudge if he asked someone if he could buy a gun but Des's eyes are fixed on Hudge whilst Hudge's eyes are fixed for most of the time on the rail of the witness box in front of him. Des watches Hudge's lips move. "Yes. Mrs Fenchurch."

"And what did she say?"

"She said 'no', 'I don't sell guns'."

"And was there someone else in the shop?"

"Yes, her sister."

"And did she say anything to you?"

"She was very angry with me."

"Why do you think she was angry with you?"

Hudge shrugs his shoulders; his bottom lip begins to tremble. He never knew why people were ever angry with him. Never knew why his stepfather took off his belt.

"Do you not know why?" Williams asks.

"I don't know."

"If people are angry with you and you say 'that your brother Des said' do you think that makes things all right?"

"Yes."

Des makes eye contact with his father in the public gallery, his father who has been given a privileged front row seat and he feels suddenly very sorry for the baby: for Joseph Hodge. He wishes for his tiny half brother the peace of Perry's sweets and quiet nights with Michael Miles but he doubts Joseph will have that.

Stevens-Sinclair is on those Jack in the Box feet. "My learned colleague is unashamedly leading this witness and putting words into his mouth."

"Move on, Mr Williams," Boney Judge says and Hudge looks up at the judge for the first time.

Williams takes a deep breath and asks the question he really hasn't wanted to ask at all. He asks Hudge if, "your brother Des asked you to go and get a gun from the Exchange & Mart?"

Hudge wouldn't say he did. He wouldn't tell that lie. Des has never discussed guns with Hudge.

"No."

Des cannot help but show his relief. Sod what the jury think.

"Then why did you say that? Why did you tell a lie?"

"I didn't tell a lie. I was getting it for him."

Des looks up to the witness box and frowns.

"You were getting your brother the gun but he had not asked you for it?"

"Yes."

" 'Yes', you were getting your brother the gun or 'yes' he had not asked for it."

"Yes, I got it for him."

No clarification here. Which of the two is this? The jury members look confused. Hudge is confused. Williams moves on. Why is he moving on? Why does he not make this clear? Des has twenty years of life hanging on this. And two years previous it could have been his head. Williams is now asking Hudge about what happened on the night in question, asking him if he saw Geoff Mabs leave through the scullery with Jean Oddy. Hudge nods.

"What happened then?"

"I can't remember."

"Well, try to remember, Mr Hodge. When Geoff Mabs left the caf through the back way with Jean Oddy, what happened next?"

Hudge stares into space.

"Did you see your brother fight with Geoff Mabs?"

Hudge looks down at Williams, briefly and shakes his head.

"Is that a 'no'?" Williams says.

Des wonders if his barrister is trying to get a court confession from his brother but Des knows this is impossible. Hudge will keep his word unless he forgets the story and Hudge is now shaking his head.

At this point the judge intervenes and says slowly to Hudge, "Did you at any time, see your brother Des fight with Geoff Mabs? Say 'yes' or 'no' to this question."

"No."

"So were you present when Geoff Mabs was stabbed?" Williams asks.

"Yes."

"And was your brother Des present?"

The courtroom sits in its strange speaking silence. And then ...

"Yes."

"And anyone else?"

"Lily Lee."

"And did you see Geoff Mabs stabbed?"

"No. But Lily saw who stabbed Geoff Mabs. Lily saw who did it."

Williams says he has no further questions because he probably realises that Hudge is not going to testify that his brother stabbed Mabs by self defence or any other means. In the end, both barrister and judge have to simply give up because all Hudge would say was that 'Lily saw who did it'. This Hudge repeats. For some time, Hudge repeats this again and again until Stevens-Sinclair rises to cross-examine him.

Speaking very very slowly ... at first ... Hudge says, I washed the dishes. I wasn't to take any money, just wash the dishes. Des said."

"You do what Des says. What your brother says, do you Mr Hodge?"

Hudge nods. Of course.

"You must answer the questions, verbally." The judge tuts and shakes his head. "I mean you must say either 'yes' or 'no'." Hudge asks 'why'? and the judge replies, "Because it is the rule," and Hudge seems to understand.

"Yes."

Stevens-Sinclair repeats, "Yes, you do what your brother Des says."

"Yes."

"Did you like working in the Oddy's caf?"

Hudge is confused. He says, 'yes,' and then, 'no.'

"Does that mean sometimes?"

"Yes."

"Not all the times?"

"No."

"Why not all the times?"

"Geoff Mabs - he crowded me."

"How do you mean, he crowded you?"

"He was a bad boy."

"Why was he a bad boy?"

"He crowded me and he crowded Jean Oddy."

"Why do you think Geoff Mabs did this - crowd you as you say?"

There is a pause. Someone can be heard chewing gum in the public gallery and a clerk of the court looks up and frowns at the offender. Des sees his father and Des stares at him thinking, Hudge knows all about being bullied. Doesn't he, Dad? Like my mother knew all about being bullied, didn't she, Dad? "Let's all be nice and quiet about it all. It's not as though I did any real harm. You're all standing. Happens in households all over the country and you got me angry. I've an evil temper on me and I had one too many ... Let's keep this under our bonnets."

"I can't tell," Hudge says.

"Why can't you tell?"

"I promised not to tell why Geoff Mabs crowded me."

"Who did you make that promise to?"

"I can't tell."

"And why can't you tell?"

"Because I promised that person I wouldn't tell and I must keep a promise."

"Yes, but Mr Hodge, you are under oath and you must tell the truth."

"Yes, but I must keep my promise."

There is another pause in the courtroom whilst Stevens-Sinclair scratches his head and then says with the huge authority that his education and experience has given him, "Yes but the truth is more important than a promise."

Hudge looks up towards the dock and straight at Des, but Des is powerless to give him the answer. Stevens-Sinclair may well have stumbled on exactly the right words to set Des free - the truth is more important than a promise - and Hudge is about to speak when the barrister says, "Was it to your brother Des that you promised not to say why Geoff Mabs was crowding you?"

Another moment lost. But Des suddenly realises that Hudge has not promised him or his mother or Lily to be silent about Geoff Mabs crowding him. He had, of course, promised someone else. Des thinks back again to the conversation he had with Hudge on the Monday night before the stabbing. Hudge had said that Lily was not his girlfriend but that he had a girlfriend. There it was. It had been staring up at him from his highly polished shoes for some time now. But he has not wanted to acknowledge that his brother kept secrets from him, like his mother had. We all keep secrets from one another. Hudge has promised Jean Oddy that he would keep quiet about her being his girlfriend. And when Jean Oddy said to Des on the Sunday night that she would get back at him where it really hurt, she had meant Hudge. It was why Jean was protecting Hudge. She was protecting herself. Now he knew: Hudge.

For Hudge, Jean Oddy had been his girlfriend. It was why Hudge had committed the crime. For Jean.

Des looked up at the witness box at his brother. Meek, mild, kind Hudge, like his brother Ben and his father Teddy Pepper before him. The physical and emotional surge of sex would have been too confusing for Hudge to understand. He would have protected Jean Oddy from anything and everything. Hudge needed protecting from himself. Des now wants to take his brother away and to the furtherest point on earth from this spot: from an unsympathetic court and an unsympathetic stepfather only feet away from him. There was Hudge's huge lower lip stumbling. But Hudge does not reply. Des loves him. This isn't fair. None of this is fair. Life, after all, is not fair.

"All right, Mr Hodge. Do you remember that Geoff Mabs had a camera?"

"Yes."

"And did he take photos of you?"

"Yes."

"And did you like Geoff Mabs taking photos of you?"

"No." Hudge shakes his head vehemently.

"Why not?"

"Jean didn't like him taking photos."

Jean.

"And on the Tuesday, on the night before the stabbing, did you see Geoff Mabs's camera lying around."

Hudge slowly nods.

"Is that 'yes' or 'no'?"

Hudge nods again and mutters, "Yes."

"Yes, you saw it lying on a table or the counter?"

"The counter."

"And you took the camera, didn't you, Hudge?"

"Yes."

Des has known this. The camera has been found under his bed. Found before September came slipping in. Found as soon as number 47 was searched. Lily told him about the night she thought he was hiding something under his overall. Had it been Geoff Mabs's camera? The overall ...

"Geoff Mabs owned a very expensive camera. Did anyone tell you to take the camera?"

Hudge looks at the rail in front of him.

The overall... Where is that overall? The overall could set them free. Lil, what have you done with the overall?

"On the Wednesday early evening of the stabbing, why did you go into the Exchange & Mart?"

"To get a gun."

"Why did you do that?"

"To kill Geoff Mabs with it."

Stevens-Sinclair pauses because he knows the nuances of a courtroom, knows that if he says nothing it will allow the court to relax, to react, for a murmur of papers and sighs and coughs to settle on the witness's statement and then he is angrily and accusingly in with, "Who did you get the gun for? You or your brother, Des?"

Hudge looks as though he is on the point of tears. "For me."

"But you would do anything your brother tells you, wouldn't you, Hudge?"

"Yes."

"No further questions."

As a uniformed arm reaches up to guide his half brother down from the witness box, Mr SS QC is looking as though that was another witness well done. But Hudge hesitates. He half turns and then grasps the rail in front of him. "Des said to say that he stuck the knife in Geoff Mabs."

Des lets out an audible sigh of relief. For the first time in this courtroom, Stevens-Sinclair is taken unawares. "Yes," he says, gravely.

"And I stuck it in."

And for the first time in this courtroom, Des thinks that he might taste freedom and the first bite is good. And for the first time he allows himself to think about the knife in Geoff Mabs's stomach, his blood and Geoff Mabs turning to him and looking at him without anger but with peace. And Des feels so sorry for Geoff Mabs, so sorry for Jean Oddy, so sorry for them all and about it all. And when Mabs turned to look at him in his final moment it was the moment that Des thought it was all going to be all right. That he was alive. Like now. Hudge's truthful confession, at this point in the trial might help them all.

Stevens-Sinclair is visibly shaken; his stillness muddied. Whilst all outcomes have been anticipated, this confession hasn't. Stevens-Sinclair bows his head, touches the scalp of his perruque and takes a sip of water. And all might have been well but for Boney Judge saying, "Mr Stevens-Sinclair, we need further clarification."

And Stevens-Sinclair takes yet another sip of water, looks up at Hudge and says, "And Des stuck the knife in too. That's the truth, is it?" Stevens-Sinclair has picked up on the little word 'and' as well.

The truth or the promise, Hudge?

Hudge looks up to Des in the dock, as if searching for the answer. Then he says with half closed eyes, "Des said he stuck it in. He tells the truth. I stuck it in. I tell the truth."

Wise Mr Stevens-Sinclair QC: the truth is more important than a promise.

Yesterday's Chip Paper Pennington Free Press - Thursday 17th March 1960

Derek Reginald Hodge, a nineteen year old former Nestles factory worker claimed self defence when accused of murdering Geoffrey Raymond Mabs, 21 year old son of Charles and Zelda Mabs, owners of the Fish and Chip shop on the Pennington Road. Hodge was accused of stabbing Mabs in Alpha Road, Pennington last August 26th but dramatically changed his plea at the end of the trial.

It was stated in evidence that just after 10.00 pm on Wednesday 26th August last year Mabs was found lying in the yard of Jack Oddy's cafe on the Pennington Road which backs on to Alpha. He was rushed to hospital but pronounced dead on arrival by stab wounds to the stomach. The police arrested Hodge at the scene of the crime and on searching his home in Peterson Road found Mabs's Ilford Witness camera under the mattress of his bed.

In Mr Williams's closing speech he said that Hodge now denied stealing the camera and said that he removed his brother's overall at the scene of the crime and took the blame himself. At the time, the defendant had no idea how much the other boys had been ribbing and crowding his elder brother Hugh Hodge. Williams said in his closing speech that the defendant said that his elder brother stole the victim's camera, took the knife and stabbed Mabs.

He left the Lees' grocery shop on the Pennington Road just after 10.00pm with his girlfriend and entered Alpha Road to see his elder brother stabbing Geoffrey Mabs at the back of the Oddy's café.

Det- Sgt H. Brooker confirmed the assertion of Mr Hodge's counsel that Hodge was of good character with no previous criminal convictions and further confirmed that Mabs had several convictions for violent offences. Alcohol was shown to be present in the dead man's blood.

Mr Stevens-Sinclair for the prosecution in his closing speech said that, "I therefore urge the jury to conclude that the case for murder of the victim by Derek Hodge has been proved beyond all reasonable doubt."

Mr Williams in his closing speech said that if the jury was not satisfied that the prosecution had proved their case then they could return a verdict of not guilty of murder.

The jury is out.

Pennington Free Press - Thursday 24th March 1960

Yesterday, the jury in number one court at the Old Bailey found Derek Reginald Hodge guilty of the murder of Geoffrey Raymond Mabs on Wednesday 26th August last year. In his summing up the judge said, "The fact that this young man tried, at the end of his trial when he could see that the evidence was heavily stacked up against him, to change his story and in so doing accuse his elder brother of the crime is unspeakably incomprehensible. I have never, in all my years in court, been witness to such a selfish plea of 'cut-throat' defence. It has been repeated by witnesses that the defendant's brother of mentally deficient means would, I quote, 'do anything for his brother'. All evidence points to the fact that this was a pre-meditated act of violence, motivated by sexual jealousy by a young man with 'an evil temper'. Under these circumstances I have no alternative but to sentence you, Derek Hodge to life imprisonment serving a minimum of eighteen years."

Speaking outside the Old Bailey this afternoon the condemned man's father, Mr Reginald Hodge said, "We shall appeal. My son would never tell a lie."

The condemned man's twenty two year old brother -Hugh Hodge, is being tried as accomplice to the murder.

Pennington Free Press – Friday 7th October 1960 Hodge Appeal

An appeal was brought by the defence in the case of Derek Reginald Hodge, found guilty in March this year of murder. Hodge is serving a life sentence for murdering Geoffrey Raymond Mabs in Alpha Road on August 26th last year.

The defence brought the appeal on the grounds that a blood-spattered overall, allegedly worn by the Hodge's elder brother at the time of the murder would prove the defendant's innocence.

Seventeen year old Lily Violet Lee, testified that she took the overall from Hodge and 'hid it in the Brambles' (sic greengrocer's) stables on the site of the recreational ground on the Pennington Road.

Percy John Brambles gave evidence that in September last year he cleared out his stables and had them renovated in order to house his new Ford Poplar van.

No such overall was found.

A roll of film taken by the victim in the week preceding his murder, which was alleged to help the case for the defence, has also remained missing.

Tomorrow's Chip Paper

Years later, Lily heard that Zelda Mabs had sold her story to a daily tabloid. It was some time in the nineties. Lily, with a naivety that she never really lost, believed that Zelda might have dropped some morsels of truth in tomorrow's chip paper and she was excited when she purchased the newspaper at Victoria station. The by-line read in bold: *The Most Pitied Woman in England during the Fifties reveals all.*

But alas, all that Zelda Mabs was capable of revealing was her cleavage, which looked as though it had been given padded upholstery. The tabloid said that she had once subscribed to the Spotlight Casting Directory. She looked at the photo of Zelda as a young woman; tried to see in the inky outline, some similarity to the boy she once knew.

The extended article simply said that Zelda had changed her name from Margaret Mara - interesting that Zelda should discard one of her prettier assets in search of something which promised more, to Zelda Steaverson. 'Zelda' had worked as a Windmill girl during the war and was short-listed at an audition for high kicking Tillers after the war. She was always somebody's girl. But Lily doubted all that. It had been so hard to get to the bottom of any truths as far as the Mabs's family was concerned and the only reference to 'what had happened' was simply stating, in black and white, the facts of the case.

She was immediately shocked by the woman's appearance. Now in her seventies, Zelda had finally achieved a cheap measure of celebrity: never having had the finance or means to bleach her teeth, plump her skin or touch up the roots and fed on a diet of Players Number Six and Johnny Walker, she looked shrivelled.

My son's father was his grandad. Or his grandad was his father, Zelda was quoted as saying.

Lily thought back to night before Geoff was stabbed: remembered the sadness in the boy's eyes. For that was the way she remembered him now: a boy who never grew up. Remembered as the Everly Brothers sang of dreaming their life away that he had said - "I wasn't his. Had nothing to do with him. Charlie told me Sunday night. Zelda had cheated on Charlie. The woman's an absolute bitch".

And Gordon had explained, when they got further enough away from 'the scene of the crime' in miles and years, from 'what had happened', that young Geoff had been sadly abused. Probably by his grandfather as his 'father' had been before him. "You see Lil," her father had said, "Man passes on inhumanity to man." It was a good phrase. Her father had read Philip Larkin - the poet - who Gordon said, "was a very clever man and had been educated at Oxford University which is ..."

"A million miles away," Lily said and then added, "He probably meant shat on from above." She received letters on HMS headed notepaper before the grocery shop was sold but these strangely ceased after the family sailed for Connecticut. She had kept sending her letters of course but Connecticut, she supposed, was further away than even

Oxford University from Alpha Road and prisons. Maybe Des Hodge had given up on her.

Gordon took up his newspaper.

"But he loved his grandad," she went on. "His grandad had been good to him. Explained about the stars - how they are there and then not there. Like Geoff," she had said, as the tears ran unblotted down her cheeks. "Yes, like Geoff," Gordon had said.

"And he knew? He knew? He knew that his grandfather had done things to him? How could he have known? He loved his grandad."

Her father was not a tactile man, but at this juncture he patted her shoulder and explained. She was in her mid-twenties by then, but she didn't know, "That sometimes," her father said, "things can happen so young that you don't remember. Or you push things back. Forget them. And that's for the best, I think, despite what Mr Freud would have us all think, but Geoff found some photos ..."

Had Geoff tried to tell her? There in the stables where she had later placed Hudge's blood stained overall. Geoff's blood. Had she not listened hard enough?

"Did he have a little sister? What about his little sister and being locked away in the caravan?"

Gordon shrugged his shoulders. "Oh, I've no idea about little sisters," he said, looking oddly guilty when Cecilia came into the room. Cecilia never liked to talk about 'what happened'. "I only read the newspapers," Gordon said.

"I don't know what you keep them for," Cecilia said with vowels that slid like Iris's now.

"For posterity," Gordon said. "There was no mention of any sister."

What remained certain was that fibs could have huge ramifications. And strangely it was the small fibs that seldom get brought into the light of day but they were forerunners of the kind of lies of which ultimately she, Des and Hudge had been guilty of. Gordon had fallen into his newspaper and they had never again talked about 'what happened'.

Lily missed her train. She stopped still in the middle of Victoria station. The newspaper article moved on to focus on the theme of forgiveness and the once most pitied woman in England was quoted as saying: *I know that the elder brother owned up at the trial, the brother who had learning difficulties.*

Lily knew these last words were those of a journalist. But she read on: *When my son's photos were found ... the roll of film which he took the week before he was murdered, it did look as though the elder brother had been having a rough time in the caf where he was working but the elder brother Hugh Hodge wrote and said he was sorry. But the other one he never said he was sorry.*

But he had. He had written to Lily in 1960, before they left the grocery shop and he had written, "I'm sorry I made you lie."

Had she ever forgiven him?

Forgiveness? Yes, I do. Because they didn't really know what they were doing, did they?

Lily could never be sure, even to this end, if Zelda was telling the truth or that her response was simply the prerequisite for media coverage. Only creators knew the full truth. She shivered and drew her Cashmere cardigan in closer to her.

On the next page was Roy whatsisname who had given up the Bingo calling and become a runaway success.

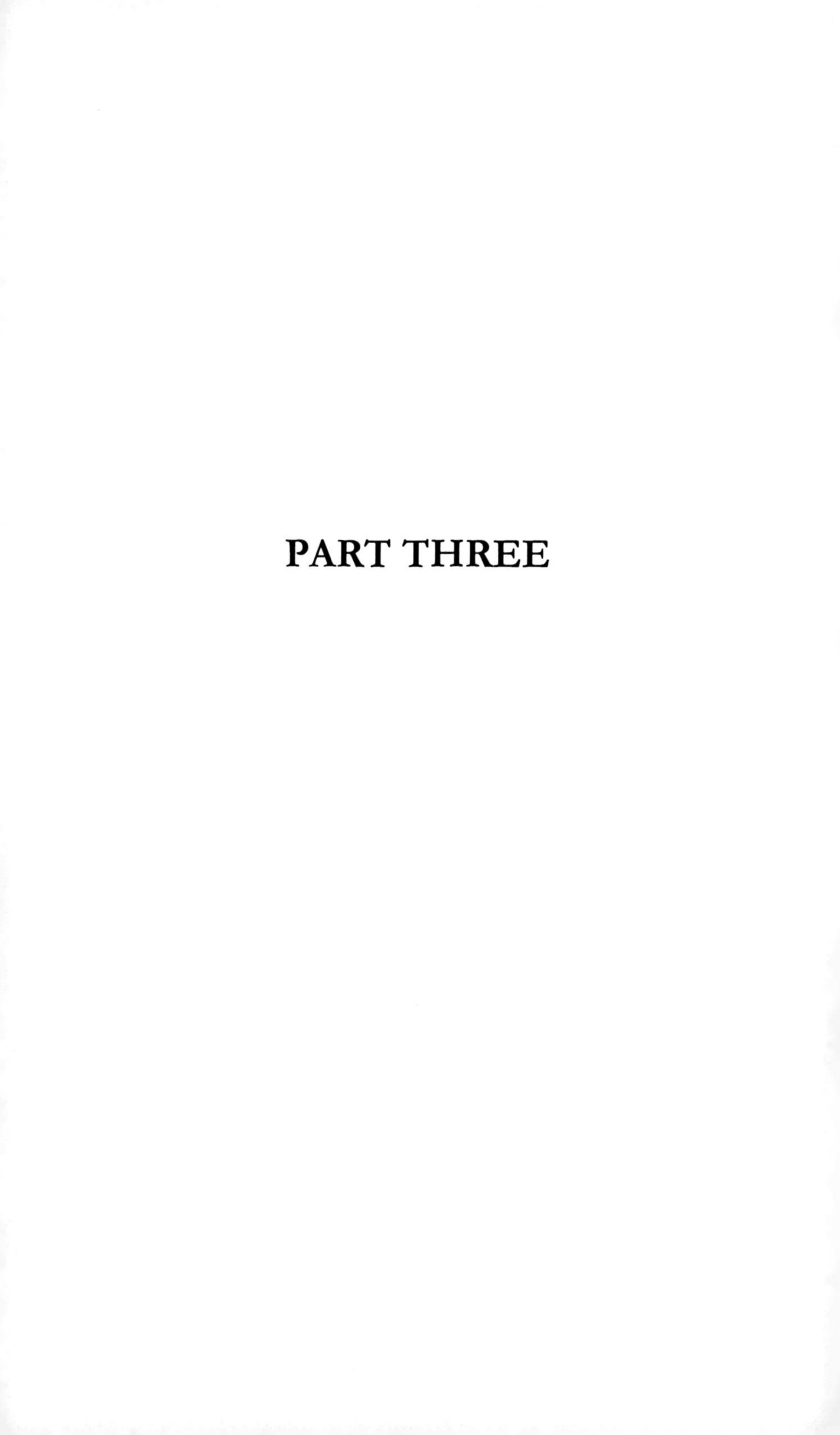

PART THREE

13

JANUARY 2006

Friends Reunited

Hi Derek Hodge,

'Friends Reunited' have contacted me, giving me your email address. Apparently you have seen some of the cine-films my father took in the fifties? I sold them to 'Friends Reunited' and they have used some of the clips for commercials worldwide. You think you might know me? My father took them of Ben Hodge's wedding when I was a bridesmaid. They said that you had been in touch with them and enquired about my identity. If you are the Des Hodge I once knew, after all this time, I hope you will be in touch, if only to put it all to bed, so to speak. My parents took me to live in Connecticut in 1960 but I returned to live in UK some twenty years later. I received letters from you but they stopped coming. Did you get mine? That is if you are the Des Hodge I once knew.

My name is Lily Ryan and I am now 62. I have not been in contact with anyone about what happened. Best regards - Lily Ryan.

Hi Lily Ryan,

The very first thing that I did when I left prison was to return to Peterson Road and open the family Bible. I had asked Jean to keep it safe. It was there that I found our passports in Proverbs 17 and in Amos I found the old emigration papers for Australia.

From my window: clusters of brick and fibro houses step up towards the cliffs ; their climb ultimately overwhelmed by the density of the rainforests. Further out noisy flocks of crimson rosellas come to feed on the berries of a silver maple; further out still eucalypt forests of Eastern blue and scribbly bark shelter red-bellied black snakes and goannas whilst the koo koo koo koo kookaburra, a squat black and white thing of the kingfisher family laughs loudly.

Here I am, well and truly in Australia, just south of Sydney, a long long way from Pennington. This is what my mother dreamed of for her sons and she got all the paperwork before she died. She talked about us emigrating for the sum of ten quid donated by the Australian government but whether she would have done anything with the papers had it all not happened, who knows? My mother loved to dream. When I was released on September 7th 1976 at 2.00pm in the afternoon, during that long hot summer when tomatoes flourished, this is where I brought Hudge. Our Australian summer was about to begin. He died a couple of years ago, aged sixty four, having spent some years in prison and in care after the trial.

We are now almost as old as the Everly Brothers but not quite as old as these rainforests ...

How our lives might have been different, had we paused for thought on that August night in 1959.

There were two things said which stood out with absolute clarity for me during the trial. The first was said by your mother. She said that the trouble with young people is that they think they will always be young and that it all goes too quickly.

It is a privilege to grow old; one that some are not given.

I missed the sixties with you. I was in the same place when hairstyles changed and when Mankind landed on the moon. But where were you? With Auntie Iris obviously. Connecticut? I had no idea. I missed your letters. Was that Fort Cecilia bloody Knox?

I missed sleeping in your arms. I missed you. I simply missed you. It all went too quickly.

The roll of film which Geoff Mabs took on his camera revealed Hudge's world that week of which we were all unaware: the ribbing, the sexual relationship with Jean and what you were up to. Hudge never could remember where he put the film. Mum must have found the roll of film somewhere in the house. I'll never know if she knew about the camera. What I do know is that she put the roll of film right where I would have known where to find it if I really wanted to, Lil. Her last words to me were: *the Bible will reveal all. The Alpha and the Omega.* And when you Bessie Fenchurch spoke to you at Mum's funeral I was standing at the doorway. Bessie said that Mum had been reading the Bible during the police search. Well, she saved Hudge years in prison. Once I had time to really think I knew that the roll of film, beginning with 'r' was at the back of the Bible, in Revelations.

When the authorities gave me copies of what had been developed I realised that this is life. Geoff Mabs's last week of life served real purpose in teaching me that lesson. There's an energy in those photos, in those last moments of youth on its road of promise. Youth can so easily destroy life by arrogance, anger and low self esteem.

The second thing which stood out for me at the trial was when Stevens-Sinclair, speaking for the prosecution said that the truth is more important than a promise.

It's important that we get the information, that we understand the story. Then maybe we stand a chance.

And to that end, I need to ask one more thing of you. Dearest Lil, I asked so much of you when we were growing up, I don't know how I can ask you now to do more. But I will.

When my mum died, it was my father who owned the house in Peterson Road. He had gone to live in Hartlepool with Jean Oddy's mother. When my father died, the house passed to Jean's mother and Jean swore she would always live there - which is what she did until her dying day a few months ago. My stepsister moved into catering, specialised in cake making, made me a cake on every birthday I spent inside and baked for Hudge every birthday until he died. She grew large, had a large family, led an ordinary life and I grew to love her as a real friend, which is the most I have come to ask from life – that it be ordinary and that I have a friend.

The house has now passed to my half brother - Joe. I don't know if Jean would have said anything to Joe about the stabbing. I don't want any brother thinking I was a turncoat. The world can think it, but not my brother. I don't want Joe thinking he is in some way tainted by blood. What happened to all of us was like the iceberg formed thousands of years before it met the Titanic. It wasn't meant to happen, it could have been avoided, but it was on course for a disaster.

If I could tell a boy on a street with a knife a story, this is the one I would tell.

Tell him the story, Lil.

Des

14

FEBRUARY 2006
47, Peterson Road

"So ..." he said. "My family are a bunch of murderers." He held up the Yale key to the terraced house; grimy windows. "I had duplicates of these made," he said, placing the key in the lock. He wasn't smiling. "Quirk of fate that I'm now the proprietor, eh lass?"

She didn't like being called 'lass'. She was sixty two. His were Geordie syllables; maybe 'lass' was a regional colloquialism, not meant to be condescending. "Call me Lil," she said. "Everyone else did." She bit her cold lip for using the past tense. The rain spat.

His dark brows sprang and arched. "Let's go inside and get warm, hen. This is bone cold for the south," he said, swinging open an unoiled door. "Excuse the turn of phrase." His lips flinched sparingly into a small smile. Did he mean hens or bones?

There had been no handshake; no warmth of palm on palm. But that was to be expected; they had never been a family for old fashioned manners. Joe had inherited more than the steel chiselled jaw.

The hallway itself was uninviting, frosty even and didn't smell the way it had done almost fifty years ago: when Lil had been sixteen, before 'it all happened'. Then there had been the warm cooking fragrances of rich dried fruit and softly sifted sugar, when words were measured, sieved and considered for their mixed worth and baked into something sturdy, crusty and deeply palatable. Half baked truths came later ...

Footfalls in the hallway ... front room to the right, stairs straight ahead leading up to the two bedrooms ...

"Did you miss him?" he said, bypassing the front room and pushing open the door to the back room, which Lily knew, led into the scullery. Joe had been here before.

The back room - they would call it a family room now - was where they had all lived, where she had all but lived: scullery leading on from the back room, where she had eavesdropped all those years ago. The front room was where Aida, her babysitter, they would call her 'childminder' now - would go to ransom her wartime past: legs running up the mantelpiece, cracking open nuts, a bottle of gin and stories of her wounded life. *God give me strength.* Aida's words bounced back from familiar walls.

Did she miss him? She pulled her coat collar into her neck, damp from the rain, protecting herself against the bleak past. Of course she had missed him, but she only said, "Still," peering into the back room before stepping forward.

Joe looked like him. Of course. All those missed years. This is what he might have looked like in middle age. Something like this. He switched on the gas fire. "Jesus," he said, "it's like a morgue in here." And for the first time he smiled broadly, blowing breath on to his palms drawn together as if in prayer. "Sorry," he said. "It's hard to be deferential."

She wondered if he really meant to use that word.

"Tea?" he asked.

Lily is met by her nodding reflection in the mirror above the fireplace. She expected somehow to see the reproduction painting of the big black woman with the green turban and the hooped earrings. But she is met by her greying bits; the painting like much else would have been long gone.

"Your sister hasn't long gone then?" she said, looking at her reflected self which was not the face of the then guileless sixteen year old. The blackberry stain had gone. Blackberries thrown at the wall on Blackberry Sunday. The wallpaper had changed. It had all gone, they had all gone; what lingered in the air she could not tell.

"Half sister. Dead," he said, as he threw tea bags into a plastic tea pot; not the brown earthenware pot that used to live here. "It's her tea though," he said lifting one of the tea bags to his nose and sniffing. "She obviously liked baking cakes." He motioned to the glass cabinet where row upon row of cake stands were displayed. "What the hell am I going to do with all those?"

She almost smiled and sat down.

"Take a seat," he said and turned to make tea.

This was his house now.

Lily used to plonk; plonk her childhood self down on this once linoleum floor; plonk with grazed, scabby knees and elbows. Plonked this old right leg which had once been young with a fresh gaping wound of her 'cicatrice' on Aida's scullery draining board. She even looked under the table to see if Aida's handbag was there. Long gone. As was the Family Bible. That, she guessed, was miles away. She smiled to herself: Revelations.

"I haven't been here since you were born," she said.

"Because I suppose," he carried on, with his back to her, not hearing, or ignoring her remark, "in a strange kind of a way I am related to them all. Or at least touched by them."

Touched. An odd little word to use.

"The Hodges, the Mabses, the Oddys ... the Lees. Lily Lee," he said turning to face her from the scullery and taking a cigarette pack from his overcoat pocket. "Lily Lee," he said, repeating her name softly, as he lit up and flirting, yes flirting across the gulf of the sixteen years between them. How very odd. Nothing changes.

She studied the tablecloth. The old tablecloth came to mind, the one with little orange and green checks: not quite gingham, but similar. It was a brief study because it was then she saw the photographs ...

He placed a mug of tea on the crocheted tablecloth before her but she was looking at the cabinet where Aida's 'precious' sideboard used to be.

"Oh, the photos," he said. "I think my brother left them here." He moved to the cupboard beneath the glass doors, searching.

But she was looking at the framed photos of children, of grandchildren, flanking the many cake stands and Royal celebration mugs and personalised anniversary crystal glasses: crammed with the sweet scents of an ordinary life. Probably not a well educated life, but a life well led in a home kept alive with cooking aromas. She wanted to move towards the photos, handle them, put on her spectacles, but even though this house might have been hers, might have been, had it all not happened, this was not her house. Odd that Joe of all people should end up ... it was a strange quirk ...

He placed a photo album on the table: a cheap, slim, plastic album. "Bloody gritty story," he said, turning his back on the cabinet, speaking across her thought. Joe looked around the tiny back room, filling it with his presence and nicotine which transported her back to familiar beginnings. "Gritty. Like the house. Am I the last?"

"I think so," she said.

"Well, it's probably just as well."

"Have you children?" she said, skimming the numerous framed photos in the glass doored cabinet behind him and reaching for the spectacles in her bag.

"I have two sons. One's close by us - at Durham university, the other at Cambridge."

"Oh, that's a million miles away." She paused. She smiled. "You must be very proud," she added. "My father would have been." With spectacles, she was now able to clearly see the framed colour photographs of an ordinary life.

"Married?" he asked, abruptly.

"Just widowed," she said, looking beyond him, but touching her single gold band. She had never believed in engagement rings: a secret superstition.

Joe thrust his hands into his jacket pockets, pulled on the cigarette, narrowed his eyes, watching her. He nodded as if he understood. "Thus this timing," he said.

"I think the young ones call it 'closure'," she said. Then added, "But I need to think there are years in me yet."

He smiled for a second time. There was something in the creased corners of Joe's eyes that reminded her of him. "And I need to switch on the central heating," he said. "Warm up the bedrooms." He crossed to the scullery.

She gazed at the family photos and then, suddenly, and expecting colour just the same, she opened the album in front of her. She was hit by dusty photographs and a heaviness beneath her sternum. These were altogether something else. They made up the missing week. These were the missing photos, so essential to the appeal. After almost fifty years she was witnessing those lost black and white moments, recorded by Geoff and nearly lost for a lifetime. It was his legacy to the future: photos of stars which had exploded a million light years from this present moment. And it was how she remembered her past: in dusty black and white, never in colour. She wanted to inspect each inch, as if the inches held clues which would yield up the truth of the matter like scouring old news reels.

"They're Geoff Mabs's photos," she said. "He took them."

"You call him Geoff?"

"It's why there are no photos of him."

Joe stood above her, smoothing the dark shadow of stubble on his steel chiselled jaw. He shook his head. "I don't feel connected to them at all. "You?" he asked. At first she thought he was asking if she felt connected to the people. How could she not be? She had been the prime witness. But then she realised that he was pointing to the fair haired teenager on a roundabout in a recreational ground. She had noticed on the way down from the station that the rec. was still there but that roundabout ... *est disparu.*

"Me," she said.

"Beauty. You were a beauty." He took another drag on the cigarette and smiled again. The room was growing warmer. "Not that you aren't now."

"I was a prig," she said.

When she pointed to a photograph of a darker, rounder girl cleaning a table in a cafe, she noticed he let his ash just drop. This was his house now. "Jean," she said. Jean Oddy leaned provocatively across the caf table and into this century. "You know," she added. "The Oddys ..." she swallowed with embarrassment, she wasn't sure how much he knew, "the Oddys," she repeated, "owned the caf on the Pennington Road."

Of course, he knew. His mother Gwen had once been an Oddy. This time, as he took a long drag on the cigarette, he narrowed his eyes but did not smile. "It's an Internet Cafe now," he said in almost a whisper.

She raised an eyebrow: faint irony. She had noticed. "Blackberries mean something else now, don't they?"

But he didn't hear. "You don't look very happy in this one," he said, picking out a photo which was a close shot of her sixteen year old face.

Ashfields Park ... Sunday 23rd August 1959 ... Blackberry Sunday ... a hot day burnt into her brain. "I ... I didn't like having my photograph taken." That summer came rushing upon us, she thought, reduced itself to ashes, went crawling into autumn. And then she said, pointing, "This is Hudge." Dear, dear Hudge. That innocent but vacant look. Dear Hudge who never ever grew up.

"The simple one?" Joe asked.

"Oh look," she said without thinking, even a photo of her trying to teach Hudge to cross the Pennington road. She never knew that Geoff had taken that photo. It was as if he had taken snapshots of her faded memory: Hudge looking for gaps in the traffic, their hands at the kerb forming a multi-knuckled fist.

"Would it be autism now?" he asked again.

There must have been nearly two dozen photos: the missing film; Hudge in the caf washing dishes. Jean taking orders with the juke box behind her. Lily's breath caught in her throat at the sight of Hudge in his white overall ... his clean, white overall.

"And this is Des," Joe said, picking out another photo, his forefinger beneath the young man's chin.

Their hands brushed as she turned the leaves. Some of these black and white photos would be missing she knew for sure: destroyed probably.

"How do you know?" she asked.

He hesitated. "I went to the Newspaper Library."

"Of course."

There was Des on the swing at the rec. It was where it had all started. Geoff had been watching? Had taken the photo of the three of them on the swings, minutes from this house but a million miles away, when they were in their teens: Des, Hudge, Lil. Des in his leather jacket, Des with his Brylcreamed dark hair, Des with his Senior Service cigarettes, a moody, dark, brittle Des. Hudge swinging high. And in the background, behind those swings, the greengrocers - Brambles' disused stables ...

There was even a photo of Mrs Brambles herself: navy cap stuck on the side of her head, canvas apron with zip up purse, fingers like the old kind of sausages that used to hang in the butchers. Dear unknowing Mrs Brambles, whose fingers wired tea roses into baskets, spun fruit in brown paper bags and created an orchard of fresh vegetables daily on the Pennington Road. Brambles the greengrocers next to Oddys' Cafe and a couple of doors up the Lees' grocery shop on the main Pennington Road. She could hear the roar of the traffic now: passing an empty shell of an abandoned shop which still bore her maiden name on the sign writing. Who owned all that unopened mail she had just seen through the dusty shop window? Brambles' greengrocers was boarded up, closed to the world. Where were all the shopkeepers? The only business which had remained was the undertakers.

"Geoff isn't here," she said again, uneasy.

"I'd like to know the story," he said. "After you emailed me last week I came down to the Newspaper Library. I looked up the details of the court case but everyone tells a different story. Do you know the truth, Lil?"

The truth, Lil. The whole truth. Nothing but the truth. The truth had only half remembered edges. She said nothing.

"I'd like to know the truth about my parents, about my family," he said. "When there's been a murder ... and more ... don't you think I deserve to know what you do?"

He was the next generation. The third generation. Lily could hear Aida's syllables and smiles stretching up to reach her. They were a balm against the greying bits; a refuge against the rains which spits. "I discovered things over the years. I've only recently learnt about you," she said. It was a small apology. "It's the story of a boy stabbed in a back street."

"Tell me," he said.

So she did.

****

There was a turn of a duplicate key in the front door lock ... hesitant at first ..

Joe Hodge smiles at Lily as the key in the lock turns. Footfalls in the hallway ... and the back room door opens ...

And there stands her friend: peppered and weathered by time, a smile on his slightly askew lips but a million miles from her Brylcreamed and leather-jacketed young suitor.

"Hello, Lily," he says.

His syllables sound different.

"Hello, Des."

Her syllables sound different.

"Some years left in me yet," he says. "Made up your mind?"

Joe stands between them, a faint echo of the past.

"This isn't where it ends then," she says.

THE END

Lightning Source UK Ltd.
Milton Keynes UK
UKOW031023091012

200300UK00002B/1/P